Jeffrey Lee was born in South Africa and educated at Oxford. He has been a BBC foreign affairs producer and Foreign Editor at Channel 4 News. After receiving an MBA from INSEAD, he is now involved in new media. Jeffrey Lee is married and lives in London. *Dog Days* is his first novel.

DOG DAYS

Jeffrey Lee

BANTAM BOOKS

LONDON • NEW YORK • TORONTO • SYDNEY • AUCKLAND

DOG DAYS
A BANTAM BOOK : 0 553 81499 0

Originally published in Great Britain by Bantam Press,
a division of Transworld Publishers

PRINTING HISTORY
Bantam Press edition published 2002
Bantam edition published 2003

1 3 5 7 9 10 8 6 4 2

On page 15, the line from 'These Are Dog Days' from *Collected Poems* by W. H. Auden (1976), is reprinted by permission of Faber & Faber Ltd. The lines quoted on pages 103 and 229 are taken from *Heart of Darkness* by Joseph Conrad (1902).

Set in 10/12pt Palatino by
Falcon Oast Graphic Art Ltd.

Bantam Books are published by Transworld Publishers,
61–63 Uxbridge Road, London W5 5SA,
a division of The Random House Group Ltd,
in Australia by Random House Australia (Pty) Ltd,
20 Alfred Street, Milsons Point, Sydney, NSW 2061, Australia,
in New Zealand by Random House New Zealand Ltd,
18 Poland Road, Glenfield, Auckland 10, New Zealand
and in South Africa by Random House (Pty) Ltd,
Endulini, 5a Jubilee Road, Parktown 2193, South Africa.

Printed and bound in Great Britain by
Cox & Wyman Ltd, Reading, Berkshire.

For my father

All people in this book are fictitious. The journalistic behaviour is true, or based on established reporting technique.

Dog Days (*Dies Canicularis*)

(i) Period of the year when the sun rises with the Dog Star, Sirius. Traditionally period of the year when dogs are susceptible to rabies.

(ii) Days of unwholesome heat, season of sickness, madness and malign influences. In modern almanacs reckoned between 3rd July and 11th August.

PROLOGUE

Time passes. People age. The date skids relentlessly as a locked wheel on a slick, fast bend on and over a jolting, undeniable millennium. Here we find a grey hair, there a certain stiffness in the morning joints or a crippling hangover, longer and deeper than blithe, youthful excess could ever imagine. Even so, despite this physical ageing, many of my circle – blood, friends, colleagues and acquaintances – when by chance they come to consider themselves, perceive someone who is single, childless, young. So much of life seems not to leave its mark on the soul.

'I feel frozen as a person,' a friend of mine said recently when I pressed him to consider himself. 'Somewhere in my twenties, I think. Maybe even a student.'

Not after days like those. Those forty days and forty nights changed lives. Such days make people different. They make us, well . . . older. They leave an impression.

Though, to be honest, I am not sure exactly what is to be learned from the tale of those long, hot weeks. It seems in retrospect like one of those television documentaries, where, if there is a key moment, it is always in the glance of the interviewee after an interview has finished, in the silence of an unanswered question. You feel that the meaning, if, indeed, there is a meaning (you can never be quite sure), is just off-screen somewhere. But that meaning tugs at you nonetheless.

It was of course, partly, the story of a death. Miranda Williams was young, idealistic and murdered. It was partly a story about wickedness, a long, darkening tunnel without much light at the end of it. There was the fact of a certain identity, of a particular evil, yes. But it was not just the killing. During that journey towards quasi-revelation under that relentless sun, you could have seen – well, maybe 'glimpsed' is better – some extremes of humanity and technology that make me wonder how far we've really progressed in the millennia since we were nomadic hunters, even in the aeons since we were apes. I knew that we were living in the information age – I once counted myself as one of the civilizing informers – but out there it was a pretty uncivilized business all round.

If this document, written by a journalist, offers few explanations, please do not be surprised. After some years in journalism, I came to believe that the profession rarely answers questions. It serves simply to raise them. Even now I make few claims to know where this story ends, or even where it truly begins. It might have begun in earnest that 3rd July, in London.

In my mind's eye I see how it might have begun a few days before, when, far to the south, out on the bulge of Africa, one of our brotherhood was spooling backwards and forwards through video sequences of violence and death. Finding the right edit point he hits the assemble button and the latest instalment is added. It takes just fifteen minutes in real time. He keeps the sound low. No-one comes in. In the half-light of the hotel room, long, competent fingers spin the control to rewind.

The images of butchery and violation pause, then Miranda Williams's last moments scuttle backwards with a high-pitched whine and blur into myriad chirping lines.

PART 1

THE LAW OF THE JUNGLE

3RD – 14TH JULY

'Yes, these are the Dog Days, Fortunatus . . .'

I

Early that July, I had the vague feeling that I was on the edge of something. I hoped it was a new beginning and not still the vestiges of the half-endings I'd just made, principally of a family life (with Claire, my exasperated wife, and Alex, our son); smoking (with Philip Morris, twenty a day); and, at least for a while, work (just back from finishing a TV documentary about African child soldiers). I was ready to slip effortlessly into one of those fallow periods which allow a certain amount of reflection to enter a normally busy mind and introduce the nagging feeling that you should be looking, however idly, for some meaning to your life. I had no need of money, though – some moonlighting on commercials for a German car maker had earned me a substantial sum – and I would never let the proddings of conscience irritate me too much. I would have been the first to admit that I was mostly just waiting for something to turn up.

It is not that I am a fatalist. In fact I tell myself, daily, that I'm the captain of my own fate. Of course everyone needs a little navigational help – even the best skippers have call for pilots from time to time – but I always felt, at bottom, that I could master the tides in my future.

Could I have known that, before first light that morning, my future was already packed into a wooden coffin? My fate was quivering in the cavernous belly of a military transport plane, flying towards me, from Africa.

Simply put, I was a relatively successful freelance TV producer waiting for a new job. Maybe something boring, I thought, 'for a change'. Well, there I was to be disappointed.

Naturally, those momentous spring tides of fortune come up in the most prosaic ways. My sense of something looming was heightened not by a thunderclap, but by a simple email from the Broadcasting Corporation. 'The Controller would like to see you – today' was the gist. I had been back from Africa less than a week.

It was an uncertain English morning, summer finally attempting to gather momentum after an unusually chill spring. The myriad windows of the Broadcasting Corporation's leviathan West London complex shimmered under the wavering sun like the scales of a giant fish.

I swiped my magnetic visitor's ID card through the slot and entered. Inside that postmodern monolith, the temperature was its year-round rock-steady average. The windows were made of an 'intelligent' brand of plate glass that darkened in response to the strength of the sun. The brighter it got outside, the darker the glass became. That day it struck me, more than ever, that no reality could penetrate the Corporation without being measured, digitized, filtered.

I was shown through the cocooned newsroom into a large, dim office where three women sat stiffly behind computers, their faces glowing in the cold blue light from the screens. Slim and suited, they typed incessantly and without a word. The only sounds were the pecking of their fingers at the keys and, from a corner, the constant whirring of a printer disgorging a stream of paper. I wondered what they were typing and imagined endless terse memos, curt summonses, form letters of redundancy, decisions on the fate of countless unsuspecting employees. And then what? – a presentiment, maybe? – my excitement grew and my feeling of anticipation crystallized into the absurd and novel idea that this meeting might decide my fate. I found that I was breathing hard, disturbed enough to wonder about smoking a cigarette. Even if I had still counted myself a smoker, there would have been no question of lighting up in the Corporation's sterilized environment.

One of the women looked at me over her keyboard. I sat down on a soft chair covered with a dark brownish material and waited, facing a wide and dark metallic door in the opposite wall. Shortly, no doubt at some unheard electronic signal, the woman nodded towards the door and I went through. Two walls of the huge corner office were vast sheets of the reactive plate glass. They were dimmed almost black, letting in just enough light for me to make out the thin smile on the Controller's implausibly youthful face. Another wall was completely taken up with television monitors, their sound turned down. Each was tuned to a different channel, many of them run by the Controller. On Corporation Channel 1, I could see veteran reporter Nick Rampling, walking through what looked like a hospital in Africa. Children with distended bellies stared listlessly at the camera. On another channel I recognized star Corporation war correspondent Judith Dart holding a bulbous microphone up to a soldier by a large tank.

Without emerging from behind his angular steel desk, the Controller quarter-rose to greet me, gave my hand a limp but dry shake and indicated that I should sit. He was a slightly built man, maybe even a little effeminate, but the Controller, or rather his official position, presided over the news of millions in this country and around the world. In his official position he certainly had power over me and he adroitly exuded the knowledge of it in every unconcerned gesture. I had never really liked him.

He tossed over a small pile of newspaper cuttings and smoothly swung round in his chair to look at the bank of muted TV monitors. Silent artillery boomed out and noiseless explosions were flashing on many channels. Where was that, I wondered – Palestine? Afghanistan? I looked quickly at the collection of cuttings. An odd chill came over me. Dormant memories began to yawn and stretch within. The cuttings were reports of a woman's death, dated three days before. A woman I knew. The first, from a popular tabloid paper, bore the headline

Aid lovely savagely slain

Most of the page below the headline was taken up by various pictures of the victim, including one of her in her nurse's uniform and another (the largest) of her squeezed into a scant bikini, captioned *Tragic Miranda on her last family holiday*.

The text was crammed into a block at the bottom left. It ran something like this:

Frenzied Killer

British nurse Miranda Williams was brutally slain in the remote, war-torn African country of Upper Guinea.

The 25-year-old beauty was tragically killed during a new outbreak of fighting between crazed tribal soldiers high on a cocktail of drink and drugs.

Former May Queen

A dedicated Red Cross aid worker, and once May Queen of her village, she had given up a promising career in Britain to help the needy around the world. Now she has been killed by the very people she went to help. Miranda's body was found yesterday by horrified colleagues.

A Senseless Waste

Back in her peaceful home village of West Dean, Norfolk, Miranda's friends and family are devastated. 'She was such a ray of sunshine,' said boyfriend Darren, 27, 'she wouldn't have hurt a fly.'

Despite many years in the news business, I have to admit I do not usually follow the news very carefully. I sometimes read a middlebrow, somewhat left-leaning broadsheet. I had read the story about this girl. It had moved me somewhat. The broadsheet report was also in the pile of cuttings I had been given. It carried one picture – a demure head and shoulders shot of a pretty blonde girl. The background to Upper Guinea's civil war was outlined, as were a few more details about 'Miss Williams's' nursing career. There was no mention of whether or not she had ever been May Queen. Her home village was given as East Dean, Suffolk. Both papers agreed that her parents were, indeed, 'devastated'. In the broadsheet, boyfriend Darren's reaction was not reported.

I had just skimmed these two cuttings when the Controller spoke. 'So, Lucas,' he said, without turning from his silent screens, 'what do you think?'

What did I think? I thought it was awful. 'I think it's awful,' I said.

As the subsequent silence lengthened beyond natural thinking time for the Controller's response, I wondered if I'd given the wrong answer. In the Controller's smooth, childish face, only his eyes moved, flicking back and forth across the rows of TV monitors.

I was mentally clawing for a saving comment when the Controller seemed to sigh ever so slightly. Then he turned back to me with deliberation, as though dealing with a slow schoolboy.

'Information rules today,' he said. 'It is the world's most powerful force. But there is so much of it. It is an overgrown jungle of facts and events. A jungle where lots of predators – competitors – are after our audience. At the moment, we are Kings of the Jungle, but we can't be complacent.

'Our role,' he hesitated, 'no, our duty, is to tell, to enlighten. But we must have an audience to inform. We need to grab a wider audience, Lucas. Our news and current affairs coverage needs colour. Take this mess in Upper Guinea. It's a bad situation, a very bad situation, and no-one seems to care. But *we* care, Lucas. We care. And we need to get people watching. So that we can make them understand.'

His soft, low voice had affected me. It was always like this. Whatever you thought of him, the Controller had a sort of charisma, a confidence in his mission, in its rectitude, in its power. Again the silence lasted a fraction too long before I realized I was expected to speak. This time I did actually have a point to make. I didn't like where things were leading.

'I don't do news any more,' I said.

'So,' the Controller continued, somewhat exasperated

(he showed this by adding the merest dash of *patience* to his even tone), 'so we are going to get some human interest into our coverage. I want you to make a documentary – not news – about how this girl came to be killed. People here will identify with her. Pretty, young, idealistic, English and now – unfortunately – dead. You know the sort of thing: What on earth drove her to go to that godforsaken place? Who killed her? A sort of in-depth "Chronicle of a Death". The story of one person's tragedy through which we learn the general lesson of the horrors of war. Any questions?'

For a moment the huge windows behind him seemed to darken further, obscuring the magnificent view away over the rooftops to the centre of London. I shook my head.

'Not really,' I said, thinking, why is it always me?

'We picked you to make this film,' the Controller went on, 'because you made that excellent documentary recently. The one on serial killers. Interesting, serious, but with a popular touch. Saw it. Liked it.'

I nodded my thanks. I didn't believe him for a second. I wondered if the Controller had ever seen any of my films.

'And as you've just come back from there . . .'

'Yes,' I said. 'I know the place. I even knew Miranda, briefly.'

On the video wall, the screens flickered noiselessly. A different Nick Rampling report was on one of the Controller's new digital channels. Rampling's earnest, concerned face was silently goldfishing through a piece to camera on a dusty street. It looked hot where he was. Perhaps he was still in Upper Guinea.

'Rampling's going to be staying out in Upper Guinea,' said the Controller – could he read my mind? 'We'll tell him you're coming back. He'll be a great help.'

Oh yeah? I thought.

And that was that.

'Good luck,' he murmured vaguely as he waved me out. 'I know you're the man to get to the heart of this. Good luck.'

The three women were still typing as I passed through the outer office. The printer whirred rhythmically. The youngest of the three got up and handed me a large brown envelope. She observed me without feeling and whispered, in an inflexion remarkably like her boss's, 'Good luck.' Strangely, she seemed to know I was going to need it.

11

Lucky Lucas. I had been that once, to a group of people with whom I had perhaps gone too far. Right now I didn't know whether to feel lucky or not. I was being hustled back into their arms. I really was not sure whether I could face another active war zone. Too much had happened to me in too many places. I had suppressed too many memories. I just didn't want to get involved any more, but wars seemed to follow me around. For years, from the springboard of the Gulf War onwards, if it was seedy and violent, I was there.

What a pack we were! JC, Lando, Rampo, Farhad, Ralph, Lucky . . . Virile and strong, we thrived on hardship and conflict. We were admirers of Hemingway and Capa. We fed off Vietnam classics like *Dispatches* and *If I Die in a Combat Zone*. We laughed at danger through the days and through the nights we got impressively drunk. 'We are of one blood, you and I,' we would chant. 'Heed the call! Good hunting all! Who keep the Jungle Law.' We chased sex like terriers and stories like bloodhounds.

War assignments had never been popular with my girlfriends.

Well, that's not strictly true. When I met a girl, here or

there, war correspondency would gild my pitch with a certain gritty glamour, but swiftly, if she developed any real feelings for me, the initial excitement would be replaced by worry and resentment. I can even remember an innocent Claire's brown eyes widening. 'Where?' she would gasp. 'What?' Her boring, bourgeois friends were secretly envious and serenely, insidiously confident it would all go wrong.

Later I saw the same eyes, glazed over by the chasm my work excavated between us, dulled with fear, sometimes with disgust, always with incomprehension.

'Why?' she would ask tiredly. 'Why do you do it?' A satisfactory answer always eluded me. I could never bring myself to say 'Because I love it.'

Of course that wasn't the only reason my relationships failed – I was generally not very good at them – but it was a major reason. When Claire fell pregnant, I eventually went so far as to promise that I would never work in war zones again. After only a few more trips, I actually stopped.

It was not easy. As much as if not more than my promises, some troubling personal events and deep-seated concerns were necessary to help me kick the habit. Certain experiences, which I had almost wholly repressed, eventually made the life untenable. For long years I stayed away, though I regularly felt the nagging desire to re-enter that dark world which still stirred such ambivalent feelings.

Giving up wars had made no difference in the long run, of course. Swathes of me remained sealed off. Experiences and skills prized in war zones are not easily transferable to the subtle, unfathomable world of normal people interacting. The scars were there, and they still throbbed. Claire had left me anyway.

'Your problem,' she would say, 'your problem is you

think you can't be really alive unless you stare death in the face.' I thought she was just complaining.

Now that she and Alex were gone, I had reasoned, I was perfectly within my rights to go to war again. I found that I was more than mildly excited by the prospect. I took the child soldiers story and filmed in three West African countries where civil wars were in a state of uneasy truce.

Looking back I can see it was like an alcoholic who begins again with just the one glass of spritzer with dinner. The lurking sights and sounds of war, even in abeyance, were enough to make me want to drink all the way through to the port. Now I had taken on Miranda Williams, in a place where war, that most chaotic horseman of the apocalypse, was riding in to enjoy one of its purest incarnations, dragging pestilence, famine and death in its wake. I simply could not raise enough objections. I wasn't even afraid.

Also, I had come across Miranda. In the small expat world of Upper Guinea, where earnest aid workers and a cynical press corps coalesced in a close, if sometimes prickly, symbiosis, it was hard to miss her.

Miranda came out of the bush into the humid capital like a breath of air. Against a jaded war-zone crowd, she stood out as incongruously fresh and innocent, but with the disconcerting hint of something hidden, coyly promised. Undeniably she had toyed with a few options, including me. I had noticed her flirting with JC and Ralphy, and, of course, with the insatiable Orlando. She looked at me provocatively, I remember. 'Why do they call you Lucky?' she asked with a sort of smile.

'Because he always gets away with it,' someone replied for me, with more bite than was necessary. Rampo, I think.

There was strain behind Miranda's eyes but they were bright and blue as lapis. Even in the tense ceasefire of Freeville, she was restless for adventure. I had liked her. I had found her attractive. Part of me was sad that she had to die.

I had one final justification for doing the film. A self-deception really, which I actually did believe, most of the time. I told myself that this was simply, absolutely, absolutely the last trip. I would make this film and that would be that. No more war zones. I would retire to make nice, interesting docs on archaeological excavations of Iron Age hill forts, or wildlife, or something.

There was a certain irony in that the film which had impressed the Corporation enough to win me this assignment was the documentary I had made on Mark and Violet Slade, the notorious killer couple of Cheltenham. Privately, I always thought it was a bit of a tawdry subject, but years of warfare had given me an affinity for the material. I certainly wasn't going to be shocked by a few dead girls. Mark and Violet's most creative vivisection could never approach the myriad churning mutilations the mindless metal of a shell can work on the human body. Anyhow, the serial-killer film was well made and it achieved a good audience rating. Apart from various awards in my news days, I suppose it would count as my one real TV triumph. Nothing exceptional followed it, and the film had also added to the mess in my private life.

Claire regarded any interest in serial killers as insidious and unhealthy.

'You are what you eat,' she said to me. 'What if you are what you see?' She was probably right. The library of morbid research books I gathered during the production was thrown out, without my knowing, in a spring clean. I did not complain. After the serial-killer project, whenever I was accused of bringing my work home too often, the unspoken reference was to the day I fell asleep in the sitting room and the research file slipped from my lap. I woke to my wife screaming at me. Our young son sat mesmerized among the scattered images of disarticulated female skeletons and sado-masochistic sex.

Back in my office I made the call with which I began every new assignment. I phoned my mother.

She answered after twenty rings. Nothing hurried Mother.

'Peter, how lovely,' she said. 'Who is Miranda Williams?'

'Thanks, Mum,' I said. 'She's the nurse who was killed in Africa recently.'

'Oh. Wasn't she killed most awfully? Oh, Peter, it sounds like another of your strange films that I'll never understand. Haven't you just come back from there? And isn't it dangerous? I thought you'd told me you were giving all that nonsense up. Leave it to the young men.'

'Mmmm,' I said. 'Well, I'm not exactly old, Mum.'

'Yes, but I thought you were at least a bit more mature. You really are none the wiser for all your travels, are you? Have you told Claire?'

I made an equivocal noise.

'You've got to talk to her, Peter. You and she were made for each other. Anyhow, there's the little boy to think about.'

'Yes, Mother.' I should have expected it, I suppose.

'Anyway, you must come and see me soon. At least before you go. You haven't been down for ages. I'll check out the charts to see if your next trip's going to be all right.'

'OK, Mum.'

'Oh and Peter, what day was Marina born?'

No matter what, my mother could always make me smile.

III

Under the fond illusion that I still had influence over my destiny, I began to plan the shoot. I picked up a new, Corporation-issue notebook – the blue, hardback kind that, for some reason, all producers use – and went down to a wine bar on the Green. I sat down in the sunny forecourt with a carafe of Chilean Sauvignon Blanc. Music filtered out from the bar. At a corner table nearby, two girls sat talking, laughing. I found one of them attractive, the sun glinting off her hair. Her teeth seemed very white. Put it down to the last shoot. Weeks in the weirdness of West Africa can leave a man a little deprived, or maybe that should read depraved.

I reminded myself that I was married and busy, pushed girls way to the back of the priority list and carefully wrote *Chronicle of a Death* on the front of the blue notebook. Looking back on that light moment of beginning, when warmth and sun were still pleasant things, I had no inkling whose death, or how many, I would have to chronicle.

I turned to the folder given to me by the Controller's secretary. In retrospect, it was a sign of things to come. My entire team had already been chosen. Someone, apparently, had already booked a crew, and assigned me an AP – Assistant Producer. Not that I was dissatisfied with the team – in fact I was pleased enough, with the crew at least. It was just unusual that it should all happen so easily, and outside the producer's control. This would remain the basic pattern through the whole journey. The destination, the itinerary, the whole package was devised and driven by others, and by circumstance. In the end analysis, I can claim only some of the optional excursions. This gave me a feeling of vague unease, but I don't get too worried about such things. My standard reaction is to go with the flow.

I still did not know how fast and high the tide was flowing. Just about then, on one of those endless Suffolk air bases, a military transport plane out of Africa was disgorging its sombre cargo into the care of the county coroner.

I carried on looking through the folder. There were more cuttings and background on Upper Guinea. I flicked quickly through the densely printed pages. My few days in the country had not taught me much about it, but this was all pretty obvious stuff – fever, poverty, corruption, civil war. I turned to a thick manila envelope instead and pulled out a group of photographs. The sunlight glinted on their glossy black and white. I felt a strange sense of foreboding. My throat tightened.

A covering note clipped to the prints explained that these had been sent by satellite just a few hours ago. The first shot showed a decaying wooden porch on what looked like a sandy street, maybe a beach. A few rangy black soldiers in motley uniform stood around idly, looking at the camera, their guns lolling. One wore a top hat. Another seemed to be wearing a sword. The second photograph showed a dim, dusty interior, presumably of the same building. There was an indistinct, shadowy shape on the floor that I could almost have taken for a pile of clothes. The shape was reflected in a broken mirror on the wall. At the sight of the next picture the world around seemed to shrink and fall silent. The piped music from inside the bar faded along with the chatter from the two girls. I flinched instinctively, and my hand reached towards a pocket for the phantom cigarette packet.

After a moment, I forced myself to look back at the photograph of the dead woman. She was naked and horribly mutilated, only just recognizable as the Miranda Williams of the newspaper pictures. She lay on her side in a sort of foetal curl. Her throat seemed to have been shredded. Her breasts and stomach were studded with punctures and seamed with long, deep cuts. There were livid bruises all over her body. I flicked quickly through various angles, all too vile for general consumption. The final picture showed a covered stretcher being carried from a doorway. Some locals had gathered by this time, standing in that semi-stiffness of people involved in an event they know has significance for others. Half the onlookers seemed interested in the stretcher with its heavy shape under the white cloth. The rest were looking at the camera. I noticed a few white faces in the crowd. There were some photographers, TV cameramen and others, probably journalists. Some of them I recognized. And behind the stretcher, a crying white woman.

I put down the photographs and looked up. I took a deep breath and a long pull of wine. The sun was obscured for a moment behind a solitary cloud. The two laughing girls were gone.

That was the end of the Miranda I had known so briefly. That was the end of the story my documentary had to tell. A grim and grisly death in a pestilential fever-hole. The Controller was right. It was a tragedy. I felt queasy and vaguely disoriented. Part of what you might term the human in me was saddened for the girl. Other parts of me – masculine? primitive? – were still drawn to her beauty. Somewhere in me there even flickered a raw anger at a world that marred and destroyed such things.

Another part of me was cheered. The filmmaker within said this could produce a good film. I am as multifaceted as the next man, and this particular aspect of my make-up was already looking at Miranda in a coldly objective light. Whatever my feelings for the once living, bleeding, human woman, her unknown life and climactic death had become the stuff of my film, material that I would have to assess, summarize on tape and then portray in an hour or so of television.

The roulette wheel of memory flung up the Miranda I had met in the breezy poolside bar in Upper Guinea's lone hotel.

'He lived here for a long time, you know. During the Second World War. Out on South Beach.' She was brushing wind-snapped lengths of blonde hair from her face and talking of a dead writer we both admired – a great, if tortured, man of letters, who had written and set some of his most moving and pessimistic works in Upper Guinea.

'He wrote a lot about infidelity,' I think she said next, smiling at me. Her eyes had held mine with a look I tried hard to recall – challenge, perhaps.

'And guilt,' I said.

I felt drawn to her, but I wouldn't say we had communicated much. I still had the impression of a desirable woman, full of energy, of eagerness. We'd talked a little more about literature, a bit about movies.

We had the novelist in common, *Apocalypse Now*, some of the same poetry . . .

It was hardly love at first sight, but, well, I would never have told Claire about meeting her.

So, of Miranda's life I knew little beyond what the papers said. We would have to dig around a bit. Miranda was, in a sense, the star of the movie, even though she was dead. Her fresh beauty, which tugged at the man, offered great opportunities to the filmmaker. With a bit of family background, viewers would quickly care what happened to her. They would, in the Hollywoodspeak that increasingly influenced our news and current affairs, 'emote'. At the most basic level, her looks would boost the audience.

I admit that right from the beginning I was deeply sceptical the film would make any real difference to the world, but you never know . . . A beautiful girl stood a better chance of bringing home the plight of Upper Guinea's people. A beautiful girl also promised a moving love angle. I turned the possibilities over in my mind. A life, a death had to be filleted and presented as a story. Once the pillars of emotion were set in place, Lucas the producer could slip in the boring bits – the politics, the geography, the facts.

Is it distasteful that a journalist can treat such things so clinically? You might as well complain of a carver not caring for trees, of a potter harming clay. Television filmmaking is a craft like any other. When the wheel spins or the camera turns, events, decisions, forms are compressed into a lasting version. The slight indentation in clay is a finger's pressure. The digital rearrangement of magnetic particles on tape is a politician's lie.

By subduing my emotions, or rather, by recognizing them and then devising how to recreate them in an audience, through the screen, I was simply doing my job. And I like to believe that I am, in fact, less cold-blooded about my work than many of my colleagues. I plead that even before I heard of Miranda Williams, I had been finding it harder and harder to forget the real lives that I sliced into sequences and rearranged, out of context, for mass consumption. That was one of the reasons I gave up news, and the extremities of war. I was never the best at laying aside human scruples. But then again, I was never the best at anything, really.

I dialled the mobile number I had for my AP.

'Hello. Marlow.' A low, precise female voice answered on the first ring. The reception was fuzzy, and in the background to her voice there was laughter, music, glasses clinking.

They were on location in Oxford, she said, about to shoot an interview in a wine bar, but, yes, she had a moment. The Controller had already spoken to her (wasn't he just so nice?) and she was very keen to go to Guinea and do the film.

'That's great. What are you shooting there? Perhaps you need more time?' I would not have minded a few more days on my own with the story.

'Oh I'm just reporting on some little sexual harassment scandal. We're almost finished. The piece is going out tonight.'

I thought I knew Laura Marlow relatively well – by sight and reputation anyway. Everyone in Corporation Current Affairs knew her. An almost sadistically beautiful young woman with apparently limitless ambition, she was already marked out for the top. The usual calumnies abounded about how little she would not do to get there. I had already told myself not to be prejudiced, but you know how it is. The Controller had assigned her to our film as a learning experience. That cast me partly in the role of teacher, not something I really felt qualified to do.

I was struggling to make myself understood through the interference, but at the other end Laura seemed to understand everything clearly. I asked over the crackling ether for her to start digging out people who had known Miranda Williams, from school age upwards. We agreed that she should set up locations and interviews, then meet us in the evening in Suffolk.

'I'll see you tomorrow then,' she said enthusiastically. Her voice had the slightest of West Country burrs to it, Dorset maybe. A rural accent that an ambitious reporter was trying to hide? Or was it just the poor reception playing tricks on me?

'We must talk about the film,' she was saying. 'I've got lots of ideas. I'm so looking forward to working with you. I'm sure I'll learn masses. Thanks so much for asking for me.'

I could have told her that I hadn't actually asked for her, but I didn't. I was quite prepared to have Laura Marlow well disposed towards me.

I phoned the production manager instead, starting her on the boring bits that I have never had much time for – the budget and logistics. I then called the cameraman, Brian, and the sound recordist, Steven. Solid, salt-of-the-earth professionals, they had filmed as a team for over fifteen years. For roughly the middle five of that, we had often worked together. That partnership had ended in, well, difficult circumstances. The fact that I was calling them out of the blue after a good half-decade did not seem to faze them at all. Nothing ever did.

'Oh it's you, Lucky,' said Brian. 'So you've given in then? Hope they made you a good offer. I suppose this is the very last time again, is it?'

I could hear him dragging on a cigarette as he spoke. He sounded the same as ever.

'Oh it's you, guv,' said Steven. 'Heard you had fallen off the wagon. Let me guess – *one last trip*? What little pleasure jaunt have you got for us this time? Another mosquito heaven probably.' Steven hated mosquitoes. He too sounded the same. Would they think I had changed? Would they trust me? I knew, whatever happened, I could rely on them absolutely.

They said nothing about the Rwandan debacle. I wondered, not for the first time, if I could take another war. I held my hands out in front of me, palms down. They seemed steady. And I had not even had a cigarette.

It was a warm night. In bed I watched for more news on Upper Guinea. All I found was a line on INN and a US Central Network report by the anchorman Ralph Reynolds. It focused on a campaign of mutilations by one of the warring factions (I forget which). Piles of amputated limbs, puddles of blood, swarms of flies – the usual stuff. Ralphy, I noticed, looked as tanned and healthy as ever. In fact his hair looked suspiciously thick. I would have to check when I got out there and maybe rib him a bit.

Flicking to the Corporation channels, I caught the Regional News and Laura Marlow's report on sexual harassment. Actually I think it was the first and only broadcast report she ever presented. All I really remember of the story is Laura's question to one of the shy student victims of the 'rampant scourge': 'What, precisely, did he do to you?' asks Laura, coldly, in a fetching close-up that accentuates her cheekbones.

At the end she delivers her sign-off straight into the camera with a promising touch of outrage.

Now, I try not to put too much stock in appearances,

but I defy anyone who sees a recording of that report not to be distracted by the beauty that was Laura Marlow then. I can't remember her pay-off words. I do remember the wisp of blonde hair that she brushed artlessly from her unlined face. And I remember noticing that her eyes were blue, a piercing, clear-blue-sky blue.

IV

Suffolk was slow and low, with black skies heavy just above the flat country. Below the weather a narrow band of air hung, stuffy and warm. The hamlet of East Dean lay in a fold of shallow, treeless hills. In the hollow, the village itself was leafy and shaded. Beech trees, sycamores and ash lined the lanes around thatched cottages, old brick houses and a simple, square-towered stone church. We filmed around the village through the morning, trying for scenes that would help illustrate Miranda's early life, but instead capturing only the listless, lowering mood of the day. If you look at the tapes the light seems faint and grainy, giving a dreamy, almost out-of-focus air to the place. The village seemed lifeless. There were no children playing, there was no merry village pub, or quaint village school. We couldn't even find a farmer at work.

There might have been the slightest awkwardness between the crew and myself at first, but we quickly slipped into a rhythm of work as easy as if we had never been apart. Brian's beard was noticeably greyer, Steven's bald patch noticeably broader. They might both have put on a little weight. No-one mentioned the past. To my annoyance they both still seemed to chain-smoke all day. Brian grumbled a little about the material. So did Steven, who regularly made us pause for a minute as he tried to record an atmospheric soundtrack of the village.

Finally he got a minute of wildtrack he liked, the buzzing of flies and bees edging out the whining rise and fall of vehicles Doppler-shifting past along the main road. 'Never know when it might come in handy,' he said.

Miranda's family lived in a small Georgian coach house, set back from the road behind a neat lawn and a wave of rambler roses. One wall was covered in honeysuckle, except for a space cut out around a jutting black satellite television receiver. A few parked cars cluttered the small gravel driveway. I left the crew filming the exterior and went up to the door and knocked.

I assumed it was the sister, Nicole, who opened the door. She resembled Miranda, but with darker hair. And she seemed a little older, a little sadder, or maybe sterner. She asked me who I was and when I told her, her lip curled and she turned back into the house. 'Another vulture,' she called down the corridor. I won't deny I felt a bit offended. I also felt a fleeting guilt that I had sensed before, but never so strongly. Perhaps I should have stopped then, when the sense of wrong was still something deniable, lurking. Before I was in too deep. Again.

'I'll put him in the parlour,' Nicole said and showed me to a small room. It was cool in the house after the heat outside. I took in a low ceiling, a large brick fireplace lined with horse brasses, and some comfortable old chairs. Before a minute had passed, a small man in a rumpled suit crept in.

'Wilson,' he said, offering a limp hand, 'from the paper, you know. I'm going to tape the interview, in case they say anything good. Look, everything you get, we get too, you know that's the deal.'

'No problem,' I said.

Miranda's family had agreed to be interviewed, but only once and only today. There was some sort of deal with Wilson's employers (a prurient tabloid newspaper) for exclusive rights to their story. They were making an exception for the Corporation because, first, we were the Corporation and second because the programme would be broadcast well after the newspaper exclusive. I had no problem with that. *Chronicle of a Death* was not competing with the tabloids, I told myself.

Nicole soon returned with her parents. They were dressed up – he, late fifties, in a grey suit and tie. His wife, a few years younger, in twinset and pearls. I tried to be as warm and comforting, as un-vulture-like, as possible. They seemed not to notice, let alone care. Almost vacantly they shuffled over to the sofa and sat down together, murmuring everyday greetings. The woman was clutching what looked like a photograph album. Nicole took it from her and handed it to me. 'Of course you'll want to see this. The vultures will want to pick the carcass clean.'

I tried to ignore the venom. 'Yes, we probably will want to film some photographs of Miranda growing up, if you don't mind.'

They didn't seem to, but I heard Wilson the tabloid hack mutter something to Nicole about her having agreed to sell the paper all the rights. Nicole gave him a basilisk stare then turned to me. 'My parents are ready now.'

'Forgive us, but I'm afraid it's going to take a little while to get the camera and lights set up.'

She fixed me with another of her repertoire of

withering glances. 'What d'you need all that for?' she snapped. 'All you people want is a bloody sound bite.'

'Now, now, dear,' said her mother. Her father remained silent, staring into the middle distance. Wilson smirked.

Brian and Steven arranged the set-up with calm efficiency. Three small, one-kilowatt, redhead spotlights were set. The key light went behind the camera, the fill light gave the scene a softer overall glow and the backlight gave it depth. Brian stretched blue transparency across the spots to balance the daylight coming in through the window. Happy with our controlled facsimile of a conversation, I sat down just to the left of the camera lens and asked the questions.

The interview was passable. There was little emotion. The two people in front of the camera were still in profound shock. All they were able to say now, they had said before, to family, friends and in interviews with Wilson's paper. With some people, the well of expression is exhausted long before the well of feeling. So it seemed with Mr and Mrs Williams. Their quiet lives had armed them with no emotional defences, no model phrases or actions suitable for this kind of upheaval. All the spontaneous, instinctive outpourings had been made over the last few days. They had already told their tales to the newspaper, and I could hear that the anecdotes of Miranda's early life were now being recited by rote, without feeling. The sentences came out slightly stilted, as if the Williamses were trying to remember what they had said to Wilson, as if there were a correct way to talk about a daughter you had, presumably, loved, and about her violent death.

There was one thing I thought might open them up a bit. 'You know, I knew your daughter,' I said, 'briefly. Out there.'

Mr Williams looked up at me sharply, as if this made me a suspect for something – violation, murder? I wondered if I had made a mistake in personalizing things. His wife was moved, though. 'Oh, really?' She leaned forward eagerly, as though she could connect to Miranda through me. 'How was she? Was she eating well? Did she seem happy to you? She sounded happy to me when she called. Tired, but happy. Did you meet her young man?'

This was something fresh. I didn't pursue it immediately. 'When did you last talk to Miranda?' I asked.

Mrs Williams dabbed away a tear with a creamy handkerchief. 'My daughter called about three weeks ago – on one of those satellite telephones. She said she was fine, but I was worried that she sounded a bit hoarse. She would never talk to me about the fighting, she doesn't want to worry me, you know.

'She said the weather was getting hotter, or rather, the climate. She said they don't really have weather there because it's always the same. It's always hot there, I think . . .' Mrs Williams paused and I waited before asking the next question, feeling that there was something more to come. Sometimes the best thing an interviewer can do is just shut up. This pause went on and on. Just as I began to ask another question, she continued. 'Miranda said she was happy. She said that she had met someone. She said she was courting.'

You could sense, rather than hear, a perking-up of interest from Wilson in the back of the room. I must say, I wondered about the incongruity of an old-fashioned, almost innocent term like 'courting' in a place like Upper Guinea. I felt asking about boyfriends was a bit close to the bone, and the last thing I wanted was to give Wilson some more intimate grist for his tabloid mill, but this angle interested me.

'Do you know who the man was?' I asked, cautiously.

She didn't and I didn't press it.

With three interview spotlights, seven bodies and the talk of death, the room had become hot and oppressive. Wilson had opened a window but that only seemed to make the place stuffier. Outside some thin grey clouds slid across the hazy sky.

'Cut,' I said.

Brian turned the lights off, but the couple on the sofa did not move. Mr Williams had said hardly anything throughout the interview. He sat beside his wife and made comforting gestures, squeezing her hand, brushing a hair from her forehead. They seemed dulled and battered, not devastated. I was not worried for the film because I knew that, properly cut, that very numbness could be accentuated and would have power for the viewer. Brian was satisfied too.

'Nice two-shot,' he said when I asked him what he thought, 'with the vase of lilies behind. And a nice close-up of the mother's hands clutching the handkerchief.'

'Hmm. Sound's fine,' said Steven.

After the interview, we shot a sequence of the mother looking through photographs of Miranda. There she was, straining to push a mower with her father at the age of two, paddling in an inflatable pool, in a party hat, face covered with chocolate. You saw her growing taller, her hair falling longer and blonder, until it was cascading down her back in the May Queen picture used by the papers. We saw her nursing a sick sparrow, riding her pony, playing with a spaniel she got for Christmas.

'She loves animals,' said Mrs Williams, 'especially dogs.' There were many more pictures of Miranda, I noticed, than of Nicole.

It wasn't clear that the sequence worked. Mrs Williams was tired and stiff in front of the camera. I decided to leave the parents be. Wilson badgered the mother some more on Miranda's sex life – 'Look, she brought up the subject, didn't she?' he whined when Nicole intervened. Then he scurried outside to file his pap through his mobile phone.

We spent some time filming just the photographs from all angles – tilts, zooms, pans and close-ups. The images could later be used individually, for atmosphere, or could be cut into a sequence of Mrs Williams looking through the album. Looking through the lens at this staccato, two-dimensional past, Miranda appeared perfect. There were none of those red-eye flash shots, none of those ones when the click catches you mouth open, face distorted in the middle of a word. She seemed to slide gracefully, inevitably, from event to event.

A life of gymkhanas, team photographs, prize days, birthdays, holidays. We would be hard pushed in the film to get closer to Miranda than these pictures. But even this, I knew, was not reality. Reality was normality and normality is what comes in between people's Polaroids. I feel we did capture a hint of Miranda's essence, though. Looking closely at the pictures, one part of the girl did seem to grow on you and come alive – her eyes. Something about them had affected me when I met her, and it hooked me again looking out from the newspaper cuttings. Now I saw what it was. There was a questing quality about them, a pleading, almost a hunger. I hoped Brian's camerawork could catch it. As always after shooting a sequence, the crew kept silent while Steven diligently recorded a minute of ambient sound – 'You never know when it might come in handy.'

We also filmed up in Miranda's old room. It had been kept girly and pinkish. There was still a soft toy from childhood by the pillow. I asked Brian to shoot the books in the lone bookshelf. There were cheap romances, some classics and a few less predictable books by famous authors – including some set in Africa, I noticed. They had been written by the late novelist we both liked. I read widely in my youth – poetry and prose – and I often wondered about the effect of childhood reading on your life. Had these books pushed Miranda towards adventure? Towards Upper Guinea? To her death?

There were also a few murder mysteries. We rearranged the books so that when Brian panned along the shelf, the shot ended on a crime title, something like *Murder Most Foul*. Thinking this was a little heavy-handed we tried it again, this time ending on Hemingway's *Green Hills of Africa*. It might make a neat filmic device to move the story to Upper Guinea.

A short while later, Brian and Steven were carefully fitting the lighting kit back into its impossibly small box when Mr Williams came purposefully towards me. All his previous vacancy and diffidence had vanished. Gripping me forcefully by the arm, he leaned close and whispered loudly, harshly, 'I'd never say this on camera, but this is what I really think. Those fucking fuzzy-wuzzies didn't deserve her. And they should all be killed. That's what I'd do. Kill the lot.'

Startled, I watched him as he released his grip and walked away, his gait falling back into the round-shouldered shamble it had been all afternoon. I shook my head resignedly. It always seemed to happen. You can be sure, if you're making a documentary, that the telling moment will happen when the cameras are not rolling. Perhaps we were merely taping dreams, ideas of Miranda, visions of her from a timeless world of ideals. I hoped that an interview with her sister would provide some franker, more realistic material.

Instead, the conversation with Nicole served only to increase my sense of this day as something remote, of a different age. When I thought of it later, it was somehow jerky or out of focus. Like a poor-quality home video or the old film of a bygone time.

Seizing a period of clear sunny sky, we persuaded Nicole to do the interview sitting on a garden seat. The family had Super 8 mm home movies of her and Miranda swinging on the same seat when they were little and I planned to use the home movie in the documentary, mixing through from the grainy old pictures to today's crisp digitape image of Nicole alone. Now, swaying slightly, back and forth, some of Nicole's hostility ebbed. She was more revealing about Miranda than her parents had been, but the otherworldly feel of the interview increased as, gradually, Nicole relaxed. As she did so, she came to resemble her dead sister more and more. When I looked through the camera's viewfinder to see if Brian had framed the close-up as I wanted, Nicole's eyes looked straight into the camera and into mine. Just as Miranda's had once in Upper Guinea, just as they had from the photographs. Did I detect that same searching desire in them?

Those hazy hours raised doubts in me about what I was doing that have lingered with me until today. It was my first real inkling that I might not be able to get away with just making a simple film, that the project might become something altogether more engulfing. Looking back, there were clues too, obscure clues to how she died. But we weren't looking for killers, we were only making a film about a girl.

'What was she like?' I would remember asking

Nicole. (In reply to this question, Mrs Williams had said she was loving, honest, clever and pretty, in that order.)

'People said we were very alike,' Nicole answered, then continued, deliberately, 'I'm not perfect. Nor was she.'

'What do you mean?' I asked, but she did not elaborate. 'Did she ever tell you anything that made you think she would be in danger?'

'Miranda was the sort of girl who always courted danger, one way or another.'

After the interview she even smiled.

'Not a bad bit of stuff,' murmured Brian.

'Hmm. Can't you keep quiet for a moment?' asked Steven, as he recorded the soft almost-silence of the garden and the faint creaking of the swing.

Nicole showed us out. 'I'm sorry for being so hostile,' she said, 'but I can't help feeling we've been used.'

'You sold the story to the newspaper,' I pointed out.

'Yes, but there were so many journalists besieging us. I decided that at least Mum and Dad could get something out of all this. And maybe one lot delving through our personal lives is better than a whole army of them.'

'Yes, of course.'

'They are so intrusive. Wilson wanted all the pictures of Miranda in swimsuits and they wanted to know all about her love life.' She sounded fierce now. 'Well, I made sure they didn't find out anything.'

I noticed, not for the first time, the circle of whiter skin around Nicole's ring finger, where a wedding band must recently have fitted. I still wore mine. For a moment I found myself thinking about Nicole's love life. I also thought briefly of Claire. I couldn't prevent a look of enquiry crossing my face.

'Look . . .' Nicole hesitated. 'Look, we all have our secrets. But if there was something about Miranda that would upset Mum and Dad, there's no way I would tell anyone.

'If you need anything else,' she went on, 'I'm quite prepared to help. Just leave Mum and Dad out of it. You're welcome to film the funeral if you want. It should be in a few days. But I'd be grateful if we didn't do any more interviews right now.'

I agreed and turned to leave but felt her hand on my arm.

'One more thing. I know you're going to talk to other people about Miranda. I'm sure you'll talk to that waster Darren. Just remember he's an oaf and he hasn't been her boyfriend for ages. He'll say anything for a bit of cash, or for his few minutes of fame.'

I nodded thanks and gave her my numbers. 'In case there was anything else you think we should know,' I said.

Just in case there's anything you might want, I thought.

Then we left her there. The last flickering film-like image of that afternoon's home-movie memory is of her leaning in the doorway watching us leave. She looked thoughtful, as though she was considering various options.

It was cooler now. The day was waning and the sun was so low that its light streamed in below the clouds. We drove up onto a rise and filmed the sunset over the village. Brian used a filter to redden the scene 'just a shade'.

'Nice spot,' said Steven, as his microphone caught the rustle of a light evening breeze ruffling the wheat fields.

V

We watched the rushes together on a monitor in my hotel room, then Brian and Steven, in the time-honoured class-divide tradition of Corporation crews, retired swiftly to the public bar. I turned my mind to the documentary and my minibar, sinking a couple of gins while making a rough outline of how the film might look.

It should not surprise anyone that I was writing a script. The idea that documentaries are truly 'documentary' is just another of many popular misconceptions about TV journalism. As a rule, such films do not simply document or record actual events. They usually begin as an idea, a 'story', conceived in a producer's or an editor's head. The skill of the filmmaker comes in devising (and then getting) stimulating images and interviews to illustrate the story.

In this case, my rough storyboard had the film opening, I imagined, with moody shots in Upper Guinea. The girl's death would be briefly outlined, then, almost like a flashback, we would cut to Suffolk. The contrast between the harsh tropics and the green and pleasant land, between the mayhem of Africa and the happy childhood memories of England – I could see it all. I even made a rough list of the interviews to be included, and some sequences: the village and the family; the funeral and mourners; the hospital in Guinea with Miranda's medical colleagues and so on. It was a strong, simple story, it would tell itself. The first day's rushes were good. I was filled with a sense of well-being. The night was still warm and I was relaxed and confident. Forgetting the doubts of earlier, I felt I had already cracked it.

There was a soft knock on the door. 'Come in,' I said. And just like that Laura Marlow swung easily into my life. I was struck again by large blue eyes, and a bow-shaped mouth. She wore no make-up.

'Hi,' she said, shaking my hand. Her grip was firm. 'Sorry I'm late. Hope it's not too late to talk.' She sat down, one slim leg crossed gracefully over the other, her skirt just over her knee, light brown, matching her jacket. A slightly austere look. She gave a half-smile. I caught a faint aura of a scent like lavender.

'No,' I said, 'not at all.'

She laughed, and the downward curve of her lips turned upwards in a smile that could one day have captivated a million viewers. I put my right hand over my left. I hoped she had not seen my wedding ring. 'Drink?'

She nodded. 'Diet Coke please.'

That wasn't exactly what I had in mind.

'Now listen,' she said earnestly, 'I've got some great ideas for the film.'

'Ah, yes,' I said, pouring her a Coke and myself a tiny bottle of whisky from the minibar. 'The film. Of course.' I wondered whether the rumours about her promiscuity were true.

'Let me tell you what I found out at the autopsy first.'

'The autopsy?'

'Well, I thought I would contact the coroner and when he said they were doing an autopsy on Miranda today, I asked if I could go along. I felt it would help me get to know her better.'

I was a little taken aback. You can imagine. One minute you're generating the first faint but unmistakable hum of hormonal interest, the next you're talking business about dead bodies. Perhaps I had drunk a bit too much. Oddly, I think I also felt irked that Laura had such an intimate knowledge of Miranda. In a strange way I was jealous. I was pricked by vague, coiled premonitions of complications and confusions. I ignored them. 'You waltzed into the morgue, just like that?'

'It wasn't so difficult,' she said and smiled again, sweetly, just as she had before, this time batting her eyelashes. I noticed the stretch of her shirt over her chest. I began to wonder whether Laura did not have certain characteristics that might prove extremely useful on a story like this.

'The thing which surprised me about the procedure was how wet it all was. Everything so squishy. Then, suddenly, they sawed into the skull and it was so dry. Bone dry, I suppose. It was quite shocking in a way. It was my first autopsy, you know.'

I wondered how many more she planned to attend. Well into my second decade of television production, I had managed to avoid going to one. Even on the serial-killer film I had not attended any of the bone-sorting sessions. Just the thought of them carefully unravelling those broken bodies, unwrapping the masking tape from the suffocated skulls, had left me nauseous.

'Amazing thing was, so much fat on her. Such a slim girl, but still, that layer of yellow, yellow fat. I'd never seen a dead body before. I still don't feel I've really seen one. You know, it's more like a hospital there. It's all scientific. Not like the terrible things you must have seen.'

She paused expectantly, perhaps hoping that I might let drop the odd atrocity story. I was not in the mood. I was wondering how much fat Laura would show, if the scalpel opened her up, or me for that matter. Would it be yellow? Wasn't everyone's?

Laura had more to tell. 'The pathologist said the wounds on her looked like she'd been mauled by an animal.'

'Well they do have lions and hyenas out there.' I was trying to make a joke.

She ignored me and carried on eagerly. 'I wondered whether it might have something to do with the Moro tribe – you know, the nomads in Upper Guinea. They're one side in the civil war and they all have vicious hunting dogs.'

She had obviously done the reading.

'Maybe,' I replied. I didn't have the faintest idea what she was talking about. 'But don't you think the mauling is probably a detail we can skip for family viewing?'

With the alcohol and the late hour, I really didn't feel like talking business any more. Laura persisted. 'But look, if we are going to find out who killed her, we need to know the facts, don't we? How can we ever bring the killers to justice if we don't?'

Oh dear! I thought. An idealist. Time to play the producer. 'Um, I think we should get some things clear from the start,' I said (gently, I thought). 'My film is not about an investigation into how Miranda died. It's a film about her life, and how it led to that death. It's about a person, and about the problems of Upper Guinea. If anything needs solving, it's those problems, not the murder. Anyway, solving things

– problems, murders, whatever – is not our job.'

I could see Laura was a little crestfallen and partly to cover up a certain embarrassment at being bossy, I carried on, 'As for justice, just how do you propose we "bring to justice" a bunch of rabid militiamen? Anyway, justice is not our job either.'

Laura's bow mouth set firm. Her eyes glinted. 'It may not be yours,' she said, 'but it's certainly part of mine. I think it would be a shame if we simply made a soppy melodrama about some poor country girl's sad life. I think this story will work best as an investigation. I think we should give *our* film a hard, investigative edge.'

Her voice sounded more West Country now she was stimulated. I wondered whether she had been to elocution lessons. Her intensity was intriguing. 'Well maybe I'll think about it,' I said, meaning I probably never would.

Laura looked at her watch and rose to her feet in one fluid motion. 'You're the boss,' she said, meaning she definitely could not quite believe it.

At that she turned and glided from the room. Partnerships had started better. A good day's work had soured. Suddenly I was annoyingly sober. My AP, my *highly attractive* AP, already thought I was a bit of an idiot.

I think Laura and I felt we were very different then. Whereas I had reached a point where little was certain, she thought she knew exactly where she was, and where she was going. She was so focused that I sometimes wonder if her thoughts were ever really free animals. For a long time I think they had been chained, tamed and trained by a mind so disciplined it surprised even her family. Family for her was an elderly aunt and uncle. Her parents had died when she was very young.

Her story, as she later told it to me, was straight and narrow – school yearbook, university newspaper, journalism college, the Corporation. Her heroes were the great reporters – Michael Buerk, Edward Behr, John Court, Nick Rampling. No girly bands, no Barbie dolls, no ponies. Just news. Journalism did not exclude men from her life, but it did exclude any serious commitments. She had boyfriends, sure, but her indulgence in them was, as she put it, purely 'technical'. Her true passion was for the truth itself, for justice. There was injustice in the world, she believed, and journalism could right it. There was truth out there, and journalism could reveal it. That such revelations would inevitably lead, she was sure, to awards, success, fame, was – how shall we put this? – no disincentive.

Laura was dedicated both to the ideals of her profession and to her career. She saw no reason in the world why the former should interfere with the progression of the latter. The Miranda Williams story was a perfect example. It was not news, true, but I know Laura thought it could be that big break many of us sense skulking just around the corner. To me, Miranda Williams was a tragic story and a poignant subject for a film. I just wanted to do my job and move on. For Laura, Miranda's death was a learning opportunity, a wrong to be righted and, it must be said, a stepping stone. Which view is more worthwhile? I don't know. They all came down to the same thing in the end.

As for me, Laura knew I was experienced, so I must have known a bit about news and current affairs. I had even won awards. Laura was obviously disappointed at our first encounter, though. I had clearly not inspired her with the drive and ambition she was expecting. As far as journalists went, she would whisper to me much, much later, I struck her as a low-key Clark Kent without the Superman. 'What's more,' she would add, 'it was always Lois Lane who broke the stories anyway.'

In any case, I was dissatisfied after that first meeting. I felt I had been patronizing and pompous. If it had even occurred to Laura to find me the slightest bit attractive she would certainly have changed her mind. Basically, I had irritated her. To Laura, I would learn, that was provocative in itself. She was the sort of girl who didn't like anybody getting under her skin, in any way, ever.

VI

The wake-up call came as requested at half past five. I never liked getting up early but it is an unfortunate fact that the best times for filming are the magic hours of early morning and late afternoon. At those times the light is clear and golden. The shadows are long and the contrasts clear, but not too harsh. Also, although it hurts to admit it, you can't go wrong shooting the odd sunset and sunrise. Cliché shots, yes, but they work, and you can slip them in almost anywhere as wallpaper for a clumsy transition or some especially banal commentary.

A greyish haze obscured the dawn. The grass was dewy, but any night chill had gone. It was going to be a warm day. My bed felt clammy. My head throbbed lightly. I felt embarrassed about the exchange with Laura. I realized that she had not told me what she had learned from the coroner, and, infuriatingly, I now wanted to know. It was going to be a long day.

She was downstairs waiting with the crew. She smiled sweetly.

'Good morning,' she said. 'Sleep well?'

Laura looked as fresh and ironed as I felt jaded and rumpled. Her hair was tightly tied back from her clear face. I caught a hint of the same lavender scent of the day before.

Steven and Brian were already smoking. They seemed bored by the early call. It was, as I well remembered, their way of showing irritation. They went about the job quietly and effectively as ever, though. Steven recorded a full-throated, velvety chorus of birdsong. Brian captured the pools of mist hanging in the shallow valleys. I tried to picture Miranda running across the fields as a child.

Laura, scrupulously polite, sat in the car most of the time, diligently making notes and phoning ahead to our next locations. She had planned the day perfectly. As the morning wore on we went back to East Dean and talked to some of the villagers. Most of them remembered little about Miranda. Apparently she had a good, strong voice when singing hymns, but then she only appeared in the church at Christmas and Easter. She was a good lass, if a little hot-headed. All those dangerous places she went to. Kept her poor mother in a permanent state.

As a peace offering, I asked Laura to handle the short interviews, which she did sensitively and efficiently. Brian and Steven said nothing, but were obviously impressed by our AP's composure and professionalism. A little grudgingly, so was I. By the time we all sat down in a doily'd village tea shoppe for a break, the ice could be broken. Laura took the initiative. 'Shall I tell you about the autopsy now?' She smiled. 'I bet you want to know what I found out.'

'Haven't given it a second's thought,' I fibbed. It had been irking me a bit all morning.

She smiled again, hitched up a sceptical eyebrow and told us. Miranda had apparently been throttled to death. She had been stabbed and slashed with a knife.

She had also been mauled – scratched and bitten repeatedly. 'The pathologist said he's seen nothing like it since the Slade murders. Some of her flesh might even have been eaten, apparently.'

'Gross,' said Steven.

'Savages,' said Brian. 'Cannibals probably.'

Laura frowned at them. She seemed strikingly unaffected by any of this. 'Actually there were some bite marks that could have been human, but the mauling was probably done by a canine animal after Miranda died. It's possible they found traces of saliva. Some samples have been sent away for analysis.'

'Did he say whether she'd been raped?' I asked.

Laura looked at me closely, as if to test the effect of her words. I suspected she was deliberately trying to shock. 'I asked the pathologist. He said, "This girl has sperm in every orifice, including some of the new ones they gave her." '

I was disgusted. Unwanted images washed over me. I thought of the run-down room, the dirt, the dying body tossed back and forth. I thought of the humiliation, the pain, the terror. I wondered how Laura could seem so matter-of-fact about such details. The words sounded so incongruous emerging from her. There was a taste for the extreme in her that troubled me. 'They?' I asked, coolly as I could.

'Well, he wasn't sure whether it was one, two or how many. DNA tests should tell.'

Silence fell. Brian was gazing at Laura with what might have been surprised respect. Looking back, I wonder whether it was wariness. Steven puffed idly on a cigarette. 'Don't suppose we should mention the sperm angle to our next interviewee then,' he said.

The next interview was with the only one of

Miranda's sexual partners we would identify with certainty, her boyfriend Darren.

Darren ('Call me Darren') was weaselly and wiry, with a head shaved to stubble. He lived in a new housing development in the 'historic' market town which was snaking its light industrial tentacles towards the village of East Dean. His house was a pleasant enough semi. Inside it was a tip. The hall was a mess of clothes, old newspapers, bills and payment slips. Darren was, he said, a 'graphical designer' and showed us some of his current projects. We filmed a stock set-up sequence of him washing the dishes, then shot the interview in his drab living room. He openly looked Laura up and down. 'She gonna ask the questions then?' he enquired hopefully. 'Great. Up close and personal, yeah?'

Laura smiled wearily. 'Tell me about how you first met Miranda,' she said.

Darren gave good interview. He had met Miranda at the Accident and Emergency department of a local hospital while she was doing her nurse's training. 'She bandaged my thumb. I'd cut it doing DIY on this old place. She was so gentle. Like an angel.'

Darren cried a couple of times. They were going to be married, he said. He was 'devastated'.

'But I have no hard feelings against the people of Upper Guinea. Their corrupt leaders and global capitalism are to blame.'

We wrapped it up very quickly. Darren waited till all the reverse shots and cutaways were done. Then, after Brian switched off the camera, Darren took the opportunity to demand some money for his pains. When Laura said that wasn't the way the Corporation did things, he became angry. When he saw that was not going to work, he became spiteful. When Brian and Steven took the kit out to the car, Darren hissed to

Laura, 'Do you know how I really met her? I first met her at an S & M club in Norwich. She was dressed in a skintight red rubber suit. She was crawling around on all fours. The suit had two holes here,' he pointed at his chest, then at the front and back of his jeans, 'here and here. She was wearing a studded leather collar. All she needed was a man with a lead. I had one. I clipped it to her collar and away we went.' He burst into hysterical laughter. 'She was taken there by her sister. All women are slags. You too.'

Laura reddened and her eyes flashed. I felt I should do something, as Darren leaned close and almost spat the last words into her face, so I interposed myself and whispered into his ear. Darren seemed to shrink immediately. He muttered a scowling apology to Laura, and slunk off. 'Are you all right?' I asked Laura.

'Yes, thank you.' She seemed unfazed by Darren's outburst. She certainly had some steel in her. There was a resolution burning in those blue eyes that affected me. I had seen something similar before. I couldn't quite remember where.

'You really gave him a fright,' she remarked with a smile. 'I'd never have thought you could be so intimidating. What did you say to him? It was very effective.'

In fact, I do not make much of a frightening figure. I had simply told Darren that unless he apologized, the Social Services would be very interested to see that he had such a thriving design business in his own home when he was claiming rent support and unemployment benefit. 'I noticed the payment slips in the hall,' I said a little self-consciously. 'One of the first rules of journalism. Keep an eye out for the details. Any small piece of information can be useful. Or harmful.' I felt like I was lecturing. I wondered if Laura had noticed that I was no longer wearing my ring.

We were silent for a while, both thinking of the same problem that had just arisen. 'Of course it's got nothing to do with anything,' I said to Laura.

'Maybe not,' she agreed, cautiously, 'but is it true? If it is, we'll have to rethink what we can use from the interview, if anything. We can't use that fairy story about the cut thumb if it isn't true.'

'Unfortunately, the cut-thumb story is good on camera. In fact it's all we've got on camera. And remember, Miranda's sister warned me about Darren. I'm sure he's just making it up to get at us.'

Laura was unconvinced. 'Nicole didn't say he was a liar, did she? Anyway, why should Darren make up something vile like this and then wait till the camera's off to say it?'

'Maybe he thought it would turn you on,' I joked. Why did I say that?

'Well maybe it did.'

She turned and stalked back to the car. I was unsettled now. Why did she have such an effect on me? I should have been more patient. She was young. She would learn. In the final analysis, television was about making do with what you had. You couldn't broadcast pictures that didn't exist. At that early stage in her short career, Laura still felt she could get everything she wanted. Then again perhaps it was envy that I felt – envy at her energy, her enthusiasm, her idealistic belief in some grand news mission. It was an idealism that had leaked out of me somewhere down the line. Since those days, in my most honest reflective moments, I have even wondered whether I ever really had it in the first place. Laura was making me ask questions which I felt I had addressed satisfactorily long ago. But maybe

I never really answered them at all. And those damned blue, steely eyes were getting to me again. Still, at least I was annoying her as well. And I was the boss. The ride back to the hotel was quiet. I suddenly felt that the night air was uncomfortably close.

It was three large whiskies later that I returned to my room. I was pleased to note that I had still not smoked a cigarette. The message light was flickering on the telephone. I rang the operator, who said that a Nicole Jones had called. It took me a moment to realize it was Nicole née Williams. She had left no message. I was mildly thrilled. Surely there was only one reason she might have called. My brain slightly fugged by whisky, I picked up the phone, but as I dialled, I realized I was calling Claire. I slammed down the phone and fell into bed. Thinking of Claire, I drifted into a befuddled sleep.

Claire's image melted seamlessly into a power-suited Laura, lecturing me on something I couldn't quite catch. I turned away and saw the girl from two days before, on the wine-bar forecourt. This time our eyes met and she crooked a finger at me, invitingly. 'You like to watch?' she asked. The finger grew a ring, and then the girl was Nicole, below me, naked, moaning. I was moving on top of her, our bodies sweaty, straining. Her head rolled left and right, her mouth opened in ecstasy and her eyes rolled back in her head. Then I saw the eyes were blank and bloody, the gaping lips were pale. I was having sex with Miranda. In the dream, I screamed.

VII

The morning marmalade was congealed into a lump. Buried deep in the foreign pages of the papers lurked reports on Upper Guinea. They were enough to make all but the most gung-ho war tourist apprehensive. Hundreds of civilians were being murdered in ever more frightful ways, thousands more were threatened by starvation. The war had obliterated agriculture. Everyone seemed to be to blame – the World Bank, multinationals, colonialism. The pundits were unanimous that something had to be done. There was talk of a UN feeding programme. There was hope that the Americans might get involved. The US, apparently, felt a bond with Upper Guinea. This was because, 150 years ago, the country had been founded by a group of emancipated slaves from the American deep south. It was another nice touch of ideals gone wrong, I thought. I wondered if we could use it in the film as a device to parallel the destruction of Miranda's hopes.

Laura had a smorgasbord of Miranda's local friends and colleagues for us to interview, and some information on the photographs of Miranda from Upper Guinea. They were the work of Farhad Morvari, a cameraman and photographer. I knew him from many places – Somalia in '92, Sarajevo and Rwanda in '94. I remembered him as a mysterious, elusive figure. The crying girl walking behind Miranda's body was a friend of hers, Lucy Chambers, a doctor. Both Farhad and the doctor were still out in Upper Guinea.

The day was spent filming in Norwich, where Miranda had trained as a nurse. Her former colleagues and the doctors who taught her spoke of her natural aptitude for nurture and healing. It seemed she really might have been a gifted carer. 'It's so unfair,' said a girl who had trained with Miranda. 'She was so *good*. Why does evil always destroy good people?'

Why indeed? I wondered.

'Hmm,' Steven said, 'great sound bite.'

Laura put in a phone call to the coroner's office. The body was to be released to the family. No new results had come through. 'What's the rush?' the assistant had said. 'She's dead, inn' she?'

The funeral would be on the eighth. Then we could go to Upper Guinea, but only after completing the Corporation's Hostile Location course.

For me, the time had come to tell Claire.

I got back late to my bare studio apartment in a moderately chic area of West London. I had taken it on a short rental after Claire had shown me the door and there I still was, four months later, still renewing the fortnightly lease, paying a fortune. There were two notable messages on the machine. One was from an air hostess who was taken with me. She was attractive and as perplexed as I was that nothing had happened between us. I suppose that even though Claire and I had split up, I still felt oddly loyal. Perhaps even then I secretly harboured some hopes of our getting back together. The second message was from Claire. It was terse, but pronounced in her I'm-very-calm voice, the one she used when she was anything but. 'Peter, we must talk,' it said. 'You haven't called for days and there's something important I have to tell you.' Then, with more than a dash of remonstrance, 'Anyway, it's not right that you don't even bother to talk to your son.'

It was too late to phone, I thought. I didn't want to make the call that wakes them up, finding them grouchy. I didn't want the call that catches them flustered in the middle of something, and leaves you convinced that the something was sex with someone else. Nor did I want the one that finds no answer and you wonder where the hell they are at that time of the night.

The temperature was rising and the city night was stuffy. I opened all the windows, fruitlessly trying to create a draught. I turned the lights off, lay in bed and planned what I was going to say. I got the machine. 'We're not in at the moment. Please leave a message after the beep.'

We're not in? Why *we*? Our son Alex, being five years old, did not get many calls. Or had it always been like that and she just hadn't changed it? I put the phone down without a word.

VIII

The day of the funeral dawned damp after night rains. The sky washed clear but the ground heavy. We arrived hours before the ceremony. The mossy tombstones were wreathed in an early mist, which gave the graveyard a mysterious air. We filmed as it dissipated, curling away and revealing the grave dug yesterday for Miranda, covered with a black tarpaulin. The pile of soil beside the grave was moist and rich. Worms coiled in it, plump and white. I lifted a corner of the sheet over the grave and looked into the hole with the idea of filming it. Shadowed in the slanting early light, its depths were invisible, black. This darkness seemed to me the final realization of Miranda's death. More even than the explicit photographs I'd seen. Steven made us pause as he recorded the graveyard atmos.

Later on, the slow weight of pallbearers and mourners trod a muddy path through the small country churchyard to the graveside. Mr and Mrs Williams were ashen, and even frailer than before. They leaned heavily on one another and on Nicole. She ignored us. By now the rest of the media had arrived. Barred from the cemetery, they lined up along the graveyard's low stone wall – three television crews for the Corporation news programmes, local, national and digital, plus a few more for non-Corporation outlets. A few photographers circled around and I thought of Nicole's description of the media as vultures. Still a bit harsh, I decided. Only doing our job. Then I spotted Wilson and his photographer and thought again. They were a bit like birds of prey, hovering in the cemetery, almost next to the bereaved family. Still, the Williamses had sold the story. They couldn't complain.

Some of the friends and colleagues we had interviewed were among the gathering. I noticed that Darren was not. I urged Brian to try for big close-ups of the mourners. A couple of crying faces can work wonders for a film. Brian complained he was too bloody far, but grumpily screwed on his telephoto lens and whirred away. Steven was listening intently to his headphones, though an observer would have wondered what he could be recording. Standing on the cemetery edge you could only catch the odd snatch of the service on the faint breeze. Even if Steven gets nothing, I thought, it's not the end of the world. We would use some sound-effects recordings of crying, or even some sad music when we cut the sequence.

The sequence. It's nothing to be proud of, the way we saw the scene. The truth is we perceived the ceremony, the grief of a family, the end of a girl's time on the surface of the world, as a sequence. That, if you are a broadcaster, is your job. All that can be said is maybe, for me at least, something was on the verge of changing.

As they lowered Miranda Williams into the cool earth, I felt troubled by what we were doing. Perhaps this film really was going to be different somehow. Beside me Laura also looked pensive. We said little to each other, but our disagreement over Darren's information did not seem to be affecting our work.

As soon as the ceremony finished, Laura got hold of the representatives from the Red Cross and one of the famine-relief charities. We interviewed them in the churchyard, framing the shot carefully. In the background the gravediggers were throwing shovelfuls of earth into the hole. 'Miranda's death', said the well-groomed Red Cross woman, 'must not be in vain. She died for the people of Upper Guinea. For her sake, we cannot forget them now.' She gave the number of a Red Cross hotline for credit card donations. The famine-relief worker ploughed the same furrow. 'Miranda's death was a tragedy. But it is just one of many tragedies in Upper Guinea. Unless the international community acts now, thousands more innocents are going to die.' He gave another hotline number.

We were preparing to leave when we saw Nicole talking to the vicar. For some reason Steven went over – he seemed to be shaking hands with him. Then suddenly, Nicole was striding up to us, warding off the attentions of various journalists.

'How dare you!' she hissed at me. 'I thought you were different from the others. I even called you the other night, to say thank you, for being so easy on my parents. But you're just like the rest. Vampires, vultures, leeches, living on the blood and suffering of others. I wish you would all disappear and leave us, leave everybody alone.' She turned away and left me, I admit, speechless.

Laura enjoyed that. 'You made an impression there, obviously,' she chuckled. 'Maybe she heard that we interviewed Darren.'

I shook my head. 'No, I don't think so.'

Steven came over from his talk with the vicar, studiously winding up a cable. 'What's the problem?' he asked.

'The sister got in a bit of a bait with Peter,' said Brian. 'Dunno why.'

'I hope she wasn't angry about me recording the service,' said Steven.

'Why should she be?' Laura asked. 'We stayed outside the gate.'

'Hmm, yeah,' said Steven. 'But maybe she didn't like the radio mike I put on the priest. Nice idea, guv.'

Laura was open-mouthed. I was a little sheepish about the intrusion, but how else were we going to get the sound? I knew that when it came to editing the documentary, I would be ready to use the sound, no matter how Steven had got the recording. There was no doubt about it. Laura's shock quickly dissipated, though. After a moment's reflection she even smiled and nodded as if she had learned a valuable lesson.

As we left the church, the NGO workers were still doing interviews and giving out hotline numbers. 'Miranda's death', I heard the Red Cross woman say earnestly to another camera crew, 'must not be in vain . . .'

It is a handy freak of nature that, when journalists go on holiday, the amount of news decreases. Now approaching the height of summer, it was officially silly season for the media. Without much competition, Miranda's funeral disinterred Upper Guinea from the morgue of dead news stories. The calls for intervention rose to a clamour. The war had still not caught the public's imagination, though. Partly because it was such a murky, complicated runt of a war, partly because it happened in Africa. After all, there have been so many wars on that benighted continent, and one is very much like another. I doubt most of you even remember this one. The last major outbreak of war in Guinea, by the way, was not in Upper Guinea, but in another place called Guinea-Bissau, an altogether different country. Confusingly, Africa also boasts a Guinea-Conakry and an Equatorial Guinea. The paucity of the colonial imagination never ceases to astound.

For those unlikely few who might be thinking of going to Upper Guinea, the country (it is not large – somewhat smaller than Ireland) lies on the left-hand side of Africa, on that western sweep of the continent that juts out into the Atlantic Ocean. In colonial times, it was part of what was called, by those going out there, the Gold Coast. Those who arrived called it the Fever Coast, or, as often, the White Man's Grave. For many years, Laura told me from her reading, there were always two open graves dug in the capital, ready to accept the next white casualties. The coast devoured the conquerors like insects.

After filming Miranda's funeral, Laura suggested a new working title for the film – *White Woman's Grave*.

IX

Laura and I got on better after the funeral. I think the underhand sound recording had impressed her. She was a stickler for authorities in journalism and according to one US network producer, whose memoirs were part of Laura's canon, to be successful in this type of journalism required 'unorthodox tactics, stamina and, for best results, a criminal mind'. I suppose mild blackmail of a dole scrounger and planting a secret microphone against the wishes of a grieving family exhibited hints of the first and third.

Thinking on it now, I would like to believe that I really did lack the full complement of traits needed by a great journalist. One famous view that Laura used to quote defines these as 'a little writing ability and ferret-like cunning'. In the book of another of her idols – one of our most fêted TV reporters, famous for his tender and personal descriptions of human suffering – Laura had underlined the passage where he writes of his 'ruthless appetite' and 'predator's instinct'. The very vocabulary of Laura's media-course textbooks seemed to promote this hunting hypothesis: '. . . the camera crew become the hunters . . . shoot it quickly before it moves . . . use your camera as a sniper's rifle, not a machine gun.'

Laura believed she had these skills within her and was keen to develop them.

'Just watch Brian and Steven,' I tried to stress. Probably not enough. They would have been far better examples for behaviour than her producer, or the few others she would emulate in her short apprenticeship. I wondered what she would make of the reporting styles she would encounter in Upper Guinea – Rampo's bull-dozing, JC's quiet efficiency, Orlando's recklessness.

Her natural inquisitive bent was irrepressible. She was always prying and ferreting into all angles of the story. She even tried to interrogate me on what Miranda was like. 'I suppose you met Miranda in Freeville?' Laura said. 'When you were shooting the film about child soldiers. She must have disappeared around the time you left. Did you know her well?'

'Ummm, hardly. We stayed in the same hotel. Seemed nice enough.' I didn't really feel I had much to add.

'Is that all?' Laura said wryly. 'No other observations about such a pretty girl?' The sceptical purse of her lips and tilt of her head seemed to imply: 'I'm pretty and nice enough – surely you would say more about me?' Now and again she would gently press me on the subject, and I didn't mind. What I didn't realize was that Laura would be quite happy to pursue her own personal investigative training whenever it suited her, without telling me.

Our digital handicam made this easier. From the start she was keen on using this small consumer camera. Most crews took them as back-up, in case the main rig – Digital or Betacam – went down. Sometimes the producer could use them on his own to get extra material – I'd often done this on my shoots. The little cameras were also useful for difficult trick or hidden-camera shots. 'Multiskilling' was one of the Corporation's buzzwords these days, so some camera operation would enhance Laura's already exemplary CV.

She knew the war-zone experience wouldn't hurt either. Everyone had to do their danger time if they wanted to get on in the business. For us, horror can be a powerful career propellant. In her stringent way, Laura didn't think much of people who hadn't been through one of the extreme stories, the big stories that really made the news, and people's names – the stories like Vietnam, the Ethiopian famine, Tiananmen Square, the wars in the Gulf and the former Yugoslavia.

There was also that glamorous something about war coverage. In her normally sheltered life, Laura had never even been slapped, but already she felt an affinity with the whine of bullets and the colour of blood. Her bookshelf was heavy with Ernest Hemingway, James Cameron, Nick Rampling, John Court. She had read all the classics of foreign correspondency – the hilarious *Anyone Here Been Raped and Speaks English?*, the emotional *Letter to Daniel*, the tragic *Death of Yugoslavia*.

Television gripped her most of all. Laura was of that first generation brought up on wall-to-wall satellite news and images of violence from round the globe, round the clock. Had anyone challenged her, she would have dismissed the idea that she had a taste for violence, but you could tell she was sure she would not flinch at danger, nor retch at the sight of blood. Miranda's autopsy, she had made clear to us, had not affected her at all. For people like Laura, the morgue is too sterile. It doesn't count.

I remember that time when part of me wanted to

experience the real smell of death. The consensus from my reading was that it is somehow sweet, but I wanted to smell and describe it myself. Back then, like Laura, I paid the usual lip service to the horrors of war, but secretly, also like her, I felt it would be a bit of a thrill to experience one. I remember looking forward to getting a flak jacket and finding out what my blood group was. I relished writing it on the front of my first helmet, like in the movies.

When the Corporation issued us with our combat gear for Upper Guinea, Laura had an indelible marker pen ready for the occasion. I saw her writing, almost lovingly, on the front of her ocean-blue flak jacket. 'L. Marlow, O Rhesus+' it said. Or something. I can't quite remember, and the jacket can't tell me. A few weeks later it was torn to pieces.

X

It is at least quaint and probably weird that, to teach its news journalists about war, the Corporation sends them to one of the loveliest, most peaceful places on earth. The Hostile Location course takes place at a Jacobean manor house buried in the green hills of the West Country. If there's any chance you might end up filming somewhere dangerous for the Corporation, you spend a few days here first.

The course's stated aim is to minimize exposure to the dangers of 'hostile environments'. It also serves insurance purposes. News organizations try and cover their backs before sending you into places where no loss adjuster would dare to tread, places where acts of God are run-of-the-mill. Laura looked forward to the training as the last stage in her preparation for the field. Brian and Steven were a little more circumspect. They had already done the course. They said it was a complete waste of time. 'Wouldn't protect you from a playground squabble,' said Brian.

'Better to send us on a driving course,' muttered Steven. And he was right – in many war zones, motor accidents injure more journalists than hostile fire.

The principal danger on the course was that

traditional journalistic hazard, 'getting excessively drunk'. So, unsurprisingly, Brian and Steven were quite happy to do the course again. That was one hazard they were sure to negotiate with ease.

Anyway, these days, there was no way the Corporation was sending anyone to Freeville without the latest 'risk assessment certificate' thingy. Upper Guinea was currently rated A+ on the Corporation's list of hostile environments. This meant that it was about as dangerous as anywhere could get, the journalistic equivalent of the Somme. Once I would have been thrilled by the rating. Now I decided that I would easily settle for a straight B.

I knew that other news organizations also sent their personnel on the course, but I was still surprised when I walked into the chintz drawing room just in time to catch a smooth, upper-class voice drawling something suggestive like, 'You should come up and see my guns some time.'

The owner of the voice had just accosted my AP. He was a tall man with an unruly nest of blond hair and a languid air. He was extremely handsome.

Laura raised a perfectly arched eyebrow.

'Oh I collect them, you know,' the man said. 'Just got a great new automatic rifle in Upper Guinea – an AK-47 actually . . .'

'Don't mind Orlando, Laura,' I said. 'He's totally deranged.'

Orlando's air of dislocated calm could be misleading. In action I had seen him work with the speed of a cobra. Now he spun smoothly round, surprise relaxing quickly into his infectious, rolling laugh, rich and textured as velvet. The sleeves of his exquisite silk shirt were rolled back, revealing the tanned, muscular forearms of a tennis player, or of the cameraman he was.

A highly unusual freelance cameraman, though. A millionaire aristocrat who jumped off the Eton–Oxford–banking conveyor belt, Orlando Harries had traded in his bonus for a Betacam, and gone tearing around the world looking for the action. I first met Orlando in the Croatian forests down near the river Sava. I would always associate him with the sickly, unmistakable smell that drifted up from the bodies of murdered villagers scattered in the long grass among the pines. Officially on leave, he came as a war tourist – yes, these people really do exist. For a wheeze he got accredited by the Croat authorities as an employee of the fictional *Daily Beast*. Arrogant and fearless, his Gulf War exploits had already given him a reputation for being indestructible. I remember him laughing off some shrapnel through his thigh in Vukovar. Later on, in Bosnia, steel slivers from a hand grenade had removed a sizeable chunk of his brain, with, it must be said, no noticeable effect unless it was to make him even more lackadaisical.

'Hello, Lucky,' he said. 'I gather you'll be coming back to Upper Guinea then. I'm going back too, you know.' He shook my hand warmly. In the heavy summer quiet, deadened by the mossy lawn and the heavy fabric curtains, you could hear his necklace rattling.

'What's that?' asked Laura.

'Finger bones,' said Orlando. 'Human ones. I collect them as well. Amazing how often you find fingers, you know, especially in Rwanda. They get cut off trying to block machete blows. It was happening all the time there.' He stopped suddenly and turned to me. 'Sorry, Lucky, I didn't mean to . . .'

Like hell he didn't. 'That's all fine now, Orlando,' I fibbed, holding back images of that time. 'Don't worry.'

Laura looked at me curiously.

'Well, whatever.' Orlando shrugged carelessly and turned back to Laura.

Orlando had been working in Upper Guinea when I was out there filming child soldiers. He had obviously been pulled out for some R & R and his current employers – a television news agency – had decided to cover their insurance obligations with this (for him) totally redundant course. He would be going back to Guinea just a day or two before us. I wasn't overjoyed at the coincidence. Across a dozen wars, Orlando and I had developed an easy enough relationship without ever being real friends. For me, in this peaceful place, his presence put a little dampener on things.

The first course lecture did nothing to cheer me up. Bill the instructor, a compact commando veteran with a heavy moustache, asked Laura where she was being assigned.

'Upper Guinea,' she replied, brightly.

The instructor sniggered. 'Oh yes, you are in the right place, love. Believe me, you're going to be grateful for this course.'

He then proceeded to reel off a menu of hazards on offer in our destination. 'You've got your grenades, rifles, machine guns, mortars, artillery, tanks, booby traps, mines (anti-personnel and anti-vehicle), machetes, bayonets, snakes, sandflies, chiggers, leeches, bilharzia, heatstroke, dysentery, gastro-enteritis, river blindness, tetanus, typhus, cholera, yellow fever, dengue, encephalitis, leishmaniasis, malaria (vivax and falciparium) and of course . . .' he seemed positively gleeful, '. . . rampant AIDS. I think you'll find there have even been some cases of that charming little haemorrhagic African concoction, Ebola. Get that, my dears, and you end up bleeding from just about every orifice. Ha. Ha. Ha.'

'He left out the cannibals,' whispered Brian.

'Yes, and the witch doctors,' said Steven.

At the time, I still thought they were joking.

Laura did not seem in the slightest bit disturbed. In her organized fashion, she had already compiled a comprehensive list of the dangers from her background reading. She had endured whatever vaccinations were available and was already taking tremendously potent Mefloquine tablets to prevent malaria. She was aware that these could have side effects such as hallucinations, mood swings and violent nightmares. She had noted that leeches can be removed with salt, ticks with alcohol and that filaria worms must be wound out of the skin gently, by the head. Laura believed in learning.

My belief was, and remains, that the main problem in a war zone was probably not the guns or mines, but the people who fired and laid them. And there is no straightforward template for dealing with homicidal maniacs high on a cocktail of drink and drugs. To be frank, I found the constant talk of danger and dismemberment somewhat disconcerting. The incongruity of the grim subject matter and the idyllic rural setting added to the growing sense of unease and unreality that had encroached on me from the first days of the project.

Laura was experiencing no such concerns. She seemed to thrive on it all. She was alert in the classes and at night she hung on every word of the experienced war reporters. From them she hoped to imbibe more of that news glamour that had once excited me. Some of the old hacks had seen more action than their military teachers. They had been sent here by their employers almost in expiation, as though a course now would retrospectively protect them from the dangers to which editors had sentenced them in the past. I did not tell

Laura that half of them were now undergoing treatment for addictive disorder and post-traumatic stress.

Seeing the light in Laura's eyes they would embellish and embroider. I don't think she ever encouraged them in the way some of them, men and women, might have wanted – especially given her sexual reputation – but, as a journalistic pupil, she was insatiable, fitting the data away in the neat filing cabinets of her mind. There were nascent doubts, though. 'They're bluff and tell all these stories,' she confided to me. 'It sounds so exciting. But nobody seems to *care*.'

No-one seemed to feel as strongly about her vocation as she did. The only person to use words like 'duty' and 'truth' was her. The rest of them talked a lot about the journalistic life, yes, but not about the journalistic project. Laura seemed mildly disappointed.

Orlando mainly listened. When Laura asked him why he spent his life travelling war zones, he said simply, 'All man's problems stem from his inability to sit quietly in a room.'

Now and again he laughed restlessly, or flirted idly with Laura.

Laura and I grew friendlier over these few days. I saw something of my early self in her eagerness. (I want to say naivety but that might not be accurate.) I also saw a reflective side, a sombreness that could come over her. I suspected a sadness in her heart.

On a certain day, in one of those strange, natural events, we found ourselves – as if by chance – alone in a spinney of beech, some way from the house. She was generally quite a barricaded person. This day, this green-shadowed, gentle moment, her guard relaxed. For a while we said nothing, simply looking out over the soft voluptuousness of downland.

'Why don't you ever talk about your past?' she asked

me. 'They all tell me you've been in the thick of the sort of stuff they're teaching us.'

'That was in another country . . .' I said, thinking, . . . *and besides the wench is dead.*

'Yes, so?'

'I mean in the past. The past is another country.'

'But you're going back now. Haven't you got anything to teach me?'

The Dorset burr sounded stronger now. Her voice had become low and quiet. It hovered in the still air and softened on the carpet of humus below our feet. Bars of sunlight slipped through the beech trees onto her face. I looked into blue eyes slightly narrowed by the light. 'That depends,' I said.

'On what?' She glanced up at me with a lilt of teasing challenge beneath long lashes.

'On the subject.'

'What about war?'

'Not much worth teaching.'

What about love? I thought.

'Well, what's it like to be under fire?'

Exhilarating, I thought.

'Hard to say, really,' I answered, evasively. 'Scary?'

'Can you tell how someone will react in the front line?'

'No, you can't.'

I've got a feeling you'll be fine, I thought. Maybe too fine.

'Why did you give it up? Brian and Steven know, don't they? But they won't tell me.'

It stirred me slightly that she had been asking about my life. The memories stirred too, shifted in their sleep. 'It's a long story . . .' I made it obvious that I wasn't keen to tell it now.

'Be mysterious then.' She smiled. 'I'll find out

everything in the end.' Then, in a rare moment of sensitivity, for her, she changed the subject. 'I come from near here, you know,' she said, looking out over the lush, quiet valley. A cool breeze rippled fields of ripening wheat across the rolling cap of the downs. On the horizon glowed the yellow gash of a field of rape. 'My family has always lived here. I know it's stupid . . . I mean, I want to travel, to be a war correspondent and all . . . But sometimes I wonder why I ever wanted to leave.'

'I know what you mean.'

We were silent for a while. Standing close. There was something unspoken growing between us. Possibilities and questions we were in no hurry to explore, or answer. Then Orlando came along – as if by chance – with Brian, and reminded us that the next lecture was about to start.

Laura, escorted by Orlando, walked briskly towards the class. Brian and I lagged behind. He lit a cigarette and gave me a shrewd look. Brian would rarely say anything directly, but I know he was thinking of previous locations, emotions and situations scandalous and tragic. Perhaps he was even thinking of Rwanda.

'Careful, Lucky,' was all he said.

I nodded. Yes, I thought. Careful.

The crew was right about another thing too: the Corporation's Hostile Location course lays effective groundwork for one staple war-zone activity – the drinking. Brian and Steven sat stoically through most of the lectures, then came alive to orchestrate the nightly bouts with monumental efficiency. Laura did not join in the actual inebriation, but she did attend. One evening she mentioned we were making a film on Miranda Williams. It turned out that Miranda had herself been on the course. Aid agencies now followed the media in preparing their staff for conflict zones.

'Yes, I remember her,' slurred our thuggish unarmed-combat professor. 'Pretty lass. Nice eyes. They were medical people that week, so we made the battle-field first-aid lessons a bit more advanced. She seemed to know what she was doing. Capable girl I'd say. Good-looking lass. Damn nice body, too. Terrible shame.'

I hope the course does us more good than it did her, I thought. It didn't keep Miranda out of harm's way. I remembered Nicole saying that Miranda courted danger.

'Bit of a goer, I reckon,' said commando Bill, 'not that I'd speak ill of the dead, mind.'

'What did you think of her, Orlando?'

Orlando was drumming a swizzle stick on the rim of perhaps his fifth gin and tonic. At the question he paused. 'I thought she was gorgeous,' he said, lazily. 'What do you think, Lucky?'

'Yes,' said Laura. 'What was she like, Peter? You must be able to remember more than you've told me.'

'Honestly, I couldn't really say. Interesting, I suppose. I hardly met her. You knew her as well as I did, Lando.'

'You really think so?'

'As well as any of us.'

Orlando gave an enigmatic half-smile. 'Georges may be a better judge of that.'

'Who's Georges?' asked Laura promptly.

'You'll get to meet him eventually,' said Orlando. 'We all do.' He drained his glass, tilting it until the ice clinked against his teeth.

Laura's thorough mind turned to practicalities. 'Let's shoot a sequence here, on the course,' she said. 'It was one of the last things Miranda did.'

'Not bloody likely,' said Brian.

'Not on your life,' said Steven.

As far as they were concerned, this was time off. As far as I was concerned, I agreed with them. Laura set her lip in a determined look I was getting to know well. The next day I noticed her filming systematically with our handicam.

I've seen her footage and, as I thought, there wasn't much worth recording. I don't think it would have been used, even if we had gone on to finish *White Woman's Grave*. It is more like home movies than anything else. There is a fun sequence of us all trying to negotiate the fiendish booby-trap course through the beech wood – if the traps had been real, we would all have died. There is a surprising amount of footage of me, sometimes filmed when I was unaware. In one shot, held for quite a long time, I am seen in three-quarter face, sitting by a window, looking out. The picture zooms in to a BCU – a Big Close-Up, when the subject's face almost fills the screen. I think I look calm, untroubled. To my eyes now I seem young. There is nothing in my face of the unease I remember feeling. In another sunny sequence that I didn't recall, I am even smiling at her, tussling with her for possession of the camera. I point it at her, and before her hand playfully covers the lens, you glimpse a pretty young woman laughing in a flimsy summer dress.

It was the last time, save one, that Laura would appear on camera.

Most of the material records classes that were no more than common sense and seem somewhat less than that in the cold light of video. A lecture on what to say in hold-ups suggests you say nothing. The same advice is given in the lecture on kidnappings. 'Just do whatever they say' is the official line, in case it happens to you.

In fact much of the course seemed to be of dubious value, designed only to increase feelings of trepidation and impotence. Camouflaged Special Forces instructors proved that if an enemy is well hidden, you cannot see him at a distance of three feet. They showed that mines can kill you in various different ways – some mines spring up in the air and eject bright steel slivers in all directions. Some spray down on you from trees. Others, the size of scones, or ice-hockey pucks, lie lurking in long grass, scattered over fields like chaff. After a graphic demonstration of knife wounds, involving a heavily tattooed Royal Marine and a side of beef, one quivering young reporter left the course never to return.

Of these lessons, what really made any impression? First aid should have, I suppose. We learned the ABC – check the Airway (is the throat clear?), then the Breathing, then the Circulation. Then there was triage – which wounds to treat first – Breathing, Bleeding, Burns, then Breaks. Or was it Breaks then Burns? I forget. I was not really much good in the simulations, always choosing the most bloody superficial wound to treat first while missing the unconscious casualty choking on his tongue.

Laura of course had it all down pat. When a famous Corporation reporter got tipsy, fell off a wall and broke his leg, it was Laura who snapped into a scarily proficient first-aid mode. I was pleased to hear later that she had asked for my help. I had already gone to phone an ambulance.

I returned to see Laura finish a respectable makeshift splint under the approving eyes of all. Her brow was furrowed and the tip of a small pink tongue protruded from her lips in concentration. Like all the best carers, she even had the patient smiling. I again thought of

Miranda Williams. It was as though Laura was becoming linked to her in my mind. She had seen Miranda's dead body and now she was learning some of her skills. There was even a vague resemblance – the blonde hair, the high cheekbones, the blue eyes. For a moment I imagined Miranda here, just a few months before. She would have been just like us, I thought, going through the motions, enjoying the countryside, the company. She would never have thought it would happen to her. But then again, who does?

There were some useful tips on how to get past checkpoints. Marketing people will be pleased to know that when bribing tetchy militiamen, brand matters – make sure you take Marlboro (reds) and Johnnie Walker. I most enjoyed the lecture on how to make a room safer under shellfire, as demonstrated in the manor-house parlour. If you are ever trapped in a plush drawing room by artillery, remember to take down the chandeliers and other heavy glass fittings. Close the chintz curtains and push the dressers, bookcases or other furniture across the windows. Sleep under a table if you can – preferably solid Jacobean oak.

There were also film shows – video nasties that the public never sees. They showed us the uncut rushes of news stories, stories sensitively sanitized when you saw them in prime time. Some of them I had seen in life. I remember the footage of charred bodies from a Baghdad bunker, the intricate atrocity of Somali revenge on dead Americans in Mogadishu, the brute carnage of the market bomb in Sarajevo – a man walking cleverly away, holding the stump of his upper arm high, finger on the artery to save blood. He found the forearm in the gutter and stuffed it in his pocket. They sewed it back later.

Some of the videos were meant to teach us what not

to do. There was the footage from the cameraman in Slovenia who was killed by Yugoslav army tanks. Moral – don't get too close. 'Yeah, but the shots are great,' said Brian, 'and they still run them.' There was the crazy footage from Lebanon filmed inside a crew car somersaulted across the road by an explosion. A mine was buried in the verge. Moral – stay on the hard tarmac where mines are not buried. There was the final footage from the US network crew annihilated by an Israeli tank in Lebanon. Moral – be careful with your shoulder-carried professional video camera – it can look a lot like a shoulder-launched anti-tank weapon.

I now wonder what made us more able to bear these scenes than the general public. What meant we were more qualified to understand and to digest violence and terror? Even there, in a place close to paradise, I could hardly stand it. I tried to tear my eyes from the series of horrors and looked out through the diamond-leaded windows onto garden walls of red sandstone, draped in flowering white clematis and honeysuckle.

The whole course was more than mildly surreal, but maybe it did serve to hint at some of the hardships ahead. If not a true facsimile of a conflict zone, it offered some worthy approximations. For someone like Laura, so open to learning, so receptive of data, it was like building a ramp for the perception, starting to unravel the popular concepts of extreme situations from their reality. Questions like 'Have you made a will?' have a certain power to focus the mind.

For many of us, apart from that tumble with the school bully, our experience of violence comes entirely from the media. In more than fifty years of war's banishment to the fringes of our planet, people have milked their thrills from screens large and small. From our jumbled, news-item inklings of the world, we imagine an affinity with the wild side of reality. I have friends who have seen so many films about the Vietnam War that they think they are veterans. Some of them even suffer from shell shock.

Even the toughest Westerns and war films still promote comforting myths, though. There is the benign-sounding 'flesh wound', for instance. The problem, apparently, is infection. A high-velocity bullet – from an AK-47, say – causes a massive amount of trauma to soft tissue as it tunnels through the body. The smashed flesh around the bullet's path dies and starts to rot. Infection can set in immediately, gangrene within hours. To avoid this you have to disinfect the wound and clear away the bits of dirt and clothing that the bullet drags in with it. Prompt surgery is usually needed to carve away the dead tissue around the bullet's route.

The tourniquet is another big no-no: a) it doesn't really work – using finger pressure to the artery is much better – and b) if it does work, you might be helping infection. You shouldn't cut the blood supply to the wound for too long. 'Taking cover' is also more difficult than you think. In cinematic gunfights, any tin-can car, plasterboard wall or picket fence seems to provide adequate protection for the hero. The final lecture on the course showed that this too is wishful thinking.

'In my unit we didn't say "like a knife through butter",' Bill the instructor recounted with relish. 'We used to say "like a fifty-calibre through a solid wall". And if you think those flak jackets you've been issued make you safe, think again. They're useful against shrapnel, sure, but high-velocity bullets? Ha. Ha. Ha.'

Then, increasingly excited, Bill demonstrated how modern small arms can propel a bit of lead through almost anything you might instinctively regard as cover. Fences, trees, car doors, girders and solid walls all succumbed. When specimen flak jackets and helmets were penetrated with ease, even Laura gulped.

The instructor reassured us that some of the new ceramic plates do stop most bullets. These plates are fitted into pockets protecting areas on the chest and upper back about the size of a table mat. They are very heavy. When Laura had twenty-five pounds of bulky jacket on, with both ceramic plates inserted, she could hardly move.

Remarkably, the instructor claimed a new generation of armour was being made from the webs of a certain Far Eastern spider. I almost had to pinch myself. From the start I had felt drawn into a web by this story. It was being woven all around us. Now a web was to be our protection. Not for the first time, I wondered whether Miranda Williams was worth it all.

In the last lesson of the course, the shadows were lengthening on the croquet lawn when Bill grandly brought out the *pièce de résistance*. He placed a large round pig's head, pink as a newborn, on a low stone wall by the summer house. The air was thick with the smell of hot mown grass. Small swarms of midges danced in the warm evening sunlight. 'Pigs are similar to humans in a lot of ways,' Bill said, as he inserted 'your bog-standard round' into a rifle and shot home the bolt with a flourish. He aimed at the head and pulled the trigger. A neat hole appeared in one cheek, and a fist-sized chunk of pig skull blew off the other side. Laura's eyes widened in shock and what I suspected might be excitement. I stood back as she joined the group to peer at a real exit wound close up. Orlando yawned.

Then the instructor loaded a 'specialist' round. 'My own private recipe from the Falklands,' he said with a wink. 'I tell you the Argies didn't like 'em.'

He squinted down the barrel, held a shallow breath and fired the bullet into the pig's blank left eye. Through the green-gold light of the summer evening, in a bright red-pink spray of bits and blood, the head exploded.

XI

Those few days in the countryside are, apparently, adequate to equip you to deal with the extremes of man's inhumanity to man. I still have my certificate to prove it. Back in London I took my new-found qualification straight to a meeting with Claire. No course could prepare me for this particular hostile environment.

Claire's bombshell would have drilled through even the latest arachnid/ceramic armour plate. 'Peter, I'm seeing someone else,' she said, as gently as she could. She sat opposite me, willowy and stiff-backed. I might have detected the slightest tremble. Alex played unconcernedly in front of us with his building blocks.

I felt a chill start somewhere deep within me. I might have murmured something. I was not surprised, just pierced. I noticed she had cut her hair. We talked distractedly about it for a while and I asked if she had slept with this man. Tears gathered in her eyes but did not drop.

'Yes,' she said.

'Here, in my, in our bed?'

'It's my bed now, but, no.'

In a sort of trance I asked who he was. She said I

wouldn't know him and it didn't matter anyway. No, I thought, no, I suppose it doesn't.

We carried on chatting aimlessly. I couldn't help feeling that some reaction was expected of me. Shouldn't I have been angry? Violently jealous? Was this all a test, however painful and convoluted? She would expect me to act indecisively, meekly. Deep down did she want me to fight for her? Did I sense an element of pleading, of regret in her tone? I didn't feel certain enough to react to it. For some reason, I was distracted for a moment by a thought of Laura, laughing in her flak jacket. The opening for action was gone. I missed it.

'Do you love him?' I asked. She did not answer.

Alex was talking quietly with his imaginary friend. Because I could think of nothing else to say, I told her, at last, about my trip to Upper Guinea. Claire, half relieved, half disappointed at my placidity, now became almost angry.

'I was going to tell you,' I protested. 'Anyway, I'll only be there for a week or two.'

It was as though the enormous fact of Claire's lover had been forgotten instantly. Maybe both of us weren't convinced it was important in the long run.

'I don't think you should go,' she said, passionately. 'You can't. What about your son?' She sounded like she almost cared. Perhaps she wanted me to stay in London, to try and win her back. 'I mean, Peter, you're a features producer now. Since Rwanda, the closest you've come to covering a spring offensive was that fly-on-the-wall film about spring cleaning. Now you're suddenly rushing back into war zones every other week.'

I nodded resignedly. The thought occurred to me that I did not have to go. I could change my mind. It was going to be dangerous. It was going to be tough. Part of me wanted to go, yes, but I also had grave misgivings.

In that moment, I thought, if Claire asks me, I will stay. If only she asks me, I can still turn my back on it all. She didn't. Instead she became defiant.

'Well, all right. Do whatever you want. You always did. You were never satisfied with your life here. You still think reality is something out there, something difficult that you have to search for. Well it's not, Peter. Reality is this. It's here. It's us. And we'll survive here and deal with it, even if you won't. Your luck's just run out.' She told me to leave and turned her back.

There was no goodbye.

Letting myself out, I realized why I recognized the steel in Laura's eyes. Claire had the same strength, the same fire. I think now that tendrils of Laura had already begun to wind through my being, but as I left that house for what I believed was the last time I grappled unhappily with the possibility that part of me might love Claire for ever.

Before I went down to the country to see my mother, I finished preparations for the shoot. I didn't want to bring those dark things with me to my family home. I went over the latest developments. Upper Guinea was becoming, if anything, more dangerous. Meanwhile, DNA tests suggested that just one assailant had sexually assaulted Miranda. Laura pointed out that didn't mean that only one person had killed her.

I sent a message to Upper Guinea with the returning Orlando, confirming that an experienced Africa hand, Jan Hartman, would meet us in Ivory Coast. I had worked with him in my brief trip through West Africa a few weeks before.

In one long and fruitful evening's work, Laura and I figuratively put our heads together. We drew up a revised structure for the film and a schedule for the shoot.

'What are you doing later?' she asked, as night closed

in outside the Corporation windows. Her fingers lightly brushed mine as she reached for a pencil. Instead of withdrawing, she left her hand there, imperceptibly reading split identity and indecision in the whorls and ridges of my fingers. Oddly, after Claire's infidelity, I felt an urge to prove myself somehow responsible, faithful. Certainly an affair with my AP was not on the immediate agenda.

'Getting an early night,' I muttered.

'Shame.' She looked me in the eye, with a quizzical smile. My scars, physical and metaphysical, burned. 'Not afraid of going to a war zone, but afraid of me? You're an enigmatic one, Peter. I'll get to the bottom of you yet.'

That night I packed my large suitcase as I had a hundred times. I always took as much as possible, including diary notebooks and a Nikon. These had always recorded for me the real life to which our filed reports approximated. Then I zipped up bleak thoughts of war and drove out into the soft countryside.

My mother seemed so happy. My sisters had recently given her two grandchildren and she showed me the latest photographs as we had tea in the favourite Crown Derby china that had always been there. It was so quiet in her village you could barely hear cups chinking over the birdsong. I had grown up in this house and I wondered what could ever bring me to desert this place for the destinations I had chosen. Why had I not found somewhere like this of my own? Somewhere where roots planted, clutched.

On a day like this I felt idiotic to be leaving. Perhaps Claire was right. I had longed for a life of starkness, right and wrong, good and bad, black and white. The complicated, everyday issues of home, of relationships always seemed so grey, so ill-defined, so inapprehensible in comparison – soft focus as opposed to the hard-edged, high-contrast world that you saw on your TV news.

Again I told myself that this trip was the last time . . .

My mother had it all worked out.

'You've got a death wish, darling,' she explained. 'You're only doing this because of Claire. She's not going to take you back just to stop you going, you know. And she's not going to suddenly think you're a macho man either. Anyway, that's not what she likes. Who is this Laura Marlow? She sounds attractive. What star sign is she? Taurus? Hmmm, careful. That could go with yours. Now don't you go getting involved again. You know it's too soon.'

'Yes, Mother,' I sighed. 'No, Mother.'

'Oh and Peter, I did the chart of that girl who was killed. You know, the one you're making the film about.'

'Miranda Williams.'

'Yes, poor Miranda. Look, her Mars was rising. She should never have gone to Papua New Guinea.'

'Upper Guinea, Mother. New Guinea is near Australia.'

'Wherever. And the thing is, the chart says her life will be short. It's quite clear. She was going to die whatever. It is also clear that Sagittarius is dangerous for her. Maybe she was killed by some hunters.'

We sat and smiled together in the cool drawing room while the day finished in one of those long, temperate evenings that so define summer for me. The scent of jasmine and lavender flooded in from the garden with a haze of childhood memories. In the clear sky, flashing blue swallows twittered and swooped to feed on the gathering swarms of insects. The low sun dipped under the eaves and poured a balmy golden light through the bay windows.

At the edge of my vision, the sharp oblong shape of a large black television squatted in the corner like a warning. My mother walked over to the set and switched it on.

Involuntarily I closed my eyes. If it was the news, I did not want to see. It would intrude on me soon enough. But instead of the pedagogical, insistent tone of the newsbringer, we heard the murmuring of the good burghers of a sleepy Midland market town, bringing their family heirlooms for valuation at the *Antiques Roadshow*.

'Oh how nice,' said my mother. 'I like this one. They find an Elizabethan poison ring, you know, and a Viking axe. Imagine, things like that sitting in someone's attic.'

As the night rose above the downs, we changed channels and watched *The Wizard of Oz*. 'It's a twister,' cries dissatisfied Dorothy, swept up from her Kansas home by something she cannot control and deposited in a land of danger and wonder. In front of her stretches a yellow brick road, the road that beckoned to all my kind, leading us off, away from our own personal Kansas. Normally it was one of my favourite films.

I hugged my mother goodnight. At the bottom of the stairs she turned to me. 'And Peter . . .' she was serious now, a mother's worry showing, '. . . be careful. I know it's more dangerous than you say.'

I smiled. 'Thanks, Mum. I will be.'

I made one more call before leaving – to a university friend who had given up war reporting for a life teaching at a very traditional English country boarding school. We had long argued about the values of news and I had often teased him for staying put in his rural time warp. I admit that I looked down on the petty politics of the staffroom, when set against the tectonic shifting of civilizations that I had witnessed. I just couldn't understand how an enquiring mind could pass up travelling the globe.

'Once and for all,' he would recite, 'there are things I don't want to know. Wisdom sets bounds even to knowledge.'

When he heard I was going back to a war zone he refused to see me. 'I can't believe you haven't learned yet,' he said, on the phone. 'Thucydides . . .' (my friend taught – intriguingly – Greek and Physics) 'Thucydides had it right more than two thousand years before us TV news goblins. That war is an evil, he said, is something we all know, and it would be pointless to go on cataloguing all the disadvantages involved in it.'

'But this is my last time. I just feel that it will finally clear everything out of me.'

'Oh, I see. Kill or cure. Like using dynamite to stop an oil-well fire, you mean. Well, possibly. I still think you could be making a bad mistake. Be careful and call me again when you've come to your senses.'

Laura's leave-taking was straightforward. She made a simple will. Everything, it appeared – her flat, her few, stylish possessions and her modest but blue-chip share portfolio – was bequeathed to her one living relative, an aunt. Her few real friends she had left behind in the West Country. She saw them so rarely it would be weeks before they noticed she was gone. After brief reflection, she left a concise, composed message on the answerphone of the man she'd been seeing. Frankly, I do not think she cared whether she ever saw him again, but Laura would think it best to be polite. She went out into the warm evening dressed in a new linen suit, the sort she knew that real foreign correspondents wear. Along with her usual large handbag she carried nothing more than a sturdy khaki holdall. No doubt she had carefully planned what to take. All the best journalists, Laura had often read, travelled light.

At the airport, Brian and Steven made a final check of the kit. The average film crew would travel with a dozen boxes or more. Over the years they had pared down the paraphernalia to just four: the cylindrical tripod case; an oblong mini lighting kit the size of a croquet set; a box for tapes; another for batteries and charger. Brian carried the camera with him always. It would be loaded with tape and ready to roll. Steven carried his sound equipment and a canvas 'Belly', a professional bag made by Bellingham. This was bulging with the vital odds and ends that made all the difference – the sun gun, gaffer tape, filters, Steven's maxi-strength DEET insect repellent and a few tubes of multicoloured Smarties. The crew was well overweight this time with permethrin-impregnated mosquito nets, extra batteries, four flak jackets plus helmets and the handicam as back-up. They were also taking more tape stock and replacement editing equipment for the two Corporation crews already working in Upper Guinea with Judith Dart and Nick Rampling.

While they sorted out the excess baggage, I heard them talking. 'This is going to be a nasty one,' Steven said to Brian.

'Yup.'

Brian lit up a cigarette. 'Do you think he'll be all right?'

They were talking about me.

'Reckon so,' said Steven, taking a light from Brian. 'Always good in a pinch. What about her?'

'She's up for it. That's for sure.'

'Do you think she has any clue?'

'Not much. But did we?'

A couple of hours later, the night sky swallowed up the winking lights of an aircraft heading south. From the ground, that sodium-yellow night was bereft of stars.

PART 2

HUNTING WITH THE PACK

15TH – 30TH JULY

'. . . in the blinding sunshine of that land I would become acquainted with a flabby, pretending weak-eyed devil of a rapacious and pitiless folly.'

XII

The heat of the Fever Coast enveloped us at 5,000 feet. It was a warm, thick dampness, heavy with mist and ozone. Plumes of water vapour curled like smoke through the overhead lockers and condensed into rivulets streaking the inside of the throbbing fuselage. The propellers seemed to be churning through a warm broth. The sweat prickled out all over your body, beaded into big, full drops on your forehead and rolled into your eyes. Laura pulled her hair out tight and tied it at the back. I saw the shine of moisture at the nape of her neck and on her temples.

Below, the landscape along the coast was a scrubby brown. Inland to the east, huge thunderheads brooded over low hills, covered by a dark green mass of forest that melted into the far horizon.

We flickered over a vast river delta, a fan of sea around it muddied brown by silt. Then there was the hint of sunlight catching reflective material, of the regular lines of human presence. The plane shuddered heavily, spun and plunged towards the airfield below in a steep spiral.

'Don't worry, my china,' shouted Jan Hartman above the roar of the engines. 'They always land . . .' he gasped as the plane gave a particularly heavy jolt, '. . . like this. It makes them a tougher target for the SAMs.'

If Laura was worried about the surface-to-air missiles, she did not show it. She was gazing, rapt, out of the small window. She licked a drop of sweat from the curve of her upper lip. I found myself unconsciously doing the same, tasting wet salt.

The plane corkscrewed violently towards the earth. Hartman laughed wickedly. He had met us in Abidjan, Ivory Coast, where we had left our international flight and loaded onto the only plane still operating into Upper Guinea. Its pilots were a couple of Ukrainian privateers left over from some defunct mercenary adventure. Now they ferried a stream of journalists and aid workers in and out of the unpleasantness of Freeville.

Hartman was an old Africa hand, a sun-dried white from Zimbabwe who had washed up in West Africa more years ago than anyone could remember and had stayed. 'For three reasons,' he would say, in his southern African drawl, 'the girls, the girls and the girls.' A stringer for one of the big print agencies, he had been in more wars than he could count. 'I set off the metal detectors in airports,' he would moan, 'I've got so much lead in me.' Then he would pull his bush hat with its leopard-skin band down on his bald head, tap his pipe and launch into one of his war stories. He invented at least half, but, as he said, what he didn't know about the continent 'wasn't worth a puff adder's spit'. He had been in and out of Upper Guinea through all nine – or was it ten? – years of civil war.

Hartman had been undergoing a spell of treatment in the relatively sterile francophone environment of Abidjan when Miranda's body was found. He was not shocked – years on the Fever Coast had left him an inveterate pessimist. 'Freeville's one of the worst places I have ever been,' he said. 'It was only a matter of time before someone got killed. And – what's-her-name? – Miranda won't be the last. If each dead whitey deserves a whole hour on prime time, Jeez, you'll end up making an entire series.

'When we arrive,' he said, relishing his guiding role, 'just stay calm. Give no money to anyone unless I say so. And don't film. They can get jumpy at the airport. Better do as I say, my chinas.' He looked meaningfully at Laura. She had wanted to film the arrival, to show what Miranda would have seen when she first hit Upper Guinea. Hartman said it was a bit risky. I agreed.

The plane thumped into the ground then turned back up the runway, bumping spasmodically over potholes in the decaying concrete slabs. There was the hint of a control tower and a dishevelled grey terminal, but the plane seemed to be moving away from them, along a runway flanked by blank green walls of forest. 'It's the Bamanda's turn today,' Hartman explained through the roar of the propellers. 'They take a split of the airport profits. The Government holds the terminal, so today we stop at the other end of the runway. Don't worry, their entry visas are just as pointless as the government ones. If anything they're cheaper.'

Opening the aircraft door made no difference to the temperature. It just added noise. The rickety steps were lowered into a jabbering sea of outstretched arms and upturned faces. Brian and Steven clung grimly to their gear and fought through the crowd, following Hartman towards a small hut on the edge of the airfield.

A group of pudgy, coal-black soldiers sat in cane chairs by the corrugated-iron shack. They were bored. African soldiers have a peculiar ability to seem bored all the time, even when they are killing people. They ignored Hartman, but there was a flicker of interest when they saw the camera gear. 'Teee-Veee,' one of them said in a slow sing-song. 'Mmmm-hmm.'

'Very dear visa,' said his friend. 'No entry.'

Two of the troops slowly got up and began to poke languidly at the gear with their rifle barrels. Steven, smoking, and Brian, camera hanging from his shoulder, looked around unconcerned. Laura looked annoyed.

Hartman pulled us into the shack, where lounged an even bulkier and more bored-looking soldier. Despite the Stygian gloom of the hut, he wore dark glasses. Hartman told me how many dollars to pay, and I put them on the table. 'Can we go now?' Laura asked.

Hartman shook his head. 'That was immigration. Now you have to clear customs.'

I laid another sheaf of bills in front of the motionless soldier. I wondered if he was asleep. After a moment, Hartman seemed to have received some imperceptible signal and we left. Behind the hut Hartman led us through the crush of Peugeot 504 station wagons and Toyota Land Cruisers towards a white, tin-can Datsun minivan. A gnomish, grey-haired Guinean hopped out as we approached. 'This is Mohammed,' said Hartman, as the driver slid open the dented side door with a wide grin. His front teeth were filed to razor-sharp triangular points. Round his bare left arm was a bracelet of black hair, hung with small green and white cowrie shells. 'He's called Mo for short.'

The camera equipment loaded, Mo hunched over the wheel with a frown of concentration. After a number of attempts he selected first gear and took off like a maniac down the road to Freeville. Requests to slow down were ignored. 'Doesn't he understand English?' asked Laura.

'I don't know,' said Hartman gloomily. 'He's basically pretty deaf.'

'Don't you think we should get a driver who can hear . . . ?' Laura asked me. Mo lurched through a particularly teeth-grinding gear change. '. . . And who can drive?'

'Yes, yes,' cackled Mohammed, loudly.

'Ach, don't worry about Mo,' said Hartman. 'He can be bloody useful to you. His clan are famous witches and cannibals. People don't mess with Mo.' He patted the grinning homunculus on the head.

The road signs gave the first hint of warfare. For some reason (perhaps because the bullets punch such nice, neat holes in the thin metal) they present an irresistible target to African gunmen. Across Sierra Leone, Liberia and Upper Guinea, they have all been riddled like Emmental; well, actually in Sierra Leone there are no road signs left at all.

Freeville, too, showed scars – gutted houses, shell holes in the walls, building fronts pitted and cratered by Jackson Pollock sprays of small-arms fire. Vultures skulked on broken lampposts. 'So bloody common, now,' said Hartman, 'they just call them pigeons.'

Packs of fat dogs lolled in the heat.

Still, it was not your image of a city under the tyranny of war. With its shabby plaster and peeling clapboard houses packed between the Atlantic and a range of coastal hills, the city was rickety and run-down, but chaotic with grimy life. Above stagnant open sewers, stalls crowding the bumpy roadway sold everything from coloured ribbons and cooking pots to piles of writhing palm grubs. In the unflagging late afternoon heat, the sweaty, salty smell of the port mixed with the fug of fires, paraffin, cooking oil and the acrid vapours drifting up from the mangrove swamp. The van's pace slowed to a crawl in the crush of pedestrians and beaten-up cars, driving on whatever side of the road took their fancy. Many of them had to swerve violently to avoid Mo, who stuck to his path, regardless. 'Lock your doors,' advised Hartman as we ploughed through a busy intersection. 'And keep your windows up,' he snapped at Laura, who had rolled hers down when the Datsun's feeble air conditioning coughed to a halt.

Lounging soldiers waved us through a couple of checkpoints. At one the commander wore a black top hat – the traditional Krio headgear. All these war-boys sported de rigueur dark glasses. Mo flashed his toothy smile at them and waved. The soldiers' Ray-Bans gazed back impassively. Some of them looked no more than ten years old – 'war-sparrows' I remembered they were called. I wondered if we had interviewed any of them during my child-soldiers shoot.

Then the van was rolling into a leafy neighbourhood. The roads widened between well-trimmed verges and high walls capped with barbed wire. Heavily armed white sentries stood guard outside buildings flying foreign flags. There was little traffic apart from the odd Range Rover travelling at high speed, chock-a-block with armed Arabs. The cars here drove on the correct side of the road. 'Diplomatic quarter,' said Hartman. 'Rich Lebanese and expats. Luckily the hotel is in this area, so it's a bit more protected.'

We skirted a high mud wall. There was a gate. Around the bulbous grey trunk of a large baobab tree waited an untidy cluster of cars and vans. Their skinny drivers stood around in flapping, multicoloured shirts, dangling a variety of automatic rifles. A drowsy attendant guarded the gate. He peered into the van, saw Mo with his white cargo, and lifted his rudimentary wooden barrier. We drove up a small peninsula, overgrown with bush and flanked by perfect beaches. Mo stopped in a sandy courtyard, in front of a long, low, double-storey block, built in an arc around the headland. A recently painted sign hanging on its weathered grey plaster proclaimed it the Cape Atlantic Hotel. 'OK,' said Hartman, 'you can relax. This place is safe.'

'Famous last words,' I heard Steven murmur.

I was pleased to be back. The Cape Atlantic was one of the wonders of Upper Guinea. Even now, it can make me wax lyrical about what might have been, because, not many years ago, Upper Guinea was a peaceful place. Its beaches, people said, were the next big thing. True, the coastline is marred here and there by coils of mangrove swamp, and north of Freeville the estuary of the Great River soils the Atlantic dirty brown. South of the town, though, long, smooth miles of soft, silver-white sand, fine as dust, stretch out along the shore. In front the coast slopes gently into a warm, clear ocean. Behind, it is shaded with whispering groves of palm and casuarina. The sea teems with rock cod, barracuda and bonito. At night, turtles creep out of the water by moonlight to lay their leathery eggs.

Along one of these beaches, on a small promontory, a French entrepreneur came to build a holiday resort. Isolated by a lagoon and thick stands of mangrove, he severed the cape from the harshness of the Third World. Behind a high wall he razed the bush and planted a lush tropical garden with tennis courts and an amoeba-form swimming pool. He lined the beachfront with secluded thatched cottages, linked by bougainvillea-fringed paths that wound between bushes of oleander and fragrant frangipani.

Just a week before the first package charter from Calais, Upper Guinea imploded. Opportunist rebels took the opportunity to visit the well-stocked kitchens of the resort. The French entrepreneur took the first opportunity to get out.

The hotel became a makeshift headquarters for some squabbling faction or other. They were comprehensively routed and the hotel comprehensively looted. The bougainvillea ran riot, spreading its spines around the ferns that seeded in the damp and decaying thatch. The trim tropical garden was reclaimed by bush. The heavy jungle vines wound in and out of shell holes in the walls. The turtles laid their eggs in the crumbling cottages.

When the civil war eventually became news, the journalists and aid workers began to arrive. They had nowhere to stay. An enterprising Guinean of Lebanese extraction occupied the hotel and put his people at the airport to 'collar the dollars'. Now everyone stayed at the Cape Atlantic. Miranda Williams had stayed here. By the time we turned up, the hotel roof was clear of foliage and had sprouted a thicket of satellite dishes. The new proprietor had resurrected the restaurant and about half the rooms. Most critically, he had resurrected the bar. For ninety-five cash dollars a night you got a room with a door that might lock. There was often electricity. Sometimes you even got hot water.

The outdoor bar offered the only possible respite from the heat. By the time we wandered out, searching for the faintest of sea breezes, the press corps was already firmly ensconced around the greenish pool. Orlando's tall figure rose to greet us in the gathering dusk. He made straight for Laura. 'Welcome to the Wild Bunch,' he said, grinning.

XIII

Orlando was drinking at a table with Hartman and a weaselly local Corporation reporter, Richard Jones.

'I see you have a new piece of jewellery,' said Laura.

Orlando lifted the white triangle of shark's tooth hanging alongside the ivory of his knuckle necklace. 'Great White. *Carcharodon carcharias*. Keeps off violence and magic of the flesh. Do you have a charm?'

'Don't be ridiculous.'

'I'd get one quickly if I were you. You can't be too careful, you know. Look at poor Miranda. She was a sceptic too . . .'

'Shut up, Orlando,' said Hartman. 'Just ignore him, Laura. He's completely mad with his bloody knucklace and his superstitions.'

'You can talk, Hartman, old thing,' said Orlando. 'Tell her about the bit of shrapnel you carry around. And while you're at it, tell her which bit of you they pulled it out of.'

Laura made a patient face. Thankfully, before Hartman could launch into his favourite yarn, Nick Rampling himself wandered over.

Going noticeably to fat, Rampling's bland face was

that of a favourite uncle beneath a carefully groomed head of bright red hair. He smiled ingratiatingly. 'Greetings,' he said to no-one in particular, 'how wonderful to have you all here.' I sighed inwardly; the young radical I started off with all those years ago had long been replaced by another Rampling – the self-elected head of the journalistic community wherever he happened to find himself.

'Hello, Rampo,' I said. 'This is Laura Marlow.'

After a blank flicker of his eyes, he completely ignored Laura. Excited to be in the presence of an idol, she looked disappointed, but next to Rampling was another of her pantheon. John Court acknowledged my presence with nothing but a brief nod. I did not mind; John and I went back a long way. He would talk to you when he wanted. It had always been like that.

'Hi, JC,' I said.

People always said John Court seemed even taller in life than he did on the small screen. Looking up at his lean figure you could see why. The lamplight threw shadows into the lines of a face weathered by Third World suns and Third World wars. He smiled slowly at Laura and I could see her quickly forget Rampling's slight. Court was the epitome of the foreign correspondent Laura would have wanted to be. Viewers liked Rampling's image. They felt comfortable with him. Court disturbed you, he goaded you into thought, he grabbed your attention. I idly hoped he didn't try to seize Laura's. She smiled back a hello and he looked her over with cool appraisal.

'Marlow,' he said thoughtfully, in his clear, even tones. 'The name of a detective perhaps. Are you an investigative journalist, Marlow?'

'I'm working on it,' she replied lightly.

'Well, I trust you will get your man,' he said, a

half-smile playing at the corner of his mouth. It was hard to place Court's accent.

Court was the best. We all knew it. The Ramplings of the world would never acknowledge it, but they knew it too. Court's only real rivals now were Rampling and Ralph Reynolds. And Rampling would never take the same risks for a story. Rampling was headed for a top spot in the Corporation, he wasn't going to jeopardize that. Ralphy Reynolds? Well, 'Hollywood Ralph', Rampling would sniff, was in the entertainment business really, not news.

Court stayed for a few minutes, chatting amiably to the table with easy charm, then joined some colleagues on the other side of the pool. Hartman nudged Laura.

'You think we're a bit odd, with our necklaces and our talismans. They say Court lugs a bloody hyena's jaw about with him.'

Laura seemed to be only half listening. She was looking thoughtfully over at John Court.

Rampling was sweating profusely. Dabbing his head with a damp handkerchief, he surreptitiously took me aside. He was one of those people who come just a bit too close to you when they talk and I drew back instinctively. 'We should fix a time to have a little chat about how we are going to co-operate,' Rampling was whispering sententiously. 'We Corporation people must stick together. You know how it is.'

He walked me a little further into the shadows of the garden. 'Now you'll never find anyone more helpful than Nick Rampling, but I don't want you to assume you're going to rely on me. Judith and I are filing just about every day. We're doing plenty of live spots, and basically working like dogs. So are my crew, fixer and driver. We certainly won't be able to spare any resources from the news effort for your documentary.'

He made *documentary* sound like a dirty word. 'Nor do we want you poaching our interviews. News, as you well know, will always have priority.'

'That seems perfectly reaso—' I began, but Rampling went on and on. It registered that the time fixed for our 'co-operation discussion' was now. It also appeared that the 'little chat', as usual with Rampo, would be a monologue. 'Of course, if you turn anything up', he continued, 'on that Miranda woman, I'd expect you to make it available to us. And if we need extra hands for news coverage, we might just have to call on your crew as well. You know, if the story gets really big.'

I was amused at his presumption. I was about to point out that the priorities for my team were 1) our safety, and 2) our documentary, when he patted me on the back. '. . . And if you find things getting difficult again – you know, like you did in Rwanda – don't worry. You can always count on me.' And he walked off to join Court and some others across the pool.

I shook my head in amazement. There were aspects of newsgathering I really had not missed. Perhaps I should go to bed, I thought. Then Steven appeared and handed me a drink. 'Hmm. Don't worry about Bigfoot Rampo,' he said, referring to Rampling's habit of clomping into a big foreign story and taking the limelight from locally based reporters like Richard Jones. 'He's about as useful as a spare arse. He might not help us, but his team will. We know them. And Judith Dart's people too.'

Steven and Brian had already met up with their fellow crews. With a lot of beer and backslapping, they all trooped off to watch satellite television on the one working set in the lobby bar. Laura was bemused. 'Are you seriously going to watch TV in a place like this?' she asked. Her eyes were bright with excitement.

'Aren't you interested in the situation? Aren't you interested in our film?'

'Not as much as England versus Poland, World Cup qualifier,' smiled Brian.

'Research and planning – that's the talent's job,' said Steven. 'You're the posh intellectuals. We're just the poor old techies, we are. You might enjoy being somewhere foreign. We just take our home wherever we go. Anyway, less mosquitoes inside.'

I whistled over a third gin and tonic with a chaser of Freeville's notoriously potent Bright Star beer. Laura frowned at me. After one drink she had turned to Diet Coke. I hoped she would not get any more puritanical, it really would be a waste. 'The tonic's full of quinine, you know,' I said. 'Good against malaria.'

'Well, you'd better drink it then,' she said, sweetly. 'Don't want you getting even more delirious.'

Gin and tropics had overcome the undercurrent of unease that had bothered me on and off since the beginning of the project. I was not keen to reawaken it by asking people about Miranda. Nor did I have the energy right now. I nursed my drink and watched Laura.

Keen to get under way, she already had an enthusiastic gathering of distinctly male journalists on hand to answer to her every requirement. Fortuitously, everyone knew some vital detail about Miranda, or at least they could nod and smile and claim to. Among them I remember a good-looking Dutch radio reporter who was, quaintly, concerned about the damage the war was causing the environment: 'The shells cause pollution and they have burned down much forest. This is bad for the greenhouse effect.'

Hartman was amazed. 'Good grief! In hell he'll complain to the devil about global warming.' He sucked on his pipe then said prophetically, 'He should worry about his own skin.'

There was also a quiet Swede and, genuinely helpful, a soft-voiced Bamanda cameraman called Sohrab. His hair and neatly trimmed beard were almost entirely grey. He had been a psychologist before the war. The pages of Laura's narrow-lined notebook filled up with her tiny, regular script.

I drank down to my slice of lime and let my thoughts drift away, out through the clouds of mosquitoes to the ocean beyond the line of palms. I could just make out the faint white lines of small breakers in the twilight. The sun really did disappear quickly here, I thought, as it dipped, blood-red, into the black ocean. It fell too quickly for the aged retainer who wandered slowly out to light the lamps. For a while it was dark around the pool.

Laura and her informants fell silent for a moment. The only sounds were the faint rushing of the waves and the pulsating chirrup of a tree frog. If this is war, I thought, rashly, I was wrong to leave it.

'It's quiet tonight,' said a disembodied voice from the darkness.

'Maybe they've run out of reasons to kill each other,' said someone else in a non-English lilt, the young Dutchman perhaps.

'I could give them a few.' Hartman's gloomy tones this time. 'Anyway, these Kaffirs will think of something soon enough. They always do.'

Then, out of the freshly fallen night, dozens of lithe young women appeared, swooping and flowing around the tables like a twittering flock of long-legged birds. Their taut skin glowed old gold in the lamplight around plastic skirts and brightly coloured material stretched tight across their breasts. Laura pursed her lips in disapproval. 'They're prostitutes!'

'Er, not quite,' said Richard Jones. 'A more accurate description might be "good-time girls".'

'Well, I bet they all have AIDS.'

'Not exactly,' said Richard, pedantically. 'More like seventy per cent of them.'

'Well it's exploitative anyway,' said Laura. 'Not only of women, but of the local culture.' She sounded disappointed that the journalists didn't act more responsibly. She also saw no-one else seemed to mind, and stopped complaining. The girls probably sensed her resentment, because, somewhat to my chagrin, they gave our table a wide berth.

I suppose the girls were part of the scene, really: cheerleaders to the journalistic team, part of the gladiatorial rewards for the uncomfortable contest against each other and against the dark things – fear and disgust – that were our daily grind. Laura noticed this on the first night. To her consternation, the death toll in the war was called 'the score'. The consensus was that some nomadic tribe was leading, though a farming tribe could nick a result in overtime. Unless the Americans came quickly, the ruling urban elite would be knocked out of the competition. Laura was a little nonplussed that her profession, there to convey the enormity of these events to an ignorant, uncaring world, could appear so frivolous. 'Anyone would think they're treating it all as a game,' she whispered to me, indignantly.

As the night thickened, Orlando and Hartman pointed out the poolside gathering to Laura. Wire reporters and newspaper journalists sat together, so did the workers from the UN and the NGOs. A clique of photographers sat underneath a tall palm tree, their table piled with rolls of film and empty beer bottles. Off to one side, a nerdy-looking couple huddled in front of a computer. 'Internet geeks,' mocked Hartman. 'Jeez, can you believe it? God knows what they're doing, filing weird pictures to Snuff Dot Com or something.'

One table was surrounded by a collection of TV techies – cameramen, sound men and picture editors. At another sat a clump of disconsolate-looking Japanese. 'Sad story,' said Orlando, chuckling. 'They ended up in the wrong Guinea. Should be making a wildlife film in Guinea-Conakry. Now they've run out of cash and can't get out.'

'Is Georges here, Orlando?' Laura asked.

Orlando seemed impressed by her memory. 'Georges Renard? Can't see him. Don't worry, you'll meet him soon enough. He usually sits over there.'

He indicated a table on the dim edge of the lamplight. It was the table where I had first seen Miranda Williams. Sitting there, alone, was a dark, bearded figure I felt I knew. He seemed to be staring over at us. 'Who's that?' asked Laura. As she pointed, the man rose and his tall, stooping frame faded into the darkness.

'That's Farhad Morvari,' said Hartman. 'Great lensman – won plenty of awards. Persian. Bit of a loner.'

I had hardly recognized him with the beard. Farhad had photographed Miranda's dead body, so we wanted to interview him. I looked over at Laura. Simultaneously we said, 'Let's talk to him tomorrow.'

'Great minds . . .' said Laura. We both grinned.

Hartman indicated the last table. 'And that's the royal court, where the big boys sit. They're all there tonight. See the woman with the breasts and the peroxide, that's the great Teresa Cellini. That's the equally great Nick Rampling and John Court who you've met, and usually, if there's bouffant hair and a big smile, that'll be Ralph Reynolds from the Central

Network. Hey, Orlando, has the Ralphy roadshow packed up and gone home to the States?'

'Yes, but I hear they're back tomorrow. They'll want him to anchor from here when the Marines come in. Big US audience.'

'My highly placed sources tell me the Marines could be here any day now,' said Richard.

'Jeez! That's going to be a blerrie mess.'

Orlando laughed richly. 'Well, if Hollywood Ralph's a-comin', it's a sure sign the cavalry are a-comin' too. They've probably worked out the invasion schedule to hit prime time back in the States.'

'You'd better hurry up and hire some local people before the rest of the Yanks get to this shithole,' Hartman grumbled to me. 'The rates will shoot through the roof.'

I drained my latest gin and stood up to leave. 'Goodnight,' I said. 'It's been a long day.'

Laura flicked her eyes up at me provocatively. 'Pity we didn't film at the airport though, isn't it?'

I came over all blasé. 'Oh didn't I mention it? We did film at the airport. Do you want to see today's rushes?'

'What rushes?' As far as Laura knew, we had not filmed anything.

'Brian filmed the whole arrival,' I said. 'Secretly. Just did it hanging off the shoulder.'

'Why didn't I know?'

'Need to know basis,' I said, with what was probably a smug smile. I winked to tease her even more and walked back into the hotel. I realized I liked the way Laura's eyes flashed when she was wound up. Behind me I could almost feel her fuming. She would soon see we had done it the best way. If you don't know the cameraman is filming, you don't act suspiciously. Brian had not told me he was doing it either.

I had left my window open and the light on. My room was full of moths swirling and bumping around the bare bulb. I grimaced. I hate moths. They remind me of death. The dusty tile floor below the light was scattered with their singed corpses. Around the ring of light on the ceiling, small geckos hunted, their long tongues flicking out to scoop in their prey.

The first-floor room looked out over the town and I could see it was almost all dark. The yellow glow of firelight flickered here and there. Apart from a few pin-pricks of light, only in the diplomatic quarter was there the usual white-blue urban brightness of electric bulbs. The only two working street lamps flickered outside the hotel gate. Under one, I could see the cluster of cars and vans that served the pack. I could see some of the drivers asleep in their vehicles. Others sat playing cards around a fire, beside a tepee of assault rifles. Circling in the pool of light beneath the second lamppost, a small boy paced. He was reading.

The thin gauze of my mosquito net allowed only the merest whisper of cooling air. My sleep was interrupted by dreams of wild tribal dances, drums pounding, heels thumping.

XIV

'Did you hear the shooting last night?' Laura asked me excitedly at breakfast. 'There was a real firefight in the town after you went to bed.'

'No,' I lied. The noise had not helped my fitful sleep, and I felt irritable. The thin hotel coffee and the gritty, greyish toast seemed even worse than they had the last time. The serrated circles of last night's beer-bottle tops still coated the grimy linoleum floor like barnacles. The sea breeze had died during the night and in the dusty bar-cum-dining room off the lobby, it was shockingly hot for eight a.m.

Laura, with her voracious urge for information, already had her crisp blue notebook open on a taut thigh. Hartman had almost lost patience trying to explain to her which factions had been fighting the night before, and why.

'The truth is,' he was saying, 'you'll never understand this place completely. There are about fifty tribes and God knows how many languages. There are two big ethnic groupings you need to worry about: the Moro and the Bamanda. The Bamanda are darker, shorter. Like . . .' he looked around, pointed at the stocky, coal-black receptionist, '. . . like Ado, or the guys at the airport yesterday. They're farmers and towns-people. The Moro are lighter and taller. They're nomads – hunters and cattle-herders. The thing is that the Bamanda and the Moro have always fought like crazy.'

He lit his pipe. It was eight a.m. for Christ's sake. I tried to wave the smoke away.

'Then you have the Krio and the Lebs. The Krio are the descendants of freed slaves from the US. They came here early in the nineteenth century and founded the city. That's why it's called Freeville. Enough of them survived the fevers and the cannibals to intermarry and keep political control . . . until now. The Lebanese are traders and run the only real business here – the diamonds.'

'So what's the latest theory on why they're fighting again?' I asked, yawning.

'I know,' burst in Laura, who then energetically proceeded to outline her version of how the debt burden and exploitation by multinationals had ruined the economy. Because of that, apparently, the delicate balance between Bamanda, Moro and Krio had disintegrated.

Hartman smiled patronizingly. 'With all due respect, my china, that's bullshit. The latest fighting was actually sparked off when the Lebanese attacked the Moro, for some obscure reason. I reckon they're all fighting over one thing – ice. Diamonds. They're basically just a bloody bunch of armed gangs, fighting to control those blerrie rocks.'

Laura bridled. 'So it's nothing to do with the economy then?'

'Trust me, china, basically they all hate each other. The Krio think their native cousins are primitive savages. Everyone hates the Krio because they're so unbelievably corrupt. The Lebanese are racists. They are rich, ruthless and everyone hates them too. Those bloody Moro nomads are ruthless, uneducated and brutal. They think the Bamanda villagers are just slave material. The Bamanda are superstitious and *phenomenally* brutal.'

Laura did not continue the discussion. She was still confident that her reading had given her a good grasp of the situation. She seemed more comfortable with the comprehensible structure it had imposed on the conflict. Many journalists prefer these academic answers, believing that there is an underlying order to things, an order that news can illustrate. I'm not sure life is like that. 'What do you think, Peter?' she asked me.

I suspected the truth lay somewhere in between their two points of view. Doesn't it usually lie somewhere uncertain? Anyway, it had little to do with Miranda Williams. She had been caught in the middle of all this. That's all I cared about. I didn't know the answer. 'I don't know,' I replied.

'Thanks a lot,' said Laura, huffily. 'You realize we'll have to make sense of the situation, to make it comprehensible in the film.'

I thought for a moment. 'I think the viewer should have some idea of what's going on out here, yes. If what is happening is completely crazy, we should reflect that. If nobody knows what's going on, why should we pretend to?'

This was anathema to Laura. 'But the duty of news and current affairs is to explain things to the viewer.'

'Yes, but to explain the truth. If the truth is nobody knows what the hell's happening, maybe that's what we should report.'

Brian and Steven, in swimming trunks and T-shirts, wandered yawning into the lobby. They were both wearing floppy, dirty-white sun hats. They reminded me of the children's TV characters, Bill and Ben, the Flowerpot Men. 'What's on today then, guv?' asked Brian.

'Yeah,' said Steven. 'Beach or sightseeing?'

Laura laughed at what she thought was a joke. My keen AP wanted to start filming immediately.

'Sightseeing if you want to,' I said.

'Hmm, I hear there's some great Gothic architecture,' said Steven.

'Beach it is then,' said Brian.

'Last one in's a Rampling,' said Steven.

Laura turned to her producer, aghast. 'You're not letting Tweedledum and Tweedledee go swimming?'

'That's precisely what I'm doing,' I said.

'But when are we going to start filming?' asked Laura. 'Drinking, TV, swimming – this is more like a holiday camp than a war zone.'

Well, actually, I thought, in some ways it probably was. A few journalists were mumbling about some aid agency press conference down by the port. Most were still in bed nursing hangovers, lying catatonic by the pool, like Orlando, or meandering down to the beach like the delightful Teresa Cellini, whose ample curves swayed by in a cerise Chanel bikini. She looked, I thought, pleasingly similar to Marilyn Monroe.

'Ciao, Looky,' she said alluringly. 'I am sooo glad you're back.'

'Hello, Teresa. Still wearing short skirts I see.' Teresa's shapely legs were pocked with mosquito bites.

'Will you go to the press conference for me?' she pouted back. 'I am off to the beach.' She gave Laura the quick once-over of a detected competitor.

'Sorry, Teresa, I don't do news any more.'

'Looky! There was a time when you would do

*any*thing for me. I hope it will come again. Don't forget, darling, I know *every*thing about you.' She smiled in a deliberately transparent fashion at Laura, blew me a kiss and sashayed off.

'What does she mean?' asked Laura, looking at me curiously.

'I have no idea.'

I returned maybe just a little too quickly to the plan, explaining that the crew needed to rest after travelling, and that I wanted to start filming slowly, giving us all time to acclimatize. No point in taking any unnecessary risks. It would be better to start with some gentle filming in the hotel that afternoon, in relative safety. Anyway, Miranda Williams, like all expats, had spent a lot of time at the Cape Atlantic, so the film needed some hotel sequences. It was already down in the structure.

XV

'Hey, Lucky, how's it hangin', pardner?'

The familiar Midwestern twang interrupted Laura and me as we toured the hotel for locations.

Here we go, I thought, bracing myself for the whirlwind that was Ralph Reynolds.

He was already clapping me on the back, bouncing around, flashing his trademark plastic smile. He was of course wrapped in dark glasses. 'And we-ell! Who is this lovely lady? You really have struck it lucky this time, Lucas.'

Ralphy was barely capable of being seen in polite society. Utterly shameless and single-minded, he had escaped from the factory floors of what he called a 'tyre town'– an urban wasteland of the known world's four largest tyre companies, decaying in the remote nothing of the Great Plains. Quite by accident, he had been catapulted to network fame in Bosnia: 'Anyone know about Balkanization?' an editor had asked. Ralph thought he had said 'Vulcanization' and stuck his hand up, or so the story went. Anyway, as Ralphy would tell you, he 'never looked back'.

'Hi, Ralphy,' I said. 'This is the lovely Laura.'

He pushed his glasses up into his bushy hair to stare

at her openly. 'If you ever get tired of that documentary stuff, babe, and want to do a little *hard* news . . . I could always use a fresh producer. Hey – *fresh* producer. I like that. Ha ha ha ha!'

Irritatingly, Laura basked in it. She batted long lashes over blue eyes and smiled coyly. She really could be a little flirt. I was sure that Ralph was wearing a toupee.

At lunchtime our local fixer and translator turned up. Malaika was a tall, coffee-coloured Moro with a Krio mother. Her hair was long and straight, her eyes darkened with antimony. She had studied International Relations in Washington DC, but the woes of her birthplace had wooed her back from a business career in the States. She was desperately keen to help Upper Guinea, to do something, anything. She had been useful on the child-soldiers film. The subject had upset her so much she was constantly crying. Her idealism made me faintly embarrassed. I hoped we would not let her down.

Malaika was serious and sad. She was also beautiful, with that aristocratic, aquiline grace the nomad women have. Her name, she had told me shyly, meant 'Angel'. I admit I enjoyed having her around, but I was a little unsettled by meeting her again – we had in fact become quite close on the last shoot. Malaika's attractions had not escaped my AP either. Laura gave me a quizzical look, as if she wondered precisely what skills I'd hired Malaika for. Malaika made no reference to my last visit and I, ever the true professional, tried to skate over it and get straight to work. I asked her to set up a meeting with the Moro chieftain and to get his permission to film in the parts of the town held by his fighters.

'I can arrange an interview with the Kane – with the chief,' Malaika said. 'The filming too. No problem.' She smiled reassuringly.

I was slightly unnerved at this. I always am when someone says 'no problem'. Malaika had little TV experience. Nothing proves Sod's Law more than making a film. Everything is a problem when you are shooting.

'What do the Moro say about Miranda Williams?' Laura asked Malaika.

'They say they did not kill her. They say they do not know who did.'

Join the club, I thought.

We began filming in the lobby, where the merest hint of cool shadow lurked in the afternoon heat. We interviewed the cheerful Bamanda desk clerk, Ado. He was squeezed into a tiny bellhop's jacket and had a vast smile. The sum total of his views was that Miss Miranda had been 'just fine'. The florid Lebanese manager grunted through his cigar that he 'knew nothing, saw nothing'. What the guests did was not his concern, as long as they died off the property.

Next was the hotel room where Miranda had stayed. It was rented permanently by the Red Cross. There was something poignant in its ordinariness, void of the personalizing images we had found in Miranda's Suffolk bedroom. We interviewed the room's current occupant, Ben, a morose Australian medic. He was Miranda's replacement, on his way to the hospital the Red Cross ran out at the creatively named Mile Sixty. 'That's a bush town sixty miles down the inland road,' he explained lugubriously. 'Nasty place. Miranda was based there mostly. She came into Freeville now and again. She was on a break here when she went and got herself killed. Horrible.'

'Could we go out to Mile Sixty with you?' Laura asked.

'I suppose so. But it is awful, you know. Only place

worse than Freeville, if you want my opinion. Wouldn't be surprised if we all got killed, to be honest. And there's not much chance of going at the moment. I've been sweating here for days. The road's closed. They're fighting, you know. Ghastly.'

Laura asked if Ben knew anything about what Miranda was doing on the day she died. 'No, not much. Well, only that she was found down on South Beach. It's in Moro territory. In the house of some famous writer. I'd never heard of him. That's all I know, really.'

'Well, do you know who Miranda's boyfriend was?'

She had to ask it, I thought.

On the recording, Ben doesn't flinch. 'No. Didn't know she had a boyfriend. Didn't really know her that well actually. Look, we were two expats out here – colleagues. That was all. Still, I'm just surprised that she would go out alone. I mean, not even Miranda went out in Freeville alone. Normally she would have told someone where she was going. That day I guess she didn't. I've no idea why. It's strange.'

'Did she leave any personal effects here?' asked Laura.

'Umm. No,' Ben spluttered, putting his hand across his mouth. At the time I thought he was simply a bit overwrought. Watch the rushes and it is clear he is lying. 'The person who knows most about all this is Miranda's, um . . .' he seems to clutch for a word, 'Miranda's best friend. She's a doctor called Lucy. She works out at Mile Sixty. I warn you, she doesn't like journalists much.'

After Ben, we interviewed the two Corporation reporters who had met Miranda. We had to coax Judith Dart from her action station by the hotel door. She seemed far away, her eyes glazed, her answers monosyllabic. She refused to remove her flak jacket even for the interview and immediately afterwards returned to her jump-off spot. Her fingernails were chewed to the quick. Steven tapped his forefinger against his temple, making a strange gobbling noise. 'Not enough action recently,' he said.

'Yeah,' said Brian. 'Going cold turkey.'

I knew they were not joking. Judith Dart's eyes could easily be the yearning eyes of the addict. She was nervous, irritable. She probably even slept in her body armour. 'Do they all end up like that?' asked Laura, appalled.

'No,' said Brian, 'some of them are dead.'

Nick Rampling was not a nervous wreck, but when Laura asked him, before the interview, what he knew about Miranda Williams, he was hardly the caring figure off the telly. 'Look, I hardly knew the girl,' he said brusquely. 'I'd seen her around. She was killed. Big deal. Working here is a risk. OK, so we did a couple of stories when she died – only because there was nothing else around.'

A moment later, when Laura interviewed him on camera, he said in a kind voice, 'Miranda was such a wonderful girl. It's one of the hardest things as a foreign correspondent to report on the deaths of those you know and like. But if Miranda Williams's death can help bring the attention of the world to the terrible things happening here, then maybe it will not have been such a waste.'

Steven stuck his finger into his mouth and mimicked vomiting as Rampling walked off. Laura intercepted him. 'Mr Rampling?' she said deferentially, still conscious of Rampo's exalted status. 'Do you have any idea who Miranda might have been with on the day she died?'

Rampling's eyes narrowed and a vein pulsed on his

temple. He fixed Laura with a beady-eyed attempt at a withering glance. 'Jesus Christ!' he snapped. 'For the last time, I have no idea. God! Next you'll be asking me if I was the last person to see her alive. Anyone would think I'd killed her.'

At the time, of course, this statement was ignored as just another Rampling tantrum. It was ludicrous to suspect Rampling as a killer. It was ridiculous to suspect any of us. Though, when you think about it, it's not as if any of us needed lessons in killing. We had all seen enough to have a pretty good idea.

That second, sweltering evening we spun through the rushes on the edit pack of Judith Dart's crew. The interviews worked. Brian had captured the starkness of Miranda's hotel room. Ben came over as miserably as he did in real life. It was a steady start. Laura and I did not find the photographer, Farhad Morvari.

The quiet local journalist Sohrab was obviously keen to make friends. We hadn't been long at the pool bar before he appeared in our group again, sitting slightly away from the table.

Eventually he leaned forward, holding a dog-eared Polaroid. 'Look,' he managed to blurt out to Laura, 'these are my children – they are twins.'

'They're lovely,' said Laura politely. 'Who is the woman?'

She passed the photograph on to me, two frizzy-haired five-year-old girls beaming proudly in school uniform. Behind them a smartly dressed, plain-looking woman with bright eyes and a winning smile.

'It was their first day at school. She is my wife.'

'I didn't know you were married,' I said.

'I'm not.' His voice caught for a moment. 'She died two years ago.'

'The Moro?' asked Laura.

'No. She died of a malaria. Nothing worth reporting, you might say. Psychologically, though, I can assure you it makes little difference.'

'I'm sorry,' we both said. We were quiet for a while.

'Where are the children now?' asked Laura kindly.

'They are in Ivory Coast. They are safe enough there. Soon I hope I can bring them back here. When there is peace.'

I remember a strong rush of feeling for Sohrab. He struck me as a decent man. I hoped – might even have prayed, had I believed – that he would survive. Perhaps of all of us, he was the one who deserved to most. By the end, he had everyone's respect. And as a mere local amateur, he had no choice but to earn every bit of it.

Sohrab coughed a little nervously and asked Laura through the hand still covering his mouth, 'Do you have any children? A husband?'

'No way. That's not part of the plan just yet.'

'You live by a plan?'

'I try to. It's the best way to get on.'

Sohrab looked sad then, for Laura's innocence or for his own derailed life I didn't know. 'I have found that plans have a habit of going wrong.'

'Not mine,' said Laura.

I couldn't help wondering where I fitted in her plan.

By the pool the pack was highly amused. They had played a joke on Teresa Cellini. Teresa rarely left her hotel room, except to sunbathe. Wherever she stayed she rented the two largest adjoining rooms and dubbed them the Presidential Suite (the pack called it the Honeymoon Suite). Many of us had passed a bridal night or two on one of Teresa's journeys. Lazy as hell, Teresa expected colleagues to brief her about events and press conferences, rather than undergoing them herself. She was famous for writing eyewitness accounts of battles that happened when she was in bed. It was meanly said the only reason she ever put on body armour was to sweat some pounds off her famously generous figure.

Normally the pack didn't mind doing Cellini's work for her – Teresa's ambition and sloth were matched with a charming innocence, and the pack loved her for being both sexy and fun. But for a long time now, she had not bothered to leave the hotel, perform a single interview or attend a single press conference – government or rebel. A few pack members decided it was time to teach her a lesson.

When she swanned in for her evening poolside entrance, Hartman and Jones made sure Teresa overheard them talking about the great story of the day – how rebel soldiers had slaughtered and eaten all the animals in the zoo. Teresa's doe eyes widened further. 'Darlings,' she cooed. 'How awful.' With what she thought was subtlety, she fished for some details then went off, saying she had 'forgotten something'.

The stranded Japanese wildlife producer had also overheard. 'I do not understand, Mr Hartman,' he said curiously. 'Freeville has no zoo.'

The table burst into laughter. Laura was looking on with increasing disapproval. It must have seemed more and more like a holiday camp to her all the time. But then, she was enjoying herself, too.

I remember way back at the beginning, when I wondered whether all this didn't undermine the seriousness of the enterprise. Should we be so carefree when there was so much suffering around? Surely war reporting wasn't all fun and games? If Laura was thinking this, she would have been reassured by a crackle of gunfire close enough to cut the chuckles short. I noticed her stiffen slightly and her breathing quicken.

Her excitement infected me. A little later, it was with a barely deniable mixture of intentions that I asked Laura back to my room – to take another quick look through our plans. As we reached the first-floor landing, a tall figure disappeared around the bend in the bare concrete corridor. Laura ran after him, her quick, feminine steps echoing. 'Farhad!' I heard her call.

I turned the corner after her and saw her think for a second before knocking on a door at the end of the passage. 'Wait,' came a muffled response from inside. After a moment, the door opened an inch. It was dark inside the room, with the hint of a red glow.

'I'm Laura Marlow. We're doing a story on Miranda Williams. For the Corporation . . . You took the first pictures of her body. We'd very much like to interview you.'

I did not think this was going to be easy. I had been around Farhad in Somalia, Kabul and a score of stories since the Gulf War. I do not think I had heard him say more than a few sentences. 'No.' His voice was deep and resonant.

'Did you know her? How did you find her body?'

There was no answer. 'Well could we perhaps film you at work?' Laura persisted, trying to peer into the mysterious shadow of the room behind the door. 'Perhaps we could film you developing a picture of Miranda?'

'No,' said the deep voice again, and Farhad blocked the gap in the doorway with his body. In the empty hall, the few working light bulbs glimmered feebly through plastic shades thick with dust and dead insects. Their dim light caught a dark-hollowed eye through the chink in the door. It reflected dully off the matt black Nikon still hanging from his neck. 'No, I'm not going to agree to that.'

'Why not?' asked Laura. But the door closed in her face.

Laura was not used to being refused. She must have learned long before how easily she could worm things out of people, especially men. 'We'll get him on camera, one way or another,' she said, almost to herself. Her determination to pin down Farhad became a feature of her private investigative project.

We turned back towards my room but had taken only a few steps when a bizarre apparition barred our way. A ratty little man, dressed in blue denim dungarees and nothing else, pulled a Walkman off his head and thrust it at Laura with a grunt. 'Leesten,' he said, in a thick French accent, '*écoutez*.'

He clamped the earphones on Laura's ears. Her perplexed expression deepened and she gave the Frenchman a strange look. 'Do you want a go?' she asked me, pulling off the earphones.

'No, thanks, I've heard it before. Haven't I?'

He pushed them at me anyway before putting them back on his shaven head and shambling off down the corridor.

'Who the hell was that? And what was I listening to? It sounded like banshees, or drumming or something. Like nothing on earth.'

'That,' I said, 'was Georges Renard. Calls himself a photographer. A war tourist really. Lost all his hair and most of his marbles during a night under artillery fire back in Croatia in '91 – in Vukovar. That's what you were listening to. I don't think he's ever slept properly since. He prefers wandering around like that, freaking people out.'

'Mmm. So that's Georges. He'll know everything that goes on after lights out.' She frowned. 'Lucas, why didn't you ask him about Miranda?'

'I'm not so sure it's worth it. Anyway, best time to talk to him is early evening. He tends to be more lucid then.'

In my room we pored over an outline of our film under the dim bulb. A closeness crept up on us again. I think the feeling came upon Laura too quickly for her to stifle. Trying to shake it off, she walked, a shade nervously, over to the window. 'Oh, you've got a land view,' she said vapidly, taking a deep breath. 'Interesting.' She paused. 'Peter . . .'

'Yes?' I joined her at the window.

'. . . Were you there, Peter? Vukovar, I mean.'

'Yes, I was.'

Her hands clenched slightly on the window frame. 'What was it like?'

We stood there silently for a moment, shoulders almost touching, our hot scents mixing at some intersecting boundary between us, working subliminally on the edge of our conscious senses. I didn't want to reach into that pool of memories. Not here, where the consequences could be too severe. Not with her. 'I'll tell you some time,' I said. 'Anyway, you might be finding out the hard way, soon enough.'

I stared out into the simmering night. You could almost see the heat rising from the corrugated iron roofs of the town. The small boy was there again, reading in the dust below his street lamp. I thought for a moment, then rummaged through my bags and went downstairs. As I passed the hotel gate, the guard shouted something at a group of waiting drivers. One of them got up and banged on a van door. I saw Mo's woolly grey head appear sleepily above the dashboard. Then he was eagerly turning on the engine, ready to go. I mouthed 'No' to him, not now, and Mo disappeared below the windscreen again. The other drivers ignored me as I walked over to the boy. Seeing me approach, he pretended he wasn't reading. He reminded me of some of the child soldiers I had interviewed for my last film. He was a skinny ten or eleven, wearing a clean but frayed T-shirt with *Grateful* printed across the chest.

'What are you reading?'

The boy looked up at me shyly. I looked at the worn cover of the book. It was a children's fantasy about a boy magician. What must it be like, I thought, not to be able to read at home, to be ashamed not to be able to afford so basic a commodity as light.

'Look, here's a torch. You can read in bed if you like. It's not good to be out so late.' The boy's eyes widened. He glanced up at me suspiciously for a second, then he reached out, grabbed the torch and fled. I watched him scurry off into the dark. The back of his T-shirt read *Dead*.

When I returned to my room, Laura was gone.

XVI

Filming in Freeville could be a chore. The day would begin with you shaking the scorpions and other night crawlers out of your shoes. It would end in a blitz of mosquitoes. We filmed dawn and dusk; at noon the unremitting top light from the vertical equatorial sun burned out Brian's contrasts and gave flat, lifeless images. It was also excruciatingly hot.

Skirmishes could flare up any time. Gangs of war-boys, drunk on palm wine, raced the streets in the open-backed pickups mounted with heavy machine guns and grenade launchers. They would place us 'under official confirmed arrest' until Malaika could negotiate our 'bail' with a suitable dash of American dollars. During one detention, Laura stared open-mouthed when the bored officer in charge, confirming every prejudice she reviled, actually read her passport upside down. Malaika was profoundly embarrassed.

The danger was greater for Guineans. The tottering Krio regime had just brought out a slogan: 'The future is in your hands'. This was a gift to the rebel public relations people ('spin witch doctors', Brian called them) who deftly ordered their troops to start hacking off the hands of government supporters. Even darker rumours were being muttered – tales of massacre, ethnic cleansing, ritual torture, cannibalism. Fresh human body parts were easily acquired for magical rituals. Freeville's best-selling VHS was the snuff footage from neighbouring Liberia showing the torture and murder of President Samuel Doe.

The Moro sector of Freeville, where Miranda had been killed, remained closed to journalists. The nomads seemed to distrust the imperialist intrusions of the modern world and its spearhead, the media. Some said their animosity was a reaction to the way the pack had reported Miranda's death. The general thrust of the media script had certainly been to cast the nomads as the bad guys.

There was plenty to cover while we waited for Malaika to negotiate access to the Moro areas. It is the job of any documentary to convey the atmosphere of a place, and, if you watch the rushes, I think you'll agree we achieved this. In the shimmering heat, Brian has maintained the impressionistic, dreamlike nature of the footage shot in Suffolk, but the feel is of nightmare, not daydream. The air rises quivering from the roadways and cars. Shot on the long end of the zoom lens, the picture swims as though taken through water. In the haze, children play in muddy heaps of refuse. In one of our first shots, you can see two bloated dogs tug at something sticking from the end of a rolled-up grass mat. I remember the conversation behind the camera: 'Hmmm. You have very fat dogs here,' said Steven.

'They have a lot of food lying about,' Malaika replied.

'Like what?' asked Laura, innocently.

'Have a look,' said Brian, pointing to his viewfinder.

Laura bent down and saw that Brian had focused on the scene. Through the waves of heat you could see the dogs pulling at something black and red sticking from the mat. She suddenly realized what she was seeing and pulled away from the camera with a cry of disgust. 'Your journalist friends call them "cigars",' Malaika said.

And the woven grass winding sheets of Upper Guinea do taper from the corpse's head down to the feet in a cigar shape.

In a sombre mood, we moved down to the port to shoot the first sequence dealing with Miranda's career. We began at the chaos of the new Red Cross hospital. Brian captured this story within a story in one telling shot. Again it is hazy as he tilts down to the new site from the burned-out hulk of the old hospital up on the inland hills. Sweating queues of women and children waited outside the shabby, breeze-block warehouses. Inside, the crowded wards were dark and boiling hot. Here and there a brick had been knocked out to let in a breath of air and light. There were no windows. The legs of the cane beds rested on small piles of bricks. 'They do that to stop the Mokolosh climbing into the bed,' said Malaika. 'The Mokolosh are wicked, and they steal the souls of the sick. They are very busy these days. Luckily, the Mokolosh are very small demons.'

We were filming the patiently perspiring patients outside the clinic, when I felt something tugging me by the elbow. I looked around and saw nothing. 'Down here, boss,' I heard, and I looked down into the big eyes of the small boy from the night before. 'I am Papus,' said the child dolefully. 'Thank you for the torch.'

'Pleasure,' I said.

'My brother says that I can keep it. But I must help you.'

'Shoo!' broke in Malaika. 'Master Papus, scoot! Peter, this boy is a nuisance. He just wants a dash. He is Mokolosh himself.'

'I am not, seester,' said Papus indignantly. Today his T-shirt said *Who wants to be a millionaire?*

'Hold on,' I said, amused. 'Let's find out what he can do for us.'

'I can help you. Journalistfellahs always ask questions. Me too. I hear many things.'

'How much would you charge?'

'First,' Papus said earnestly, 'long-life batteries.'

After a brief negotiation, I had another employee. His first payment was actually Smarties from Steven's Belly bag. Papus wandered off on his first mission 'to find out what was going on'.

To complete the sequence at the hospital, we interviewed a doctor about Miranda. 'I miss her,' he said. 'We could not afford to lose Miranda. I wish she were still alive.'

Good stuff, I thought.

'Were you and Miranda close?' Laura asked, eagerly.

'Oh, I don't mean in any sentimental way. What I mean is she was another pair of capable hands. We are seeing an increasing number of severely malnourished cases, especially children. Today we have had our first instances of cholera. I am afraid we are on the verge of an epidemic. We are lucky the rains haven't come yet. When they do, it will get worse.'

It was quite good material, but maybe better for news than for us – it could date quite quickly and it wasn't very revealing about Miranda.

We were about to leave the hospital when Papus came trotting up again. 'Come and see my friend,' he said, and led us behind one of the concrete blockhouses to a patch of waste ground. A family group stood over the delicate body of a small girl. 'That's tee-tee Dombe,' whispered Papus. 'My friend.'

Instinctively, Brian and Steven began recording the

scene. It appeared to be a funeral service. A young man placed a peppercorn and a knife in the dead girl's hands. He stood up and turned to the girl's mother. 'OK, Mammy,' he said.

The woman spoke directly to the corpse. 'Kill whatever killed you. If you cannot kill it, throw pepper in its eyes.'

Then she and the rest of the family walked off. There were no tears. The young man rolled the body up in a grass mat and carried it over to a large, freshly dug pit. He simply tipped the mat up and the girl's body slid out of it, all flapping loose angles of elbow and knee. It hit the bottom with a muffled thud.

'Do you want to film?' the man asked, politely.

We peered into the pit. Some bones had broken in the fall. White splinters poked out through the skin. Laura nodded – it was such a shocking picture – but Brian shook his head and I just looked away. For some reason this crew and I drew a line in the same place. The funeral – yes; big close-up of mangled child's anatomy – no.

We were all quiet for a while. It was obvious the pit was far too large for one small girl. The hospital was expecting a lot more deaths. As we left, another knot of people emerged onto the waste ground, carrying a cigar-shaped package. 'Why aren't the news crews doing this story?' Laura was confused again. 'There's famine and disease right here and all they do is sit around and play stupid jokes on each other.'

'Ask them,' said Brian.

Laura asked Hartman that night, but he was in a grumbling mood. 'Ach, we've done that sort of thing before,' he said. 'And even if we wanted to revisit the story, that skellum Teresa has gone and single-handedly redefined our agenda for today. Can you believe she actually filed that stupid story about soldiers eating the zoo animals?'

'So your joke worked,' said Laura. 'So what?'

'Joke's on us, I'm afraid,' said Richard Jones. 'They splashed Teresa's story and our editors want to know why we haven't got it. Now we've all got to go and make it up.'

'It's all right for you johnny writers and radio hacks,' complained a passing photographer. 'I've got to try and cook up some pictures.'

Laura's journalistic training courses had covered political bias, editorial influence and the possibility of inaccuracies creeping in when reporters were under pressure. Her lessons had not suggested barefaced invention of stories, certainly not staging pictures. This was, to her, incredible. Simply repellent. Laura saw that John Court had appeared at her side. Turning to him, I noticed, not to me, she asked, 'That photographer. He's joking, right?'

'I very much doubt it,' said Court.

Laura's already large blue eyes widened perceptibly. 'What do you mean?'

'I recall, in Sarajevo, seeing that very gentleman slap a child in the face, thrice, to make it cry. He then took a series of profoundly moving photographs. Those lachrymose images of Bosnian suffering won him a major international award. I shouldn't think he'll have much trouble locating a cage and dressing it up with some maggot-infested haunch of raw meat.'

Laura was shocked.

'Please do not be shocked,' said Court. 'It may seem a poor excuse for journalism, but regrettably, it happens all the time. Would you care to join me?' He pulled out a chair for her at his table.

Laura looked at me. I pretended to be engrossed

in conversation with Malaika. 'I'd love to,' she said.

There was no doubt Court could be quite charming, especially if, like Laura, you hadn't heard his diatribes before. His blue eyes burned into you with passion when he talked. He seemed closer to the reality, deeper in the understanding, more lucid in the analysis. Secretly, I think Laura permitted herself the audacious thought that Court was a kindred spirit. He used the same vocabulary. He would go on ('and on and on', Ralph would say) about Mission and Responsibility and Justice. He had a strong moral sense too; he was legendary in the pack for never cheating on his expenses. Sometimes I'd wondered, though. You see, when it came to reporting a story Court felt the ends justified the means. He would do anything.

Laura was glowing that evening. There was a little flush of righteousness at the pack's trivialities, there was a little blush of sun on her cheeks. There was a gloss of pleasure at a successful day's shooting – the rushes were potent, easily evocative of a variety of Mirandas we might want to construct for the viewer. But I suspect there was another reason why Laura seemed so satisfied with that first full day. It was only as I was about to go to sleep that I recalled the glazed expression on her face when she looked into the broken girl's burial pit.

That day, my AP had seen her first real live dead body.

By the pool she relaxed enough to drop her professional reserve for a moment. 'You know, I watched you take that torch out to Papus the other night. I thought it was very sweet of you. I never knew you had such a soft side.'

I tried showing her a harder side by grunting noncommittally. I have never been able to handle flattery.

But then I receive it so rarely. 'I don't know about sweet,' I said. 'It's not a word I'd use to describe myself. What about tough or macho?'

'No, sweet's OK. I like sweet.'

We quickly gelled into a cohesive unit. The fighting dwindled in daylight hours and a combination of Malaika's charm and greenback-greased palms soon made filming relatively routine. The Moro rebels remained a shadowy force, glimpsed across the front line with their dark hunting dogs. Papus proved himself a treasure, trotting in each morning with all the street rumours – where the fighting had moved, where the new checkpoints were, which unit was the most drunk. I also asked him to listen for any information on the 'nurse seester'. His salary was a box of long-life batteries and $1 a day.

Brian and Steven would methodically record the sound and vision that I requested. I had obviously convinced them that I was not going to run amok, and they trusted my direction. At least I had a good idea of how the finished film would look, so they felt there was a reason for everything they shot. There is nothing a crew hates more than shooting pointless hours of general views and interviews destined only for the cutting-room floor.

And Laura, well, she researched diligently, was bright, creative, and handled the interviews cleverly. Behind her rigid self-discipline and drive, I still felt something of the ineffable sadness in her. In the supercharged air of Upper Guinea, she was utterly irresistible.

Each evening, before adjourning to the bar, we spooled through the day's rushes on our portable edit pack. Laura would log the shots and the interviews.

Brian and Steven had used their relationships with other crews to get hold of tapes we would never have seen back home. This included footage other crews had shot of Miranda Williams's body. I had seen some of it before this trip and watched reams more now. It did not bring Miranda's spirit any nearer for me. I felt her more in the air of Freeville than in the 625 lines, 25 frames per second of our edit screens.

One viewing sticks in my mind. I was watching with Laura. Or rather, most of the time I was watching Laura, her profile, in nothing but the dim, bluish light of the screens.

It was video footage of Miranda's corpse in the silence of a dilapidated house. There was the darkened room, the broken mirror. I had seen quite a lot of this already. It was boring to me now. I was more drawn to the strange kinship I felt between the eager, questing girl in the dark beside me, and the dead girl in the machine. The very glow on Laura's face was thrown by electronically agitated pixels decoded from Miranda's carcass.

Laura pressed 'play' on the second machine and a similar image appeared on the edit suite's left-hand screen. Again it was of Miranda's body, lying in that fatal, foetal question mark. Somehow, it had a different quality to it. What was it? I looked carefully, with a worrying sense of recognition. Well, it was handicam quality. 'So we've got some non-pro footage as well.'

'Is there something different about it?' Laura wondered.

On the soundtrack, waves crashed heavily on a nearby beach. I rubbed my eyes and looked more closely into the myriad pointillist dots. The minivideo picture lacked just a touch of the professional camera's sharpness of colour and range of contrast. It was softer, grainier. I just looked and said nothing.

Laura had noticed something. 'Hold on,' she said. 'I'm rewinding.'

Laura spun back, and allowed the sequence to play again. The sound of breaking waves made a powerful contrast to the stillness of death in the dusty room. 'There!'

She stopped the tape. 'That's a much better shot, isn't it? Better light.'

There, across a few frames, as the camera panned down the body, were slatted shadows and bars of light, the light as through a Venetian blind, or a louvred shutter – or a badly boarded-up window. Undeniably it gave the scene an extra mystery and power. Laura noted it down in her shotlist. I glanced at the tape box. It was unmarked.

'Silly amateurs,' muttered Laura. 'Who doesn't mark their tapes? I think it's a pool cut. It could have come from any number of different camera teams. I'll check whose it is and get it cleared.'

I do not know what would have happened if she had.

XVII

Four days into the shoot, Malaika wangled permission to interview the Moro chief, Madiba Kane. We drove carefully through the front line and on up to where Freeville's fungal slums began their crowded climb into the tree-covered hills behind the town.

Moro gunmen in a dented pickup guided us into a large shabby compound of beaten red earth, ringed by a low wall and a few windowless mud huts. In front of one, a striking woman stood, sweeping the dust. She wore gold earrings so huge they rested on her shoulders. The yard was busy with slender, light brown Moro men, stripped to the waist. Their upper bodies glistened as they unpacked and assembled an arsenal of mortars, heavy machine guns, gleaming Kalashnikov assault rifles and, carefully arrayed along one wall, row upon row of long, curved swords. At the door of the largest hut stood two intimidating figures. They wore the flowing royal blue robes of the desert, crossed with bandoliers of ammunition. Exquisitely engraved scimitars hung curling by their sides. A small number of knotted leather thongs hung from their belts. They carried their long rifles as idly as toys. Next to each guard, unleashed, but statue-still, stood a magnificent waist-high hunting dog, saluki-lean, jet black.

The guards chatted amicably with Malaika then pointed to a carved hardwood chair under a thorny acacia tree in the courtyard. 'They want us to do the interview there,' she said.

Brian and Steven went to set up, while Laura and I were shown inside to meet Madiba Kane. In the gloom of the interior all we saw were his eyes, glinting at us from the one chink open in the blue swathes of robe and turban. The ageless gaze was bright in the darkness. I recognized the piercing, unblinking stare of a predator. From beside the Kane I heard a growl and saw a flash of white teeth as his dog, black as the shadow around it, yawned in warning. Then the Kane's eyes smiled and a low voice said in clipped English, 'Good afternoon. You're from the Corporation, aren't you? Tremendous. I listen to your International Service every day. *Spotlight on Africa* is a very fine programme. Shall we go?'

Brian set up the camera in front of the acacia and Madiba sat in its lightly dappled shade. His dog settled down in the dust by his seat, warily eyeing Steven's waving boom mike. 'Turn over,' I said.

It is a great shot, even if I do say so myself. The background is one of the copper sheen of sweating Moro bodies and the cold gleam of gunmetal. Madiba did not lower his turban for the interview. On the recording you can hardly detect his mouth moving as he speaks. All the movement and expression is in those hawk's eyes.

Despite his excellent English, Kane insisted on answering in Moro, with Malaika translating. Laura started the interview on general topics. 'What are your aims for Upper Guinea?' she asked.

'The Moro will take power,' said Madiba simply.

'What about the Government? What about the Bamanda?'

'The Krio ruling class are buffoons in their top hats. The Bamanda are slaves. If they try to stop us, we will kill them.'

'What if the Americans come to make peace?'

'We want peace. But if the Americans come to stop us taking power . . .' he seemed to yawn behind his turban, '. . . we will kill them as well.'

He said this matter-of-factly, as though defeating the most powerful nation on the planet was something the Moro could do without thinking, before breakfast. The way he said it, we did not doubt him. And events proved him right, of course, to an extent. After a few minutes of general discussion, Laura moved on to the subject of Miranda. 'The Moro seem to be good at killing,' she said, boldly. 'Why did your men kill Miranda Williams?'

The warlord's eyes signalled surprise, and anger. The girl had guts. For a moment I feared she might have been too direct. If the Kane got angry, we could expect more trouble than we could from 'Call me Darren'. In the event, her challenge worked.

The Kane reflected a moment. 'Yes, we can kill. We are warriors. You see these?' He lifted his curved red scabbard to show a hanging line of knotted thongs, too many to count. 'These show how many men I have killed. You are not a man until you have killed.'

He looked away from Laura and addressed his next words, in English, straight into the camera. 'But – by the Koran I swear – no Moro killed this woman. I send this message to all who would hear.'

'She was killed on your territory. People say it was a Moro who killed her.'

The Kane looked back at Laura. He shrugged. Still in English he said, 'That is untrue.'

'People say she was attacked by dogs. You have dogs.'

The eyes proclaimed pure incredulity at the accusation. 'Our dogs do not eat human flesh. Only Bamanda.'

Laura changed tack. 'In that case you're saying that you do not control your territory? Who can kill freely in Moro territory then? If Moro did not kill Miranda Williams, who did?'

The Kane's eyes flashed warning now. He was unused to being challenged in any way, let alone by a young white woman. He switched back to Moro. It was a long answer. Malaika stammered out a much shorter version. She seemed upset. 'We control our territory,' she translated. 'We do not know who killed this woman.' Kane waved the interview closed.

Laura ignored him and asked, 'What if you find one of your men did kill her?'

Kane switched to English again. 'He will die. And if anyone, like yourselves . . .' he panned his unblinking view around the crew, '. . . brings shame on us, by accusing us of this crime, they too will die. Of course,' he concluded meaningfully, 'nobody is going to accuse us of this crime any more.'

'Cut,' I said. 'Everyone out of the sun.'

It was a wrap. 'Good work, Laura,' I said.

We stood in the shade of a hut and Mohammed came chattering up with some water from the van. We all drank deeply. Steven tut-tutted a bit about the sound. 'That bloody turban muffles him slightly. Should be all right though.'

Brian had shot some of the interview in BCU. 'It's great,' he said. 'All you see are these amazing eyes. Got some great cutaways of the dog looking mean as well.

Evil-looking mutt. It could help you in the edit suite if you want to make him look like the bad guy.'

Laura wiped her forehead. 'If he is the bad guy.'

'They did not kill the nurse,' said Malaika, still upset for some reason. 'He is telling the truth.'

'I agree,' said Laura. 'He's cruel, yes. But he's – well – noble.'

She had a point. There was something pure, almost refreshing in Moro savagery. It was hard to believe they would senselessly focus it on a woman. Laura frowned thoughtfully. 'But if the Moro didn't kill Miranda, who did?'

Malaika soon demolished our sentimentality. Logging the rushes of her chieftain that evening, I noticed the long last answer and Malaika's short translation. 'What does he really say here?' I asked.

She looked sombre. 'He says that if we use any of this material wrongly, he will blame me, even though I have Moro blood. He says he will have the other half of me raped and crucified. Whether the Moro side dies is up to God.'

Malaika began to sob uncontrollably. I was amazed she had kept her calm so long. I put my arms around her and she cried into my shoulder – great, rolling tears that soaked through my light cotton shirt and wet my chest.

I told Rampling and Dart that the Kane interview was strictly off limits. Normally we might have given Corporation reporters access to the material, but Corporation news items could be seen in Guinea on satellite and I didn't want to risk Madiba Kane's anger, at least not until we finished filming in the areas he controlled.

The next day Malaika was still jittery, but she refused to stay behind when, with Kane's permission, we slipped back through Moro lines to film the place where Miranda's body had been found. A baffled Papus guided us. He thought the visit was idiotic, if not downright dangerous. Everyone knew the place to be haunted by the spirit of a white man who had lived there once. But Papus knew South Beach well. He lived in the slum behind it.

The once imposing double-storey house was on its own, not more than a mile or two from the hotel. It crouched on a low rise of sand dunes behind a wide, sloping beach, untidy with sharp tufts of spiky grass. I wondered whether anyone bathing on the beach would have heard Miranda's screams over the rolling surf. I wondered if the famous writer's ghost had heard. He had written here through the six long years of what civil-war-weary Guineans now dismiss as 'the short palaver', and which was, in this part of the world, principally a war against the Vichy French.

The wooden, plantation-style building had since been approached by the mushrooming shanty towns of Freeville and it now lay marooned between a squalid bidonville and the ragged dunes. A cracked stone veranda ran around the ground floor of the house beneath a wide wooden balcony, which encircled the upper storey. It was a dreary place. The floorboards were rotting and the delicate tracery was cracked. The pale blue paint was peeled and flaking and the tiled roof was almost all gone, looted by the more daring slum dwellers.

Laura had forced herself to read some of the author's West African books as part of her research. I had been reading him for years and in a way his ideas had worked their way into me. I could picture him now sitting on his veranda, gazing out over the featureless sea into the uttermost west. Perhaps his ghost sometimes still did. His ideas of sin, redemption and futility had left me moved and bitter. The fate of the house seemed to fit with the bleakness of the writer's universe. In *White Woman's Grave* I planned to use this fate, this location, not just as the setting for Miranda's death, but as a metaphor for the whole colonial legacy in Upper Guinea. It was a grand structure, riddled with decay, swamped by chaotic semi-development, gone to the dogs . . . and now full of death. This was an important sequence, so we took our time, framing each shot with care.

'Perhaps Miranda came here sightseeing,' said Laura, a hot wind flicking tendrils of hair around her sunburned face. 'She was a fan of his writing.'

'You'd have to be one hell of a fan to want to come out here,' muttered Steven.

'D'you think she'd come here alone?' Brian asked. 'I wouldn't.' He panned across the scene, his viewfinder revealing a desolate beach at low tide, a barbed-wire fence around derelict, overgrown grounds, blotched with black scars of shadow from the baking sun.

'Hmm. Not even a tough cookie like Laura would come here alone,' said Steven, his headphones catching only the faint surf and a gull's cry.

Laura smiled. She took it as a compliment. She agreed with Brian. I could see her mind whirring, thinking, 'So who did Miranda come with?'

We moved up the shallow dunes and climbed into the grounds through a gap in the wire. Papus refused to come. He sat unhappily on the sand, clutching the little gri-gri around his neck. Inside the house it was gloomy and silent. With the tide so low you could not hear the surf. Shards of light filtered in laser-like rays through cracks and bullet holes in the plank walls. Our footsteps stirred up dust, which swirled in the sunbeams. The air was oppressive. I felt short of breath, suffocated by the murk, by the closeness of Miranda's fate. Maybe the house really was haunted, I thought.

You couldn't miss the place where her life had ended – in the centre of the house. The blood was still there – a shapeless dark red/black stain soaked into the dry boards. A broken mirror on the wall appeared clearly in Farhad Morvari's photographs. This dim, windowless hall was where they'd found her. You could follow the trail back from here, a wide, dark swathe, as though a wet mop had been swabbed through the inch of dirt that lined the floor. Had she still been alive? I saw her being hauled, with those injuries, through the splinters and dust, into this gloom. I saw her final, dying curl.

This absolute trail of Miranda Williams's life led back to a small room on the other side of the house. This was where she had been ended as a person. The slaughter room was lit through gaps in a boarded-up window. Sharp, bright slats of sunlight fell in a strong, barred pattern on the stains of old blood. It was all over the room. On the floor there was an eerily symmetrical central patch like a mutant Rorschach ink-blot test. All the walls were spattered with dark splashes, as though they had been sprayed. Memories I wished to keep well out of waking hours came rushing back. My head whirled and the bars of light blurred together like a strobe. I felt like vomiting and went quickly outside. I stood on the beach and focused on a point where the waves broke.

Papus came wandering up with some friends from the shanty town. 'So you have seen the ghostfellah then, boss.'

I nodded. 'Something like that.'

Papus tilted his head vaguely to take in his urchin companions. 'Now my friends heah the nurse seester was killed by a red demon. This is a very bad fact.'

'Yes, Papus.' I looked at my hands. They were shaking. I craved a cigarette.

Inside, the crew carried on without me. We had brought Farhad's photographs along. Brian tried to frame matching shots on the Betacam that would allow us to mix through from our coloured empty tomb to Farhad's black and white death scene, or vice versa. These filmic transitions may be contrived, but they can be very useful in a documentary. They link sections, make points and they have a certain artistic power.

I could hardly bear to go back that evening and film the sun setting over the sea behind the house. The tide had surged up the beach; straining breakers crashed just below the porch. I decided to wait in the van.

XVIII

Most of our film's building blocks were stacking up neatly but we were frustrated in pinning down one part of the structure – Farhad Morvari. Doyen of cameramen and photographers, his harrowingly graphic work – in still black and white or moving colour – included some of the defining images of modern warfare. In those days, I remember, he was also experimenting with digital stills, streaming video and the Internet. For Farhad, war had become the medium for his art. Reclusive and aloof, he went about his business with complete dedication. He would slip out of the hotel early in the morning and spend the day alone, shooting. Almost every evening Laura would try to persuade him to talk about finding Miranda's body. He would refuse. More than once, after a tense day's filming, Laura banged on his door in frustration. 'Why won't you talk?' she would shout. 'Have you got something to hide?'

No answer would come from the blank wooden door.

Another niggle was Mo the driver. He turned the

simplest journey into a white-knuckle ride of mis-heard directions and close calls. He could not get his air conditioning to work and his car was constantly breaking down. Mo especially annoyed Laura. When, trying to park beside a checkpoint, he managed to reverse carefully into a large pickup full of tetchy gunmen, she made her sternest protest yet: 'He's a constant threat to life and limb of everyone anywhere near the road, both outside and inside the vehicle. Lucas, I think we should replace him.' She always called me Lucas when she was cross.

Malaika, after pacifying the angry rebels with a sizeable dash, translated the crew's complaints to Mo. He listened intently, then shook his head. Jabbering, he pointed to the leather bracelet on his left bicep and pulled out a small hide pouch and a large cowrie shell hanging on a thong around his neck. 'It's his gri-gri,' said Malaika, 'his ju-ju. He says it protects all of us. It protects him from bullets. They will turn around and not hit him.'

'This gri-gri stuff is superstitious nonsense,' said Laura. 'Tell him, Malaika.'

'Well,' said Malaika, sheepishly, 'actually, I have one too.' She pulled out a postage-stamp-sized leather wallet from where it hung on her chest. 'I know it seems odd, but this is part of the wisdom of this particular place.'

Laura sighed. 'Didn't they teach you anything in Washington?' But my AP's curiosity was one of her most winning traits; it got the better of her here. 'Well, whatever . . . Tell me. What's in those things?'

'It is usually the 113th chapter of the Koran. The Chapter of the Dawn, we call it.'

'What's in Mo's?'

Malaika spoke quietly to the driver.

'Yes. Yes,' he nodded and emptied the pouch to show us. Laura groaned in disgust. Cupped in Mo's yellow parchment palm were a shrivelled big toe, a mummified ear and an eye. All human.

'Cannibals,' said Brian. 'Knew it.'

'Yup,' said Steven.

Mo nodded knowingly, convinced that he had reassured us with the strength of his magic. I felt highly convinced, but then I had also noticed the cold steel barrel of a more modern type of ju-ju poking out from under his driving seat. I reckoned Mo could look after us, one way or another.

On one of those featureless tropical days that folded damply into another, I let my grateful AP lead the team out to film in Freeville – just routine General Views, but it would be good experience for her. It would also give me a chance to relax and reflect. I tinkered with the film's structure, but found my thoughts roaming far beyond the blue notebook on to what I loved, what I cherished, who I was. Taking the satphone up to the roof, I phoned home. My former home, I remembered, when the new, painfully Australian nanny answered.

'Is Mrs Lucas there?' I asked.

A pause – remembering orders, perhaps? – then, 'Oh, you mean Ms Rowan? She's away for a few days.'

'Business?'

'On holiday.'

I gritted my teeth. Who takes a summer break alone? Alex was asleep, the nanny said.

'Wake him up, please.'

'Oh, I'd rather not.'

So now some bottle-blonde surf bunny, fresh off Bondi beach, knew what was best for my son.

'Just bloody wake him up, will you.'

For a while I waited there, perched on the parapet of the hotel roof, the dull concrete expanse curving round the head of the promontory. The hard plastic of the phone was hot against my ear. I could look almost straight down at the breaking waves, a heavy swell rolling in from the Azores, ending in a crash of white spray on the humps of smooth, dark rocks, their lower parts encrusted in a mat of limpets, mussels and anemones. The other way I could see back across the overgrown garden to the hotel wall, with the gate towards one end, the gloomy mangrove swamps at the other. Behind them simmered the town in a fug of lunchtime fires.

After a conversation with a dopey and yawning but happily surprised son, I was beset by a troubling mixture of bitterness and loss; I tried to wash it away in the clean Atlantic.

The ocean was fierce, a high spring tide curling and pounding up the beach. I swam out through the churning surf to where the water rolled smooth, deep blue and cool.

I thought back to a moment years before, with Claire, in a tideless sea – a colourless, caressing Aegean – off an island she loved. I do not think I had ever felt further from the shadow of war. That same day, we suspected, Alex was conceived.

Cares sloughed off me in the clear water. I thought I saw a dolphin surface to breathe. For a moment I was glad. Then I wondered whether Claire was lying in that same gentler sea right now – with him. I was still a little angry when I found myself, as if fated, by Teresa's boudoir on the beach.

'Ciao, Looky,' crept the velvet tones from beneath a large white parasol. 'Where are you being all my life?'

I bent under the umbrella to see her stretched out on

her lounger. Her peroxide-white hair hung down almost to the sand. A skin-coloured bikini made her look naked. 'In spirit, I've been right here, Teresa.'

I sat down beside her. In the thin shadow of the parasol, her fleshy, reclining body was covered in a sheen of lotions and perspiration. 'Now tell me, Looky, honestly. What is so interesting about this girl of yours?'

'Laura? Well . . .'

She laughed knowingly. 'Ah, so you do like her. I will be jealous. No, silly, I mean the other one of course. The dead one – your Miranda. There is some great story there that I should know?'

My Miranda!?

'Not really,' I said. 'She was an ordinary girl, I suppose.'

'Just the kind you want. Watch out for that prim little Miss Laura Marlow. You stick to Miranda. Live women are much more trouble. Especially for a married man.'

She smiled. Possibility-eyes beneath a fringe flicked up towards her dark, fan-cooled room, then, archly, back at me. 'But then, you still like trouble, don't you, Looky?' she purred. 'All kinds of trouble.'

Afterwards, when I awoke, the crew had still not returned. I was spooling for inspiration through the rushes when I heard the usual commotion of a Mo arrival in the courtyard. A few moments later they hurried in. Laura's face was shining. She looked triumphant. 'Miranda's not the only one,' she said, proudly.

'What do you mean? Miranda's not the only what?'

'Just watch this.' Laura plugged in a tape. Her jumbled explanation poured out alongside the steady, linear storytelling of the unwinding video.

Off-screen a voice calls out. The camera swings off

the tripod and catches some heavily armed Arab gunmen. With a nonchalant wave of their assault rifles, they cordially invite the crew to accompany them for a meeting. It takes Laura less than two seconds to cordially agree. Brian, of course, calmly, secretly, keeps rolling.

I could watch the story unfold on tape. The sound is painful for Steven – it comes from the inferior camera mike – but you can keep track of what's happening. 'Malaika was petrified,' said Laura, laughing. I noticed Malaika casting her an offended glance. 'Even Mo looked frightened. I think maybe his magic doesn't work on Lebanese.'

On the screen Mo's van was sandwiched between two black Range Rovers bulging with militiamen – 'Like being back in Beirut,' said Steven. They rush through the diplomatic quarter and way up the hill overlooking the embassies and the Cape Atlantic Hotel.

I saw spiked iron gates swing open and the van approaches a villa behind a high concrete wall, topped with silver coils of razor wire. Brian stays on the wide angle to catch a jet of water jigging around the neat green lawn. The sprinkler's spray casts a rainbow in the sunlight where two plump Arab toddlers play under a black maid's watchful eye. There is some jabbering in Arabic, a brief tussle as Brian refuses to let go of his camera, then the guards relent and the view passes into a white-tiled interior. 'Air-conditioned,' said Steven, regretfully. 'The only time we'll be cool on this trip.'

There is a shot of Malaika gazing at the ostentatious décor with undisguised loathing. 'I was really worried Malaika was going to freak,' said Laura. 'But I must say well done under pressure, everyone.'

Brian and Steven raised their eyebrows.

A squat Lebanese in jeans and a striped T-shirt squints up at the team from an ornate desk. On its black morocco top lie a jeweller's eyeglass and an unfolded sheet of newspaper, on which nests a handful of dull, glassy stones. 'Sit down,' he says, in a thin voice with a heavy Arabic accent. 'Tea?'

The team sits on a collection of mock Louis XIV gilt armchairs covered in shrink-wrapped plastic. I wondered why Arabs often have such kitsch taste. 'Yes, please,' comes Laura's voice, indignant at the whole diversion. 'And by the way, who are you?'

For just a raised-eyebrow instant you see the Lebanese is surprised that the woman has spoken. In that instant he reassesses the situation and continues calmly. 'I am Mansoor.' He pours out the mint tea in a thin, splashing stream, holding the teapot high above the small glasses.

'Just as a matter of interest,' I said, 'what's all this got to do with Miranda?'

'Just wait,' Laura said.

'I gather you are researching the death of the British nurse.' Mansoor addresses this question to Laura.

'I am the Assistant Producer,' she corrects him. 'That's senior to Researcher. But, yes. Now what do you want?'

'I think you should see this.' He hands her a handful of Polaroid prints. 'We believe whoever killed your nurse killed our Yasmeen also.'

I turned to look at Laura. She was looking at me expectantly.

'Good grief!' I said.

'Yes, isn't it amazing? But there's more.'

The on-screen Laura in Mansoor's study looks at the pictures, swallows hard and nods her head.

'She was the daughter of one of the leading families of our community. We believe Moro killed her.' Mansoor looks darkly off camera – towards Malaika, I think. 'Yasmeen was killed just a few days before your nurse. Like your nurse she was killed in a Moro area. She was killed in that . . .' he gestures at the Polaroids, '. . . in that terrible way.'

Laura makes an affirmative sound the camera can't quite catch. Mansoor takes a loud sip of the bright green tea.

'Look,' Laura said. She dug in her pocket and passed a Polaroid over to me.

I shut my eyes and sighed. A brief glance was enough. The flesh had been scored with the same deep cuts, especially round the breasts and throat. The body was curled in the same foetal curve, like a comma, or a question mark. It was grim, shocking, and unexpected. I certainly did not have time just then to work out how this affected our film. The rushes ran on.

'Listen,' said Laura. 'Listen to this.'

On the screen Mansoor says, 'It is because of this barbarism. That is why we fight the Moro.'

Laura responds with feeling, 'Why? Just because one girl was killed?'

In front of the humming edit pack, I could see she was still astonished. The media had filled acres of newsprint and hours of airtime explaining the deep-seated social and ethnic reasons that had set one faction against another in Upper Guinea. Meanwhile the Lebanese and the nomads were fighting a simple vendetta. On the tape Laura pleads the Moro's innocence. 'Are you sure the Moro killed her? Their chief swore to us on the Koran that they did not. And he doesn't strike me as a liar.'

Mansoor seems to think about this seriously. 'Yes. It is a pity. Normally you can do business with the Moro. They are savage, yes, but not as primitive as these vermin of Bamanda, who eat excrement, by the way.

We Lebanese are few. All the people here resent us. If we do not respond with force when we are attacked, soon we will be wiped out. Just be aware. If you require help, we can provide it. There are not many of us, but we are strong.'

'You're rich,' Laura says. She looks at the pile of uncut diamonds on the desk. They appear to range in size from an apple pip to a large almond.

'OK, rich.' Mansoor smiles, sifting the stones easily between his fingers. 'But money buys you a lot of guns. And experience. Believe me, without our help, no-one can win this war. Many of my men have fought in battles from Beirut to Bosnia to Afghanistan. For their beliefs, or for money.'

Just like half the journalists here, I thought.

'My advice to you is to be careful. You don't know what kind of people these Moro are.' Mansoor looks again at Malaika, malevolently. 'They do not like the media and they are ruthless savages. My men will escort you back through the Hospital quarter. We captured that area from the Moro a few days ago. You can see what they did to it.'

Behind us in the hotel room, Malaika made a spitting sound. 'Thieves and liars,' she muttered. 'This is a bad man.'

The meeting continued just long enough for Mansoor to give them his mobile telephone number, and categorically refuse Laura's offer of an on-camera interview. 'Once is enough,' he says, turning to Brian. 'So I hope you got all that. Next time, please do me the honour of asking first.'

Just before the team is bundled back into the Datsun, Brian's tape runs out.

'What shall we do with all this?' asked Laura. 'We can't ignore it.'

I still wasn't sure. 'The deaths do look similar, but we can hardly be certain. Not certain enough to complicate our film, anyway.'

'But someone – Moro, the Lebanese think – is out there, killing, raping women.' Laura did not mention her hard, investigative edge again, but she was thinking it.

'Laura, lots of people are out there doing that. And even if we found them . . .' There was no point in reminding her that there was no police force here, no law.

'But there is an international war crimes court in The Hague. And with Mansoor's help . . .'

'We can't even be sure it was the same killers . . . Let's think about it. OK?'

'You're the boss.'

How did she manage to make that sound so ironic? It was not our place to explain the war. It was not our job to hunt down murderers.

Our work in the Moro areas was exclusive and stirred up a lot of what we took to be competitive interest. Ralphy Reynolds had the gall to try and poach Malaika to fix for him. Nick Rampling asked in a lot of detail about precisely what we had found on the old writer's house and the Moro situation. He then immediately tried to get into the Moro sector himself. He lacked Malaika's diplomatic skills, though, and I wasn't surprised when we spotted the beacon of his red hair amongst a crowd of war-sparrows at a Moro checkpoint. He was blustering with his usual energy and lack of sensitivity.

Rampling waved us down and we stopped without a second thought, little knowing the effect the next few minutes would have. Mo pulled up a few yards before the checkpoint. At a gesture from her boss, Rampo's dowdy producer trudged up to the van, trailed by a scrawny Moro boy soldier in ragged combat gear many sizes too large for him. The producer was clearly suffering the strain of working with Rampling.

'What's going on?' I asked her through the open window.

'Rampo wants to go down to the beach down there. Something about the house of a famous writer. Says he wants to use it for colour in his next piece.'

'Is that so?'

Rampo imperiously called the producer's name. Her shoulders slumped and she turned back. 'Her master's voice,' she explained, ruefully.

Rampo shouted from the roadblock. 'Hey, Lucas. Help me get these bloody . . . imbeciles . . . to let us through.'

I wondered if any of them understood English.

We got out of the van as Rampling came stomping over.

'These savages won't let us film. Lucas, are you going to release the material you shot in Moro territory – the interviews and the house on South Beach?' He was standing just that fraction too close, as ever. He smelt strongly of stale sweat.

'Sorry, Rampo, no can do.'

'I can order you to, you know.'

'You can try.'

His face went a little red around his button eyes. 'I'd hate for you to misunderstand me, Lucas. If you've turned up anything interesting, you'd do better to let me know. It might be a news story.'

I wondered if the murder of Yasmeen and its repercussions was a news story and decided, potentially, yes.

'Nothing interesting, Rampo,' I said.

'Good,' he said. 'But just remember, Lucas, I'll see your material eventually, so you had better be telling the truth.' He seemed genuinely relieved. 'Now tell her – your, uh . . . companion,' he indicated Malaika, '. . . to come and help.'

Irritated, I turned to Malaika. 'Why don't you see if you can help.' And then I made one of those spontaneous, common mistakes. If I hadn't given Malaika a conspiratorial wink a lot of nastiness might have been avoided. 'Remember how Mister Rampling hates to be misunderstood,' I said. 'Make sure you translate *everything*.'

Malaika gave a knowing nod.

'Steven, could you give me some Smarties, please,' she said, then she went over with Rampling to the cluster of boys still arguing with his producer.

Laura tapped me on the shoulder. 'He's really glad we've got nothing. Do you think he has something to hide?'

'No more than the rest of us, I think. He's just glad we're not going to come up with a big scoop.'

Malaika came back to the van and we drove off.

'So bang goes our exclusivity on the house sequence,' said Laura.

'I wouldn't be so sure of that,' said Malaika, mischievously. 'They really liked the Smarties and I told them Mister Rampling has dozens more tubes hidden in his car. When they don't find any, he's not going anywhere. Anyway, their English might not stretch to the word "imbeciles", but I had to make sure I translated *everything . . .*' She gave me a warm smile.

We looked back to see Rampling gesticulating wildly at the war-sparrows who were methodically beginning to unpack the camera gear from the back of his Land Cruiser. He might even have waved his fist at us. He certainly did not forgive me, or Malaika. He was the sort of man who bore grudges, and the possible consequences might have occurred to us, but that evening we were given more to think of by Papus.

In his shanty town behind the haunted house, Papus reported in hushed tones, the people now whispered that the red demon who killed the nurse seester was 'a Franji' – historically, a Frankish Crusader, literally, a Frenchman, a Christian, a WHITE MAN. Someone apparently had seen this foreigner. At first they thought it was the ghost, or a devil, but now they were saying maybe it was a white man. And, if you thought about it, Papus had a point. 'Only whitefellah can go into that bad place. Your ju-ju too much. And even devilghost is a Franji devilghost. Why else did he not attack you before?'

I was dazed by this. The team did not know what to make of it.

'A Franji killed her? Did a Franji kill the Lebanese girl as well?' Laura asked.

'Papus has no ansah, seester,' said the little boy.

We could not really ask him to go and find out. He couldn't spend too much time out on the street these days – kids as young as nine were being press-ganged into the various militias.

'Maybe "Franji" could refer to a mercenary?' suggested Laura. 'Wouldn't it be ironic if a white man had actually done it?'

It was a tantalizing idea for the film. The murder of Miranda Williams had been reported as a typical example of African savagery. The twist appealed especially to Laura, chiming as it did with her view of the West's rapacity as the root of Upper Guinea's ills. 'I'll ask around,' she said, without much encouragement from the rest of us.

'I mean,' she said, almost to herself, 'what if it were one of us?'

We ignored her, but, as a gesture, I told Papus to keep his ears open. The consensus was that this Franji demon was probably just a rumour, but Papus's story served to reawaken that nagging sense of unease.

It also offered Laura a new Pandora's box to open, a new puzzle for her impatient mind. As any TV journalist knows, judgement or definition is not much more than a question of focus, or point of view. A shift to the left or right and a man's profile looks very different. Meet him yesterday or tomorrow and it's his character that seems to change. For Laura, it was not much of a step for the inhabitants of the Cape Atlantic to warp from a group of superficial colleagues to a hotbed of secrets, vices, crimes.

'Which of them do you think might have done it?' Laura whispered to me, teasingly, that evening. 'There's you of course. You had opportunity . . .'

'Very funny.'

'. . . though I'm not sure about motive.' She looked at me archly and chuckled. 'Then there's that awful Nick Rampling. You know, there are some pretty odd rumours about him and women. Apparently he beats us up.'

We all knew Rampling's reputation. Amongst other things, there was an inconclusive but very messy scandal with a feisty local fixer in Sarajevo, a Muslim girl with hair yellow as hay and sapphire eyes. In normal life – I remembered for some reason – she had been a cellist. She played sometimes for the media in the Holiday Inn, and Rampling had not been the only one of us interested in her. Her complaint against Rampling never reached Corporation head office. The cellist was killed soon after the incident. By Serbian militia, people said.

Laura, I was sure, was only fractionally serious. Could she really have felt it amongst us then? Blink now and I can see us as if through an X-ray camera – a bubbling rich potion of motives and desires, seasoned with Bright Star beer and the heady local variant of *Cannabis sativa*. Rampling may have wanted power, Teresa money, Ralph perhaps fame, Orlando, God knows what. There was hunger there, ambition, maybe a touch of mania, but no, you couldn't have expected her to see murder.

Laura's glance would hardly have paused on the stalwarts like Richard Jones or Felipe Deflores. The unsung bedrock of the pack, they attended every press conference, reported every new development. Felipe, a portly gourmet, suffered terribly from the appalling food. Richard was plagued with regular bouts of malaria. They filed their stories diligently day in, day out, succumbed to or battled their demons and got stolidly, steadily drunk at the bar.

The cameramen and photographers might have made more likely suspects. They sailed closer to the action and many of them were as mad as any definition of the word. If people like Orlando treated their own lives as completely worthless, Laura might have reasoned, how much value could they give to others? The only man who was crazy enough to work with men like Farhad and Orlando was Georges Renard, another lunatic if ever there was one.

If Laura had included the entire Franji community in her enquiries, there were other, equally bizarre subjects to eliminate. Among the UN observers, for instance, were two highly camp, bespectacled Danes who sat on the hotel roof all day listening for the 'impacts'. Every evening at six thirty sharp, they would provide a breakdown to journalists of the type and number of detonations.

'Not much today,' I remember them mincing that evening, 'only ninety-eight impacts. And small stuff, really. Mostly grenades.'

The Upper Guinea record so far was 315 in a twenty-four-hour period. Their best day, they would proudly inform you, was in Sarajevo when they recorded 3,887 rounds, hundreds of which were 'heavy ordnance', 82 mm mortars, tank shells.

Short-sighted sexagenarian Scandinavians presumably did not fit Laura's mental photofit of a red-demon murderer. I don't think she gave them a second thought.

As for the senior members of the group, Laura simply could not suspect them. For her the Courts and Reynoldses of the world held that infallibility which favourite teachers hold for an eager pupil. Neither I nor the reader can blame her for not looking harder back then, we who have missed the traitor beside us in our bed, who have overlooked the crookedness in our own heart.

That night, I remember, Court was talking about the mission, the responsibilities of the news journalist to 'make a difference'.

Orlando was disagreeing idly. 'Nothing ever changes, JC, you know that. We are not here to make a difference. It's not our war. It never is. Our job is just to report and have done with it.'

'You are naive, Orlando. What happens to this country depends on what we report. Just as Miranda Williams will be judged and remembered by Lucas and Marlow's film, so what the world thinks and does about Upper Guinea is judged and decided through the prism of news.'

'You're right,' said Sohrab. 'For us Africans, your news agenda can be something like a new type of colonialism.'

'Not for me,' said Orlando blithely, 'I just film what I see. No more, no less.'

'It strikes me that Sohrab is right,' said John. 'We have all seen it – the TV station replacing the governor's mansion as the epicentre of power. Like it or not, Harries, we are the nabobs – you and I, Farhad, Rampling . . . in the future, perhaps even you, Marlow.'

Laura shifted on the white plastic cords of her seat. I could see Court made her feel guilty of self-indulgence and disloyalty just for joking about a murderer amongst us.

'But we have a duty,' Court went on gently to Sohrab, 'like the colonialists before us. We are taking the power of civilization into the deepest reaches of the wild.'

'Perhaps,' Sohrab said respectfully. 'But remember, for us, colonialism was not always such a good thing.'

'Without journalism,' Court was lecturing a bit now, 'these places would remain dark, incomprehensible, remote. No aid, no attention, nothing. Your people would be allowed to sink quietly into oblivion. You need us. We bring the spotlight.'

We were all saying that once. I too used to think that we could bring that beneficial light. Remarkably, Court was still saying it. More remarkably, alone of all of us, he still said it as though he believed it. Listening to him, Laura saw her half-formed suspicions as absurd. She felt confident that we were light-bringers, and that she was one of us. That pleased her.

Still, looking back, it is odd that she could believe this so happily. Glancing around the Cape Atlantic Hotel, you would have seen few specimens who would excite suspicion as killers. You would also have seen few who deserved to be dubbed true emissaries of light. Most of us were simply there, observing and reporting the nastiness in front of us. It takes no special IQ, no exceptional skills, no notable emotional intelligence to be horrified by war.

XIX

The next day it tried to rain. Out of a dull sky like gun-metal, with no visible clouds, leaked a dry, sterile drizzle. In the terrible heat, the drops evaporated before they hit the parched ground.

In the Cape Atlantic, it was as if manna had fallen. Reporters who had been idle for days flexed their typing fingers and juiced up their laptops from the dicey generators. Editors back home harried producers for constant updates. Teresa actually arose from her beach lounger, like Botticelli's Venus, to grace a government press conference. Ralph was jittering in a hyperactive funk. Upper Guinea had been resuscitated as a news story.

Recently the coverage had stagnated, kept alive only by a lucky series of decapitations, which bred reports with headlines like *Horror of the Headhunters*. The head-hunter line had played well in the UN general assembly and Washington DC.

So the United States had ordered a fleet to Freeville.

Over the next twenty-four hours, a flash flood of new blood rolled into town. The old hands observed the newcomers with contempt.

'This', complained Richard Jones, 'is not journalism. It's a circus.'

'Infotainers,' scoffed Hartman. 'Let's see how long they last when the shit starts flying.'

Laura took their view. She already felt like a veteran. 'These people aren't news,' she snorted, 'they're showbiz.'

Strings of network employees trudged in lugging shiny piles of satellite equipment, icemakers and crates of Perrier. Earnest young producers, brittle with ambition, fussed around clutching their clipboards. These insipid invaders had not the slightest interest in where they were. Some of them did not even know. The only wars they were interested in were ratings wars. The only politics they cared about were back at head office. They eyed each other with suspicion, fretted about audience figures and schemed over how best to save on their per diems, already the equivalent of Upper Guinea's average annual wage. In the evenings, frightened production assistants and make-up girls gathered gingerly by the pool, lathered in insect repellent. There was a cacophony of complaints about the bar girls, the food, the lack of hot water, the bugs, the heat. These were swiftly silenced when sustained shooting broke out in the town. The American invasion plans had provoked a spasm of nastiness.

'That's more like it,' said Judith Dart, licking her lips.

The newcomers went quiet at the noise then scuttled back to their hotel rooms. The old hands laughed derisively. Laura sat with them, listening to the rising sounds of battle and playing one of the games that sorted the men from the boys. I had stopped playing years ago.

'M-16,' said Richard Jones, after a high-speed burst of gunfire.

'AK-47,' countered Orlando, as a staccato rat-a-tat-tat replied. 'Moro,' he added (you got more credit for guessing the source of fire).

A loud whoosh and a blast sounded from up the hill in the colonial quarter. 'RPG-7,' said Hartman, 'Bamanda.'

Laura was impressed. I don't think it occurred to her to wonder how valuable their knowledge was. The fighting excited her. I knew how she felt. That evening the frogs and surf were drowned out by a night chorus of shooting.

Not long after that, the sun rose on the first American ships. Their grey bulks lay wallowing in the slow Atlantic swells, just out of artillery range. Pointed black helicopters buzzed around them like gnats.

Onshore, the network teams ran cables from their satellite dishes down to the beach and the reporters did their stand-ups to camera with the ships as backdrop. On the Cape Atlantic's lone TV set, you could see the INN pictures from the beach a few heartbeats after they were filmed, the signal bounced back via New York and a series of geostationary satellite transponders. 'Operation Peace on Earth,' the reporters would intone in that weighty way they tend to adopt on screen, 'will begin as soon as the Marines arrive. That could be as soon as the day after tomorrow. Until then, this country remains in a tragic turmoil . . .'

You know the sort of thing.

Around the news crews, hundreds of townspeople mingled, trooping quietly through the lights and camera tripods like tourists amongst the menhirs of Stonehenge. A temporary ceasefire seemed to be in place. The media had turned peacemaker, and gunmen of all factions wandered together down to the water's edge to look out at the warships. The long pipes of a cruiser's guns were clearly visible. The Guineans peered curiously at the journalists as they went through their obscure nodding rituals, trotting out their litanies into the bulbous black sticks. Enterprising Krio sold their top hats to the dollar-heavy network employees. Fat Bamanda fighters posed for the camera in their fancy-dress blend of tribal and Western clothing. The slender Moro feigned aloofness, but hung around gawping at the cameras, smiling bashfully as awkward children whenever they were filmed.

Later that day, chugging helicopters began to ferry journalists out to the fleet for press conferences. Even Teresa took a ride, to the whistling appreciation of the perspiring sailors. Out there in the bay, the ships were like floating ovens, their metal hulls blistering hot. They rolled slowly in the boiling haze, waiting for the Marines.

Ralph Reynolds became insufferable. 'This is going to be my war, man,' he boasted. 'Rampo, JC, they're going to take a back seat to ol' RR. This is going to be an *American* war.' Ralph was hoping for a swift invasion. He needed the Marines onshore. If he was going to compère this show for a worldwide audience, he needed the performers. When the Marines did not turn up, Ralph became even more pushy and impatient. 'I could kill for a story,' he moaned. He was livid over the delay and took out his insecurities and anger on hapless navy spokesmen in press conferences on the cruiser. 'Boy, we did for him in there,' he would say. 'There was blood all over the floor.'

Ralph and I talked quite a bit over those frustrating days. It's possible I was just about the only person he really talked to. Almost everybody disliked him and I pretty much felt that almost all of them were almost right. I did feel an odd sympathy for him, though, which presumably he detected. I felt he was a bit shy, underneath. Anyway, I think I know what he was after, and I don't think I let down my guard.

'How's it hanging, pardner?' he would say, then start to reminisce. 'Do you remember Sarajevo? Hey, those were the days, man. "We are of one blood, you and I." Remember, Lucky?'

I remembered all right.

Somehow we must have seeded suspicions in his fertile mind. When we first arrived, Ralph had studiously ignored our project. We were making a documentary and as far as Ralph was concerned, if you weren't doing news you were no better than a war tourist. He must have thought, along with everyone else, that we would find out nothing about Miranda's death. Ralph did admit remembering Miranda – 'Yeah, attractive, blonde hair. A nurse, no?' – but he gave the impression that he couldn't have cared less about her.

Somehow, though, he must have heard Papus's rumour. Was he listening when Papus told us? Perhaps. I can't be sure. I do know that Ralph had cultivated the eavesdropping capabilities of an AWACS surveillance plane. Whatever you think about Hollywood Ralph, he was a brilliant journalist, when he cared to be. In his time he had been as ruthless as John Court and as reckless as Orlando Harries. In short, Ralph was a professional. When the bombs were falling and the deadline spiralling near, you could rely on him to stay calm and deliver a polished, unruffled performance. In the excitement of the fleet's arrival, I suspect Ralph salted Papus's titbit away. Later, faced with a long, idle wait for the Marines, he must have decided to act, setting in train his own subtle investigations and their unsubtle consequences.

Meanwhile the circus put everything in place for D-Day, plotting communications and camera positions, scripting the story. The transformation of Upper Guinea into a fully fledged mass-media spectacle meant events needed to gel into a simple, comprehensible formula. The circus settled on 'Krio good, Moro bad'. The top-hatted 'democrats' were more media friendly, and of course descended from freed slaves. Decisively, they were – at least nominally – Christian. In media terms, the townspeople were practically Americans themselves. They were us. The nomads were anything but. Their culture was unashamedly medieval, openly violent, autocratic and indecipherable. To the chagrin of the circus, they just would not perform adequately. The Moro refused to give interviews or allow filming in their areas. Their eyes peering threateningly from indigo turbans, their opaque amalgam of paganism and Islam, it all added up to an image of profound otherness. The Moro were definitely *them*.

Hollywood Ralph shamelessly sifted the shifting web of gangs and alliances into 'democrats versus terrorists'. He was never one to get bogged down in subtleties – they were unlikely to play well with the good folk of Tyretown, Ohio, or wherever he was from. I remembered him taking me aside in Northern Ireland. 'Listen, Lucky, you know this story pretty well,' he said. 'Hey, it's a big story, especially for the Boston affiliates. There's just one thing the audience has a problem with. It's all these . . . letters.'

'Letters?'

'You know – IRA, UVF, UFF . . .'

'Acronyms.'

'Yeah, acnoryms. It's confusing. You've also got the Loyalists, Republicans, Nationalists, Sinn Fein, Unionists, SDLP . . .'

'Yes?'

'Well, can't I just go on and call them all the IRA?'

The ludicrous pressures from the home front were no

help. When a manager told him the Network was holding up a broadcast of one of his war crimes reports, even Ralph was amazed. 'So this business manager says to me: "I've got the lawyers looking at it. We've got to be safe on this: can we really refer to this government death squad as 'ruthless'?"'

You had to sympathize.

One urgent editorial requirement was a standard death score. So far, different networks had been using figures ranging from 12,000 dead (John Court for International Network News) to half a million (Ralph Reynolds for the Central Network). Viewers were confused enough about Upper Guinea without such discrepancies, so it was agreed to use Red Cross estimates as a neutral, mutually acceptable figure. I think the number chosen was 250,000. Laura saw this as an admirable example of inter-agency co-operation.

'How did you come up with those figures, Ben?' she asked the stressed Red Cross man after the meeting. He seemed to have aged ten years since we first saw him.

'Well,' he said slowly, 'I used a selection of the many accurate information sources on offer. I went to the central bureau of statistics then I added figures supplied by the rebel factions, the military and the bush hospital information Internet site . . . How the hell do you think?' He paused, then went on tiredly, 'I made them up of course. Nobody has a clue how many people have died in this awful war.' Ben sighed. 'We guess, basically. Then each week or two the media add another few thousand. The key thing is not to underestimate. The aid donors and the media editors need big numbers. In Africa, that means a lot of zeroes. Ghastly.'

Laura protested. 'But if we didn't push the stories and the numbers to the limit, the Americans wouldn't be coming. Then where would this place be?'

Ben shrugged. 'Yes. I know. And look, we're as guilty of it as anyone. It just depresses me that there is always this drive for bigger numbers, better pictures, more explicit violence. Sad faces aren't enough, you people want tears. We show you hungry children, you people want starving. Sick is not enough, you want dying.'

'But surely that's a good thing,' said Laura. 'There's always room to go a little further, get a little closer to the real truth. If people are crying, starving, dying, that's what we should reflect.'

I could tell she had been speaking to John Court.

The locals' reaction to the Americans was impenetrable. Every morning, cloaked men from the Poro, the Leopard and other secret societies gathered chanting on the beach in their diabolic belled masks. This alien sight was not recorded by the pack. Many of them were still in bed and most of the rest thought it would be racist to show such 'primitive' images of Africa. 'A shallow, colonialist image of the black man, Lucky,' Ralphy told me, 'confirming low stereotypes and prejudices. There would be an outcry from every black organization in America.'

Others were not put off by political correctness; the scenes were simply too strange, too far removed. 'People at home just couldn't understand,' Rampling would say, as though he did.

A few of us recorded this tectonic awakening of the tribal gods. I was attracted by the eeriness of the rituals and shot some moody sequences, which might conceivably have fitted into *White Woman's Grave*. Otherwise I only saw Farhad, with Georges Renard, and John Court. JC wove the impressionistic images into a report on the tribal background to the conflict. I'm not sure it ever ran. The pack slumbered and awaited the invasion.

Meanwhile the marabouts, griots and medicine men crept down past the well-prepared camera positions on the beach. Hidden in costumes of leaves and straw, coated in ochre and streaks of red mud, they cast fetish charms into the breakers and wove intricate spells on the obstinately silent grey behemoths. You could not tell whether the witch doctors were hoping the ships would depart, or praying for them to intervene. In the event, they just stayed put.

On or around 27th July, a grey mood fell over the hotel. Isolationist votes in the US Congress had postponed the Marines' arrival, perhaps permanently. Onshore the story had flagged as well. 'Your countrymen are letting us down,' an ambitious circus producer whined to Malaika and Sohrab. 'There's just not enough fighting.'

I was affected by creeping guilt over a now undeniable attraction to Laura Marlow. By the time I next came to phone my erstwhile family, desire and guilt rose together in my gullet like a remembered indigestion. Up on the roof, burning heat exacerbated the incipient heartburn. I tried to huddle in the meagre shadow of a network satellite dish while my satphone launched its electronic pulses up into the endless blue nothing of the air.

I was prepared for another unpleasant encounter. Whenever Claire had been home during those first troubling weeks, she had passed me brusquely to Alex. But 27th July was our son's birthday. This time she seemed genuinely affected. She sounded soft, emotional, like a voice from a pleasant time that I could not place. I heard the laughter and shouting of a children's party in the background.

'How is it there?' she asked. 'It looks pretty awful on the TV here. I don't know how you can stand it. I've been thinking about what you do, Peter. If only you people could make it look less wicked. Wickedness has its attractions. You should try and make it look vulgar. I'm sure it's vulgar.'

'This really is the last time, Claire. The very last time.'

'Yes, of course.' She sounded sad. 'Pity it's too late.'

I almost asked her who she had been on holiday with.

She called Alex to the line and his voice echoed down to me, hollow and faintly distorted.

'Mummy wouldn't give me a rifle,' he complained. He meant a toy one.

'Don't worry, Alex, I'll bring you a TV camera instead, when I get back.' I meant a toy one, too. The Freeville street kids made them from wire coat hangers.

'When's that, Dad?'

'Soon, Alex.'

'Then you'll be back with us for ever? With Mum?'

'We'll see, Alex.'

The party noises in the background whooped closer to the phone. They almost drowned out Alex's 'Bye, Dad,' as he was whisked off by Red Indians or Delta Force operatives or whoever boys were these days. Usually that would be the end of the call.

'Love you,' I said, into what I thought was a dead line.

'Do you?' Claire was still there. 'Did you really ever love me, Peter?'

My unruly mind threw up images of past betrayals, of the faithlessness of war, of Laura Marlow.

'I'm not sure,' Claire went on, in the same tender tone. I remembered the voice, it was the Claire of a time long past. 'But I know Alex loves you, Peter. And he misses you. Sometimes I . . .' Deep down the web of twisted copper cable, optical fibre, digital interchange and satellite transponder, I heard it teeter on the edge of her larynx: '. . . miss you too.'

'Yes?' I rubbed the spot where my wedding ring once clung.

'. . . Oh, no, it's nothing. Just . . . just be careful, Peter.'

It was enough to make me wonder. It was enough to remind me that we would be home soon, that there was life out there. It was enough to make me swear to myself, again, that nothing was going to happen with Laura Marlow.

The hotel was plagued with frustration and apathy. Amidst the relaxation of social norms and civilized mores for which war provides a useful excuse, the bar girls thrived. They appeared each evening like clockwork, just as the bats began swooping low overhead. The circus had increased demand. Knowing journalists well by now, they even provided receipts labelled 'food' on hotel headed paper. 'Big meal last night?' was the standing joke.

The girls gathered around the poolside tables, ignoring the politically correct outrage of the network staff, and flirting with a frank, open shamelessness found only in Africa. 'I am soup and jolof rice,' they might say, or simply, 'Eat me!' They could be as direct as walking up to you and grabbing you between the legs – a greeting known as the 'Freeville handshake'. They were persistent too. Soft knockings and whispers would come through the door at night. 'I just want somewhere to sleep,' they would lie, giggling. 'I just want to use your bath.' There was an engaging freshness, almost a naivety about the girls, and, AIDS-ridden or not, many of them were beautiful. I, of course, maintain that I kept my door firmly bolted.

'You are not hungry?' a very attractive example

asked me one night. She was checking coyly why I did not seem to partake of the joys on offer. 'Maybe you like to watch?' The girl stroked the hair of a giggling accomplice. Echoes of indulgences past sweated me for a moment.

'I'm not against all this,' I replied, 'it's just not for me.'

'Hmm. So you won't mind us helping out the local economy, then?' asked Steven, who had been adopted by a plump young woman from an inland tribe notorious for their sexual depravity. He was paying her in food and cigarettes.

'Just make sure you're condomed to the hilt,' I said. 'There's no point in bringing a flak jacket then not protecting the rest of you.'

'No problem, chief. It's double sock all the way.'

Laura still did not approve. 'Why do you do it?' she asked Brian.

'I feel sorry for her.'

His nubile young lady was betrothed to a Swiss photographer who had left some months before. She was still cheerfully awaiting the air ticket to Zurich he had promised.

'Why don't you just give her the money and not, well, not sleep with her?'

The girl seemed to understand. She said something to Malaika, who translated. 'She says she would not accept that. Why should she sleep with someone else, if it is Brian who gives her things?'

'It's disgusting,' said Laura.

Malaika looked serious. 'It is natural. This is a dangerous place . . . What do you say – a hostile environment?'

'These girls are a bloody hostile environment,' said Laura.

Malaika went on. 'Here you might die at any time. Maybe it is not so wrong to enjoy your life . . .' For a moment her gaze seemed to rest on me. '. . . It may be short.'

I looked at the two young women talking in the warm evening. The light and the dark. Malaika's profile, Laura's eyes. I thought of Laura's lavender aura by the window in my room. For an instant my gaze met hers and I felt like casting my obscure resistance to the wind. Claire had dumped me, damn it! Then it passed. I looked away. At the time I thought Laura was disappointed, but I decided I was imagining it. I suppose I was holding lots of things back on this trip. It would be too easy to lose myself in the intensity of it all. And once in, well, I didn't know how deep I would go. I did not want to get lost.

'Watch out! Hyperactive superstar alert.' Laura's stage whisper warned us of the appearance of an increasingly restless Ralph Reynolds.

'Hey, guys! Come on, let's liven this morgue up.'

Ralph trotted over to the thatched bandstand and had a word with the band. They opened up a passable rock and roll.

'I don't dance,' Laura protested feebly. She cast me an imploring glance but Ralphy had already pulled her onto the floor. 'Yeah,' whooped Ralphy, swinging her almost violently. 'Ride 'em, cowboy!' He danced surprisingly well, holding her closely but lightly, and Laura giggled like a child as he manoeuvred her across the tiles. He turned her now and then in intricate twirls.

'Hey, this lady spins like a feather,' he said admiringly as he returned her to her seat. He winked and snapped his fingers at me – an annoying habit he had – ending with his thumb raised and index finger pointing at you like the barrel of a mock six-shooter, 'Mind she doesn't blow away.'

Laura looked flushed.

'You're a bit of a dark horse, Ralphy,' drawled Orlando. 'Never took you for a dancer.'

'Some of us have hidden talents, Lando, baby,' smiled Hollywood Ralph. 'You aristocratic Brits might find it necessary to show off. Some of us more modest Midwest folks hide our light under a bushel.'

'I'm surprised any bushel can conceal your blazing talent, Ralph.' It was Jan Hartman, well into his favourite local gut rot.

It seemed to be open season on Laura. Even the tubby little Sohrab screwed up his courage and asked her to dance. It was a slow number and he, timidly correct, held her stiffly, almost at arm's length. I think he might have looked up once and she smiled at him. I saw a beatified glow on his face. The top of his greying curls came only to her nose.

Felipe Deflores cut in next with a flamenco flourish and I felt I shouldn't mope about.

I looked at Teresa and inclined my head towards the dance floor. She raised her eyebrows.

'Now it is I who am Looky.'

Teresa felt voluptuous in my arms. She danced heavily, but with an instinctive, sinuous rhythm.

Poor Teresa. I liked her. Everyone did. You couldn't help it. She might infuriate you and nowadays she was often kitsch and indolent, but she had worked hard to get where she was. And she knew nothing of malice. In my arms she sighed and put her head against my shoulder.

'I'm tired of all this, Peter,' she said. 'I want to go home soon.'

'We all need a break now and again.'

'Not a break. For good.'

'You're going to settle in Rome?'

'That's not my home. You know I come from a small town in the south, in Calabria.'

I realized I knew so little about her, about her family, about what mattered. Presumably there were two old people in some dusty hilltop village who were thinking about a Teresa they knew. I saw her as their memories might paint her, the child running amongst olive groves, the troublesome girl, coyly entrancing village boys in a sunny piazza, the itinerant woman saying yet another hasty goodbye. I pictured a dignified old man with a flat cap and a woman all in black. They would be proud of Teresa, they would be worried about her. Then again, maybe there was no-one.

'But I thought you liked this life,' I said.

She was silent for a while.

'I miss love, Looky. Where is love out here?'

That was a question I really did not feel qualified to answer.

More people were dancing now. Even the Internet geeks had got up from their keyboards and were boogying around the table where their laptop screens glowed eerily.

Orlando had whisked up Ralph Reynolds's producer, a cheerleader-pretty Californian blonde with a skirt as short as some of the more daring local tarts. Dancing in front of her hero Ralph made her blush deeply. The dashing Orlando danced with the same infectious energy he brought to his camerawork, and the beautiful couple returned laughing and panting to the table. He ordered ice creams and she ate hers with a girlish relish, licking and sucking the cone with a virginal eroticism. She looked as if it wouldn't melt in her mouth.

'I like you, you know,' Orlando said. 'I bet you actually believe that George Washington never told a lie.'

'He never did.' She batted her eyelashes and looked at him, wide-eyed. I thought of deer and headlights. 'I also believe in Mom's apple pie and in health, wealth and the pursuit of happiness.' Orlando laughed his rich, infectious laugh.

She dabbed him on the nose with her ice cream and her bare heels flashed white in the torchlight as she ran giggling off towards the beach.

'Well, I suppose I should pursue,' grinned Orlando. He darted after her into the dark.

'Great girl,' said Ralph ruefully. 'Bit innocent though. I hope she doesn't fall in with that maniac. She really has a lot to learn.'

'Yes,' said Hartman, 'sleeping with you would be much better for her career.'

'You got it, man,' chuckled Ralph.

'She is nothing but a child,' said Teresa.

'If she's on the road . . .' Hartman said.

'. . . she can take the load,' laughed Ralph.

'Old enough to dodge a shell . . .'

'. . . old enough to put out as well!' Ralph and Jan exchanged high fives.

'So it is actually true.' A smiling Laura shook her head in mock disapproval. 'You men are all the same. I would have hoped war would cool you down. It seems the opposite is true.'

'You are sooo right, darling,' said Teresa, reaching forward to touch Laura on the forearm. 'They are all peegs. Here they have an excuse to behave like it. Deep down they all 'ate women. And they love war.'

'Hey, I love women,' protested Ralphy. He raised a single eyebrow at Laura. 'Wanna see how much?'

Ralph could be entertaining company, but he could also really make me seethe.

XX

Only a few stray members of the pack were interested when the Red Cross secured safe passage to Mile Sixty, the bush hospital where Miranda Williams had worked. We needed to film there, but the old hands were dismissive.

'A lot of sick people,' smirked Rampling. 'So what?' He was too busy hounding his producer into bed.

Judith Dart shrugged her shoulders. 'I'm a Combat Correspondent. If you want to cover Mile Sixty, send the Development Correspondent, or the Health Correspondent maybe.'

Mile Sixty was a long trip if you weren't sure of a story. Some years back the European Union had funded a gleaming new road, which cut the journey time to about an hour and a half. Relentless heat melted the asphalt, peasant builders stole the gravel underlay for their concrete. Degradations and diversions of neglect and war had pulverized and corrugated the track. Somehow the journey had stretched by about forty miles. It would take about five hours, according to the perennially pessimistic Hartman.

'What's it like?' asked Laura. 'No, on second thoughts, let me guess. Ghastly, right?'

'Blerrie arsehole of the world,' Hartman chortled. 'You must go. I guarantee you'll hate it.'

We set off at first light. The faintest of morning hazes soon burned away, replaced by a scorching, cloudless sky. Inside the van we yearned for a breeze. The rutted dirt roads, in even worse condition where washboard-ridged remnants of tarmac still lingered, slowed our speed to an airless crawl. Behind Mo's Datsun bumped some other vehicles containing Miranda's gloomy replacement, Ben, and a group of the recent arrivals. None of the long-serving brigade was there, apart from the relentless Orlando Harries, who always gaily wanted to go everywhere. He was hoping the journey would not be as peaceful as the Red Cross had promised. None of us was wearing a flak jacket. Orlando had advised us against taking them at all. 'I wouldn't bother with that,' he told Laura, airily. 'You'll never wear it. You'll be sweating worse than a paedophile in a playground.' It was his way of trying to impress.

I kept half an eye on their interactions, but decided she was not interested. Orlando was a romantic figure in some ways, with a predatory sexual history, but I suspected he was too cavalier about journalism for Laura. Also, although there was a touch of lunacy to all of us, Orlando was obviously, overtly, certifiably insane.

So too, you might be forgiven for thinking, was our driver. Mo, eagerly leading the convoy, took a series of wrong turns, got totally lost and held up the entire line of vehicles. Jabbering happily to himself all the while, he was in thoroughly bad favour by the time we got to the city rim. That is where the jungle starts. It looked thick and impenetrable, dark green and shining with damp. The narrow, pitted path that ran through it was almost a tunnel. It was also Upper Guinea's main highway.

We had only been driving through the forest shadows for a few minutes when the shells began to land.

Imagine the loudest sound you have ever heard. Then double it. Then double it again. That is like the sound of a shell exploding nearby. It's too loud to be anything but pure noise. If it is anything, it is an earth-shattering, gut-thumping, breath-sucking, ear-blasting *crack!*

On your television, you never really hear the noise of close shellfire properly. The sound is too loud for microphones. Sound recordists use limiters to muffle the din. This stops their eardrums and the delicate recording membranes of their equipment being destroyed by a blast. It also means that loud bangs can appear as mere pops or thuds. Properly recorded effects can always be added later in the edit suite.

The first explosion pounded the air out of my lungs and set my eardrums ringing. The Datsun was buffeted by the shock waves. Then another shell exploded, and another. They seemed to be all around us. Some detonated in the undergrowth, shearing off branches and sending fountains of dirt, twigs and leaves out across the road. The panicked drivers of the other cars careered madly off into the bush. Oblivious to the mayhem in his vehicle and all around him, Mo carried serenely on his own sweet way. Within moments we left the explosions behind and glided to a gentle halt some way up the road.

A shaking Brian and Steven automatically broke out their camera gear and filmed the scene. The other cars, smashed up against trees or jammed in ditches, had to endure another few moments of barrage. It occurred to me that we might be filming the death of some of our colleagues. What would we do with the footage then? Would we use it? Put it in the archive to sell as library pictures to war documentaries?

'Are you all right?' I asked Laura and she nodded quickly, giving my hand a brief squeeze. In fact I was amazed at her calmness. I was quivering like a leaf, but she seemed happy, if anything. The shells stopped and after a few minutes of ringing, humming, absolute silence, we walked gingerly back down the road, in our flak jackets now. Funnelled down the soundproof green tunnel of the track, Orlando's velvet laugh rolled faintly up to meet us on the thick, hot air.

No-one was killed, but Ben was groggy after banging his head on the windscreen. Orlando, smiling broadly, had a small gash on his chest. 'Chalk another one up,' he joked. 'Suppose you think I should have been wearing my flak jacket.' He smiled flirtatiously at Laura as she helped Ben wind a bandage around his scarred, hard-muscled body. 'Ow!' he yelped as she gave the dressing a deliberate tug. Apart from Mo, the drivers were nervous wrecks.

'That's the advantage of a deaf driver,' said Steven.

'I take it all back, Mo,' said Laura, 'you're a star.'

'Yes, yes,' said Mo. He grinned wildly at her with his vampire smile.

Malaika was very worried. 'I was sure that the road was safe. If this has happened here, so close to town, I can't think what might happen further out. It's dangerous.'

'Of course it's dangerous,' said Orlando, laughing. 'That's the whole fun of it. Every time you survive, you can say to yourself, I'm alive! I am alive!'

I knew what he meant. You felt it even more when someone else died.

The attack hadn't given us time to be frightened, and

now it was over, any fear I felt was mixed with the thrill of our narrow escape. I could no longer deny it was there, growing and welling up, hot and deep within me. That roiling mixture of body chemicals and psychosis that means war. I felt a stab of desire for Laura, who looked strangely elated. She was panting, but it wasn't with fright. It was adrenaline. She patted the dressing on Orlando's pectorals and breathed deeply. I remember looking at her as we drove off. Her eyes were bright, her cheeks flushed. I realized she was, frankly, exhilarated.

Most of the expedition turned back. A few others crammed into the least damaged Jeep, which bumped and crawled after Mo's Datsun along the crumbling track. The rest of the trip was like a tense dream journey in slow motion through heavy heat and hushed jungle. The scene flows by in the rushes like silent history; you could almost be looking through Miranda's eyes when she passed this way. Our hearing dulled, we rolled slowly past the rusting hulks of ambushed vehicles. In some of them, the charred remains of drivers still sat at the wheel. The fast-growing jungle trees were forcing their way up through the burned-out cabs, and vines wound through the windscreens and knotted around the blackened axles. The villages we passed were silent too. Their people had fled from fighting and from forced recruitment by the rebels, the Government, whatever. The reed fences were broken down, the mud walls blasted with rocket fire. Here and there long grass grew up between bleaching human bones.

Mile Sixty was just another broken settlement in the heart of the great bush, swamped by the tides of war and the erosion of the wild. The only difference was that in some past time, when there was still something to administer, Mile Sixty had been declared an administrative centre. The only remnant of this function was the checkpoint – now just a flimsy bamboo pole slung across the road. Until recently the Government had maintained a major garrison here. To pacify the local savages, the enlightened commander cut off a number of heads and mounted them on stakes around the checkpoint. It wasn't long before the local tribes went over to the Moro. The regular soldiers promptly deserted, leaving only some spindly ten-year-old boys in oversized uniforms to await their capture and execution whenever it took the rebels' fancy. When we arrived, the few surviving child soldiers smiled listlessly for the cameras among the mocking, toothy grins of the dead.

Around the checkpoint, Mile Sixty was a straggle of huts in varying stages of decay. There were signs of a rubber plantation, clogged with lianas and jungle shrubs. The parched fields were fallow. A lone stall made of crooked branches sold dented tins of Nestlé powdered milk and lumps of high offal with a coating of flies thick and black as an oil slick. A ragged mesh fence surrounded the Red Cross compound. Inside the precinct hundreds of patients wandered like lost souls around a group of square mud huts. Three large tents formed the wards and operating theatre.

Of the news journalists, only the local producer/cameraman, Sohrab, and the young Swedish reporter found anything worth covering. The rest of the pack was disappointed. There were no overt signs of war here. The careworn head doctor said that yes, many civilians had been randomly killed. Some weeks ago a lot of limbs had been chopped off by retreating government troops. Now, the place was just full of the usual ailments of the bush. There were many septic abscesses and suppurating ulcers. An old man had a spearhead in his thigh from a hunting accident. There were legs swollen to bursting by elephantiasis, skin eaten away by lupus, bellies bulging with the extreme malnutrition of kwashiorkor. There were patients covered in the raspberry-like pustules of yaws. There were children with rickets and ringworm and chiggers. The white of one child's eye was a writhing mass of active filaria worms. Some of them were burrowing under a ridge of skin across the bridge of his nose to the other eye. One large tent was full of quivering, sweating cases of malaria and cachexia, a wasting disease that turns its victims into walking skeletons. The nightmare sense of the place was exacerbated by its quiet. Now and again a soft moan would escape a fever case, a dysenteric baby would have a swift cry. The jungle absorbed and deadened even these rare sounds, and, normally, the patients suffered in stoic silence.

At Mile Sixty there was no mass starvation. There was no genocide. There was just the usual round of parasites, disease, deprivation and premature death. None of these endemic problems would be deemed newsworthy.

'Got any AIDS out here?' asked one reporter. AIDS at least was something with which his readership back home could empathize.

'AIDS out here might be a blessing,' said the doctor.

'Ebola?' asked the reporter, hopefully.

The doctor only just thought better of hitting him.

The news journalists were gone within the hour, hoping to make it back to Freeville before nightfall. The idealistic young Swede stayed behind. Moved to tears by the dark frightfulness of the place, he had decided to remain, to write about it, and to help if he could.

We also stayed on. Mile Sixty and its horrors were central to our film. This was the life Miranda had led, this was why she had come to Guinea. And to the people here, Miranda really had been an angel. Malaika found two small boys, missing most of their toes from a mysterious local disease known as ainhum. They remembered how Miranda had nursed them, cured them and brought them a football. A mother of two girls, with a terribly swollen spleen, cried when she heard Miranda was dead. Malaika translated the woman's sobs. 'She says Miranda brought light.'

The place was terrifying.

'We call these ones spiders,' the doctor told Laura, pointing at some hopelessly emaciated children, breathing hoarsely in a gloomy tent. 'Like spiders swirling round the plughole.'

A few of those lives would be swilled out that night.

The lens usually offers cameramen protection against the reality it deciphers. But the tragedy of Mile Sixty was strong enough to pierce the glass barrier and reach even Brian. It was the sequence on the local diet that finally made him grimace and pull away from the viewfinder. The war and the abnormally late rains meant that fields were untended and crops meagre. People had already resorted to digging up anthills for seeds and scraps collected by the insects. Now the only available meat was 'bush meat' – the flesh of rodents and snakes, or, more often, rank cuts of chimpanzee, monkey and the fast-dwindling population of gorillas.

'That's sick,' said Steven.

'That'll get the complaint lines ringing back home,' said Brian. 'You'll have to put a health warning on it when it goes out on air.'

It is one of those odd things about our audience that they are much more shocked by, and less tolerant of, cruelty to animals than cruelty to other humans.

Miranda's friend returned late in the afternoon from

an inoculation tour in outlying villages. She was one of just two doctors at the post. Strained and tense, Lucy Chambers made it clear she had a very low opinion of journalists. 'They've been here, like a pack of hyenas,' she said. 'Why do you think I made sure I wasn't here today? I wasn't going to be part of the circus all over again.'

She looked at the crew. 'I'm only talking to you people because of Miranda's mother. I spoke to her by satphone. She said you', Lucy pointed to me, 'were very kind. So I don't include you lot when I say that journalists make me ill.'

We interviewed her that evening after the day's last patients limped out into the bush. At first she was a bit nervous and the same old platitudes sounded in Steven's earphones as she praised Miranda's goodness and mercy. Not for long. It was as though the harsh world around Lucy Chambers had stripped from her any ability to gloss. Relative to the brutality of life at Mile Sixty, Miranda's death was hardly the sack of Rome by the Goths. Lucy's frankness reminded me of Madiba Kane. They had the same clinical approach to life, and death. Lucy could steel herself and refer to Miranda in a cold, objective way, despite being her best friend. In fact, seeing the way her face clouded over when she talked of Miranda, I wondered whether there had not been something more than platonic friendship between them.

In the recording Lucy looks tired, but her features reveal an inner strength. She smokes a cigarette during the interview, and a blue haze drifts up through the shot. 'Do you know what *le cafard* is?' she says at one point. 'It is a French word for the madness which seizes people in the wilderness. Many of the French colonists and legionnaires who invaded these countries perished from it.'

Brian cleverly zooms in here, so the rest of what Lucy says is accentuated by the power of eyes and expression that fill the screen. This close-up reveals the lines of care etched upon her face, and the flecks of grey in her hair.

'*Le cafard* comes from solitude, from suffering, from boredom. From the endless, hopeless round of extreme conditions in a harsh and unforgiving land. I won't say Miranda had *le cafard*, but she was close to it. What you see here, day after day, can drive anyone mad. We sent her back to Freeville. For a break. I was worried about her. I thought it would do her good to get out. She was tough, yes, or I wouldn't have kept her out here with me, but she was still not much more than a girl. She still had so much to learn.' Lucy said they had spoken for the last time two days later. 'Miranda was due to call again the night after that, but never did. After a few days I got worried and returned to Freeville. So I was there when they found the body.'

'Why did she do this work?' Laura asked. 'Why do you do it?'

'We talked about that . . . We talked about a lot of things . . . Here, you are doing good in the worst place in the world. A small thing in the West is a small thing, is nothing. You can waste your life away on colds and backaches. In Mile Sixty, even soap is a revolutionary medicine. A simple antiseptic is a lifesaver. An aspirin is magical. Chloroquine against malaria is a miracle. I think Miranda felt that as strongly as I do.'

After a few minutes, we came to the question that I thought Lucy – perhaps only Lucy – might be able to answer. Knowing her opinion of journalists, and guessing at her feelings for Miranda, I thought it was going to be touch and go. Laura of course went ahead and asked it brazenly: 'Did Miranda have a lover in Upper Guinea?' For an awful second Lucy thought deeply. I wondered if she were going to say it – I think I held my breath – but she replied calmly that she didn't know.

Inevitably, as soon as the camera was switched off, we began to find out what she had held back. Firstly: her tears. Just four of them, rolling in big diamond drops onto the thin grass of the compound. A little later, over a whisky or two: the fact that Miranda had met someone when she returned to Freeville for her final break. 'I was devastated,' said Lucy. 'I was afraid she would never come back. The patients needed her, you see . . . I needed her.'

'Did Miranda tell you who it was?' Laura continued.

Lucy sounded bitter now. 'No. I never mentioned it because she didn't. I didn't really want to know. I suppose his identity hasn't emerged because he's either married or an uncaring shit or probably both. It would make sense – he's a journalist. She told me that much.'

'Why do you dislike us so much?'

'I'll give you just one example – that tosser, Rampling. He turned a day here into a story of rebel atrocities.'

'But weren't the rebels chopping off people's hands?'

'It has been known. The point is, the man Rampling filmed that day had been injured in a hunting accident. I amputated the hand myself. And Rampling knew it.'

'Well, but it managed to illustrate an important story.'

'That's not the only reason I'm suspicious of journalists.'

'What else then?' Laura was a little offended now.

Lucy paused for a moment. 'I think many journalists mean well, they might even yearn to help people. Saving people isn't just good, it makes you feel good.'

'What do you mean?'

'I'm not exactly sure, but it is more than just a warm feeling inside. It's intensity. It's excitement. Sometimes

I feel there is almost an attraction – no, maybe not an attraction – an addiction, in the power you have, maybe even in the suffering you witness. I've seen it in some of my colleagues too. Even Miranda. Her devotion to the task could be, well, almost excessive. It's as though the extremes of the job lead to you craving such a stimulus.'

Laura looked sceptical.

'Anyhow, that's just my view,' continued Lucy. 'Maybe because I've felt it. As a doctor, you really notice it when you get back to a safe technological environment where you make little difference, where you don't have this power. Where what you do doesn't really *matter*. That can be tough.'

Laura nodded as if she understood. Maybe she did. After the intense contrasts of Upper Guinea, how would she be able to report with enthusiasm on, say, some grey political controversy about local tax regimes? It was obvious to anyone that she reacted differently to the extremes around us. No fear for her, no worries about the past, about what happens when you become swept up in war. Not even the stoic, professional self-preservation of the crew. The truth is, she was thriving. I could see she was a little troubled by this. Perhaps, in her way of following authorities and teachers, she wondered what she should think of herself. Was it bad to be healthy in the midst of illness? Surely not. I decided then that I would have to talk to her about it. I also knew what Lucy meant. I felt the same attraction. I had felt it very powerfully in the past. Now I distrusted it, and resisted it. I felt I knew where it could lead.

That night, after a day buried in her country's abasement, Malaika cried. I put my arm round her shoulders and comforted her. As I said, we had been close before, on the child-soldiers shoot. Then too she had cried, and I remembered a night in Freeville, when I had held her, with a similar murk of motives in my circling embrace. Jan Hartman, that nosy Afrikaner, had seen the whole tête-à-tête. When Malaika went off to dry her eyes, he shuffled over and leered at her burnished caramel curves swaying gracefully into the hotel. He chortled wickedly. 'So, my china, you're going to go for a bit of cross-cultural intercourse? Good for you . . . Of course, you realize she's circumcized.'

'What?'

'Yes, all those nomad girls are. They cut away the clitoris, the labia. In fact anything that sticks out. Then they sew it all back together with acacia thorns. Painful when it's done and bloody painful when it's undone, I hear.'

'Thanks for that information, Jan.'

'No problem. Now if you want my advice,' Hartman went on conspiratorially, 'you'll concentrate on the nipples. Their senses there are enhanced. You know, like blind men get a better sense of smell.'

'Jan.'

'Believe me, they can orgasm through their nipples.'

'Just shut up, Jan.'

That night I kept Malaika in the hotel. In fact I led her to my room. There I discovered that she had indeed been excised. When she started to explain, I quietened her with a finger to her lips. 'Shhh. I know.'

I then applied myself passionately to Hartman's advice, with results that were charmingly and vocally successful.

It had not helped me plead my case to Claire. Could I really blame the hothouse of war for these infidelities? Or was it me?

Malaika and I had ignored the 'incident', but now, after a disturbing day in Mile Sixty, in her tent, she lifted her face to mine and I was taken unawares as she kissed me warmly through her sobs. I was laying her down on her camp bed when I heard a sound behind me. I pulled away from Malaika to see Laura looking at me with – what? Reproach?

'Laura, I . . .'

She turned and walked out. I followed her quickly, but could not see her in the dark. When I turned back to Malaika's tent, the flap was zipped shut.

'Nice work, Lucky,' I said to myself, and cursed silently. I looked away into the croaking, humming jungle night. The trees rose in steep black walls around the camp. Low on the horizon was the thinnest crescent of a waxing moon. The night sky was a cauldron of stars.

The next day, high nimbus clouds appeared, cutting out the blinding sun. 'Maybe it will rain,' said Malaika, looking hopefully at the darkening sky. She said nothing about the previous night. Back on the road to Freeville, the clouds dulled the glare, but not the heat, which settled from a blazing grill to a steady, steamy oven. Attempts to talk to Laura were rebuffed with the scrupulous politeness that I now recognized as anger. The journey through the sweltering, silent forest was uneventful. Close to where the mortars had hit us on the outward journey, I told the team to put on their flak jackets. There was the merest murmur of protest and we had just lifted Laura's into place when Mo skidded crazily to a halt in a spray of dust. A huge yellow stinkwood tree crashed groaning across the road in front of us. There were voices raised from around its base. Out of the dust cloud loomed a spectral shape wearing a diaphanous white wedding dress and a red American Football helmet – the Washington Redskins if I remember correctly. He carried an enormous machine gun, a long belt of ammunition looped over his shoulder. Behind him, faces painted white, came four others, their muscular, mud-smeared bodies almost naked apart from leather G-strings. They were armed with bulky, home-made wooden muskets. Axes and machetes were strapped across their backs. One man's outfit was completed by a wedding veil and green wellington boots. Another wore inflatable yellow arm-bands around bulging biceps, and carried a bow and arrows.

'Nobody's going to believe this,' murmured Brian as he instinctively pressed the record button on his camera. Strangely, this gave us all a brief charge of confidence, as though the camera offered some mystical line of defence. Surely we would not be killed on camera. It was a confidence that began to evaporate as the ghostly figures came closer.

Well, if we die, I thought, at least they'll be able to run something on the news.

Laura looked thrilled and frightened in equal measure.

Malaika looked simply terrified. 'Bamanda,' she whispered. 'In their war magic.'

In silence, the dreamlike apparitions drifted towards us. The forest was still. In the van the only sound was of Brian's Betacam softly whirring. No-one moved. It felt increasingly hot. Malaika looked more and more worried. Mo, if he had noticed anything, showed no concern. There was a crunch of twigs as the Bamanda approached. Laura drew back as the leader shoved his face into her open window. His eyes were a livid yellow, lined with a river delta of lurid blood vessels. His forehead and cheeks were studded with heavy ridges of tribal scarring that matched the protective grill on the football helmet. On his wrist he wore the same bracelet as Mo. The cowries clinked against the side of the car. He snarled an order, which Malaika quietly translated as 'Get out.'

His followers hovered anxiously by the side of the road. Mo, of course, seemed completely oblivious. He stared straight out through the windscreen, chewing on a kola nut. 'What will they do to us when we get out?' whispered Laura.

I felt a sudden, feverish chill. 'We're not getting out,' I said. 'Nobody move.'

The phantoms glared and levelled their weapons at the van. The man with the bow put an arrow to his string and drew it back. Malaika began to whimper softly.

Trust Laura to remember her training for this type of situation. 'Do what you're told' was the lesson for kidnaps, checkpoints and robberies. She would have been within her rights to think this could qualify as any of the above. 'I think we should probably get out,' she said.

Mo chose this moment to turn to the gang and begin shouting. He pulled his gri-gri out of his shirt and waved it at the gunmen. He licked his lips with great smacking sounds and looked the four white-faced tribesmen up and down with naked hunger. They quailed visibly. Their ringleader in his wedding dress hesitated, then gave a harsh laugh. He rattled his own gri-gri then raised the machine gun and repeated his guttural command.

'I think we should get out,' said Laura again.

'Don't. Fucking. Move,' I said.

Laura persisted. She repeated her first question. 'What will they do to us if we get out?'

'They will kill us,' I whispered. My scars throbbed painfully. 'Now keep quiet.'

The tableau was frozen for what seemed like an age. Sweat gathered on my forehead and pooled in my eye sockets. I could feel thick drops running down my spine, into my pants. Mo reached slowly down below his seat. I could see his fingers close gently on the gun barrel. Then there was the sound of roaring engines, a new dust cloud on the other side of the fallen tree. Brakes squealed and a cluster of Arab fighters spilled from two Range Rovers. The Bamanda hijackers froze in confusion.

A tall Lebanese shouted something to the man in the bridal gown and waved him towards the bush with his handgun. His followers took a few steps backwards, towards the jungle fringe. Their leader shook his helmeted head and stood his ground. In the blink of an eye, the Lebanese lifted his pistol to the side of the Bamanda's helmet and pulled the trigger. A fist-sized chunk of head and helmet blew into the bush.

The man simply slumped, crumpled to the ground in a billow of white lace. The other hijackers gave a cry of shock, let fly once at the van with a crash and a pall of gun smoke, and disappeared into the undergrowth in a hail of Lebanese bullets. Then all was silent again.

One home-made musket ball had gone in through an open window and out through the van's roof. Mo peered at the neatly punched hole and shook his head sadly. He muttered angrily when he saw an arrow lodged in his rear tyre. The Lebanese rolled the dead man off the road with their feet. 'Savages,' one muttered. He spat on the ground by the body.

Inside the Datsun, the air was heavy with damp heat and the smell of sweat. The plastic-covered seats were slick with it. I sat numbed, breathing deeply. Malaika's eyes were wide with horror. Laura got out, hoping for some air. It was just as stuffy outside the van. She was panting, her eyes shining as they had after the mortar attack. 'Are you all right?' I asked.

'Yes,' she said, 'I'm just finding it a bit hard to breathe. Like I've been punched in the chest.'

Steven and Brian lit cigarettes. I tried to ignore them. As we waited for the Lebanese to clear the road, Brian reviewed what he had shot in the playback facility of his Betacam. 'Take a look,' he said.

I put my eye to the sticky rubber of the viewfinder. In its black and white playback, I saw the helmeted face of the now-dead man loom suddenly to fill the screen as he looked into the van. He was already just an image. In my shocked state it occurred to me with a rare clarity that Steven and Brian had thrown up a wall. The very reason for confronting the nightmares – the filming – had become a defence against them. For Brian, lifting the camera to his face was an act of protection. Concentration on the process put you at one remove from the immediate circumstances. It also reduced what you saw to a two-dimensional, digitized abstraction of sound and vision. This sequence was a virtuoso performance. As soon as the Lebanese arrived, Brian had lifted the lens above the bottom of the car window and pulled out to get the wide shot. I watched spellbound as the camera, in perfect focus, caught the death of the warrior in his bridal finery.

'Thought we might call it *Blood Wedding*,' said Brian, as though nothing had happened.

Steven chuckled. Still, as the lighters flared to their cigarettes, you might have noticed their hands shaking, just a fraction.

Outside the van, Mo was still cursing the Bamanda under his breath while he changed the tyre.

Laura asked Malaika, 'What would have happened if we had got out?' She obviously hadn't trusted my judgement.

Malaika looked her in the eye. 'They would have killed us.'

Laura said, 'Well, we're lucky the Lebanese came.'

Without looking up from his wheel, Mo said something. Malaika translated. 'He says no. We were not lucky. His magic protected us.'

'Well, magic didn't protect that man in the dress very well. His bracelet didn't turn the bullet around.'

'Yes. Mo is surprised that this man was killed. He had strong ju-ju.'

Laura still looked flustered in her hot and heavy flak jacket. She should take it off, I thought. She leaned against the car as if she were dizzy. 'If he had strong ju-ju,' she went on, 'why did he die?'

Malaika translated again, 'Mo says that he neglected to use the ju-ju that lets you know when you're beaten.'

The wizened driver cackled and Malaika continued, 'Anyway he's very complimentary about your magic. He would like some of your chest magic.' Malaika seemed perplexed. 'What does he mean?' she asked, looking closely at Laura's chest. Then she cried out in anxiety.

We gathered round, concerned. Laura became unsteady on her feet. When she fainted, I was there to catch her. Even in her body armour, she felt surprisingly light in my arms.

I looked down and gasped at the charred round hole in the blue fabric of her flak jacket. I ran my hand over the ceramic plate. It was dented in the centre. The bullet had not gone through. We gave Laura some water and tried to lay her down on the rear seat. Almost in a trance, she sat up again and relived the details of the incident. She put the arrow from the tyre tenderly into her carry bag, and carefully wormed the ring finger on her left hand up through the bullet hole in the roof.

The Lebanese escorted us the rest of the way back under the leaden sky. Their leader explained that Mansoor had heard of the earlier mortar attack on the outward journey and had alerted his men to provide protection for our return. He still hoped our film would expose the Moro as the sadistic killers of Yasmeen. But Mansoor also had a message for us: 'It might be healthier to leave the country.'

'In case we hadn't noticed,' said Steven.

XXI

Back at the Cape Atlantic, Malaika took a shaky Laura to her room. The rest of us made straight for the bar and a large restorative on the Corporation. I was not scared, I was angry. So much for my attempts not to get involved. I did not mind going to a place where you put yourself in a general kind of lunacy and danger. But a place where your team was mortared or held up by mad highwaymen every day – that was another matter. Returning to war as a documentary producer had not insulated me. Quite the reverse. I couldn't take the danger. I couldn't take the thrill. I was responsible for the team's safety. I knew Laura was not going to like it, but it was definitely time to leave.

The pack had heard of Laura's narrow escape, and gave her a rousing reception when she emerged, wet-haired and brave-faced, into the humid evening air. I could have sworn she almost blushed. I was struck by how delicate she was. Her drive and determination so often concealed it. She looked fragile as a bird. 'I'm all right,' she said. 'Just a bit bruised here.' She rubbed the place between her breasts and, to admiring calls, showed off a flattened lump of lead the size of an acorn. She had found it in her pocket.

'Give that to me,' said Orlando, 'I'll get it mounted for you.'

She smiled shyly. It was her first real souvenir. Laura Marlow had looked death in the face. She had joined the pack.

Her celebrity status was doomed, though. I didn't like alienating Laura – the incident on the road from Mile Sixty seemed to have eclipsed any resentment over Malaika and brought us closer again – but I gathered the team at one table and explained that we were going to leave Freeville. 'I really see no good reason to remain. Least of all for you, Laura. In any case, we've got just about everything we need for *White Woman's Grave*.'

I didn't have to point out how close she had come to the end of her career just a few hours earlier, but the injury only made her more eager to stay. It had re-invigorated her investigative impulse. She grimaced from the ache in her chest and disagreed, passionately. 'We can't just leave. We could be onto something. The hijackers might have been after rich white journalists, but what if they were after us? Maybe someone is scared – scared of what we may uncover. If we stay we may even find out who killed Miranda, who killed that poor Lebanese girl, who nearly killed us.'

Malaika leaned forward and said gently, 'Laura, there are robberies and murders all the time in this country.' She looked at me for support and I obliged.

'Nice try, Laura. I know you want to stay, but it's just too dangerous. And Malaika's right. In any case it's not vital for our film to know which particular band of renegade soldiers murdered Miranda. Even if we did find out who killed her, and we could prove it, we are hardly going to take them in like a couple of bounty hunters. We should take Mansoor's advice and leave.'

'But it's our duty, Lucas,' Laura almost cried. 'If you don't follow the Truth, the Truth will follow you.' She was speaking pure John Court. 'And anyway, there's a chance one of us might be involved. I don't know why you're so reluctant to look into this, Lucas. Honestly – it's almost as though you have something to hide. We have to stay, or we'll just be running away. We'll always know we gave up without finding the truth.'

She was provoking me. I'm not sure I managed to conceal my irritation. 'The Truth? The Truth is, no-one knows who did these things. Probably no-one will ever know. Even if we did find out, so what? What would it explain? What would it teach us? Look – we've done our job. Now we're going to pull out.'

Laura turned to the crew for support.

'He's the boss, Laura,' shrugged Brian.

'Hmm, anyway, it's time to get out,' said Steven. 'We've got a bad feeling about things here.'

Brian nodded slowly. 'Yes. Have you noticed? There are no bar girls about.'

'And I'm almost out of mosquito repellent. Anyway,' continued Steven, kindly, 'it's just a film. There will be others, you know.'

'I don't know about you, but to me journalism is not "just" anything.'

Nobody noticed at the time, but of course we remembered later, that Ralph Reynolds had been at the next table. From the way he was sitting quietly, if you'd thought about it, you might have said he was listening very closely.

And you would probably have assumed he was desperate for a story. The American warships floating blankly off Freeville had taken on the aura of painted scenery. The action on land was in a definite intermission. Pack life was in limbo as Upper Guinea dropped off the news radar. The choppers still flew round trips to press conferences on the hot metal ships, but now they took off empty. The Marine landing was postponed again and a presidential adultery scandal was diverting US media attention.

The world's editors were edgy. They were haemorrhaging thousands of dollars a day to keep their teams in Upper Guinea. If the Americans did not commit to invasion, even Nick Rampling saw his career prospects improving somewhere else. As he put it, and no member of the pack would have gainsaid him: 'We've squeezed every drop of blood out of this story.' The pack had covered Upper Guinea from every conceivable angle. Amputations, executions, kidnappings and massacres had all been reported. Any more of this, editors said flatly, would be boring. Even the outlandish fashion sense of the Bamanda warriors had become clichéd. Everyone knew they had been dressing more and more absurdly simply to get on INN.

Increasing the death score was no longer effective, either. 'Estimates' had steadily increased from 250,000 to 500,000 in the past week, but after a while numbers, well, numbers numbed. Shocking pictures might still get a story to run, but the images would have to eclipse Orlando's horrible footage of a supposed rebel being dismembered alive. Orlando filmed this alone one evening, after, he said, taking a wrong turn in the front line. 'Only just avoided getting the chop myself,' he laughed. He sold it to Ralph Reynolds for a Central Network exclusive. Serious, 'big picture' stories like impending cholera epidemics and mass starvation were not enough to make bulletins bite, either. 'Maybe we'll run something when they actually start dying,' said the editors. When their journalists said people were starting to die, the editors would add, 'In reasonable numbers, of course.' The runes were clear. It was the story that was dying. The thicket of satellite dishes on the hotel roof thinned out as the circus dismantled its gear.

'Yes, RR is frustrated, Lucky,' moaned Ralph to me that night, some time after Laura stormed off to another table, 'I really am. You know that limb-from-limb stuff Orlando filmed – Christ, what a bloodthirsty freak that dude is, man! – that was my only prime-time piece in an entire week. You know I haven't been interviewed live on air since they postponed the Marine landing?' He was a bundle of nervous energy, foot tapping constantly on the tiles, fingers drumming on the table.

'And now there's zippo happening here, and zippo on the horizon except those goddamn useless ships! Man, my story has slid *way* down a news snake.'

So by now I think he was well into hunting down exactly what we knew. Say what you like about Ralphy, he was cunning, he was ruthless and he was a journalist born. Like all natural hacks, he followed his instincts. Having scavenged with the pack for so long, it wouldn't be surprising if he had scented something.

'So what's the score on the girl, Lucky?' he asked me, with a bland look of disinterest on his face. Ralph could be so transparent as to be almost charming. It was obvious he was digging.

'Well, I think we've finished the film,' I said. 'We'll be flying out tomorrow.'

'No, I mean the live one, you moron. She's a good-looking girl. Hell, she's *great*-lookin'. You, well . . . ? Heh, heh?' He gave a suggestive wink and wriggle of his head.

You know, for all the attraction, I think that was the first time the possibility really occurred to me in a concrete way. Luckily it was quite impossible now that we were on our way home. 'Don't be ridiculous,' I said.

'Nothing wrong with it. Hey, man, Rampling's got a wife and four kids and he's doing his new producer like he does all the others.'

'Well I'm not "doing" my AP.'

'Hey, hey. No big deal. Then maybe you'd prefer to tell me about that Miranda chick . . . Any interesting angles there?'

I thought for a minute. I would never give Rampling any good leads – he was too much of a bully. I would never tell JC – scooping people made him too supercilious. But there was just something winning about Ralph. He really seemed to think he was being subtle and sophisticated. Of course it is possible that his crassness was itself an act.

'We think the same people who killed her also killed a Lebanese girl,' I told him. Ralph's eyes narrowed. For an instant, his foot stopped tapping. He made some jottings in the small wire-bound notebook he always carried.

I didn't say any more than that. I didn't tell him about the white man, the red demon or anything else. But I got the feeling he already knew. Ralph nodded patiently. 'Fair enough, Lucky. But I hope you get everything over with soon. Close those deals. Know what I mean? You don't wanna be scooped, do you?' Suddenly, his voice seemed to take on an undertone of seriousness, almost of menace. He was referring to the documentary, but also to Laura. 'You know that once RR gets his teeth into a story . . . or into anything else . . . he's gonna worry it to death.' He six-gun-clicked his fingers at me. 'Catch you later,' he said. 'We should do lunch some day,' he added sarcastically, referring to the missing buffet of bar girls. Then he went straight over to sit by a frustrated but very fetching Laura.

Ralph had irked me before with his ingratiating advances to my AP. Looking back, I'm sure that his approach that evening was as much to do with information as flirtation. I could see him pumping her with his over-loud laugh and matinee-idol grin. Laura made sure I saw just how much she enjoyed his heavy-handed attentions.

I found his behaviour unacceptable. Ralph's enthusiasm and almost childishly obvious self-interest could be disarming, but, I'm ashamed to say, that night Ralphy made me angry. I almost went over and ripped off his absurdly lush hairpiece right there and then.

I am still not sure what Laura told him, but by the end of the evening I think Ralphy must have felt convinced that we were onto something. We'll never know for certain if he and Teresa Cellini discussed it. In hindsight it's the most likely explanation. Gossips – well, Georges Renard anyway – whispered that Teresa was his lover, though I know for a fact she had others. Perhaps he murmured something later that cloudy evening, with the lights of the American ships winking offshore like stars on the black sea face. It probably occurred in that spacious suite, that suite where Teresa saw a lot more action than she did on the battlefields she described so vividly in her reports.

Laura fumed. Where many would have been shaken and desperate to go home, my AP had been stirred by her close brush with the eternal. Now she was defying me. I couldn't help being impressed by her passion, by her convictions, by those steely eyes. Beneath furrowed brows they flashed across at me now. There was accusation in them, and disappointment. But when all was said and done, we were here to do a documentary, and the documentary was finished. 'The film's in the can,' I said to myself. 'Time to go.' I knew what might happen if we stayed. I did not want to be responsible.

The hotel band rolled out a soft Congolese zouk rhythm. As quickly as they had come, most of the circus journalists had already skipped the country, and the terrace bar seemed lonely. I thought about home and my son and my wife. I could tell her that nothing had happened on this trip. I had come out here and not surrendered to the obsessions and excesses that would usually make my homecoming such a wrench. I would try to convince Claire again, I decided, try to make a go of it. I would see her tomorrow night, as soon as I got home. I felt relieved, encouraged, as though I had escaped. I had no regrets that this would be my last night with the pack. Worryingly, the bar girls had still not turned up.

The pack sat mulling over the dismal prospects for the story in low tones. Then, over in the town, the nightly drumming of gunfire suddenly heated up. At the table where Laura now sat with Court and a few others, the conversation halted for a moment at a flutter of shots. 'Krio. M-60,' said Laura, who had paid attention during the previous sessions.

'Bamanda. Rifle grenade,' said Hartman, as an explosion thumped in reply and a flare lit up the underside of the heavy clouds. There was a crackle of small arms. Some dogs barked.

'Moro. Yorkshire terrier,' said Orlando. There was a subdued chuckle from the table. I looked at Court's gaunt face in the candlelight. He seemed to be listening for something. I glanced around and saw Teresa with Ralph. They were talking animatedly and seemed deaf to the gunfire. Teresa was laughing and drinking heavily. She looked repeatedly over at our table. I could have sworn for a moment her eyes met mine and she winked slowly, enticingly. I felt an inevitable stirring, but looked away and noticed Farhad Morvari, sitting on his own as usual. He also was staring over at us – towards Laura, I thought at the time. Like Court, he seemed to be listening intently.

There was a thumping volley of gunfire. Then more. Then more, until it was almost constant. Tracer flickered up into the hills from government positions in the town. The night chorus of fighting swelled from chamber music to a full orchestra. 'They're jumpy tonight,' said Hartman. For a moment we all paused to listen and the town, too, chose that moment to fall silent. Then the drumming exchanges began again, back and forth, ebbing and flowing. When it reached a certain level, the hotel band stopped playing and hurriedly packed up their instruments. Farhad rose deliberately from his table and left.

'Fifty-calibre?' guessed Laura at another heavy, pounding burst.

'No,' said Court, softly. 'That's real drums. Moro drums. It's coming.'

Nobody spoke. Like the rest of us, I noticed only that the night was as hot as ever, and that there were no stars. Probably the storm clouds were obscuring them. It still had not rained.

The morning brought a fell mist like none of us had ever seen.

'They call them "smokes",' said Hartman, grimly. 'They used to think it brought the fever. Still think it brings bad luck.'

It was like smoke – a hot, stinking, grey smoke. Thick tendrils of it coiled silently from the mangroves and slid in over the town, swamping the morning haze of cooking fires and dust. It banked up over the greasy shallows, filled the valleys and sidled its way damply into every crevice. The grey-green American ships vanished suddenly as if behind a falling curtain.

Looking back at that day is like seeing a series of filmed sequences, cut and recut in different ways. You can't remember exactly. Everyone remembers differently, anyway. What you do remember are impressions, general emotions. I felt increasingly tense, as if the past was catching up with me. I feared becoming trapped.

In the grimy mist, we loaded our gear into the Datsun. Laura was sulking. The Japanese natural history crew packed up too. They had finally got hold of some cash to pay their hotel bill and for tickets out. They chattered gaily to each other as they prepared to leave, seemingly unaware of the mist and the air of foreboding it brought.

I was disappointed that Papus had not appeared to see us off. I remember Mo seemed unhappy, clucking constantly and waving his hands about in the mist. 'He doesn't think you can leave today,' said Malaika.

'Because of the fog I suppose,' said Laura, hopefully. 'These can last for days, right?'

I suspected it was something else.

Mo rummaged around under his seat and brought out two large leopard cowries. He gave one to me and one to Laura. 'He thinks you need them,' explained Malaika.

Mo indicated that we should listen to them.

We dutifully lifted the smooth green-and-black-spotted shells to our ears. The low, constant echo of my circulation throbbed and roared like a warning.

'Yes.' Laura nodded, as if humouring a small child. 'You can hear the sea.'

Mo looked at us sharply, as if at idiots, before responding. Malaika translated: 'Mo does not understand. He says what you hear is not the sea, but the very blood running from your heart around your body. He says the seashell keeps its creatures safe inside. It will keep you and the blood in your veins.'

That cowrie is my only visible memento of those days.

The hotel crackled with rumour. The Bamanda had attacked the Moro. The Krio had attacked the Bamanda. British mercenaries had assassinated the president. Someone saw the spears of Moro war parties in the mist. In the small hours, someone else saw them in the hotel garden with their dogs, crying havoc. Someone had seen Orlando slipping out at daybreak, Betacam in one hand, AK-47 in the other.

We had heard it before, but this time I was worried. I had passed a terrible night. It appeared I was not alone. Rampling looked edgy and strained. His hair was uncombed, his eyes bulging with suppressed tension. Hartman was anxious, Felipe Deflores pensive. Ralph for once seemed silent. In the grip of an odd aura of calm, he seemed exhausted, or drugged. I remember wondering if Teresa had given him a hard night.

Two signs really worried me. First, Brian and Steven were impassive. Only I could see their apprehension in the obsessively methodical way they checked and prepared their gear with just that little bit of extra care. Their instinct had never been wrong. Secondly, there was no sign of Orlando Harries, John Court or Farhad Morvari. In the pack, anyone's absence could be a source of speculation. If none of these bloodhounds was around, then, as Richard Jones put it, something was definitely up. It was time to leave. I just hoped we were not too late.

Suddenly there was a rumbling sound from the

direction of the town. 'Thunder?' asked Laura, still hoping the weather would cancel our flight. 'The rains maybe?'

Malaika looked unhappy. It was a sound she knew too well. 'No, I'm afraid not.'

A hush fell in the bar. The pack pricked its ears. Ralph Reynolds's breathless producer skittered in on her endless legs and whispered something in his ear. Ralphy got up and sauntered slowly from the bar, trying to seem casual. 'There's a story brewing,' said Hartman. 'Or I'm a monkey's uncle.'

Then explosions could be clearly heard, thudding nearer, distinct. Machine guns clattered. Richard Jones scurried over in excitement. 'It's a big rebel attack. It's the Moro. I think they're trying to take the city.'

It was a story. There were whoops from the bar. The pack scrambled. Producers scattered to their satphones to contact base. Rampling, with my approval, asked Brian and Steven to act as an extra crew. Calmly, if resignedly, they agreed. Rampling also asked for a distinctly jittery Malaika as his translator. I looked at her carefully and when she nodded, I said all right. She smiled at me then went out.

I let Laura work as Judith Dart's AP. Almost beside herself with excitement, Laura beamed at me, all differences immediately forgotten. She squeezed my hand and ran to dig out her flak jacket. 'Just don't get in my way,' I heard Dart tell her. 'And go to the toilet now. When you piss yourself, you won't get too wet.'

Jan Hartman rubbed the lucky shard of shrapnel that hung round his neck, pushed his battered bush hat down onto his head and wearily picked up his notebook. He set off reluctantly towards his car. 'It's going to be bloody ugly, china. Mark my words.'

Then the hotel was suddenly empty. The engines of

the hunting pack receded, leaving just the rising noises of battle to echo through the hollow lobby.

The Japanese natural history crew came in from their car and trooped back to their rooms, dejected. 'Mr Rucas,' said their producer, gravely, 'I feel these latest developments are very unfortunate. This place is bad for the mind.'

I was left alone in the lobby. There were still no bar girls. If they did not bring their goods to market, the fighting was serious. Steven and Brian's girls hadn't turned up to say goodbye. Nor had Papus. I hoped the boy would not try to reach the hotel.

To a distant background muzak of shot and shell, I cracked a Bright Star, sat down in a cane armchair and looked out at the mist on the still sea. I knew what it would be like in the town. I could almost feel the shells whirring overhead. I knew they would be travelling at about 300 miles per hour, fizzing their path through the fog. I could hear the crack of bullets as they whipped past faster than the speed of sound. I could sense the singing ping and whine of ricochets. I would have none of it. It was not because I was afraid.

Oh I was scared enough, yes, but no more than anyone else. Something had got hold of me – a fear of something internal, a nebulous suspicion of my own motivation. It was all part of the unease about the entire trip that had returned with the visit to the ghostly house by the beach. Miranda. The Lebanese girl. Mile Sixty. The attacks on the road. It was all shocking, but I knew I was most shocked by something closer to myself. It was the very attraction I felt that repelled me. It was like, yes, it was like a siren song.

I had seen the thrill on the faces when the story finally broke. In a mirror, I might have seen it on my own. Like hounds that spot the hare, I thought. Like circus animals finally allowed to perform their tricks. I could not, would not, be one. I was in the bar to stop my ears with beer. But there were internal senses that I could no longer fool. I could curse the memories I tried to repress. I could swear to myself that I never wanted to see another war as long as I lived. That didn't make it true.

After a while, Farhad Morvari came in. Draped in cameras, his khaki photographer's waistcoat bulged at every pocket with digital discs and canisters of film. He was grimy as a coal miner, eyes looming large out of a smoke-blackened face. He was streaked with stains of sweat and what might have been blood. Farhad gave me a searching look as he stalked silently through the lobby towards his room.

Court was the next to return. He too was unkempt, dirty, face set in a half-frown of concentration. He walked straight through, holding a handful of small mini-dvc videotapes, and headed directly for his edit suite. To cut a piece in time for the INN bulletin at noon GMT, I supposed. I was left alone again.

I drank another beer. Now and again some frantic TV team, up against a deadline, would clatter across the tiled foyer and dash up to the roof to do a live interview by satellite with some faraway newsreader. If the mist cleared, the previously dull background of the dusty brown town might be enlivened by columns of smoke, and, if lucky, the odd explosion.

So I was the only person in the lobby when the news came. The news that ensured Upper Guinea would make bulletins across the world. Papus came running up to me, eyes wide. His T-shirt today sounded like something out of *The Wizard of Oz. You're not in Kansas any more*, it read.

'Come quick,' Papus panted, tugging my arm urgently

and leading me out into the dense mist, down through the hotel grounds. Way down past the tennis courts, where clumps of oleanders grew poisonous and thick. A line of hook-beaked vultures eyed me from the green wire fence. Papus pulled me with his tiny hand through a tangle of new-grown bush, towards the sea and the mangrove swamp. By one of the broken-down beach-side cottages, overgrown by a coiling thicket of thorny bougainvillea and blazing red flamboyant tree, the fat Lebanese manager stood, sweating, biting his nails. The mist swirled about the crumbling rondavel.

The manager gestured to me to look inside, but made no move to enter. I did not want to go in, either.

I was amazed by my own numbness.

Two weeks ago, if I had even been able to look, I would have retched. Now, when I went into the hut, I looked, I saw and my digestion did not register a murmur. For a moment, yes, the world seemed to recede and close in at the same time. There seemed to be no sound except the hiss of the waves on the beach. Then, from over behind the mangroves, the distant stabbing of gunfire came back to me. I remember sweating heavily as I came out of the ruined hut, thorns plucking at my clothing, damp with the condensing miasma. For a moment a ruffle of breeze lifted the fog and I gazed out over the sea. There, looking almost close enough to touch, were the American ships. I saw some shark fins cutting through the deep swells off the reef. I took a deep breath of the hot salt wind.

Out of nowhere Farhad Morvari appeared, Nikon snapping. I wondered vacantly how he had heard so quickly. How did he know that Teresa Cellini was dead?

PART 3

IN AT THE DEATH

31ST JULY – 11TH AUGUST

'Imagine the growing regrets, the longing to escape, the powerless disgust, the surrender, the hate.'

XXII

War journalists weave a fanciful web of invulnerability that serves us well. However many of us die – over eighty this year, perhaps a hundred the next – we still manage to convince ourselves that we are somehow separate from the conflicts we describe. It is as if our supposed neutrality and our return tickets give us some sort of immunity. Of course, our aloof status as observers, as non-combatants, never cuts much ice with a plunging mortar round or a dumb landmine, but you can't help hoping, believing that it should.

The experience of war also builds its own carapace. Unconsciously, with the coldness of each corpse, the buffeting of each bullet, our minds, like coral polyps, secrete their own durable exoskeletons of protection against the horror. It means you can bear what you see; it also makes you numb. Teresa Cellini's death punctured only briefly this invincible aura. There was the usual outburst of self-examination, the anguished search for explanations – none of them satisfactory.

Teresa did not deserve to die. She may not have been the most conscientious of reporters, but from some Calabrian semi-desert she had ploughed her way to the top. Who would not have taken it a bit easy once they got there? More than one of us who had been her lovers would miss her guileless generosity too, of body and spirit. Cynically, of course, Teresa's death also meant – knowing lightning never strikes twice and so on – that the odds on anyone else dying had been significantly lowered. The rest of us were still alive, and when someone that close to you died, you felt that much more full of life.

We lowered Teresa into the cool earth in a hurried ceremony at the decaying parish church. There was no way back to Calabria for Teresa now. The airport was closed, the roads blocked. The skeleton staffs of the foreign embassies showed up, so did the Krio prime minister, complete with frock coat and black velvet top hat. Only the rebels were not represented. Most of the pack came.

Ralphy still appeared to be in the grip of an uncharacteristic placidity, drained of his usual energy. Maybe he really did care about her, people muttered, surprised. He and Teresa had seemed so close that night.

'The finest *female* journalist of her time,' Nick Rampling called Teresa in his gushing Corporation News tribute, 'and a firm friend.' But he was far too busy to attend her burial. He sent his browbeaten producer instead. She looked so shattered I wondered if he battered her physically as well.

Orlando stood in the front row, his expression blank. He was fidgeting restlessly. Itching to get back to work, perhaps. Farhad Morvari caught my eye across the grave. He looked at me balefully, with a meaning I could not catch. What did he make of Teresa's death, I wondered? Some new photographs for his portfolio, or did he know more? I felt troubled, and not just by sadness. Teresa's murder raised unwelcome, uninvited questions. Laura, I was sure, felt them too. A wayward, whirring shell blurred high above the cemetery to remind me of even more pressing concerns – like our own survival. The congregation shifted uneasily. All around the middle distance, small-arms fire crackled like a pan of spitting oil.

Beside me Laura was quiet and drawn, her gaze downcast. Once she smiled up at me, comfortingly, with moist eyes. Her head came up to my chin. I felt her warm hand steadying lightly on my forearm. Part of her must have been eager to investigate what happened to Teresa, to work out how it might fit into our documentary, but this was not the right time.

'Ciao, Teresa,' I murmured, and paused a moment over the dark void. Handfuls of gravelly dust thumped onto her hardwood coffin. Behind me the pack hustled back into action.

The previous morning, Teresa's body had been found early enough for reports of her death to run the same day. Some reporters filed stories focusing on the danger to foreign nationals. They drew parallels with Miranda's murder just over a month before and pointed to the more recent, repeated attacks against aid workers and journalists on the road to Mile Sixty. John Court even speculated in his report that there might be a faction who wanted all of us out of Upper Guinea.

Yes, I suppose we all heard echoes of Miranda's death, more or less clearly. But in the fear, confusion and clamour of war, those echoes were soon drowned out. Today, a long twenty-four hours after her death, Teresa herself and threats to journalists in general were yesterday's story.

For many of the pack, Teresa's funeral was a chance to interview the important mourners. 'Like Mistah Winston Churchill said. We will fight them on the beaches,' intoned the corpulent Krio prime minister into the greedy microphones. 'But we will also fight them in the jungle. We will fight them in our fetish houses. We will never surrender.'

A group of Lebanese in leather jackets looked on. Broad, moustachioed thugs surrounding a man I recognized from the rushes as Mansoor. Noticing Laura, he came over.

'A good morning,' he said, 'and a sad development.' He was surprisingly short in real life.

'Thank you for your help on the road the other day,' said Laura. 'Your men came just in time.'

Mansoor inclined his head to accept her thanks, then looked thoughtfully over at Teresa's grave. 'Perhaps you should have taken my advice and left. It really does look as though someone is out to get you journalists. Well, it is, as they say, your funeral.' He shrugged and pushed a fat cigar between plump, moist lips. Instantly a flunky leaned forward to light it. 'I'll tell you something else,' he said, jerking his thumb towards the Krio representatives. 'Those clowns are finished. The Moro will soon get rid of them.'

'I thought you weren't going to allow that?' Laura said, slowly, as though waking up. 'Aren't you fighting them?'

'No more.'

'Oh yes? Why not?'

'I have changed my mind. Since you so persuasively spoke for the innocence of the Moro, in the killing of our Yasmeen, we have contacted their chief, Madiba Kane. Let us just say that we have no more problems with the Moro. We told them yesterday they could attack the city, so they did. It will therefore fall within two weeks.'

He said it with complete, convincing certainty. And

he was right. About everything.

'If the Moro did not kill Yasmeen,' asked Laura, more sharply now, 'who did? Did they kill Teresa too?'

'We don't know.' Mansoor looked piercingly at her. 'You are investigating. What have you found? There are rumours that . . . well you know the rumours. He is perhaps closer than you think . . .' He puffed thoughtfully on his cigar. 'Of course, if you can point the killers out . . .' His eyes glittered like cut diamonds.

I did not get the impression that much judicial process would be involved in any punishment. I reminded myself we had Mansoor's mobile number on tape. I might come to need it.

The fighting had trapped us and fate, in the form of the Controller, ordered us to stay put anyway. Miranda Williams? Well, Miranda Williams, the Controller said, 'would keep'. Teresa's death had already superseded Miranda's, and hundreds of new deaths superseded Teresa's every day. We were reassigned from *White Woman's Grave* to provide the Corporation with 'bodies on the ground' for the maturing news story. I was to be the Corporation's head producer, Laura a field producer.

I did not want to be too close to the action. Laura saw this and I suspect it made her wonder if I was afraid. Truth be told, I think I did experience fear more acutely than Laura – sometimes in that period I wondered if she truly felt anything at all. My reluctance to plunge into the thick of it was not founded on fear. It was all the old reactions welling up again: the almost perverted thrill creeping over me, the old numbness seeping into my body – the numbness that enabled me to see death as a broadcast commodity. It disgusted me. And this time I was determined not to succumb. My equanimity at the sight of Teresa's mutilated, naked corpse, curled on the floor of a ruined hut, was the sign for me; I had had enough.

In the first flush of violence, I became acutely aware of my mother, of Alex, and even, lurkingly, of Claire. Vivid images of them erupted unbidden into my mind's eye, like geysers. I had promised to be careful, and parts of me still intended to keep that promise. As the Corporation's central contact man, I spent most of my time inside the Cape Atlantic. I organized satellite feeds, co-ordinated the efforts of the three Corporation crews in-country and kept abreast of the footage agency crews were shooting. Still, risks were impossible to avoid. The work was hectic and often took me out into the field. I collected tapes from the front line, passed on information, provided support to the crews and to Richard Jones who was working mostly for radio. I carried Mo's magic cowrie with me.

Sometimes, I admit, I probably went out when it wasn't strictly necessary, just to see Laura, or with my mini-dvc, just to see battle. I don't know. I think the excitement and attraction of the two were already becoming entangled in my mind.

War consigned Miranda Williams to a bottom drawer of my consciousness. That is where I also, all too soon, hid all thoughts of Claire and of my son. We dumped long-form documentary skills too, for the ruthless formula of one-minute-thirty: cue, action footage, sound bite (fifteen seconds max), pinch of hardship, dash of blood, sign-off; no shot longer than four seconds; drum the points into the audience – the Corporation mantra: 'Tell 'em, tell 'em you've told 'em, then tell 'em again.'

I was a newsman again. And I'll tell you now, parts of me loved it.

One evening, on the brief edge of twilight, I waited for Laura on the hotel roof. We were preparing a live satellite two-way between Judith Dart and the studio. Laura was due to produce the feed, but had not appeared. Brian and Steven were muttering around, setting up lights, and I was there theoretically to supervise – to hang out with Laura, mainly – savouring the humid, chirruping dusk.

She surprised me, coming up the dark outside staircase flushed and excited, two drinks in hand. She handed me one with a sly grin.

'Don't look so surprised, Peter. I'm not teetotal, you know. And I am human.' She glanced briefly at the set-up and at her watch, then took me by the elbow and led me over to sit side by side looking out at the sea.

'A living, breathing, *female* human,' she added in a mock whisper, as though cueing me to treat her a little less like a colleague. More like a – what? I wondered whom she had been drinking with in the bar downstairs – Orlando?

The thrills of war, combined with the pummelling shock of Teresa's death, had kneaded away some of Laura's rigidity. In the faint glow of starlight and guttering torchlight from the pool bar below, her supple skin seemed to shine with excitement and youth.

'I feel like – like I'm living out history,' she said.

Laura had read about the Holiday Inn in Sarajevo. She knew about the Commodore in Beirut, the Al-Rasheed in Baghdad, the Caravelle in Saigon. Now it seemed the Cape Atlantic would join that league of legendary journalist hotels. This time, she, Laura Marlow, was there, and she slipped as snugly into this life as Cinderella's foot into her missing slipper. It was as though she was coming back to a world she knew. It occurs to me that some people may only feel comfortable when they find a life that reflects the war zone of childhood.

Steven switched on the redheads to test them. Immediately a cloud of moths and midges swirled into the blinding glare.

'So, talk to me, Peter?' Her voice was husky, softened by hormones, heat and alcohol.

'About what?'

What if she says 'About us', I thought, or something corny?

'What did Mansoor mean by saying *He may be closer than you think*?'

She was looking out across the beach that ran down one side of the peninsula towards the mangroves. In that darkening tangle behind the beach I could just make out the hut where Teresa died.

The crew turned the lights off and we were plunged in blackness as our eyes readjusted to the night.

'Search me.'

'Maybe later – a personal body search,' she chuckled. 'But listen, what if . . .' She leaned towards me whispering, slurring her words slightly. I had not seen her remotely tipsy before. '. . . What if one of us really *is* the killer? I mean, the same person might have killed Teresa and Miranda. And . . .' she hunched forward conspiratorially over her drink, '. . . if one of us were the killer, he . . .'

'Or she.'

'. . . *He* might have been doing it for years. Say it was Ralph . . .'

'What? Ralph?' And I'm ashamed to say I began to laugh. Well, the idea just seemed so ridiculous.

She gave me her patient look. '. . . or Orlando then. If they were real psychos, they could have been killing people from Bosnia to Kabul to God knows where. You'd never find the bodies, would you? Needle in a haystack, no police, lot of opportunity – why are you staring at me like that?'

'Sorry. It's just that, well, you don't look too bad when you're drunk.'

'Even you don't look too bad when I'm drunk.' Laura was trying hard to stay serious. 'OK, whatever. Anyway, plenty of journalists were here when the Lebanese girl died and when Miranda died. A lot of those people are still here now.'

I nodded, biting back a smile.

'Stop it,' she gurgled. 'Just be serious. There's Rampling. We know about him and women. And then of course John Court was here.'

'He didn't do it,' I said.

'Why not?'

'He'd have reported it already just to get the scoop.'

Laura chuckled again, but carried on. 'Orlando and Farhad were here. So was the Frenchman.'

'Georges? Wouldn't hurt a fly.' Immediately I said this I wasn't so sure. What did I know about Georges, after all?

'Well, he looks dodgy to me. So does that weasel Richard Jones. But he's far too skinny. Teresa would have beaten him to a pulp.'

She really had given this some thought. 'What about Ralph then?' I asked, playing along.

'Yes, I really wonder about him. In his own way, he can be charming, but he is a creep. Plus, he and Teresa were together in the bar the night she was killed. And the way they were getting along, they might have been together afterwards. He's also been acting pretty strangely since she died.'

So she'd noticed as well. But then I wondered how

normally I had been acting since Teresa's death. I thought Laura was going to remind me that I had been in Freeville for all three killings – I have never denied that I had no alibi – but it would take her much longer to come back to that in her deductions. It was still no more than a game for her, I thought. A challenge, yes, but just a game.

'Are you two lovebirds quite finished?' Judith Dart snapped behind us.

'Lovebirds? Is she deranged?' Laura winked at me and slipped me her drink as she stood up.

'OK, Judith, we're live in ten.' Her tone was clipped again. 'Come on, boys, let's hook up.'

I hadn't finished my whisky, but I sipped hers – a faint taste of lipstick on the warm glass. The redheads went back on, bathing Judith in artificial light. Steven was wiring her up with earpiece and lapel mike. Behind her the town seemed to pulsate with heat. Some burning houses glowed in the blackness. 'OK, London,' Judith said, in response to a voice we didn't hear. 'We're ready this end.'

I saw Laura looking around at the encircling night. Above us the Pleiades winked and glimmered. Geckos skittered around the cables beneath our feet. Distance-dulled sounds of cries and gunfire reached us from the city. Orlando's mellow laugh floated up from the pool bar. Another crew appeared and began mutely setting up to follow us onto the satellite.

Smiling to herself, Laura took a deep breath of pungent, war-torn Africa. 'Perfect,' I heard her murmur. 'Almost perfect.'

XXIII

Those were field days for the pack. We plunged baying into the feeding frenzy of combat. 'The story is your prey,' Rampling explained to Laura. 'And there are no restrictions on how to bring it down.'

The battle lines were confused, buckling and bulging in waves. In a war like this you encounter none of the problems with access, accreditation, censorship or military control that disfigured the Gulf War, say, or Kosovo. Combatants on all sides are too disorganized, too frightened to bother about cameras at their shoulder, so the only censorship you deal with is your own. It is you, the team in the field, who selects, edits, filters, changes, censors, sensationalizes or sanitizes what is happening and reassembles it in your own television mosaic. The chaos means journalists have great freedom to work. It also means that work is extremely dangerous.

Laura, swept up in the rush and turmoil, was brushed again by death. Judith Dart came back one day cursing me: 'Why do I end up nursemaid all the time? Haven't you taught her anything, Lucas? Doesn't she know she should never stand behind a firing rocket launcher? I had to knock her down to save her from the recoil.'

Laura laughed breathlessly when she told the story. 'It was my new gri-gri that saved me,' she joked, pulling out the flattened musket round that now hung on a silver chain between her breasts.

'Bloody fool,' I muttered, but I could muster little conviction. I knew how she felt. She felt immortal. Laura was surfing that extremity of combat that assailed all your senses. It assailed your very soul. I could see it working on her, awakening things buried beneath her professional shell. The violence, the fear stirred primitive instincts in all of us.

Half the pack was high on a cocktail of adrenaline and alcohol. Orlando Harries, seemingly addicted to war itself, was in seventh heaven, plying the front lines and the fine lines between life and death in a near-trance state. He had Georges Renard mumbling by his side and a wild look in his eye. He was, as we would openly tell him, completely mad. 'Of course, old thing,' Orlando would say proudly. 'Aren't you?'

A few days in, I was up with the crews, working near the port clinic. Friendly puffs of white on the ridge, a few seconds' wait, then explosions nearby. By one breeze-block ward, full of refugee women and children with the eyes of the damned, Rampling ordered his harassed producer to 'go in and find a good atrocity story. There must be someone who saw her children killed in front of her, or something. And who can speak English.' Rampling himself stayed outside 'because of the smell'.

Orlando scuttled in and out of the smoke in a half-crouch like an ape, camera held in one hand, low-slung. Snatches of his resonant laughter carried to us in the tumult. Brilliantly, he caught an explosion in the clinic courtyard that left three people hurt. His colleagues congratulated him with high fives – a meal-ticket shot.

I had also filmed it with our mini-dvc, opening the

angle wide, estimating the shell's trajectory and pointing the handicam around the corner of a building, using the exterior LCD screen to frame.

'Nice work.' Laura nodded at me. 'Maybe you have got a bit of the Superman in you after all.' She made her flak jacket look like haute couture.

'Thanks, Lois,' I said.

'Can you get it back in time?'

At the hotel, Judith Dart was already cutting her piece for the early evening feed.

'If Mo can get us out of here,' I said, wincing as another shell whirred overhead. 'This is all a bit close for comfort. Don't you think?'

'Getting some good stuff, though. We can use this for *White Woman's Grave*.' She paused. 'Can you feel her here? Miranda, I mean. Sometimes I think she's stalking me, trying to tell me something, to warn me of something.'

I started. Even in the confused smog of war, a part of Laura could focus on Miranda. It might have been because we were beside the clinic, but I wondered whether Laura's drive to uncover more about Miranda had not become something of an obsession. In some way perhaps she felt drawn to the dead woman. In some way they were coming together, or was it only in my mind?

The hefty figures of Jan Hartman and Felipe Deflores lumbered up suddenly and threw themselves down where we huddled behind a solid-looking warehouse. They were white-faced, perspiring.

Felipe took a long pull at his water bottle. He closed his eyes and took deep breaths.

'Christ, it's hot,' moaned Hartman. He pulled off his hat and mopped the blotchy skin across his scalp. He looked queasy.

'Are you sick?' asked Laura.

Hartman squinted over at her. 'No,' he said slowly. 'I'm afraid, you idiot.'

Laura shut up. In a lull, a few moments later, Brian and Steven came trotting over with the permanently rumpled figure of Richard Jones.

Brian yawned deliberately, lit a fag and reloaded his camera, handing me the shot tape. 'Light's going to go soon,' he said. 'Not much point in staying on here, is there? It's pretty hairy too.'

'You don't say,' grimaced Felipe, opening one eye.

'We're not going anywhere just now,' I said as another burst of fire crackled overhead.

'This is all too much for me,' Felipe sighed. 'You know, Jannie, I am thinking of a new career.'

'What else can you do?' asked Hartman, doubtfully. 'You're ancient.'

'I am in my forties,' said Felipe, indignantly.

'Very *late* forties,' said Richard Jones, conscientiously cleaning his battered digital cassette recorder.

'Ai, Ricardo. Do you always have to be so fastidiously accurate a reporter? The point is I am now in my prime. And I'll have you know I am a Spanish grandee. My family name is actually Deflores y Lobo. We own banks in Barcelona and Valencia.'

'And how, pray, will twenty-five years of murder and mayhem be of use to a banking career?'

'Ha! You should see the way my brother-in-law's taken over. He is the most ruthless pig I've ever met. Apart from those murdering swine up there.' He put his head above the wall for a second. '*Cabrones!* Bastards!' he shouted, waving his fist at the Moro lines then ducking back smartly as another shell boomed over towards the hills. He pulled an immaculate red silk handkerchief out of his linen jacket and wiped his forehead. '*La pobre Teresa,*' he said.

'How many of those things do you have?' asked Hartman.

'You know I remember, in Beirut, I saw a man dead. His nose had run all over his jacket. I thought, I will never die with a snotty nose. And a handkerchief is useful for other things too. My grandfather used to say a gentleman should always have a handkerchief.'

Widening smoke rings blown by Brian and Steven floated lazily overhead. In the short pause it didn't take long for Laura's restless mind to throw up its default thought. Perhaps if Felipe had not been there, she never would have thought of talking to Georges Renard. She might not have stopped searching, but at least she would not have heard certain things.

'As we're stuck here, Felipe, what do you think happened to Miranda Williams?'

'Ah, the unfortunate Miranda. She was a lovely woman. Good to have around, no, Lucas?'

I grunted evasively.

Felipe thought for a moment, then looked up at Laura, squinting a little into the sun. 'You could also speak to Farhad. Farhad was the first person to find her body, I think. He found Teresa too . . .'

'No,' said Richard, pedantically, looking up at me, 'that was our friend Lucas.'

'Oh yes, of course. Anyway, if Farhad won't talk to you, don't worry. He doesn't talk to anybody. So maybe you should ask Georges Renard. I believe he hears and sees a lot. Insomniacs often do. Of course you may not understand a thing he says, and even if you do, you may not trust it. What do you think, Ricardo?'

'I'd second that,' said Richard, absently. He blew a large puff of dust off his microphone and tapped it.

'Sorry, what?' shouted Laura above a new burst of firing.

'Can't you stop gossiping a moment,' Richard complained. 'I'm trying to get some action wildtrack for tonight's radio piece ... It's no use if you're blathering all over it.'

'Waste of time, mate,' said Steven. 'She'll never learn.'

'Oh, you keep quiet for a change, Steven.' Laura turned back irritably to Richard. 'I am not gossiping. It's called research. God, you're sexist, Richard.'

'Sexism.' Hartman shook his head. 'Where did you find this one, Lucas? Laura, haven't you got more immediate things to worry about here? Next you'll be complaining about journalistic cynicism – or Lebanese racism.'

'Well, yes, actually. I do find that quite unpleasant.'

'Recently I have begun to worry that I suffer from ageism,' said Felipe.

'Since when?' asked Laura.

'Since attractive young women such as yourself have shown no romantic interest in me whatsoever.'

'I'm a fan of escapism,' I said.

'Yup,' agreed Brian, 'escape from here. And as soon as possible.'

'Hmmm, yes,' said Steven, plaintively. 'It's getting dark.' Some shots zinged past off the corrugated-iron roof. 'Did you bring any mosquito repellent?'

When the shelling lifted, I took the tape back to the van, where Mo chanted quietly to himself with the engine running. Laura decided the crew would stay. Behind the clinic, an agency cameraman slid down onto the putrefying bodies at the bottom of a burial pit to film the next corpses being flung in from above. I can still almost feel his heavy boots sinking into the spongy, decomposing flesh with a hiss of gas and a vile smell. I can still hear Judith Dart's sound recordist putting his microphone into the mouth of a dying girl. 'Can't you keep quiet?' he shouted at Laura, who was talking to the dazed doctor. 'I want to get the death rattle.' I remember that child quivering across that fractional boundary between life and death. I couldn't help the irrational feeling that the camera team contributed in some way to her extinction. Superstitious tribesmen, they say, believe the simple stills camera can steal a fragment of your soul. How much more then must the thirsty microphone, the ravenous video camera, suck from their object's essence? Now I saw the dull, accusatory stares of the Guineans differently. To the natives, we must have seemed like incarnations of the soul-stealing Mokolosh.

'You are what you see,' Claire warned me once. I wondered what that made Orlando and his front-line close-ups. What did it make Brian, eyes glued to the violence? What did that make any of us? I wondered what it all made Farhad Morvari. No matter that the camera turns reality into two dimensions, distances and protects. No matter that the pictures may emerge in unreal black and white, shaky streaming video. He still saw so close, in telephoto and in colour. He sucked all he could from the conflict, reaping thousands of images of indigestible barbarity.

I recall the sequence he shot of a government outpost overrun by rebel fighters. The soldiers had been stripped, tied together in a circle and their faces skinned. In the pictures, their huge white eyeballs stare wildly out of the fleshy skulls. The composition was artistic, rather than documentary. The sequence was far too horrible to publish.

I asked Farhad, one evening, what purpose was

served by shooting it. 'It was disturbing,' he said, as if that explained it. 'You know everyone finds a skull more interesting than a naked body.'

Farhad still refused to tell us about Miranda, or about finding her corpse. He would not say anything about Teresa either. In fact he kept mostly to himself. I did see him talking with the Internet geeks, and now and again with Georges Renard.

'He's weird.' Laura shivered. 'Sometimes – out there – I think he's taking pictures of me.'

'It's just what he does,' I said. 'Don't worry about it.' I felt protective towards her. I even felt something which, in different circumstances, I might have termed 'love'. But perhaps I had grown too wise for that. Most emotions are wasted in a war zone. Better to save them, the wary mind says, for those situations in which they mean something, for those places and people you really care about – and have the resources to care about. If you have any sense, they are your mundane family and your quiet home.

As usual in Africa, there were not many casualties in combat. Untrained, unpaid thugs on all sides tended to shy away from heavy firefights. The main exception to this was when one group of crazies or another would suddenly convince themselves of the invincible aura of their ju-ju and charge directly into defensive fire, expecting the bullets to turn aside, or into water. No self-respecting soldier, bent on loot and mayhem, went into action without his ju-ju, reinforced by the pungent palm wine and black-market plastic sachets of neat medical alcohol, sold off from aid agency supplies.

Most of the killing would come in the aftermath of a clash. 'A-wa-o! A-wa-o!' the winning side would whoop as they hunted out civilians and fighters of the losing tribe and shot them down like snipe. Live captives were slaughtered with all the unoriginal variety offered by wars the world over. You saw the same mutilations, decapitations, exit wounds as you would anywhere else. On many of the corpses you could see how the wrists and fingers had been severed trying to fend off machete blows, just as Orlando – and I, all too well – remembered from Rwanda.

Laura's suspicions and priorities fluctuated with the violence. To her credit, she was open-minded enough to try and evaluate some of what she saw and did. She even came near to questioning the fragile journalistic fantasy of separation from the events we witness.

I told her what my physics-teacher friend had told me about something called, if I remember rightly, Heisenberg's Uncertainty Principle. It states that, at the sub-atomic level, the act of observation changes, or brings into being, what is being observed. My friend's point, which I argued against vehemently for many long-distance-travelling, short-sighted years, was that, in observing events, reporters – wittingly or not – do the same. In Freeville, as elsewhere, Laura soon saw that our presence constantly influenced events, for good or ill.

After a few days of fighting, Laura asked my opinion of what proved to be a particularly effective demonstration of the Uncertainty Principle. It happened during a ceasefire, which had held for a promising twelve hours. 'Some young government militia saw us coming up the road. They started to strut around – you know how they do – twelve-year-old killers who can scarcely lock and load their M-16 assault rifles.' (Laura was quite keen to show she had identified the weapons.) 'We've already got masses of child-soldier footage, so, to start with, the cameraman held his fire. Then the children started shooting, for the camera.'

'That's pretty normal,' I said. By now there wasn't a gunslinger in town who didn't know the media wanted *action*.

'Yes. One of the kids even told me that some crews were giving out coloured sweets for firing off a burst. Still, I was a bit shocked when Judith told the cameraman to turn over. I really don't think you should film faked shooting. But then again, Judith hadn't actually *asked* the soldiers to start firing. And, actually, the pictures were pretty good.'

Well, it's not the end of the world, I thought.

'But then, you see, some nearby rebels thought the boys were breaking the ceasefire. They began shooting back.' She looked at me worriedly, biting her lip. 'I think we broke the ceasefire, Peter.'

Cretins, I thought.

'These things happen,' I said. 'It's not your fault.'

Laura remained blithely ignorant of what happened next, but I heard it from Malaika. With their satellite feed time approaching, Dart's crew only stayed a few minutes. They missed the slaughter of about a dozen boy soldiers when the angry rebels swept down the road. After that there were no more ceasefires.

Laura's inquisitiveness would always conquer her doubts. A day or two later, even though she knew it was a very African display of media management, she went along when the government's spin witch doctors staged a show of strength for the dregs of the Krio regime. The usual sullen soldiery paraded three trussed-up rebels down to the coast in wheelbarrows and tied them to palm trees. From their silent ships, the naval emissaries of Western enlightenment could see it all in their binoculars. Onshore, the janissaries of the fourth estate jostled for the best view.

'Ready . . .' a barefoot, top-hatted officer called to his threadbare firing squad. 'Steady . . .'

'Hold it!' Ralph Reynolds's cameraman held up a hand. His tape had run out. There was an awkward pause. One of the condemned men coughed.

'OK,' the cameraman said, once he had reloaded. He gave the thumbs up. 'Go ahead.'

Rampling had sent Malaika, Laura and Brian to cover the shootings. Brian resolutely refused to film the men knotted to the bullet-scarred trunks, preferring to point his camera at the faces of the fascinated crowd. Many of them were children, more interested in the camera than the killings. They had seen plenty of the latter.

Malaika turned away and closed her eyes. Laura, convincing herself she did it out of duty, watched attentively.

'Ready . . . Steady . . . Fire!'

And Laura had the tingling reward of seeing invisible bullets pluck at the blindfolded figures. They slumped against their bonds and that was that. The Krio left them there for the vultures and the medicine men. Blood seeped down the limp trouser legs into the yellow sand.

Laura's inchoate concerns were voiced by Sohrab, who refused to film at all. Later on, I remembered his explanation. 'These men died for the camera,' he said. 'I use my camera to try and save lives.'

He had his soft, middle-class hands full by now. There was no electric power in the town. No food, no fresh water. Shops had been ransacked, storehouses looted. Hunger and disease had wormed their way firmly into the fabric of Freeville. Cholera and malnutrition doubled, then tripled the battle casualties. Unburied bodies in 'cigars' stacked up in stinking piles at street corners. You could not kill the senselessness that was engulfing Freeville. Nor could you stop it by throwing pepper in its eyes. The increasingly erratic government death squads left their victims where they fell, or flung them into the coastal swamps. Children were not immune. Sohrab filmed the capture of a young boy rebel and his mother – Laura and I watched the rushes in Brian's room. You see Krio soldiers clamp their victims' mouths with traditional calipers (to stop them screaming), then break their jaws with mallets. They tell the boy to rape his mother. He refuses. They shoot the mother and drag the boy to the van, wailing. Sohrab tried to follow, but they shot at him, too, forcing him to stop. The sequence's final scene shows the van disappearing down the dusty road towards the swamp. 'Fish food,' muttered Hartman, when he saw it. Laura watched it all without flinching. 'Good material,' she commented in a hard voice. But afterwards she turned her head away quickly. I had caught the gleam of tears in her eyes.

Sohrab was distressed by the incident. He was more upset when he discovered that only a small part of the footage had been shown anywhere. It was generally regarded as too shocking for living-room consumption. That night by the pool was the only time I saw Sohrab in despair. 'It's wrong. People must see. They must see it all. Why do you all accept it?' I could have sworn tears dropped from behind his fat lenses. 'Tell me, why do you film things when you know they will not be shown? Do you film them for your own private use?'

Nobody answered. I think we were all a little embarrassed, but if one of us dwelt at all on what his questions implied, it was for no more than the time span of a sound bite. In a quiet moment, I did ask him why he saw himself as any different from the rest of us. He was still very upset, perhaps a bit angry too.

'Whatever I film, Lucas, I would be prepared to transmit. For me this is not, it's not . . . Hollywood. It is not about getting the best shots, the best story. This is not about ratings or career. It is not something I feel I have to decode, explain or justify. I am not obsessed. This is the only war I will ever report. I simply want to record, and show. After all, this is my life. This is my reality. It is not yours. Why do you people choose to do this?'

'Do what?'

'Come here and stare, interpret and preach? Why can't you be satisfied with your own reality?' Clearly Sohrab the psychologist had developed his own theories about us journalists and our motivations. 'I think many of your friends are afraid – maybe you as well, Lucas – more afraid of their lives at home than they are here. Here things are simpler. Here in some foreign chaos, it is easy for you to come in, look at us crazy natives and impose your ideas of right and wrong, define good and bad. You cannot be so cavalier in your own country.'

I was coming to see his point. The simple, straightforward, white-knuckle fear we knew in war was somehow more bearable than the unease over undefined personal problems, the veiled menace of ageing. Here, where emotions flailed unmistakably from peak to trough, was an escape from the muddled, comparatively insipid fluctuations of family life. With the remoteness, the anarchy and the violence came a freedom to impose comfortable, clear explanations and simplifications that would founder in a second against the subtle political shades and personal repercussions of home. Life, work, success: here they really were easy. You simply had to be here, and survive.

In those few days, as Freeville tumbled from one

rung of the inferno to another, I began to ache for Laura. I needed to know where she was, if she was safe, whom she was with. I looked forward to seeing her on the front line, or returning to the hotel with tapes for editing, dirt-streaked, bright-eyed from danger. I could see that she was – for the first time since I'd known her – truly happy. At times she was confused, shocked, appalled, but any doubts she might have had about the conduct of her colleagues, about her profession, about herself, would be pumped away in an instant by another heady rush of adrenaline.

Working with Judith Dart, Laura saw war at what she came to think of as 'its purest'. They were found where the bullets flew thickest, where the blood ran deepest. They became known as the angels of death. Some said they brought it with them. Danger was Dart's great talent. She had no sensitivity, no real intelligence and no real education. She was sometimes white-faced and shivering, but overcame her fear with a truly demonic courage. She was different in that from Laura, because Laura was not brave as such. It was just that she did not experience fear. Objectively, she knew about the dangers. Viscerally, she did not feel them. I think she soon realized that she was not afraid, and was proud of it.

Only Orlando and John Court rivalled the two women. Danger called loudly to all of us, but they ran close enough to hear it whisper. Orlando ranged the battlefield arrogant as Achilles. He seemed to have no concept of danger.

Court had too much imagination to ignore death, but he had absolutely no fear of it. The only time he wore a flak jacket was for pieces to camera, to prevent watching suits back home moaning about insurance. Day after day his crew emerged from the crucible pale and quivering, but with incomparable material. The crew's work was enhanced with footage shot by Court himself on his mini-dvc, forging reports of chilling realism and awesome immediacy. Allied with Court's research and intellect, they also analysed and explained.

In the sheer artistry of his coverage, Court also outdid the rest, once even managing to perform a piece to camera next to a hunting sniper. The soldier fired some shots (as arranged) during Court's sign-off. It is still regarded as a classic of the genre – part of every broadcast media course. Court is on one knee. He has put his flak jacket on for the piece to camera. His blue eyes, so haunted by the horrors he is reporting, bore straight into you out of the screen. 'John Court . . .' it goes, '*bang!* . . . International Network News, Freeville. *Bang!*' Court does not even seem to notice the gunfire just behind his right ear. Apparently the second shot killed a man across the front line. The rushes after the sign-off show the sniper whooping and dancing with delight. If you look closely you can see the fuzzy human scalps hanging from his belt.

There was a ripple of ironic applause as Court emerged that evening.

Hartman cleared his throat, turned to Orlando and asked him, overloudly, 'Hey, Lando, did you see JC's piece tonight? Wasn't that a great last shot?'

'Which one?' Orlando shouted in return. 'The camera or the rifle?'

JC came over, looking a bit sheepish. 'Was it really that bad?' he asked.

Hartman whistled. 'Bad? It was un-be-fucking-lievably . . . great!'

Orlando chipped in again sarcastically. 'Yes, I like the understated, banal edge you put on war in your reports, John. Never one to glamorize, are you?'

'Hey, he's blushing! Well, people, I do believe our own Sniper John is a little embarrassed.'

'Point taken, Jan. Maybe it was a bit overdramatic.' Court grinned ruefully. 'Well, I suppose drinks are on me.'

Court took the banter in his stride. He knew, as we all did, that the comments came more from envy and grudging respect than from disapproval. Only Rampling gave any sign of being genuinely offended. 'Overdramatic?' he muttered. I could see his teeth grinding and his pudgy fingers clench around a bottle of Bright Star. 'It was complete hammed-up nonsense. Faked from start to finish. The man has no respect for news.'

I don't think JC heard. He wouldn't have let it go. For JC, news was everything. That was one of the reasons he liked Laura.

'Your assistant producer is as courageous and committed as any journalist I have ever seen,' he reported to me that evening. 'She has formidable – how shall we put it? – potential.'

They had been pinned down together that day during some hard fighting at the airport. 'She did not moan once.' JC smiled. 'In fact she mentioned to me some interesting aspects of the Miranda story you are producing. Have you made any advances in your investigation?'

'Now, JC, you know I can't tell you that. Anyway, it's not meant to be an investigation. That's Laura's idea.'

'I see. She is driven, is she not? I wonder what interests her so much about our late lamented Miranda. Have you noticed the similarity between them? It is not just in the looks, but in the . . . searching? – the hunger? I cannot quite put my finger on it. No, you must have noticed. You are too good a journalist not to, Lucky. Pity this whole news crescendo means you cannot complete the Miranda tale. I think it could have proved instructive.'

'You never know, JC, we might get it finished some day. If Laura has anything to do with it we will.'

It worried me, slightly, that Laura was talking so openly about Miranda.

'In future, I'd be careful what you tell Court,' I said to her. 'If he believed there was a story there, he'd lift it without a second thought.'

'Oh, no, John's far too ethical for that,' she said, but she looked pensive. 'He agreed with you about one of us being the killer – said it was nonsense. He told me to ignore Papus's story about Miranda being killed by a Franji. Said even the red-demon story was more likely.' She seemed disappointed. I think it was the first time she had thought, or hoped, that JC might be wrong about anything.

It made no difference.

On one visit to the front line, I saw them together under fire from Moro gunmen up on Hospital Hill. They were sheltering from sun and sniper in the shadow of a low wall of mud brick. Streaks of red dust lay beneath Laura's cheekbones like rouge. Her eyes were bright, her teeth very white in a face dirtied by battle. Court's long frame reclined languidly up against the wall. He could have been resting on the beach. His chiselled profile turned towards Laura, breaking into an easy grin. A pang of jealousy gripped me.

A bullet clipped the wall close to their heads and ricocheted away with a whine, peppering their faces with fragments of red clay. Court just laughed. Laura joined in and in the midst of hell, I could just catch the peaks of their laughter floating across to me amongst the chattering gunshots.

I suppose Laura saw men like Orlando and Court as the antithesis of me. Everything about them was larger than life, passionate, intense. I was more cautious, more circumspect, more, well, ordinary – graphite to their diamond. I do not think she allowed herself to conceive of her intercourse with Court as flirtation – she would have boxed their relationship tidily under 'professional'. Court, on the other hand, was, I am sure, well aware of the effect the potion of adrenaline and his attentions would have on an impressionable young woman. War was working surreptitiously on her sensuality like a spiked drink.

War is high-calibre ammunition for the libido and the pack's collective sex drive rose in direct proportion to the violence. The few enterprising bar girls who made it back to the hotel found business brisk. The nerdy Internet pair had taken to canoodling openly and there were rumours of NGO orgies in the Camfam office. Orlando Harries finally seduced Ralph Reynolds's svelte producer with the aid of her pronounced shell shock and a bouquet of bright orange strelitzia flowers stolen from the abandoned French embassy garden.

I can also confirm what I am sure some of you have wondered. Yes, for a number of us, the action itself provided the sexual thrill. A suspicion of voyeurism, of pornography, hovers over watching the stuff at home, screen-shrunk, pixilated in a cool and leafy lounge. Imagine the aphrodisiac allure of the real thing, man-size, breathing, assaulting all five senses on a baking plain.

'Do you know,' Laura confided to us, 'I think Judith actually gets aroused in combat. She always insists on doing pieces to camera when things are most dangerous. She starts to breathe deeply when the gunfire is all around her. It's weird. A sort of deep red flush spreads up her neck from under her flak jacket and she starts to hyperventilate.'

'That's nothing,' said Steven, 'you should see Rampling. I worry about poor Malaika working with him. He gets really turned on by the RPGs. Shellfire sends him over the edge.'

'Yeah,' said Brian, 'gives him a bloody great erection. Filmed it once.'

Laura did not comment. The truth is she felt a bit of it too. Her exhilaration in fear on the Mile Sixty road was nothing compared to the exultation of combat in Freeville. The abomination fascinated her. It revolted and attracted.

'I don't know, Peter,' she would say, hoping I could sort things out for her. 'It feels . . . wonderful.'

I couldn't help her. The fact is, war is meant to be hell, but, for journalists, it really can be fun. It was an almost perfect existence; after a day of being more alive than you could ever imagine, you could prolong the high of fear and loathing with alcohol, drugs and sex. In the violet evenings, you could relive highlights of the day's play to the accompaniment of the Freeville armament chorus and look forward to a violent dawn. Carried on the thick night air, the drumming of gunfire called to us like the drums called to the tribesmen of old Africa.

A morning's work would yield mileage enough for the day's story. Then, in the midday cauldron, you could wind down. Afternoons would be enjoyed on the beach. It was peaceful there. Now and again a hot shard of shrapnel would fizz into the water with a blast of steam; more often the spouts were from the blowholes of the dolphins which humped unconcernedly in the breakers.

The pack basked, sated, on the sand. It was a holiday camp again and this time Laura joined in. I remember walking down to the beach with her in our swimming outfits. We ignored Rampling, who frowned as we passed through the shady palm grove where he was preserving his waxy, redhead's complexion.

Amongst the rock pools, Orlando was lazily stalking octopus then catching them with his bare hands in sudden blurs of ink and motion. As they desperately swept through their rainbow hues, he would wrench them quickly inside out, as you would a sock. Stretched out stark naked on some nearby rocks was Ralph Reynolds's producer, sunning herself like a *Playboy* centrefold version of a marine iguana. Laura barely stifled a puritan gasp.

As we walked towards the rocks, Laura gave me a sideways glance to see if I was looking. But I had already fixed my eyes innocently on one of the American ships, a horizon away from the tanned limbs, the curved hip bones below the flat stomach with its gold navel stud, the sheen of sweat and lotion on the firm breasts and so on.

As we got closer the naked figure rolled over into a more acceptable position. From her neck hung Orlando's shark tooth. I saw she was reading a novel by the old author who lived on South Beach.

'I didn't know you read books,' said Laura acidly. 'I mean – I didn't know you read his books.'

The china-doll blonde head gave no sign of having noticed the slight. 'I don't, as a rule,' she said levelly. 'In fact at Harvard we spent more time on Fitzgerald and Faulkner. But I do think he's a great writer. Orlando gave me this book. He's a real aficionado.'

'Well at least you can see not all us blondes are dumb,' a chastened Laura chuckled, when we were a little further down the beach. By now she had lost any scruples about enjoying herself. She felt she had earned it. Over those days she relaxed enough to talk to me with a familiarity, almost an intimacy, which, blended with the raw stimulant of combat, set my pulse racing. I suppose she had begun to see me as a reliable, if baffling, part of this world where she at last felt fulfilled. 'Everyone here talks about you like a friend, Peter. I had no idea you had done so much of this. Why did you give it up?'

'Give what up?'

'This life. How could you? Didn't you like it?'

'Too much.'

A perfect forehead furrowed slightly, a puzzled purse of bow lips. Did she suspect I had lost my nerve? I do not think that she could conceive of any other reason to throw in life on the road – well, apart from death of course, and maybe severe injury or senility.

I had developed a theory about war. There were roughly three ways of reacting: you numbed, you loved, or you left. After plumbing the depths of the first two, I had left. If you didn't get off the carousel of death and destruction, I thought, you were looking at one of the other two outcomes: you can become numbed by combat, or, like Laura, you can revel in it – war is a place where you can live utterly. Either way, you run the risk of an addiction as profound and hard to shake as any narcotic. Now the whirlpool pull of all-out war was sucking us down.

Following the impulses of our blood and senses – perhaps even our emotions – Laura and I allowed ourselves to drift together in the sun. We cooled off in the quick, cold current that swept along the shore. We caught mackerel in the deep blue water off the point. We collected seashells for Mo's fetishes and mussels for us to eat. Laura's slim body went a golden brown.

On a clear evening, we sat together and watched a

perfect flaming sunset slide down behind the stark silhouettes of the American ships. 'Shouldn't we be filming that?' asked Laura. She leaned back on Teresa Cellini's old lounger, her swimsuit stretching taut between her legs, over her breasts. Her delicate hand held, I think, a banana daiquiri. Her dark glasses reflected the red sun.

'We've got enough sunsets for one film. Anyway, I'm glad we're not working. I'd rather just enjoy the moment . . .' I avoided saying 'with you'.

'Yes. Me too.' Her voice was low, almost husky. I heard the West Country in it and thought back to a clear English day in a beech wood.

I could feel her eyes on me from behind the blank lenses. She reached over to where I lay on a towel and gently slipped a smooth, dry hand into mine. The sun disappeared in a flash, leaving us in the dim light of the swelling moon. You could hear the low crackle of crabs scuttling from the water and the croaking of frogs from behind the tideline. The slightest of breezes ruffled the casuarina trees. Faint, suggestive sounds carried from down the beach where the entwined figures of Orlando and Ralph Reynolds's producer had vanished in the gloom.

Again the potentials, the questions welled pregnant between us. This time, I bent over Laura and answered them with a kiss.

XXIV

The very next morning, soft black shapes with grey-white blotches began to flop up on the beach. The bloated humps of body lay slumped along the high-water mark in ragged-edged shapes, butchered by the saw-teeth of tiger and nurse sharks swarming to the smell of blood. The dolphins melted away; there was no more swimming. Death squads were dumping their victims in the swamps. Borne up with the tide of bodies, a smell floated in from the mangroves; a sickly sweet smell. You could just catch it in the stagnant air, piercing and insidious. Then the thick mist came up again, and, unbelievably, the heat. The air was now like a simmering stew. The mist condensed on contact and mingled with your perspiration in a grimy film. Your bodily cooling system broke down as the moisture on your skin refused to evaporate. In the excess humidity, the very air seemed to sweat.

With the mist, the heat, the smell, came claustrophobia. As a warning, Moro gunmen had cringing Bamanda captives dig two grave-sized holes under the baobab by the front gate. The threat was superfluous; only the most foolhardy journalists now dared leave the hotel. Bands of marauders roamed the streets. The

Cape Atlantic was now on the front line and constant gun battles raged outside. The road in front of the gate was a glittering brass carpet of ejected cartridges. Mo was the only driver still to be seen. Often even he bowed to the ju-ju of discretion.

Superstitions spread throughout the pack. One reporter refused to take off his white suit; another would only enter the hotel through a blown-out window. Sometimes the hysteria became near-dementia: Orlando Harries painted a multicoloured target on the back of his cameraman's jacket, the bull's eye red between his shoulder blades. Hartman began calculating his stringer's fees per death reported, rather than per line.

The plucky Japanese wildlife crew decided that, especially with the thick mist, the hotel grounds were wild enough to double for the virgin rain forest of Guinea-Conakry. They found most of the plant and animal species they had intended to film and happily started to make their documentary in the garden. One early morning, I found them fiddling around in the thick brush near the mangrove swamp. Their producer politely explained that they were setting up an automatic camera. He was the only one of the team who ever spoke. 'We leave camera out overnight to film nocturnal mammals in swamp. Maybe crab, maybe mangrove rat. When rat crosses beam, camera films with night sight.'

'What will you do about the sound? The explosions, the machine guns? It won't sound much like a remote virgin forest.'

'No problem, Mr Lucas.' He smiled patiently. 'All wildlife films always put on sound in studio anyway. If a dragonfly cleans its wings, we rub rice paper. If praying mantis eats head of its mate, we bite apple.'

It was nice to know their material could be as grisly as ours. And as manufactured.

Brian and Steven seemed to like the Japanese – 'No bullshit,' explained Steven – and spent a lot of time working with them in the garden. They had enlisted the help of one of the few remaining retainers, the aged hotel groundsman. Gnarled and glaucomic, he proudly taught them about his domain. He could name every plant, in Latin and English, and was honestly upset when they were damaged, especially by artillery.

Ralphy was slowly emerging from his strange mood. In the days since Teresa's death he had often been uncharacteristically quiet, even withdrawn. Sometimes he would not leave his room, even for meals. He stopped flirting with Laura and when he removed his dark glasses, his eyes had a distant, almost haunted look. He scribbled constantly in his notebook. On some days he would only appear for an intense burst of drinking, followed by the short moonlit walk to the Network edit suite, to voice reports cut and scripted for him by producers.

A few of us tried to find out what was up, but his producer shrugged her slender shoulders and Ralphy just would not explain. Or at least we thought he didn't. Maybe he did, but we just put his efforts down to inebriation. 'My father', I remember him saying drunkenly, 'is a Vulcanizer. He's hardened tyres for all his adult life. You know, this is the only story of mine he has ever been interested in. When I told him I was going to Upper Guinea, man, was he excited. Rubber! he said. It's a crying shame, he said. They've got the world's finest rubber there, whole jungles full of rubber. And it's all going to waste. Son, won't you stand up and say something worthwhile? Why not say something about the rubber? he said. That's what people here care about. Not those spear-chuckers killing each other over nothin'.'

Perhaps the closest I got to Ralphy's state of mind was an evening when he drank himself into a stupor unusual even for the Cape Atlantic. 'Enough,' I think I heard him mutter to himself, head bent down among the Bright Star bottles, 'enough.' At the time I thought he meant he'd had enough booze.

At other times he seemed to be snapping out of something – like a man recovering from a massive anaesthetic. Now and again he would go up on the roof for a live two-way with New York. An assistant would whip make-up over the dark bags around his eyes and rub colour into his sallow cheeks. Then, in the lights, he would brighten, and the old Ralphy would be there, telling it like it was with that rolling intonation, the phrases interspersed with pauses, presumably to make them digestible to an audience the network thought half-witted: 'Upper Guinea reels under the nomadic assault . . . like a punch-drunk boxerrrrr . . . but the valiant Kriooo . . . descendants of American free men . . . refuse to concede defeat. Can they hang on until the Marines throw their hat into the ring . . . or will they have to throw in the towel? Every dayyyyy . . . the people of Freeville pray . . . for the world to interveeeene . . . that they may remain free.'

XXV

Hartman's gloomy prediction that more 'whiteys' would die was again vindicated. One otherwise non-descript day, the young Dutch radio journalist tried to leave the Cape Atlantic and was gunned down just out-side the gate. Orlando and Farhad tried to recover his body but were driven back by warning shots. The Dutchman's sprawled limbs stiffened in the dust amongst the cartridges. When he loosened up enough, some Moro thugs rolled him into one of the graves under the baobab. That night a few of us crept out and pushed dust over him. I thought of Hartman's flippant remarks about global warming in Hell, and wondered whether the dead boy had made the trip up or down. There was no film commissioned about him – no *Dutchman's Grave,* no Teresa Cellini-style international outcry. He was about twenty-five years old and now I can't even remember his name.

After the Dutch reporter was killed, none of the foreign hotel inmates dared leave openly. Some, like Orlando, JC, Farhad and Georges Renard, still slipped out now and again, but secretly, on their own. Rampling talked about it, but didn't go. Even locals like Sohrab and Malaika were now staying in the hotel –

Malaika in Miranda's old room. I made it clear to Rampling that Brian and Steven were now barred from leaving the hotel. I didn't want him getting any funny ideas about sending a crew out to do his dirty work.

The Cape Atlantic was now cut off. To stop American helicopters landing, Moro soldiers ostentatiously scattered home-made landmines on the beach and stitched deadly accurate warning bursts along the sand with heavy machine guns. The Lebanese manager disappeared, so Ado the receptionist took over the running of the hotel. This was an increasingly tricky business. Fuel was short and the stuttering generator usually ran for just four hours a day, to coincide with the peak demand times for the TV editing – half around six p.m. for Europe's evening bulletins, the rest around midnight for the States. The hot-water tank was blown up and the plumbing broke down. Latrines were dug in the garden. Luckily there were large stores of tinned food and bottled booze. The hotel began attracting more attention from the rebels and the overgrown garden became a dangerous place. Orlando Harries carried his AK-47 with the safety catch off. When he said he was going shooting, you wondered if he meant with bullets or tape.

For almost forty-eight hours, Laura and I avoided the subject of the kiss. We hardly talked at all. She seemed to spend time with everyone except me. I even saw her talking to Georges Renard and, more than once, to John Court.

On the second afternoon I found him in the first-floor corridor watching rushes. 'Where's that?' I asked, casually. 'Doesn't look like Guinea.'

'Hello, Lucky. Doesn't it?' He didn't elaborate. 'What can I do for you?'

'What's this with Laura, JC? Are you after her?'

He chuckled in his musical way, not taking his eyes off the screen. It showed a scrawny African family in the blackened ruins of a house. 'Are you by any chance in the vice-like grip of the green-eyed monster, Lucky? She is a beautiful girl, your AP. And exactly after your taste, if my memory serves me correctly.'

'No, I'm not jealous.'

Not very.

Court nodded sceptically. 'No, of course you are not. Laura and I talk. We discuss. That is all. Yes, naturally I find her attractive. Which self-respecting, hot-blooded male would not? Moreover, I like her. She has something of fire in her. She is eager to learn, willing to listen. She will, I have no doubt, go far.' He knew he was taunting me gently. John and I had never made a fuss over women in the past. We tended to leave the competition vague, or simply ignore it. In fact I was sure that Teresa had been one of his conquests. With something as fleeting as Miranda, I didn't mind; over Laura I didn't feel so generous. 'Just don't encourage her to take too many risks, JC. She's young. She's got plenty of time. And she's my responsibility.'

'May I recommend that you simply relax, Lucky?' He turned to face me. 'If she is giving you cause for concern, I will take her off your hands, quite gladly.'

He paused the tape on a close-up of a baby, I could not tell whether alive or dead. Some red dust was falling onto its distorted face, as if through sifting fingers.

'Just be careful, JC,' I said.

I think I let a hint of warning creep into my voice. John Court laughed, richly.

'I know what you are capable of, so I will take you seriously. This place is making its mark on you, Lucky. Mind you, I suspect that it is having its effect on all of us. Ralph has been acting strangely since Teresa died. I think Rampling has too – have you noticed? He has been somewhat agitated. The time has come to conclude this business. I don't mind telling you that I have some quite exquisite material up my sleeve and that I have more exceptional footage on the way. I plan to force the American hand. I anticipate that Upper Guinea will soon be at peace.'

That was JC. He had absolute conviction in his own powers, in his ability to realize his goals. If he saw a task ahead he would never compromise. I don't know whether I was jaundiced by a little jealousy, but that day I felt there was something almost demonic in his self-belief.

Laura admired his intensity, his ideas. That was clear. I knew Court told her about his night forays into the town. He hinted at contacts he had forged amongst the warring factions and the secret societies. He promised an excitement, a risk and reward that she had not yet experienced. Eventually, during one of their long discussions on the meaning of journalism, Court asked Laura to accompany him on one of his excursions. Of course she was flattered. She was tempted. She was scared. That siren summons of pure danger was sounding loud in her ears. Laura still had some stays of sense lashing her to the mast, but they were elastic and they were fraying. She said she would think about it.

I yearned for more of her. Contact, kisses . . . more. Some time of an evening I manoeuvred Laura out of the lamplight and guided her through the palms to the edge of the dark beach. There she hesitated. We were not touching.

'Peter, I want to ask you . . .'

'Yes.' What did I expect – a declaration? An

understanding? Laura was much cleverer, more ambitious than Miranda, but physically, sensually, there was something . . .

In the pallid moonshadow filtering through the casuarina trees, I was reminded of the dead girl. Miranda and I had talked on the sand, one dark evening. 'You, Peter, are just a flirt,' she said. 'You're all talk. I don't believe you'd ever do anything . . .' It was an escape clause and a challenge all in one. '. . . You being a married man and all. And anyway, I'm just a poor innocent nurse.'

I thought . . . well, you know what they say about death and nurses . . .

I remembered a coy giggle, an artless promise of some future indulgence. Would Laura promise as much?

'Look, that's Orion,' I said, pointing up to the hunter's jagged constellation. 'The three stars in a row are his belt. And see that fan of stars – that's Sagittarius. Just over the horizon you can see his bow.'

Laura was shy. It was our first real conversation since a kiss that had burned on my lips for days. 'Peter, I want to ask you something.'

'Go ahead.' Perhaps she wanted to know my intentions, what I thought, what I felt.

'Should I go out with John Court?'

'*Go out* with?'

'I mean film with him, at night. I could get some great material. Rampling's quite keen for me to film some good stuff for his next piece.'

Yes – and to take the credit, I thought.

'I don't think you should go,' I said.

'Why not?'

Obviously I did not want her to go out with Court at night.

'It's dangerous. It's not worth it.' This was true as well.

'But don't you think it's worth telling the real story of what's happening here, rather than sitting in the hotel? To get to the truth we must ever go a little farther.'

She was aping Court again.

'Laura, don't you understand? I don't want you . . .'

To go with him, I thought.

'. . . to get hurt.'

She smiled. 'Don't worry about me.' She leaned closer in the half-light, putting her warm hand on my shoulder, and whispered in my ear, breath hotter, damper even than the humid Guinea air, 'Anyway, I won't be going tonight. What will you be doing?'

Before I could answer, she left me to the sighs of sea breeze and breakers, trailing her hand down my arm with a teasing smile. I longed to tell Laura some things I knew about Court. About the time he siphoned petrol from his colleagues' cars so he, and only he, could get a story out of Groznyy. About the time he paid Palestinian kids in Gaza to stone Israeli troops. About how he had no limits . . .

I'm not sure she would have believed me, or whether she would have cared. For many in the trade, his actions were known and regarded as triumphs of journalistic technique. But I can tell you now, it was not just my jealousy speaking. I was not the only one to warn her about Court.

Laura had many qualities that could have made her a successful journalist, energy and tenacity among them. Her hyperactive mind had been mulling over Miranda Williams and the enforced lull in news-gathering meant that she turned quickly back to the dead girl and her private investigation. Laura had a hunch, and she knew from her studies that all good journalists followed their hunches. Not even Farhad Morvari's impassivity could deter her. It was that same evening she saw him, sitting as usual on his own. I watched her take a deep breath, undo a button to reveal more than a hint of cleavage, lick her lips and go straight for him.

'No, I won't do your interview, Marlow,' he said before Laura could open her mouth.

'Just checking,' she said lightly, leaning onto the table and looking him in the eye. I was sure he could see straight down her shirt. 'But could you just tell me why not?'

'I do not know the whole story yet.'

'Mmmm. Cryptic. What story?'

Farhad drained his beer and made to leave and I saw Laura grab him by the shoulder. I could feel the intensity of that grasp. A sinew pulsed in her neck, her eyes burned. Beads of sweat thickened in the sudden forehead V between her eyes. 'Farhad!' she grated. 'Tell me. How come you're always first to the dead bodies? Why won't you let me into your room? When will you do the interview?'

Farhad said nothing for a long moment, then: 'I'll tell you under one condition – that you come out with me filming at night.'

'What's that?' she asked mockingly. 'Some kind of test?'

'Perhaps.'

Laura shivered and relaxed her hold. 'I'll think about it.'

'And Marlow.' He was almost whispering now. 'I think you should watch out for Court. He is a rabid dog.'

Long, firm fingers unpeeled her hand and he walked away. She shivered again. 'He's creepy,' she said, to no-one in particular.

'But he has a point,' said Sohrab, who had overheard.

We had all come to like the quiet psychologist. Laura had even grudgingly come to admire his journalism, despite his lack of formal training. But this attack on Court made her indignant. 'He has a point about John? Are you mad? I'm sure Farhad's just jealous I spend so much time with John. I always see Farhad staring at me, filming me. And he takes the most disgusting pictures. There's no way I'm going out with him. The guy's a freak.'

Sohrab placated her. 'Oh, I don't mean that Mr Court is rabid. Oh, no. I think he is a great reporter. It's just that, well, maybe he goes a bit too far sometimes. I have seen him forget that people are people.'

Sohrab became bolder. I think Laura overawed him at first, with her looks, her confidence, but over that time in close proximity perhaps he had seen a tender side, or wanted to believe he had. He certainly felt he could say things to her. 'Still, I would love to train in England to learn journalism properly,' he went on hopefully, 'to learn skills like John Court.'

'First thing to learn, Sohrab – John does not go too far. How can you go too far when you're after the truth?'

XXVI

Burying itself in beer and brutality, voiding itself in violence and vodka, the pack was drunk. Ado gave up charging for anything and everyone just helped themselves. 'The lunatics', Brian commented, 'have taken over the asylum.'

Things were spiralling out of control.

One evening, the Japanese wildlife producer, Ito, came up to me. 'We have been talking, Lucas,' he said, bowing with a slight wobble. He pointed back to his team, looking over expectantly from a nearby table. 'We would like to make a respectful comment.' Ito could become very grave when drunk.

'This job you people do, Lucas. It does not seem very instructive. For us it is hard to learn from the incomprehensible, from the unimaginable. Is it not the same with you?'

The nights and days blur and fluctuate. The memories of that night – I think it was 6th August – are crystalline in my mind.

With Malaika staying in the hotel for safety, we were spending more time together, and on that particular evening she drank a little too much of the Bright Star. Under the yellow tropical sky she leaned over towards me as she had in the tent at Mile Sixty. She took my hand and murmured, 'Peter, I want you. I am not a silly young girl after – how would you put it? – a holiday romance.' I thought of a kiss, days ago now, on a sunset beach and wondered if she was referring to Laura. 'I know what I am doing. I can see you are a good man.'

'That may or may not be true. But I am married.'

Marriage as self-defence – it was a very useful excuse. I knew I would not use it if Laura were saying those things. I realized I burned for Laura to say them. 'I'm married,' I repeated. 'You're a beautiful woman, Malaika, but it's impossible. I don't want to use you. What – what happened before was a mistake.'

'Ah, but maybe I want to use you. Are you being honest, Peter? You were not so married last time.' Her long-lashed impala eyes impaled me, sadly. 'Maybe it is her you want to use. Will you be married when she comes?' She nodded her head towards where Laura sat, imbibing the wisdom of an increasingly erratic Ralph Reynolds and a typically pedagogical John Court. She was keeping us under observation and fleetingly our eyes met. I hoped she hadn't seen Malaika hold my hand. My heart pounded. I was relieved when Rampling called Malaika away to translate an interview.

The hotel smelt foul that night. There was no breeze to wash away the stale odour of spilt beer and marijuana that lingered in the bar. It mingled with the stench of excrement from the latrine and the ever-present hint of death. Around the stagnant swimming pool the pack drank ferociously – alcohol and neat, distilled fear. Out on the beach, the shamans – marabouts from the secret societies – combed the tideline for useable body parts. Court had learned a lot about these societies in his weeks here. 'They excise the liver, genitals and palm of the hand,' he was explaining to a wide-eyed Laura. 'Those are the principal ingredients of the necromancer's medicine pouch. The medicine is then anointed with oil distilled from the fat of a woman's internal organs.'

You can imagine. It was so easy not to think of normality, reality, fidelity. Claire, Alex, my mother and our country home – they could not have been more distant had I been marooned on the dark side of the moon.

When Malaika returned from Rampling's edit suite, she had sobered up. She seemed troubled but would not say why. Foolishly, I did not ask. 'I must go home,' she forced out eventually, 'I – um – my mother needs me.' I saw it was a feeble untruth but because I wanted Laura, I let it go.

'Will you be safe? How will you get through the Moro lines?'

She picked up her bag and touched her gri-gri. 'I am a Moro. They will probably let me pass. I don't know if I will be able to come back though.' She really did not sound her usual self.

'Malaika.' I was unwilling just to let her leave without some sign that I cared. Whatever his attachments, I suppose there is something in every man that regrets relinquishing a beautiful woman.

'Malaika, how does it go? The 113th chapter of the Koran, I mean.'

She closed her eyes for a second as she concentrated.

'In the name of Allah, the Beneficent, the Merciful.
Say: I seek refuge in the Lord of the dawn,
From the evil of what He has created,
And from the evil of the utterly dark night when it
comes,

And from the evil of those who blow on knots,
And from the evil of the envious when he envies.'

Then she kissed me on the cheek and walked off into the dark.

I looked up and saw Laura staring at me strangely, across the pool.

That night, I remember clearly, was carbon black, the crescent moon hidden by clustering clouds. I had not long turned out the light when, like the fragment of a dream, Laura Marlow glided into my room. She fluttered into my bed like a soft moth. I felt no phobia. Her hair floated free and her clothes drifted to the floor like gossamer. In the bars of light that filtered through from the lamps outside, I saw the lingering bruise between the rising swell of her breasts. In heat and arousal her smooth skin already gleamed with the faintest silver lining of sweat. Her warm scent engulfed me, lavender and summer forests. Her eyes glinted impossibly blue in the darkness. She was all taut skin and shyness and fire. Whatever had built up in us – suffering, anger, passion – spilled over that night. I forgot myself so much I worried what I might do.

Laura's cries were lost in the percussion of the Freeville chorus as it rose to a full symphony of violence.

XXVII

I woke up with a hammering inside my head. Never mix your poisons. This was a killer cocktail of alcohol, embarrassment and guilt. Claire would say it proved I didn't love her. Laura might think it proved I did love her. It was unprofessional – she was my AP for God's sake! It was the sort of crass thing Rampo did. It was just another sign that I was losing control. Why had I done it? I groaned and buried my head back into the hot pillow. The sheets were damp and pungent. Outside the gate a heavy machine gun clattered like a pneumatic drill.

'You're awake.' Laura's low voice came from the other side of the room. She was already dressed. She looked pure, radiant, happy, terribly desirable. So that was why I had done it. I felt a warm, pleasurable, almost contented flush.

'I have to go,' she said, smiling. 'Judith wants to do some filming from the roof.'

'See you later then.' I just nodded to her and squeezed her hand tenderly as she left. Jesus! Did she even know I was married? As if it made any difference in this mess.

A couple of minutes after Laura swung through the

door, I got out of bed in my shorts and went looking for a smoke.

In the stuffy corridor, I took a cigarette from Rampling's bored TV editor, who was cutting an atrocity sequence – a technique called necklacing, learned from South Africa. On the video monitors, their screens blotchy with the fat bloodsplats of swatted mosquitoes, a chanting mob wrapped a skinny young man's arms to his body with barbed wire and hung a burning tyre around his neck. I drew deeply on the cigarette.

Ralph Reynolds passed by, still not quite his old, frenetic self. 'Hey, Lucky!' he said, tiredly. He gave me a perfunctory slap on the back and lifted his wrap-around shades to peer closely at the pictures. 'Firestone SR5,' he decided, after a moment's thought. 'Fine choice. That particular rubber mix burns at a higher temperature. Waste of a good tyre though.'

Through the rising swirl of smoke I watched the editor lay down the chanting first, then add a background drum beat. He timed the victim's movements to the rhythm. Whenever the dying man swayed too jerkily, he used a touch of slow motion to bring the death throes back in sync with the music.

At the time, in the midst of that lunacy, it didn't strike me as odd. Recently I bumped into the editor again. He could hardly remember Upper Guinea, let alone this report. He had worked in three wars since then. 'Oh that piece,' he said, once I'd reminded him. 'Yes, I liked that one. Won an award, you know. Creative, you know; sometimes the pictures just need a bit more oomph. People are so used to straight violence these days.'

Strange how in even this extremity of experience, professional observers could still fall back on fictional creativity for some of the most memorable moments. One of the most famous photographs you will have seen from this measly, pigmy war happened thus: on a quiet afternoon, a group of journalists spotted some kids playing football in a burned-out building. Sensing good shots they hurried over. The kids fled. Well, wouldn't you? Hulking great men charging towards you, metal cameras looming, spear-like boom mikes thrusting? One little girl was left behind cowering in a blackened pit, staring up at the flashing lenses and furry gun mikes with big, frightened eyes. You'll remember the shot: she wears a bright yellow dress and blue plastic sandals; one hand is raised pathetically as though warding off evil.

The still cameras snapped; the videos whirred. Only one photographer had the sense to transmit the picture, captioned: 'Girl, four years old, separated from her family in a bombardment.' That was the picture on every front page.

At the front of my mind was Laura. There was no water at all in the hotel that day, so no washing, and her scent lingered on me. Now and again I would catch it and think of her. I wondered if anyone else could smell it. In that half-conceited way new lovers have, I kind of hoped someone would. I was a bit put out to see her spend a lot of time with Ralphy and John Court, as though nothing had changed. It is odd that consummation makes you more jealous, not less. Laura had now ably demonstrated her desire – maybe even her affection – for me. Logically, I suppose I should have minded less about their attentions to her. Of course it wasn't like that. I knew Court and others were still pressing her to go on their nightly excursions. She was canvassing others for advice as well. Brian was amongst them. 'I'm worried about that girl,' he said to me around noon. 'She'll soon be going out with Court or with some other maniac like Orlando. It's all going to her head. And by the way, boss . . .'

'Yes?'

'. . . You didn't, did you?'

'Have you got a cigarette?' I asked.

Brian handed me one. 'You little devil,' he grinned. 'Don't say I didn't warn you.'

I think only the doubtful propriety of working alongside competitors of the Corporation dissuaded Laura from taking up the dares of Farhad and Court. Some of the rules still held a tenuous sway over her. In this increasingly fevered environment of lust and danger, I wondered how long their hold could last.

Far backstage of our antics in the Freeville spotlight, fate – international diplomacy this time – was scripting the next act. Prompted by the terrible news stories – the pack had rocketed the death score to 850,000 – the New World Order ground into motion once more. A Washington PR agency, hired by black groups with Krio sympathies, found a pretty African woman to sob out how rebels had ripped sick infants from their incubators. It was a hoary atrocity fiction that had worked well for Kuwait in the Gulf War. Freeville of course had never seen a baby incubator, but if any reporters in Guinea bothered to point this out, they were ignored. Pressure for intervention became irresistible. The clincher was a US opinion poll suggesting that black voters were overwhelmingly pro-invasion. They wanted to save their civilized Krio brethren from the heathen nomad hordes.

The morning after I had sex with Laura – the mist prevented us from seeing, but we were told – Marine amphibious assault ships anchored alongside the impatient US battle fleet. You could sense things heaving to a climax. In the west, the world's greatest power marshalled its forces. To the east, huge storm clouds shimmered through the heat. The smoky air was pregnant with the threat of rain and violence.

If the Americans hoped to intimidate the Moro, they were wrong. The nomads redoubled their offensive. The government-run TV news reported a famous victory at Mile Sixty, so we assumed the outpost had fallen to the rebels. The tottering regime gave up the ghost and a string of small boats crabbed out to the US ships, laden with top-hatted Krio dignitaries including the prime minister. His promise to fight them on the beaches was evidently better carried out by his disintegrating army, some tattered units of which were driven back to the Cape Atlantic. They lurked behind the wall and took pot shots at rebels from the scarlet canopies of the flame trees.

In the late afternoon a Moro truck turned up at the hotel gate and unceremoniously disgorged the filthy survivors from Mile Sixty. The doctor, Lucy, was among them, overcome with fatigue and grief. The Swedish journalist had survived as well. Miranda's replacement, Ben, was dead. Most of their patients had also been killed. Laura was outraged. 'You should write the true story of what happened,' she said to the young Swede. 'Tell the world.'

'What should I write? That I have seen unimaginable horror? What will that do for anybody? It is unimaginable. It is incomprehensible. It would be no use.' His eyes were as empty as any man's I've ever seen.

'Why do you do it then?' Laura asked. 'What are you a journalist for?'

'I'm not a journalist any more,' he said. 'I quit.'

I knew how he felt. Sometimes I worry that ou

is often useless for anything more than voyeuristic titillation, as instructive as a rubbernecking drive-past view of a motorway accident.

Laura, of course, disagreed. For her, as for artists like Farhad, the extreme was the soul of journalism – Miranda's life, for instance, would have been of no interest if not for the manner of her death. I had begun to wonder by then whether we had ever achieved anything with our extremes. However far into the darkness we penetrated, there was always pressure to go deeper. And just as the darkest recesses were being revealed, our wavering candle would shift somewhere else. News hungered so much for violence and catastrophe that the supply was never-ending. Each man-made or natural disaster we covered simply served to blot out the one before. Sometimes I think all news does is contribute to a kind of collective amnesia.

I lose track of how often we were frustrated at our lack of impact. Sights that harrowed and hounded us, war stories that swallowed up dozens of our colleagues, thousands of participants, would gargle down the news pan in one minute thirty, leaving not a trace behind. Maybe it is not so surprising. The very size of the screen diminishes the impact of television. I even remember a haggard Ralphy after Teresa was killed, quoting despondently, 'TV news is just pictures of people three inches high shooting at other people three inches high.'

In any case we hardly ever kept focus on a story. [illegible] the 'Bang-Bang' disappeared, so did we. Every [illegible]n we covered was soon replaced by the slime [illegible]eaucracy. It is hard, out of the cold light of [illegible]member a dawn that was not false. [illegible] right on doing it. [illegible]apped in a sort of adolescent limbo, testing ourselves on the edge of the rigours of adulthood. Sohrab described it as a 'constant effort to come of age'. Timid he may have been, but not in his analysis of the pack, especially not after a few beers: 'Most traditional cultures have a form of initiation into adulthood which revolves around extremes of self-denial or pain. Sometimes violence may be involved – for the Moro or Danakil, killing a man. For the Masai, a lion.'

I thought I understood. These are the same razor-sharp edges to life that journalists crave in war zones.

'With a significant difference,' Sohrab continued, warming to his theme. 'In tribal society the rites of passage are endowed with formal structures, preparation and mystic explanation so deep that they are in a sense rendered ordinary, or at least comprehensible, meaningful. They are pregnant with age-old wisdom, with lessons on how to live. They fit into a cohesive social framework that makes sense. Often, in the rites, the extremes are sublimated into symbols, which, because of their potency in the mind of the acolyte, satisfy that urge to cross some sort of boundary.

'Your culture', he indicated me and Laura, 'has lost its symbols, so your colleagues – you yourselves – seek out the real thing, and end up watching it. But a jour[illegible]list at war may approximate the hot blood of a [illegible]sai lion hunt, the searing pain of a Bamanda circumcision – having your penis flayed to the root is not something you would want to emulate, I can assure you – he may feel the drugged confusion of the initiation dance, but he will not be able to reconcile it to anything el[illegible].'

Laura [illegible] frowning her disagreement.

'OK,' S[illegible]ab said, 'think about it. I've met lots of your colleagues who say they can't seem to communicate their experiences properly. They get frustrated. They blame the audience back home – their ignorance. But is it so surprising? Typically, tribal societies recognize the incommunicability of their socializations of the extreme. They know no-one else will understand. The acts remain secret.'

It was advanced analysis for a beer-sodden brain, but Sohrab had a point. We members of the pack do feel ourselves, with an almost affronted pride, to be misunderstood initiates of an elect, almost a race apart. Over a forlorn forest of empty Bright Star bottles, I felt convinced of it. The experience leads from nowhere to nowhere.

Sohrab was arguing openly with Laura now. 'What are you going to say about Miranda Williams that is meaningful? That she was a good person? That she was a nice person? That she had plans?'

'We can at least say who killed her!' Laura was almost insulted by the little Guinean's attitudes, analysing the pack as an anthropologist analysed primitive societies, societies like his.

'Is that so enlightening?' asked Sohrab. 'That is just a fact, like the length of the Great River, or the existence of Moro violence. It says nothing.'

He was right. What would remain of Miranda's life once it was squeezed through a lens, onto a thin loom of tape, across the ether to a cathode ray tube and out into a diffusing sitting room? Only a digitized fraction of a girl's daring character, her high ideals, her faults. Who killed her? I almost found myself saying, 'Who cares?'

That night some tapes went missing from Brian's room. I am embarrassed to say I actually found myself complaining about how 'things aren't what they used to be'.

JC shook his head with mock concern. 'Tut, tut, the things people get up to these days.'

'All that hard work . . .' Rampling smirked. 'Nothing important on them, I hope.'

'Hey, any incriminating home movies?' sniggered Ralphy. Annoyingly, he seemed fully restored.

It was pointless, but I went to put a note on the lobby board in any case. Ado the receptionist read the note as I pinned it up and his eyes widened.

'Ah! That – beg your pardon – strange Mistah Georges. I done seen him up by Mistah Brian's room not so long since.'

'Georges is always hanging around.'

'Ah-ha! But he was acting strange.'

'Ado, Georges always acts strange.'

'Yes, Mistah Lucas, but this was real strange. He did not even ask me to listen to his noisy tape.'

Later that night I found Georges on a small seaside terrace off the curving ground-floor corridor. He was whittling a stick the length of his forearm with what looked like a flick knife. I could hear crabs scuttling over the rocks below.

I brushed away his offer of the Vukovar headphone experience.

'Georges, did you take some tapes from our suite?'

'Now why would I do that?'

'I don't know. You tell me.'

He whittled, whistling like the incoming whine of a shell, ending with a *boom!*

'Crash and burn!' he murmured. 'Your friend was asking me questions.'

'Friend?'

'Your *belle amie* with the blue, blue eyes. She looks everywhere with those blue eyes. But she does not see. She will put herself in danger, *non*? Unless she is careful. She asked me who Miranda's lovers were.'

'And . . .'

'I told her I didn't know. I had never been inside Miranda's room.'

'Did you tell her who went to Miranda's room?'

'Yes. She also asked me about what I know about some dead girls.'

'What did you say?'

'Of course I said "Which ones?" '

'What do you know, Georges?' I said, as patiently as I could.

'Look! Nothing is safe here. People are dead. People die in millions of ways. Why do some women die the same way?' He sketched the shape of a question mark in the air with his knife. 'Then I told her some of us are artists who are above, beyond. Some of us care for truth, for art, not for trivial gossip about dead nurses. If I have something worth saying, it will be said.'

He really is barmy, I thought to myself. I worried then that Laura, freely indulging her embryonic journalistic instincts, would smell some method in his madness. Unfortunately, my AP had not developed the equivalent analytical skills to control the dangerous conclusions she came to.

'Your friend,' Georges said, 'she wants to fight evil. To defeat it with our craft.'

'She's young.'

He gave me a conspiratorial smile. 'You too are an idealist, Pierre.'

'I was once,' I said, 'maybe.'

'Oh I have seen you this time too, Pierre. I have seen you. You still care.' He poked the blunt end of the stick against my chest. 'Something in you still hurts, *non*? Still burns.'

'What did you tell her, Georges?'

He shrugged. 'I warned her that he who would fight monsters must take care not to become one.'

A sliver of wood curled from the sharpening point of his whittling stick. He looked at me slyly. 'I told her someone has to keep watch.'

'What for?'

He giggled and gave me a wild-eyed glance. His pupils flicked left and right. His stick was now as pointed as a stake for a vampire's heart. He weighed it in his hand. 'I think you know.' He put on his headphones and waltzed off down the corridor to the strains of the Vukovar overture, mimicking, it seemed to me, the bowing of a stringed instrument, a cello perhaps.

When Brian next looked, the tapes had reappeared. He wondered if he had been mistaken about the whole thing.

That same day, 7th August, rebel warriors had attacked the US embassy. The uproar carried clearly to the hotel. Choppers screamed in through the smog to help the small garrison. An exploding curtain of machine-gun and rocket fire beat off the assault. The Moro had effectively declared war on the United States. Scandalized reports from Ralph Reynolds and other US correspondents finally formulated the conflict into neat, Manichean terms of good and evil. But if the nomads fell on one side of this simple construct, we in the pack had slotted, far too neatly for my liking, into the other.

The Moro left us in no doubt about their view of the media. In one of those sudden, inexplicable lulls in the fighting, a van roared up to the hotel, bulging with nomad fighters. They chatted quite amiably with the Bamanda gunmen by the gate and smoked a few cigarettes. Then they took a matt grey, 24-inch Sony television from the back of their pickup and without taking off their Ray-Bans, they executed it with their Kalashnikovs. The tube exploded in a spray of glass and electronics.

'A-wa-o! A-wa-o!' they called, then laughed uproariously. But the gravity of the message was lost on no-one. Later that day the Japanese wildlife team brought in some small, putrid-smelling fetish bags and voodoo effigies that had been flung over the wall. There was one hollowed like a satellite dish, some shaped like video cameras. All were daubed in a fatty, oily substance and fresh blood. Apart from the ancient gardener, the hotel staff turned almost white with fear and fled.

'Hmm. So I guess they're not good-luck charms, then,' said Steven.

I thought again about the threat Madiba Kane had made to Malaika during his interview. Malaika had not managed to return to the hotel and I regretted allowing her back out into the city. If the rebel chief was displeased with his bad press, Malaika could be in danger. I was glad at least that I had not annoyed the Kane by allowing news access to his interview.

Only a select few were undeterred by the threats to journalists. Somehow, Orlando, JC and Farhad even procured images of the American embassy battle. How they crossed the Moro lines was a mystery. Papus also managed to come and go at will. Every day I told him not to risk coming back, but every day he popped up like a stubborn Mokolosh. Each time I was both annoyed that he had risked coming and relieved that he had made it. 'You my papa, Mistah Lucas,' he explained simply.

I thought again with anguish of my son back home. Was I closer to this barefoot boy killer than to my own child? I was encouraged as well. Maybe I did have it in me to be a father figure. Papus certainly did not come for the Smarties or for more torch batteries. They were all long gone. He was wearing his Grateful Dead T-shirt again. I asked him how he got to the hotel. 'It's soo-oo easy, boss. You can just go through the mangrove waterplace. There are old treeboats. Any fellah, he can use them. That is how Mistah Lando goes out. And Mistah Court. And the dark Franji. I see them sometime.'

I grabbed the small boy by the shoulders, knelt down and looked him in the eye. 'Papus, you must not try to come here again. Stay at home with your brother. Promise me.' Papus nodded. 'Tell Mohammed not to come as well, and tell Malaika. She must not try to get to the hotel. She must stay out of sight. It's too dangerous. Too dangerous. Understand?'

Papus nodded again. I hoped he would obey. Again I wished that I had kept Malaika at the hotel. Why hadn't I told her to stay? I had known it would be dangerous for her out there. Perhaps I just wanted her away from me and Laura. I didn't know.

Everything was out of control. It was almost impossible to work any more. That day the roof of the hotel was abandoned as a camera position after the Moro took to raking it with long, juddering bursts. The large satellite dishes were destroyed and served as perches for the swelling flock of vultures. Only a handful of reports could be satellited on the 'Toko' boxes. These devices took hours to digitize and transmit a two-minute news piece via satphone in very poor picture quality. Only two were working.

A tropical concoction of heat, dirt and humidity had played havoc with our delicate broadcast equipment. Sand scratched lenses and videotape. Filth covered filters and viewfinders. Damp infiltrated sensitive electronics. Dust clogged complex engineering. Batteries oxidized. Edit packs simply packed up. Tempers frayed as we all jostled for the declining number of edit and feed slots, restricted even more by the increasingly eccentric hotel generator. Meanwhile the Internet reporters still filed their kilobytes happily via telephone.

In the afternoon, Ralphy sent me a message. It was delivered by his comely and increasingly terrified producer. A diet of tinned food, constant fear and Orlando Harries had left her looking tired and drawn. 'Ralph would like to speak with you this evening,' she mewed. She should have been presenting rush-hour traffic reports in Santa Monica, not ducking and weaving in a war zone.

'Tell Ralphy I'll be here. Just come and get me.'

'OK.' She hunched herself nervously against a distant explosion. She seemed reluctant to leave. I gave her an encouraging look.

'Well, it's about Orlando. You're British. Maybe you understand. I mean I like him and all. It's just . . . He's been acting, well, a bit weird.'

'Don't worry about him. He just tends to get a little overexcited.'

'But it's . . . What with his guns and knives and all . . . And he's very strong. Sometimes he gets, you know, scary.'

'It'll be OK. It's happened before. He'll calm down when all this does.' I waved my arm to indicate – what – the war? Life in general? When would it ever calm down for Orlando?

She gave a faint nod and a wincing, hopeful-grateful smile. As she turned to go, she said, 'Oh, can you tell Laura that Ralph wants to talk to her as well? Could she go up and see him later?'

'All right, I'll tell her.'

No, I would not.

Laura came again that night, ghosting into my room. Without hesitation, we embraced somewhat violently.

'Over the edge,' she urged me in a whisper. 'Over the edge.'

I remember her face below me, taut in that gasping extremity of pain and pleasure. I felt she revealed lonely depths of need and sadness. Afterwards she sobbed. Tears mingled with the sweat on our chests. She murmured to me of childhood loss and pain. Of confusion and doubt. I think she formulated something about 'love', but it was muffled, so I could not be sure. I held her tighter just in case, to show I'd heard. What I revealed I don't know.

We were grateful for the Hostile Location course. A blast shattered my windowpanes. Luckily I had remembered to shove the mahogany wardrobe across the window. With Laura in my arms and in my bed, I did not care where Ralph Reynolds was.

In the hot night, the fighting picked up again. The UN impact counters registered 477 detonations before eleven p.m. From somewhere deep in the garden rolled a rich, triumphant laugh. Around the hotel, dogs howled at the waxing moon.

XXVIII

In the early hours, I awoke to a sense of wrong. I felt there was a dark figure stalking me. It was as if I was back in Rwanda, violence at my right hand. The evil was almost part of me. I wondered whether this was why I had felt so uncomfortable about this whole trip. I bent over Laura's naked form for a moment, then left her breathing gently in the bed and picked up my handicam to do some filming.

Just outside the hotel I found a scene of carnage that hurled me back to the market mortar bomb in Sarajevo. A Bamanda gunman was dying in agony. I shot him with the mini-dvc. I pointed the camera at another. His life soul seemed to come whooshing out of him, sucked straight into the lens. His body implodes like a deflated balloon. The dark presence is by my side now. The camera in my hand is like a live thing. It points at a disoriented woman walking by. It strips her naked and I record the sway of her hips. As she turns to me I see it is Malaika. '*Je suis innocente,*' she says and her face melts into a grotesque African mask. Then another shell takes her head off and I focus on the pool of blood, oozing dark red in the camera light around the gleaming carpet of cartridge cases. Camera melts into machete in my hand and it is red with blood. The ground is trembling from shellfire. Sohrab's voice is shouting in my ear that this will never be broadcast. A dark figure is bending over me, grasping me. My world is being shaken, roiling. Into half-light. Shit, no, someone is shaking me awake, a demonghostdevil-Mokolosh.

It is Papus. He is filthy, shivering. I am alone in the bed. It is drenched in sweat. Laura must have slipped out during the night. The floor is studded with wood slivers and shards of glass.

'What the hell are you doing here?' I growled at him. It dawned on me that he was terrified. I softened my tone. 'I thought I told you to stay at home.'

'Seester Malaika. She dead.'

I was numb. My mind reeled. I groped around for reactions. I should have made her stay with us. I should have insisted . . .

'Are you sure? Where is she?'

'They done take her down mangrove way, Mistah Lucas.' He pointed at his eyes; he had seen it himself. I choked with disgust and loathing. I saw a vision of Malaika, jaw clamped and pounded to silence her screams. Malaika's ideal form disfiguring in that stinking soup of death.

I shouted now. 'Where? How? Who killed her, Papus? Who?'

Papus said nothing. Tears welled in his eyes. He was murmuring something. I was worried about his bare feet on the broken glass. 'Franji,' I made out at last, through his sobs.

I was confused. 'What? How could it be him?'

'Who, boss?'

'The white man. The one who killed seester Miranda?'

'No, boss. I think it was Moro, boss. Madiba Kane made them kill seester.'

'Why? Why do you say Franji then?'

'Moro done the killin'. But Franji killed her. That Madiba Kane. He see pictures of him talking on TV.'

Rampling.

I understood. Now I knew why Malaika seemed troubled after translating for Rampling. The shit had taken our Madiba Kane interview and used it in his last report. He had even made Malaika translate it – *all* of it. In her stoic way, she had not complained. The report must have been transmitted on a satellite with a footprint in Upper Guinea. Papus was right. Whether it was thoughtlessness or petty revenge for the joke we had played on him at the checkpoint, Rampling had as good as killed Malaika himself. Failure, grief, guilt assailed me. I had just wanted to make a film and go home. I had not wanted to get involved. But I had tempted fate. Now, everywhere you looked, people were dead. Rage usually came slowly to me. Not this time. 'Go to seester Laura's room,' I told Papus, 'and stay there.'

I went looking for Rampling.

I had not gone twenty feet before a hyperventilating Richard Jones bumped into me.

'Jesus, Lucky,' he puffed, 'have you heard? They've killed Ralph.'

At just after nine p.m. the night before, Ralph Reynolds had goodnighted his two-way with the network and walked down the unlit outside stairwell that was the quickest way between the roof and my room. He never made it. Early the next day, Ado went out to dig a new latrine and found Hollywood Ralph's body in a clump of carnivorous pitcher plants. The smiling receptionist finally lost his grin. 'Mistah Reynolds,' he told us in awed tones, 'his hair been sliced off. His throat, they done chop it, heah to heah.' He drew his forefinger from ear to ear in that universal, unmistakable, final arc.

I saw a scarlet echo of Hollywood Ralph's on-screen smile.

When they machine-gunned the television, the Moro had executed the medium. Now, the pack perceived, they had moved on to the messenger.

Ado and the hotel gardener dug a shallow grave in the sandy soil under the beachfront casuarinas, but the US navy commander risked a helicopter and flew Reynolds's body back, under heavy fire, to cold storage. There was no way we would ever find Malaika's remains. I wondered if her mother even knew.

In the hotel, a shaken news tribe clotted in the bar for what turned into an impromptu ritual of remembrance. There were a few half-hearted tributes to Ralphy Reynolds, and Ado opened some bottles of blood-warm Muscadet he had found hidden in the absconded manager's cupboard. Ado had collected the personal effects – torn clothing, empty wallet – scattered round Ralphy's body and now they sat in a forlorn pile on the bar counter. In a daze I leafed through Ralphy's blood-stained notebook. I noticed vaguely that there was nothing in it about me, Laura or Miranda Williams, but then many pages had been ripped out.

Rampling's crew gingerly brought me a glass of tepid wine. 'I'm terribly sorry,' his producer whispered. 'About Malaika. We all are.'

I glared at her. She had obviously been crying. 'Rampo lied to us – he told us you'd cleared the interview,' she snivelled. 'We've always known he had an evil streak, but we never thought he'd go this far.'

'We never would have allowed that shit to use it otherwise,' the grizzled picture editor said, 'I swear.'

I barely acknowledged them. To be frank, with Malaika's death, Ralph's murder, the double intensity was almost too much for me. I wanted to retreat to a place within myself. I felt on the edge of surrender, complete capitulation . . . to anger and to hate.

The pack was simmering close to panic. The aid contingent decided to evacuate as soon as possible. Some of the journalists agreed. Felipe Deflores, whose view carried weight, stood up and quickly quietened the hubbub. He was still wearing his linen suit and a no doubt pristine handkerchief still peeked from its breast pocket. He spoke reasonably for a while. Some people, even surrounded by darkness, can retain their dignity.

'You all know', he finished by saying, 'that I am not a coward. But I think we journalists are being deliberately targeted. I think we have to take the responsible route and pull out.' He did not get a good response. I saw just a few resigned nods from the gathering. Orlando's eyes looked empty and blank. I noticed he was wearing a large knife in his belt. Georges Renard was whistling to himself with his eyes shut. Farhad wasn't even there.

Stomach churning, I spoke up in support of Felipe. 'Remember, Ralph wasn't the only journalist to die yesterday. My translator, who most of you knew, was also killed. As a direct result of our work here.' Malaika had never hurt anybody. She was kind and decent. It was a disgrace. Unforgivable. I looked directly into Rampling's eyes and held his gaze for a second, trying to control my anger. He smirked and looked away. 'If you count Miranda Williams and Ben from the Red Cross, Teresa, and . . . that Dutch boy, that makes seven of us in the last month. It's just not worth it.'

I saw Laura looking at me regretfully. I think she might even have been shaking her head. I'm sure I didn't sway her. I probably swayed no-one. I never was much of a public speaker.

'We're all sorry about Malaika, Lucas,' said a calm voice. It was John Court, effortlessly taking control of the meeting. 'But I'm not convinced. This story is still worth it. We all know what the people of this country are going through out there. I for one am not going to give up on them. These deaths are tragic and unfortunate, certainly, but even if Ralph and Teresa were murdered by the same perpetrators – some group that hates us – you cannot connect them with Malaika's killing, and surely not with the murder of poor—'

Typically, Court used the Dutch boy's name. I think he was already the only one who remembered it, maybe the only one who really cared.

'They shot a fucking television for Christ's sake!' It was Ralph Reynolds's distraught producer. 'Do you think that has no connection?'

She began to wail uncontrollably. 'What's the point? This is not a civil war, it's more like a fucking slaughterhouse.' Mechanically, Orlando tried to quiet her but she shoved him away. 'Fuck off! You're all just glad it wasn't you. None of you gives a damn. You actually like all this shit!'

'Everyone,' Court interrupted, calmly, 'when they come here, knows the score. It's dangerous. That's the deal. That's why you come and not the others.' Laura joined in a general murmur of agreement. 'If anyone wants to leave, you can always try and hitch a ride out to the ships.' This was a little disingenuous. Nobody was going to leave if the others stayed. Some would never run the risk of being seen as a coward, others would just never gift competitors the story.

An ostentatious clearing of the throat and Rampling stood up to speak. Somehow he had managed to get even fatter despite the limited rations of the Cape Atlantic. Dark sweat patches spread from under his arms and down his chest. Years ago, in the Gulf War, Rampling had left Iraq on editor's orders and so had not seen the first air raids on Baghdad. Since then the fear of missing anything exceeded all other considerations. It was certainly greater than any consideration he may have had for his crew. In his blustering voice, he refused point-blank to leave. 'Now, now, no need to get hysterical. This is all just a bit of bad luck. And we mustn't exaggerate the numbers. Amanda Williams . . .' I ground my teeth in anger. '. . . was not a journalist. Nor', he said, turning to me, 'was your unfortunate translator, Lucas. As a matter of fact, I gather she was providing you with a much deeper introduction to local culture . . .'

He tossed the last sentence out as a low aside, which maybe only I heard. I didn't care. I walked over, in full view of everyone, and punched him, hard, in the left eye.

Unfortunately, although they blatantly gave me time to land a few satisfying shots, Rampling's crew pulled me away before I could do him any lasting damage.

It was stuffy in my room. My back itched with prickly heat. My clothes were damp. I dipped my reddened knuckles into a basin of tepid water. They ached. Good, I thought, imagine how his face feels. I had not fought many times. I was a professional *observer* of violence. I had beaten up a bully behind the bike sheds and fended off a scrawny mugger in Madrid. Once, travelling on the London Underground, I stopped a man bothering a slight, pretty woman and got well thumped. The woman was Claire. I recalled her face. Grateful, thoughtful. She had been impressed enough to take my number, and to use it.

Now, in this surfeit of brutality, my attack on Rampling impressed Laura. I had worried that beating up an idol might cool her ardour, especially after my public plea for us to flee. I was wrong. I heard her knock and wiped my eyes as she came softly up behind me at the basin, placing a gentle hand on my shoulder. Her mood might have been almost as sombre as mine. 'Peter, I'm sorry about Ralph, and about Malaika. I know how much you . . . cared for her. We all did.' I turned to face her as she continued, 'You know, I . . . I still think you're wrong about leaving here, but oh, I did love it when you clobbered Rampo. He really is a complete tosser.'

Did all women like their men violent?

'Thanks, Laura. Look, I still think we should get in a chopper as soon as the Yanks send one. Then we should take their first supply boat to Abidjan.'

My AP might just have gone along with this. My lover certainly would not. 'No chance,' said Laura. 'I'm staying.'

'Well . . . but I will need you to cut the film with me.'

'Ah, that's sweet,' she said, cupping my face in a soft palm, 'but I'm sure you can start without me. We probably won't be here much longer, but I don't want to leave until I have to. And remember, I'm a field producer now. I'll help you with the structure while you're still here though.'

Could I really leave without her? Could I really leave her here, drinking the ambrosia of violence, in the clutches of men like Court?

'OK,' she said eagerly, after a pause, taking my silence for encouragement. 'What do we know about Miranda? Let's see: masochist, according to Darren; bisexual, if you're right about Dr Lucy; miracle worker, if we believe her patients. Why did Miranda come to Guinea? She came because of: a dead writer; an adventurous spirit; a benevolent streak . . .' She was enjoying this now. 'And she was murdered by: Moro nomads and chewed by their dogs; Bamanda renegades; a mysterious white man; a red demon. Take your pick. It's not very neat, is it?'

'No, it's not. Are you saying your personal investigations haven't turned up anything?'

'Oh, so you're interested now, are you? Well, I'll let you know when I've found something. That is, if you deserve it . . .' She tilted her head tantalizingly.

Perhaps I wouldn't leave immediately after all.

We literally put our heads together for a while. Laura would never see the structure again. Faint turbulence from the fan and our lovemaking fluttered the rough opening shot list on my bedside table, its corner wrinkled with the curved brown stain of a coffee cup. It looked like this:

PICTURE	**SOUND**
A darkened room	Distant hiss of surf
A suggestive shape in a mirror	
Photograph of a smiling young woman	Sound of surf swelling
A shape on the floor	
A young girl laughing in the Suffolk sun	
A bleak African beach	
The most tasteful image of Miranda's bloody corpse	Loud crash of waves

'That should get them sitting up in suburbia,' Laura had said.

In the depths of the night she stirred. The gunmen were taking time off and it was silent. The moon had set and her voice came to me husky out of the blackness where my shoulder cradled her head.

'You know, tonight I felt something I never felt before . . .'

What? I wondered. Was it that the earth had moved? No, that mechanical achievement came easily enough to her. Was it love perhaps?

I tensed but said nothing. She could sense I was awake and waiting.

'. . . I suppose I felt, I felt, well, mortal.'

'What do you mean?'

'I'm not sure, but despite all this *mess* . . .' (yes, that was really how she described it) '. . . I feel these days are so – wonderful . . . beautiful.' She held me tight for a moment. 'Whatever happens, Peter, I want you to know, you've made me happy. The excitement, this night . . . you and me . . . I used to dream and hope times like this would come. Now as soon as they come, it's odd, but it keeps occurring to me that they are finite. I realize I will only have so many days like this in my life.'

I couldn't remember how long ago I had realized that.

'Don't you have anything to say?' There was the merest hint of reproach in her tone.

I was thinking that, for all she knew, this was her last day like this. 'I didn't know my influence was so morbid,' I said.

'Don't be silly. It all makes me feel more alive.' Warm lips searched for mine in the dark and I could feel her naked weight shift. The rustle of sheet and creak of springs told me she now lay back, ready, in the heat of the narrow bed.

'Didn't they say "die", in olden days, for climax?' She was almost whispering now.

'I believe so.'

The whisper came out of the pitch black. 'Well, kill me again, Peter.'

XXIX

Even more than the attack on their embassy, the killing of their famous anchorman infuriated the Americans. In the mist you could hear, rather than see, the venomous Black Hawks clattering low over the tide-line. As night fell, Moro machine-gunners fired warning bursts in their general direction. The tracer rounds arced out over the sea, glowing like meteors in the mist, dimly reflected in the dark water.

The frustrated Marines' rules of engagement banned them from unleashing their highly primed ordnance unless attacked. So they held their fire then sped their gunships high over Moro areas on whisper mode, hurling sandbags from their open doors. The fifty-pound sacks were daubed with slogans like *On your own head be it* and *I've got a crush on you*. They plummeted silently, unseen through the smog, slammed through roofs and smashed bodies with the force of solid lead.

The Moro blew up the hotel's satellite receiver, so the World Wide Web was the only place reporters could see how their material was being used in the outside world. Even Hartman grudgingly took his turn on the nerds' fancy hardware as the pack surfed the online sites of their networks and newspapers to see their copy and pictures in jerky, low-resolution streaming video. The technogeeks accepted this change in their popularity with smug equanimity.

The hotel television now only received the local channel. Somewhere between six and nine p.m. most days, the government broadcast a 'news' bulletin, which consisted of absurd victory claims, set to grainy 1970s archive of a military march past. The rest of the bulletin would be long, gruesome rushes of the torture and execution of nomads. Most of the time (if there was electricity) there was the test pattern, accompanied by Sousa marches and jazz samba. At unpredictable intervals they would transmit an unsteady version of *The Wizard of Oz*.

I remember watching it a couple of times through a haze of hemp smoke and Bright Star. If you go searching for your heart's desire, I think the moral goes, you needn't look beyond your own backyard.

I had forgotten everything beyond. I had forgotten Miranda Williams. I had forgotten my life. My family was Laura and Papus, my friends were Brian and Steven. My reality was a beleaguered hotel. That night, 9th August, the TV screen pinged to a white dot and went to random, flickering hash. When the signal reappeared, it was clear the Moro had captured the station. They transmitted, over and over again, the gory murder of Liberia's President Doe. It was a pretty clear signal to the ruling elite. Sousa and samba were replaced by droning Arabic recitations of the Koran. I wondered if they included Malaika's Chapter of the Dawn.

You knew things were bad when Brian described the situation as 'difficult'. Bullets were zipping through the sand walls of the hotel as if they were papier mâché. The rounds drilled out little piles of dust like the effects of woodworm. Artillery bursts outside the hotel sent small splinters tinkling onto the concrete around the pool. Large fragments spun whistling through the air and sliced off palm leaves, which drifted down on the heads of the journalists below. Fear finally seeded, pushing its slow roots throughout the pack. As usual in hotels under siege, the occupants of exposed rooms retreated to sleep and work in the corridor or in the relative safety of internal bathrooms (no windows there and the bath offers good protection).

Late at night, ululating Bamanda dragged a captured Moro into the hotel grounds, his jawbone crushed, elbows knotted together with picture wire. His captors laughed and smoked some cigarettes, slicing and stabbing him absent-mindedly with bayonets. They took him into the bushes. Two shots rang out. Then they wandered away, celebrating with lazy high fives. A salvo of mortar shells straddled the tennis court. Laura watched, mesmerized.

I thought I saw Orlando watching her. Ralph Reynolds's producer had locked herself away from him and his eyes now focused on Laura. I saw Orlando go up to her and ask her something. I saw John Court go up to her and whisper in her ear. I imagined they were asking her to work with them outside the hotel, at night. This time she barely refused. That sulphurous night, in the chaotic upper corridor of the Cape Atlantic hotel, JC produced the masterwork of his career.

Laura and I met only briefly that night. We did not sleep together. The barrage had finally shredded the wardrobe across my window and forced me from my room. For some unspoken reason we kept our – liaison, would you call it? – under wraps, briefly squeezing hands and brushing lips in a darkened corner.

Georges Renard surprised us, shambling into our

clinch and appraising us for an instant with wild eyes. Still, I gripped her wrists tightly behind her back and quietly sipped the scent of her from the hollows and planes of her neck. I ran the keen edges of my teeth over her throat and lips and kissed her eyelids. Then she slipped off to the safer, seaward room she now shared with Lucy from Mile Sixty. I suppressed an idiotic, almost delirious worry – or was it fantasy? – of lesbian complications and tried, feebly, to sleep in the crowded corridor. The night was a furnace. Sweat soaked my sleeping sheet, trickling down my chest, between my thighs. I wondered if I had a fever.

In Laura's room, whispered conversations and revelations would bring careers and lives to a crisis.

Outside the hotel, the hot mist swirled. Storms were lowering, fanned by boiling winds fathered far north in the Sahara. I heard a 105 booming and knew its bulky offering would land with a blast that would uproot trees like asparagus and slice up tarmac like a knife through soft belly flesh.

Papus slept soundly, curled into a ball at my feet, his thumb in his mouth.

In the morning of 10th August, the whispers went round about John's report and its impact in Western capitals. We gathered to watch, awe-struck. His editor played back to us two-minutes-thirty of sublime beauty and majesty. Even in the clean lines of its master cut, the report surpassed the most potent news item I had ever seen – Michael Buerk's 1984 report on the 'biblical' famine of Ethiopia.

I think the master is lost, but I have studied an off-air videotape at home. Generations of Toko box encoding, satellite transmission, recording and re-recording have given it a shimmering, mirage-like quality, which if anything adds to its almost magical power.

The first shot is a long, slow pan across a smoking warscape. It holds your eye as the tension builds; all you hear is the crackle and spit of unseen flames. Then the low, loaded voice comes in: 'The morning mist rises to reveal the scale of an infernal catastrophe. This is the abode of war . . .'

The depravities of war unfold to the viewer one by one in unstinting but unimpeachable horror. The pictures are neither vile nor bloody, but, even at a few inches high, they shock and appal.

To a professional, the piece is ideally constructed, balancing perfectly around a central hinge – John Court's smooth, steady walk down the middle of a terminal ward. Cholera patients rack in agony left and right. He carries it with gravity and an undercurrent of barely suppressed outrage.

Every image in the report is telling in itself, but Court brilliantly outlines the big picture as well. The viewer learns of the nomads' ruthlessness and of their vicious quest for power against the elected government. We gather that armed intervention is Upper Guinea's only hope. All the key facts are there, too – the number of casualties, the number of refugees, the shortfall in aid. Court's estimates are far lower than the lottery numbers hatched by the rest of the pack. The impact of the report loses nothing because of it.

The hook of a personal story maintains human interest: we meet Mary, the refugee mother, gasping with cholera. Through the close-ups of her miraculously healthy newborn child, Court even injects the vital ingredient of hope into the darkness. 'Lord only knows', reports Court, freely translating Mary's brief but harrowing interview, 'where the rest of my loved ones are.'

The piece ends with JC in another blackened ruin. 'I

found Mary's family,' runs the commentary, 'but bleeding war had ridden in ahead of me . . .'

This section is filmed on consumer dvc. You can clearly see the change in picture quality. The camera picks out bodies in the rubble. In one masterful shot, the image focuses on what looks like a pile of dirt. You seem to realize along with the camera that it is a body. It is as if you are there. Then the picture cuts to BCU. Underneath a transparently thin film of reddish earth you can clearly see the distorted, cherubic face of a young girl; her eyes, milky as unpolished diamonds, stare up glassily into yours.

The final shot is still dvc. It's a piece to camera, filmed from a fixed tripod in one static midshot; a grimy John Court, your vicar to this nightmare, is kneeling at its centre. In his arms he cradles the shuddering body of a teenage girl. We learn that it is Mary's sister, raped and now likely murdered by persons unknown. It is unclear to the viewer what ails her, but it is clear she is dying. There is a choke in Court's voice now. '. . . Unless the world comes to the rescue, nothing will remain . . . John Court, International Network News, Freeville.'

And the girl dies with a sigh in his arms.

Brian and Steven were quite interesting about this report. They had spoken to John Court's crew.

'Remember the sound of flames at the start?' said Brian. 'Nice touch. That was recorded from Ado's cooking fire in the hotel.'

'Hmmm, yes. He was roasting a spitted goat.'

'And the woman. Her name wasn't Mary. It was something like Inolobumi.'

'Yup. And *her* baby belonged to some other woman. And the sister at the end – JC's crew don't have a clue where any of that dvc material came from.'

It didn't surprise me. Look at any of Court's reports. Context is not his primary concern. If something fits, it is used, for effect.

They say the instant Court's report ran on INN, the US president lifted his phone and told his task force commander to 'Get those goddamn dying black girls off my screen!' Court's private crusade paid off. It was JC who finally activated Operation 'Peace on Earth'.

XXX

We had enough on our plates without still worrying about Miranda Williams, but Laura had been tenaciously pursuing her own private mission. She just refused to let go. Later that dreadful day, she called Brian, Steven and me to her sweltering room. Laura was perched on the rumpled double bed. I hadn't realized she and Lucy were sleeping in the same bed. She was holding a cardboard shoebox. We all sat down around her. The close air was laced with mingled female scents. Laura's blue eyes were flashing with conspiratorial excitement. 'I think Papus was right,' she began, firmly.

'About what?' I asked. I really didn't want to know.

'About the white man.'

I tried to sound patient. 'We've discussed this, Laura. As soon as we can, we're going. I'm not staying to find some mythical white killer. Even your friend JC thinks this is all barking.'

'We have been through this before, Laura,' agreed Brian.

'I think Papus was right,' Laura continued confidently. 'And I'm not leaving this shit-hole until I find out who killed that girl. I think the answer will mean something. I think it is one of us.'

We groaned.

She opened the box. 'This might change your mind.'

She shook the contents out onto the bed.

There was a long silence.

What I was staring at made me think at first of Mo's fetishes. A studded collar. A wriggle of toothed clips on thongs. A small black whip. Four velvet-lined, dark leather cuffs, linked by metal chains.

'Hmmm,' said Steven.

'They were Miranda's,' said Laura.

'Where . . . ?' I began.

'I got talking to Lucy last night.'

I jerked my head up to find her looking at me. I remembered the expression from what seemed like an age ago. It was the same testing look she had that balmy, distant day she described the autopsy to us.

'We had a very *intimate* chat.' She was deliberately pushing me now. Despite myself I wondered just how intimate the 'chat' had been. 'Lucy told me everything. She and Miranda were lovers, of course. Miranda apparently had certain – tastes. When she came to Freeville on her last leave, she brought this box with her.'

'So?'

'So there's something *missing* from the box. It wasn't among her other belongings either . . .'

I felt a chill. 'Yes?' We were all definitely listening now.

'A red leather mask.' She paused for effect, but she needn't have.

The Franji Papus talked of was a red demon.

A distant clatter of machine-gun fire sounded dimly. The constant rustle of the waves came up from the beach like background tape hiss on a poor recording. I said nothing.

'So, basically, it's a bad situation, then,' said Brian, grimly.

'Hmm, yes,' said Steven. 'We're almost out of smokes.'

'Can't you be serious, just for once?' snapped Laura.

'I'm not going to get het up over one measly homicidal maniac,' said Brian.

'No way,' added Steven with a wan smile. 'There are already thousands of the little swine out there trying to kill me.'

They lit up two of their last remaining cigarettes. 'Give me one,' I said, taking it from the packet.

Steven lit it with a flame that quivered, and I drew deeply. I was stunned. 'Call me Darren' had openly said it. What other clues had been left in front of our noses like that? I racked my brains. Bars of light flickered in my mind's eye. Perhaps if we went through the rushes we would find something.

The crew agreed there was little point in telling the other hotel inmates. In the first place, we might alert the killer. 'If Laura hasn't already. Telling half the world her theories,' muttered Brian.

Secondly, we would be wasting our breath. The word was that the Marines would land the next morning. Crews were grabbing long shots of the smoking town from the hotel windows and there was action footage aplenty just in front of the gate. There was eyewitness atrocity testimony from the Mile Sixty survivors. Everyone was filing or drunk or high, or all three. I intended to be drunk soon, too. I was already smoking as heavily as I could. To Laura it must have looked as though I was cracking up.

Believe me, if *I* had told the pack one of them was a murderer, they would just have thought I'd finally broken down. They would already have scented it in the Rampo episode. They might well have thought he deserved thumping, but they would also suspect he had a point about Malaika. They would have nodded kindly and agreed to watch out, thinking, 'He's lost it because of that translator he was screwing ... Well he lost it before, didn't he?'

And it was clearly a bit crazy, in the midst of hell, worrying about one specific kind of evil. As if there wasn't enough around anyway. 'All in all,' I said, 'the best option is probably just to be careful.'

Predictably, Laura disagreed. She thought we should investigate. She even had a prime suspect: 'Farhad. He was the first there when Miranda was killed. He had all those pictures of her. Why has he refused to talk to us about Miranda? What is he hiding? Georges Renard was protecting him, I'm sure of it.' Her mind was buzzing now. 'And he's clearly a complete psycho. Have you seen the pictures he takes?'

Brian and Steven were not convinced. I was not really listening.

'Look, let's just check it out,' pleaded Laura. 'What have we got to lose?' She was in the grip of it now. The fervour of the chase had taken over. Her passion and determination were overpowering. When I showed no opposition, Brian and Steven shrugged their agreement. 'What the hell,' said Brian, 'it's not as though there's anything else to do.'

First we toured the hotel. There was no sign of Farhad. He could have been off on one of his solo trips. We went down to the lobby; it was dark and humid, echoing with shouts and explosions from outside. There were spots and trails of blood on the floor. Judith Dart, her eyes staring into space, sat rocking on her chair by the door, mouthing silent nothings. Ado the clerk cowered behind the desk, his teeth chattering in fear. A row of bullet holes had been stitched in the wall behind, just above counter height. Laura simply reached over and took the spare key for Farhad's room.

'What if he's there?' asked Brian.

'We don't tackle him,' said Laura. 'We just ask him again if he'll do an interview.'

'Bit of an odd time for it,' said Steven.

What sounded like an RPG 7 rocket landed not fifty yards away on the beach. Through a blown-out corridor window I saw it erupt in a fountain of sand. I don't think Laura noticed that I was the only one of us not to flinch. 'Odd time for anything,' I said.

I knocked on the door. There was no answer. Laura turned the key and we entered. Steven stayed outside.

The bedroom was hot and dark. Thick blankets hung over the window, stifling the rising moon. Our mini-dvc began to purr as Brian laid the surreal scene down on tape. A red glow seeped from the bathroom. Farhad had transformed it into a darkroom. Hanging over the sink in the sickly red light, pictures of death dripped the remnants of their viscous fixing fluid. The room was like a sauna. In the dark cube, Laura was dripping sweat. It looked like blood.

Assailing us silently from the walls, taped edge to edge, screamed Farhad's jagged, black and white encyclopedia of man's inhumanity. 'Must get this wallpaper for the kids' room,' said Brian, adding false levity to the defence he had already raised with his camera. 'Remind me to ask him where he got it.'

A laptop computer blinked. I struck a key and the grey screen glowed into a hi-res streamed slideshow of violation and perdition. My fingertip slid over the slick mouse pad to click on an icon labelled *Marlow*. A slow-motion sequence of Laura flickered into life, lithe in her linen, close-up laughing, spinning round, camera in hand, blonde hair flying. My head spun.

Death, dismemberment and mutilation were all around me. The images stabbed into my mind, merging and whirling in the hot red light. I felt anger again. Hate. The pointlessness of it all. 'Peter,' Laura whispered. 'Look at these.'

Somehow amidst that nightmare vision, she had managed to pick out a triangle of pictures: a woman clothed, her throat cut, curled on the floor of a hut – Teresa Cellini; two photographs taped below it – two women curled on two floors, in that almost foetal position. Their postures mirrored Teresa's. Strands of flesh hung off their necks like paper from a shredder. One was Miranda Williams. The other was a mystery. Like Miranda she had been blonde, pretty, the black and white print capturing the deliberate arrangement of the body, crisply artistic. A curled shape, a question mark posing the problem. I felt a strong spike of recognition. I could not place who, or where.

In an instant Laura's logical mind whipped the chaos into a neat equation. 'Jesus,' she whispered, 'he kills people. He kills them and then shoots them. He killed Teresa, too. Oh fuck, what shall we do?' She wiped perspiration from her face. There were dark patches on her shirt where each breast rose against the cotton.

My mind began to race. It was coming back to me. She was the fixer, the cellist who had accused Rampling of assault in Sarajevo! Who else knew her? 'Put the pictures back,' I said, calmly. 'Let's get out of here.'

Did Farhad know something about these deaths? Perhaps. Perhaps it was just an aesthetic arrangement. Farhad, a visual being, living through his eyes, might simply have been struck by the death patterns. I walked quickly from the room. Laura hurried after me. 'We could tell Orlando, get him to come with his guns and arrest Farhad.' She was babbling now, swept up in the madness.

'Don't be ridiculous. You should go easy on the Mefloquine, it's making you see things. We wait for the Marines tomorrow. Until then, we tell no-one.'

Laura was taken aback. 'Fuck you, Lucas!' – all right, so she was more than taken aback, she was incensed – 'I must be mad. I must have been completely mad to . . . I knew it . . . You're just a – a – coward! You were even too scared to tell me you were married. I'm a journalist for Christ's sake. Did you really think I wouldn't find out? I should have listened to them. Rampling told me why you don't like him. It's because he knows what you did in Rwanda, isn't it? Rampling warned me you couldn't hack it. He told me how you ran away in Rwanda. How you just left your crew in danger. Now you won't even bother to protect your own colleagues from a serial killer!'

Looking at her, her hair falling over her shoulders, damp with sweat, her eyes flashing, I could not speak. I knew nothing.

'Hey, hey.' Brian held her by the shoulders for a moment. 'Calm down! I think you've got a bit mixed up here.'

Everything was becoming mixed up.

'Yes, Laura, actually,' Steven was mumbling, 'it wasn't quite like that. Anyway, just because Farhad took their photographs doesn't mean he killed them. And we haven't found the mask.'

'OK. Well fuck both of you as well then.'

I watched her stride away. Maybe she was right. The deaths of Teresa and Malaika especially had sapped my resolve. I felt responsible. I felt like a fool. I felt drained. 'What are you going to do?' I shouted after her. 'Tell everyone Farhad's a twisted pervert? We know that already.'

It was all insane.

When I next saw her, later on in the twilight of that momentous day, I could not help my heart contorting again. She was talking earnestly with John Court, the tall figure and the short silhouetted against the flashing white background of the distant storm. Above the hills, giant webbed forks of lightning flickered. A bullet, fired from somewhere amidst the gathering storm, cracked between them. Laura ducked. Court did not stir. Only his eyeballs rolled coldly to survey me, and the minute muscles at the corners of his mouth shifted, pulling upwards into a thin smile.

I almost went over to try and explain things. Perhaps I should have spoken then about the cellist, perhaps I should have told her that Court . . . but no, she would never have believed me. She thought Farhad had killed those girls. But why not red-haired Rampo? I could tell her about him and the Muslim girl in Sarajevo. Why not JC, or Lando, or any of the others who were in both places? Why not me? She saw me hesitating. She stared at me defiantly and turned back to Court. She looked up at him as though he was the answer to her prayers. I tried anyway. 'Laura . . .'

She turned angrily towards me. She was wielding our handicam, pointing it into my face. 'I didn't trust Rampling, so I checked. I know all about you in Rwanda. How you killed that girl. How you filmed it. How do we know you didn't kill Miranda? You were here. Did you like Miranda Williams? Georges Renard tells me you two got quite close. I should have listened to him.' Her voice was bitter now. Was it love she felt for me, or hate? 'Did you and Miranda get on? We know you like it rough. Don't we, *Lucky*? Did you *screw* her? Did you kill her?'

I was reeling. Everything had been leading to this. I had thought I could keep it down, hold back the past, the wickedness. It was impossible. I could say nothing.

The blank lens dug into my eyes, mined the memories embedded behind my forehead. I saw Court standing behind her, arms folded, looking on, in satisfaction.

So Court had told her.

Yes, he knew. Court knew.

And yes, I have killed.

'Laura . . .'

'Don't come near me.'

I wondered if I had lost Laura, let her slip through shaking fingers . . . lost her to Court. I stowed myself in the bar with the crew and the rest of the bedraggled pack. We did not see Farhad. For all we knew he was dead as well. On this night, 10th August, the Moro launched their final assault.

'It looks like it'll be game, set and match to the rebels,' said Rampling in his voiceover for the Corporation's late news. On the piece to camera his head is skewed awkwardly away to hide his black eye.

With the game moving towards the final whistle, the battle built to a crescendo. Georges Renard came giggling into the lobby to report that he had seen Rampling masturbating on the roof. Georges was the only person comfortable under the bombardment. For the first time since Vukovar he forgot his trauma and his tape and slept like a babe. He smiled happily in deep, warm dreams as horrible screams quavered from the undergrowth. Moro death squads were mopping up. At about midnight, after 1,984 impacts, the Danish

UN observer gave up counting with a sigh and trudged down to join the rest of us in the bar.

A white South African mercenary with a bleeding sword slash across his face wandered up to the pool. He stood swaying by the water, singing a soft lamenting song in Afrikaans. We could just hear him from the bar. 'What's he singing?' Richard asked, in a strained whisper.

' "Sarie Marais",' said Hartman, who started humming the tune nervously along with the wounded soldier.

'What does it say?'

'It's about ordinary things – crops and trees from his home country. It's a song about home and the woman who stayed there. Good things. The sort of things we should never bloody leave.'

Then, efficiently, the mercenary shot himself. His body toppled into the pool and sank slowly to hang just above the bottom of the deep end. His blood floated up in strings that mingled with the glutinous strands of green algae, frogs' spawn and mosquito larvae. We carried on drinking. When I was too drunk to swallow any more, I clambered to the upstairs corridor and dozed fitfully in my sticky clothes, Papus's head on my thigh. Brian and Steven grabbed a few more Bright Stars from the bar and sat at Judith Dart's edit pack, spooling through some rushes.

It was impossible to sleep. The heat was unbearable. Alcohol and shooting drummed in your head; edit suites whizzed back and forth at screeching high speed. Someone moaned in fear. Mosquitoes hummed around your ears. Hallucinatory Mefloquine stoked your dreams. So long suppressed, the magma of memory surged up at me, lava-hot.

Rwanda.

My God, there was so much blood. Blood and bodies everywhere. The rivers were clogged with bloated corpses.

I was filming for the Corporation. Banana groves and deserted homesteads. Dead feet sticking out into dirt tracks from the bush. Entire families hanging from the thorny acacias, like carcasses in a butchery.

I still believed in truth. I still believed in justice. For years I had delved, exposed, judged. When I found one of the killers I could not control myself. They said her radio broadcasts had fed the genocide. I interviewed her on-camera; a striking woman, ebony-skinned, high-cheekboned, oryx-eyed. I filmed her cooking, talking to her daughter on the telephone. I filmed our sexual act.

I remember a big close-up of her face: sweat beading her upper lip, teeth slightly parted, staring deep into the lens. It tormented me. Part of me desired her. Part of me despised her. Part of me despised myself for feeling both. Churning years of dirt, suppressed emotion, blunted lusts, stunted rage came welling out of me. Court in those days was my oracle. He advised me, so he knew. I told the vengeful rebel army where to find her. I guided a squad of them up there in a Jeep. A sombre lieutenant pulled off his belt to strop his machete with slow, deliberate strokes.

'You like to watch?' he asked.

'*Je suis innocente,*' she said. That same look into my lens, into my eyes. I pointed the camera and before I closed my eyelids I saw blood bright red. It spattered into the lens. I remember the three fingers, hacked off in self-defence, the layer of fat appearing under the spreading rips in her smooth, taut black flanks – yellow. I heard the chunking sound of metal in meat. I think she tried to repeat the phrase about her innocence. It came out as a gargle of the blood filling her throat. I had no doubt that she had orchestrated the deaths of thousands. But I did not murder her for justice.

I did it out of anger.

I did it because I wanted to . . .

I did it for me.

XXXI

An icy chill of suspicion brought me round. In my almost-sleep it had crept up on me. She might be spending the night with Court. I opened my eyes in a cold sweat. I dismissed the thought – Laura was not like that . . . Feverish, I tried to hold my shuddering eyelids shut. The atmosphere felt electrified. The cloying air was rich with acrid ozone, harbinger of a tropical thunderstorm. In the flickering light I stood up and picked my way through the restless, sleeping bodies in the corridor to where Brian and Steven were watching rushes, surrounded by empty Bright Star bottles. Steven paused the edit suite and took a swig of beer. Brian looked up and offered me a cigarette. I took it gratefully, with shaking fingers.

Both monitors were frozen on video footage of Miranda Williams's crumpled body in the beach house. Steven pressed *play* on the right-hand screen and the digital pixels scattered, then reformed into moving pictures. He did the same with the left.

'There it is again,' slurred Steven, after a moment.

We stared vacantly into the images. They seemed meaningless to me. I couldn't see the point.

'Do you mind telling me what's going on?' Bleary-eyed, I felt tired and exasperated. My head was hammering.

'There's something weird here,' said Brian, staring into the monitors. 'We can't work out what it is. It's in the picture somewhere.'

'Just listen for a change,' snapped Steven. 'Listen! I'm telling you it's the sound.'

He rewound and in a fluster played both tapes at once. I closed my eyes, covered my face with my hands and concentrated. Through the storm and confusion my ears tried to shut out the noises of the night, to take in and distinguish between the two soundtracks. There was something . . .

'Rewind,' I said.

Steven looked at me anxiously and played the material again.

On the left-hand screen was dvc footage of Miranda's body, shot from all angles. It looked like material Laura and I had watched before. The soundtrack was full of the loud crash of waves, bursting close by. I tried to concentrate.

On the right-hand screen was Betacam footage shot by an agency crew. The same body, similar camera angles. You could hear other crews in the background, the pack milling around. You could not hear the sea.

Sound. Tides moving up and down. Time passing. Between the first and second recordings, time had elapsed.

I looked at Steven, aghast. 'The tide. There's a time difference. At least six hours.'

He nodded grimly, understanding too. When the dvc footage was taken, the tide was high. By the time the pack arrived, the surf had retreated way down the beach.

'Jesus. This material was filmed hours before Farhad arrived to take his stills.'

It was still dawning on me.

'Rewind,' I said.

'Yes,' said Brian, sober now. 'I'm not sure, but I think there's something different about the light as well.'

We played it again and I saw those slats of sunlight striping Miranda's naked body. I realized what it was now. 'Jesus. The only light like that was in the room where she was killed, not the room where she was found.'

Brian and Steven looked at me, waiting for my lead.

'Whose footage is this?'

'We checked with his crew. It's—'

'It's John Court's,' said Steven. 'He filmed it himself. On his own.'

John Court.

'Laura!' I said, and ran.

I flung open her door with a bang. A lightning bolt lit up the stuffy room and a semi-nude Lucy Chambers, sleeping on top of the sheets, her arm outflung towards where Laura should have been sleeping.

'Wha—?' she began to ask, sitting up and pulling the sheets up around her naked torso.

'Where's Laura?' I asked – I may have shouted – from the doorway, Brian and Steven panting behind.

She shook her head – she didn't know. If she made any verbal answer I didn't hear it. We were already off and running in different directions.

As I rounded the corner into the lobby a hand grasped my shoulder and spun me round.

I was looking straight into the dilated pupils of a perfectly calm Georges Renard.

'Jean Court, il est toujours à la recherche de nouvelles conquêtes, n'est-ce pas?'

'What? Georges, I'm looking for Laura. Have you seen Laura?'

'John Court. He takes a new lover tonight. You like the same kind of girls as him, no?'

Miranda. Teresa. Laura.

I ran outside to where I had last seen them together. I found myself in the dank glimmer of false dawn. I seem to remember Papus appearing behind me. I hardly tried to warn him back. 'Laura!' I shouted. 'Lau-ra!'

Through the growing thunder in the mountains I heard the distant crack of an old 75, the whirr of the shell and knew it was coming close. Some lessons can be useful sometimes. My trained subconscious calculated the danger and I went sprawling in the dirt. The projectile exploded nearby, the shock wave rolling violently over me, the expanding fan of shrapnel screaming a few feet above my back. Half-winded, I stood up, swaying, only to see one of the Japanese wildlife team wandering obliviously up the path. He seemed utterly unconcerned about the danger. 'You look for Miss Marrow?' he said.

Hazily, I understood that he was asking something about Laura. I nodded, my head pounding.

'This morning, automatic camera switch on. Early morning. Very early. On tape we see Miss Marrow and Mr Court.'

'What?'

'We film her with Mr John Court. They go to swamp.'

My heart pounded now as well. My mind swam with images of Laura and Court together. Fear cleared my thoughts. Farhad's photographs, flickering bars of light, dead girls, suspicions and resentments, all resolved into a clear picture of what I had to do. I was meant to be good in a pinch. Well, this was a pinch, all right. I raced back into the hotel and paused just long enough to spool through our rushes to a certain point. I watched for less than thirty seconds then made one quick call on the satphone. A moment later I was off and running down through the grounds.

What had Papus said? There were some canoes?

My mind whirling, I ran clumsily down the overgrown garden path, past the beach hut where Teresa died, down to the foetid lagoon which separated the hotel peninsula from the town. Dark tangles of mangrove squatted around it. There were a couple of dugout canoes on the bank, each carved from the trunk of a single tree. I pushed one out and began to paddle like a lunatic towards a narrow channel between the knotted trees. Swiftly the mangroves swallowed me up, surrounded me in a web of twisted grey roots. Their closely knit branches let in little of the early morning glow. In the darkness of the swamp, wraiths of the smoky mist still lingered, wrapped around the stunted trees. The clinging dampness of the fog mixed with the reek of black mud and the whitening flesh of the corpses bobbing amongst the roots, worried by swarms of small brown fish. The dugout rolled alarmingly, threatening to dump me in the mire. I refused to look. Maybe I would see Malaika's dead face. In the distance thunder boomed. Or it might have been artillery. I paddled strongly, bathed in sweat.

I came out of the swamp into a polluted stream, which trickled out over a grey beach. Bloated body shapes, half-buried, washed gently back and forth in the small waves. A dark triangle of elbow jutted above the sand. The sky was black with storm clouds. Behind the beach the town was under attack again.

Pillars of smoke rose from newly burning fires. Geysers of flame and dust were thrown up by exploding shells. I saw another dugout canoe on the far bank of the dirty stream. I landed beside it.

Out to sea the American battle wagons rocked violently and began spouting fire and smoke. The boom of the guns rolled over to my ears and shells whirred overhead an instant later. The bombardment crashed and boomed like an immense roll of thunder. Sheets of lightning on the hills blended with the flashes of exploding shells. An explosion far down the beach sent grains of sand stinging into my cheek. I put my hands over my ears and closed my eyes.

Up ahead loomed the solid stone remains of an old colonial slave station, remnant of the last, bitter imperialist adventure on this coast. I ran up to it. Ducking into its dankness I heard a voice. Voices. I ran in. A flash of silver on the ground – a video camera. A dark corner, a high walled room in the early light. Two naked bodies, murmuring. One bent over the other – in pleasure? I was frozen in rage and fear.

Marlow's thoughts were fuzzy. She felt weak, drained. But she was cool. Her eyes opened slowly to a dim morning light. Someone was undressing her. She was almost naked. An unbreachable corner of her mind, precise and alert, began to decipher what had happened.

When they set off from the hotel, the swamp had been eerie in the moonlight. The moon looked full. The bulge-eyed mudskippers fluttered amongst the mangrove roots. Her camera caught the bodies of murdered corpses. She could see the cords that bound their arms biting into the swelling, softening flesh. Marlow was excited. This was the plunge, the dive. The rest had just been a dipping of toes, a testing of temperatures. Now she was in, up to here. Her heart pumped. Weeks of dangers faced, violence witnessed, welled up within her in an almost unbearable pleasure. She thought the adrenaline might burst her. Damn Lucas and his safety first. Damn his doubts and his guilt. In fact damn Lucas altogether. John lived the way she wanted. He lived utterly.

She had doubted the wisdom of going. By this time, though, she was not very wise. In the weeks with the Freeville pack she had unlearned so much. The excitement of uncovering Farhad had finally seized her. She felt invincible. And Court was so persuasive. She was so drawn to him. Into his dream she melted.

She took the handicam from Brian's kit. This footage would make her name, she thought – the first footage from the conquered city. No Rampling, no Dart, no Corporation person had dared Freeville after dark. Only John. She looked at him in the rear of the canoe, a powerful, dark figure. As they slid along beneath the branches, the strong moonlight through the bars of the canopy flickered on his face like a strobe. Unusually for him, he was smiling.

They grounded the canoe and walked up the beach. Filming, they hardly felt the passage of time. The streets gleamed like a silver sea in moonlight reflected on the carpet of shell casings. The cartridges rolled and tinkled under their feet as they moved through the town like two ghosts. Two kindred spirits. At the corner of a street three bodies lay. Marlow got down close to film, smelling the decay on them already. The Moro had taken this central district by storm. In their wild rage against modernity, they had simply destroyed. Huge holes gaped where rocket-propelled grenades had been pumped at random through the sides of office buildings. Computer screens had been ripped out and blown up with bazookas. The central bank had exploded that afternoon in a mushroom cloud of worthless banknotes, which had fallen like autumn on Independence Square. The slightest of breezes flickered a few into the air as Marlow waded a foot deep in the crinkled, empty promises of the finance minister to pay – on demand – one hundred, one thousand, one trillion guineas. Here and there, naked corpses lay half submerged in the tattered images of noble-looking nineteenth-century presidents. They filmed these scenes too, down low at death's eye level. A mutilated body in rigor mortis, banknotes sticking to his wounds. On the digital footage, using maximum brightness gain, the scene in the moonlight shows grainy and ghostly.

It was beautiful, and almost certainly unusable, the wounds too graphic, too terrible to be shown. Court's camera catches Marlow's whispered question.

'Don't you understand?' Court responds in a murmur. 'They're for me. For us. These pictures are for us. Only we know. We know what it's like.'

Marlow did know. This was an indulgence. No, it was an epiphany. She took a deep breath and she knew that she had finally sucked in a lungful of the smell of death. Its stench had at last overwhelmed the city smells of sweating, living humanity, of cooking fires, food and defecation. They hid at one stage from a Moro patrol. Spears glinted silver in the moonbeams. Court reached out a strong hand and pulled her in behind a pillar of the ruined old cathedral. In the Gothic-arched silver shadows, on the rubble of porticoes and capitals, he hushed her surprised gasp with a kiss. Does she kiss back? The cameras, crushed between their bodies, go black for a moment.

Heading back down to the beach you hear him mutter something. He must have hit her, done something. I am sure she would not have obliged him otherwise. She was still sort of on her feet when he half dragged her into the slave quarters. Inside the doorway, she dropped her camera. It is still rolling . . .

Now, his clothes folded neatly to one side, his actions considered, deliberate, defined, mechanical, Court is opening his mouth and words are coming out. Laura is on the floor, semi-naked, sluggish. I wonder if she can still hear. On the tape there are words sounding like an explanation, like a speech someone has uttered before.

'In my mind's eye I see my mother. Blonde, blue-eyed. The image of her is fogged. I know not whether by time or tears. Her mouth is open in a kind of loathing. Her hand is blurring down towards me.'

Here Court is performing something with his right hand around Laura's crotch.

'Laura, your life is painful, I know. You are tense and unhappy. You are dissatisfied. You suffer. I can help you. I can bring you peace.'

He has pulled off most of her journalist's linen suit, leaving her bare from the waist down. Now he crosses limp arms above a blonde head and slides off her T-shirt. His hands run over her breasts, go around her neck. In a last effort Laura seems to try and throw him off. She succeeds only in ending up with her long, naked legs spread around him. He seems to choke, to pause. Is he crying? The camera does not reveal. What seems clear is that Laura Marlow is at the mercy of John Court.

By his side I swear I saw a long knife, serrated. In his hands I swear he holds a contraption, articulated. It is the jaws of a hyena. We know that in their natural owner they can pierce metal dustbins. They can easily deal with the soft, downy throat of Laura Marlow. Off-screen, I act.

Court's camera is dropped now, but a viewer would know that Lucas leaps at him, knocking him from Laura's prostrate form. Court has the strength of demons. A blur in the shot is a loose stone seized from the slaver's wall and dashed against Lucas's temple. For a moment we are all motionless in the small space, panting. But Court again raises the large stone over Lucas. There is a sudden brightness. Artillery? Lightning? Then the light blazes again, followed by a wall of sound and wave of pressure that shakes the room. John Court steadies himself. Laura moans something (to him?) and he hesitates a second or two, lowering the stone and saying something in a low voice. If you boost the volume on the tape and lose some treble, you can just make it out: it sounds like he is repeating the word 'horror'. Then everything goes white and black and points of light mosaic and white noise and hissing grey hash.

Since that day I have never once wanted a cigarette.

It could easily have been different. He was half-upright when the shell landed, so he was the worst hurt by the blast, but I was also wounded and Laura was pretty far gone already. Thanks to him. I still reckon he might have finished me off, if he had wanted.

Of all the dreamlike moments of that time, those minutes – I suppose they were minutes – were the most unreal. The room was rolling, slowly, nauseatingly, like when you're drunk. I was drifting in and out of consciousness. Dim daylight was seeping in through a large hole in the wall. Roiling black titans of nimbus clouds choked the sky. The heat was infernal. My sight was hazy. The earth was still vibrating now and again from the shock of shells. I remember him crawling towards me on all fours. I think he was unarmed. They must have come then, and stopped him.

I heard scuffling, felt arms around me. They seemed to be helping. I believe I could hear a low moaning, but I don't know who it was. It may have been me. I think I saw a group of men standing around Court, talking in low voices. Some tall men in blue robes. A couple – a few – stockier men, in leather jackets. There might have been a flash of silver, some screaming. Then they were gone and Papus was there, crying, and Mo waving something black and chanting, and Steven was bent over where Laura was before. He seemed to be doing something I'd seen on a course somewhere. Or was he covering up a shape? Was Laura dead? And Brian was there, for some reason carrying two cameras.

'Cut,' I mumbled.

As I passed out again, I realized it was raining.

Then there were piercing whistles and the roar of massive engines. Voices shouting, a southern American twang. 'Oh my God.' A sandy confusion of buff khaki and camouflage. The shouts of 'Medi-ii-ic' I knew from Vietnam movies and I was being treated. Fat drops of rain were thwacking heavily into my face. I saw John Court when they stretchered me away. He was curled into a foetal position. I won't detail the terrible mutilations. I'm not sure how well I saw them through my hazy vision in that tropical downpour. Anyhow, the reader has enough data to guess how scores are settled there.

His wounds were put down to shrapnel. The closest shell might have sent a few splinters of metal into his back and arms, but I knew that the mincing of his throat had been effected by a razor-edged Lebanese knife.

Yasmeen had been avenged.

XXXII

It rained for days. Cool showers and ocean breezes rinsed the sticky heat from the cruiser's decks. Laura and I stood together on the gently rolling bridge and looked back at the grey land. Under beating squalls of rain it seemed far off, past. Distance lent it no enchantment. It was unspoken but obvious – for both of us, that way of life was over. Laura had a different look in her eyes. They had lost some of their piercing sharpness. They seemed softer now. The faintest of lines had appeared at their outer points. She was, if anything, even more beautiful. When we kissed, gently, it was a different, tender embrace.

After a few days of peace, Farhad Morvari came out through the storm on a helicopter. He was still angry about our breaking into his room, but also apologetic. 'I did suspect there was a killer amongst us. I just did not know who. I even thought it might be John Court. I'm sorry I did not say anything, but I knew you'd think I was mad. And . . .' he gave me a searching look, '. . . I also wondered if it might be you.

'It was the shape, you see. Working in black and white you get a smell for forms. The curled-up arrangement of the body was actually very specific. When I photographed Miranda's, I thought immediately of the fixer's body in Sarajevo. When I shot Teresa, well, then I was convinced. After Teresa died, I felt Court was the most likely. Georges Renard saw most goings-on at night, so I knew her sleeping partners . . .' He glanced at me again. '. . . all of them.'

He presented Laura with a picture of her in combat. I feel free to tell you that she threw it overboard. This will not hurt Farhad – he died recently, in a car accident.

We were also overjoyed – and amazed – to see Malaika. When Madiba Kane saw his interview on the Corporation's satellite news, he was enraged. He ordered his men to take care of Malaika. Some boy soldiers picked her up and took her down to the swamp to be killed. We had filmed some of them in our documentary on child soldiers. They remembered Malaika, how she had been kind to them, how she had given them Smarties and Corporation ballpoint pens. The war-sparrows hid her away then released her to the Americans. Malaika was finished with Upper Guinea. She was going to go back to the States with her mother.

A child-soldier had also played his part in saving us. When I took the canoe, Papus told the crew where I had gone. Brian had then grabbed a satphone – throwing Rampling off a live studio interview with London – so he could call Mansoor for help. I'm sure he was surprised to find Mansoor and his killers already alerted by a previous call, already out looking for 'John Court the murderer'.

Still, I was cross with Papus. He had been lying. He did not even have a brother. Papus cried and would not let go of my jacket. I gently disentangled him and passed him to Sohrab, who put his arm around the narrow shoulders. I gave all our remaining dollars to Sohrab and asked him to use it to look after the boy. I also gave Sohrab my flak jacket. Mo the driver took Laura's. It had been mangled by shellfire on the beach, but Mo was happy to incorporate it into his magical inventory. He was convinced that only his magic had saved us, the fetishes locating us in the slave prison and protecting us from the explosions. Well, so little do I know now, I cannot say he is wrong. Enough exposure to magic and perhaps anyone becomes spellbound.

You are what you see. After a few days on the ship, Laura and I entered John Court's room in the Cape Atlantic Hotel. It was like walking into a man's mind. The room of this man so meticulous, so refined, stank of sweat, dirt and urine. 'It's like a sty,' Laura said, 'or a kennel, maybe.'

Filthy blankets and sheets had been ripped off the bed and wound into a circle on the floor. Videotapes and photographs were scattered everywhere. It was as though someone had ransacked the place. Old news scripts, interview transcripts, pages of poetry, sections of journals had been torn up and mixed with the blankets in a kind of nest. 'Look here,' I said, showing Laura a torn red leather mask, with redder streaks, and a bloody toupee.

It was like a deranged collage of our culture at the climax of that unfettered century, good and evil churned as if by shellfire and reassembled out of context. There were drafts for an award acceptance speech and a treatise on journalism's role, commissioned by the same left-leaning UK newspaper that I read. There were dozens of crumpled attempts at a long letter to Court's editors, complaining about their plan to stop him travelling and make him studio anchor. Mixed in were pages torn from Ralph Reynolds's notebook, pages that show just how much Ralphy had managed to learn about Miranda Williams.

Enough to get him killed, perhaps. I also found evidence Court had tracked our investigations – copies of the videotapes borrowed from Brian's room.

Piecing the fragments together was a painstaking and disagreeable task. Many had been soiled. Laura later tried to arrange them in some sort of chronological order. Towards what she judged to be the end, Laura tells me they become increasingly violent and confused. Many are incomprehensible, insane. It is reasonable to assume that the leftist paper would have been reluctant to run Court's proposed solution to the problems of Africa: 'Kill them All. Exterminate them. Cow after Cow, Village after Village . . .'

I'm not sure if we found all Court's videotapes. I have heard rumours that various appalling images have recently appeared on a certain Internet site. I have not visited it. I can't see what good it would do me, or anyone else.

Of course we tried to work out as much of the story as we could. My version would be the following: poor, trusting Teresa had been Court's lover. Pillow talk meant she knew that Court had been Miranda's lover too. Ralph Reynolds, perhaps looking for a gofer, perhaps in the throes of passion, told Teresa of his suspicions that one of the pack was a killer. Maybe Teresa had then suspected Court. Foolishly, she had nosed around. He had killed her. Before she died, perhaps she mentioned Reynolds. Perhaps Reynolds became so jumpy because he was scared, because he thought one of us was a murderer. He might even have suspected Court. He might have suspected me. After all, I still to this day do not know why Ralphy wanted to meet me that fatal night, or why he wanted to see Laura. To warn her?

Laura and I departed as soon as the Marines secured

the airstrip. I insisted that Brian and Steven accompanied us. The Corporation wanted them to stay. Their professionalism and their stoic home-from-homeness gave them the protection of a tortoise's shell, but even tortoises get tired, hiding in their armour.

'Good of you to take us this time, chief.' Brian's beard was a tint greyer.

'Hmm. Yes, makes a change.' Steven's sunburned crown was a wisp balder.

I was not going to leave them behind as I had during my breakdown in Rwanda.

On the way back through the town, we saw what Laura and John Court had filmed that night. There had been complete and wanton destruction. 'Mashed', I recall, was Steven's word for it. It was as though the rootless nomads had vented an age-old anger against anything fixed. Overcoming the city, that sink of corruption and iniquity, was not enough. They had to grind it into the dust. Then their marabouts decked the lampposts with dead crows, with cursed dolls and charmed human body parts. Mixed with these macabre greetings, the Moro welcomed the Americans with the less subtle salutations of mines, booby traps and snipers.

Always ready to cut to the chase, the Americans decided to kill Madiba Kane. Kill the head, they believed – following a line Nick Rampling had been pushing – and the body would die. Soon after we left Freeville, Marine attack helicopters encircled Kane's compound and pulverized it with rockets and Gatling guns. They killed Madiba Kane, one of his four wives and both his sons. The Marines declared the bad guys dead, the war over. They had missed the point and they had missed Kane's nephews. The complex Hydra of Moro clan structure was not something they could have gleaned from the media. Two days after his death, Kane's clan retaliated. Dozens of Marines were stripped and butchered with scimitars. Their bloody corpses, worried by Moro dogs, were dragged through the streets in triumph. The images, filmed by Sohrab and Orlando, were piped directly into the global living room. They demolished American resolve.

I'm sorry to say that while filming, Sohrab, taken for a UN soldier in his blue flak jacket, was shot through the neck by a Moro sniper.

Our documentary was never made. The rushes, some thirty hours' worth, gather dust in my garden shed, in a locked trunk. My son is banned from entering. No doubt, one day, curiosity and perhaps daring will take him in there. Hopefully by then Digibeta and handicam dvc will be obsolete curiosities left indecipherable by mutating technology.

Laura and I convalesced together. You might say we coalesced – for a while. The possibility of 'love' was floated. Often it was on the tip of my tongue.

But, eventually, you do realize things. In the reason, the reality of your daily life, you know enough to be suspicious of constructs thrown up in the white heat of war. How sound can their foundations be? Well, you wouldn't expect Orlando to stay with the network producer, would you? You would be surprised if Brian and Steven introduced their strapping bar girls to their happily married wives.

The passions and patterns that brought her and me together had not, we both sensed, been that healthy. We were determined never to indulge in them again. And, after all, I do love my wife, and my child.

One clear, cool winter day, not so long after these events, when we were both as well as we would ever be, Laura looked at me with the new-found gentleness in her eyes. 'It's time for you to go back,' she said.

And in that deep place, wherever you feel these things, I knew she was right. 'What about you?' I said.

'I'll be all right.' She had dropped the clipped, elocuted Corporation speak and let her soft Dorset burr return.

'I know. I mean, what will you do?'

Laura had spent her whole life believing she was one thing. Something she could now never be. 'I've been contacted by a charity. They do a lot of work with disturbed children. They need someone to fund-raise for West Africa.'

I raised my eyebrows.

'No, don't worry. It's all UK-based. In fact I'll be living back at home, in the West Country.'

We said goodbye as lovers. I still see her now and then. We communicated, usually by telephone, in the writing of this memoir. She still has the bullet that magically flattened on her breastbone. She has her own scars, which the old Laura might have worn with pride. Sometimes I know she will feel the tug, but she hardly ever watches the news, and then only local. The bullet lives in a box in the attic, with the other evidence of that time. The scars, well, they are kept hidden from all except her husband and their children.

When Laura left, I wept.

The winter cold warmed and refreshed me.

My mother sped the cure. 'I knew something was bothering you, Peter. Now it's gone. I don't have to look at your chart to see that. Maybe you can now stop fussing about around the globe everywhere and get back to real life. Look. Here's a postcard Claire sent me in the summer. I think it was really sent to you.'

It showed a perfect curve of rocky cove and a crystal

sea I recognized. It had been posted from an island in the Aegean. Claire had gone there with an old, old friend. A woman.

Another card arrived just before Christmas. Above the opaque 'All my love, Claire', it conveyed the season's greetings and the suggestion that I might like to take Alex out on Boxing Day. My wife, it appeared, was not spending the holiday with anyone else.

That crisp morning after Christmas, when I picked up my son, I caught a glimpse of his mother smiling at us tenderly from a window.

Back at my mother's, before I could stop him, Alex grabbed a large cowrie from the mantelpiece and put it to his ear. Then he thrust it towards me. I prepared myself for the roar of blood and memory.

'Listen, Daddy,' he laughed, 'you can hear the sea.'

And when I bent down so he could push its smooth coolness clumsily against my ear, that was all I heard.

EPILOGUE

It did not take long for media interest in Upper Guinea to ebb. The pack moved to new hunting grounds, following violence as wolves follow the migrations of the moose. There was the war over the diamond fields of South Africa, the Islamic revolution in Egypt, the invasion of Taiwan . . . Upper Guinea has long slid into the archives and out of memory, each incarnation of news erasing the impact of the one before.

After six months of attrition in Freeville, the Marines crept away in the night. Now, if you check the surname of Upper Guinea's presidents, you will find it is invariably Kane. The country is at peace. It exports diamonds, coffee and groundnuts. In a typical sign of reconciliation, Sohrab (who survived his throat wound, though with a hoarser voice), a Bamanda, was offered the post of Minister of Information. He declined and helped reconstruct the health system instead. He adopted Papus and spends a lot of time counselling former child soldiers of the civil war.

Film rights to the lives of Teresa Cellini and Ralph Reynolds were sewn up within days of their deaths, after furious bidding. I hear the Teresa script is already written. It was always 'more of a runner'. The glamour thing, you know. Its working title is, I believe, *White Woman's Grave*. No researcher for either project has yet made a trip to Upper Guinea, nor do they plan to. I cannot say I blame them. To my knowledge, no-one has yet proposed a film about the Dutchman.

Nick Rampling inherited the Controller's job at the Corporation and is still that well-respected, if pompous, public figure you all know and, I hope, mildly abhor. Judith Dart still reports wars. Orlando Harries was killed. Somewhere in the Caucasus, I think. Or was it Colombia, or the Spratly Islands? Somewhere like that, anyway. Brian was sacked for pulling Rampling off his live two-way. He joined Steven in a highly successful company making gardening programmes. The Japanese wildlife film won a major award.

Why did John Court kill? A narrator is not omniscient. Heisenberg's Uncertainty Principle states that the act of observation changes not just what is observed, but the observer as well. Perhaps what Court saw simply made him mad. Certainly his work awakened base instincts, brutal instincts that haunt all our dreams.

In a way perhaps he succeeded too well. He went too deeply into the darkness, and it swamped him. I can sense it at my back even now, gathering in the corners of the room, here in the soft English hills, so far away. Maybe Court was unstable from the start, and it just got out of control. As we know, it was so easy out there, where there are no controls.

Laura is more inclined to look to Court's upbringing. It turns out he had a troubled childhood. His true parents treated him cruelly – like an animal. So, the theory goes, he became one. Miranda, Laura and the rest simply fitted an unfortunate pattern. You cannot say that Court had no choice, though. Plenty of people see what he saw, and are decent enough. He left a sizeable estate, which was bequeathed, in its entirety, to an elderly couple up in Worcestershire (foster parents, I think). His sizeable public reputation remains essentially intact.

Court's funeral was perhaps less well attended than it might have been. Rumours will circulate, you know. I hear his tombstone bears the epitaph he wanted: *Hypocrite Voyeur, mon semblable, mon frère*.

Still, the full story of John Court has never really emerged. Not yet, anyway. The tapes and papers from his room are under lock and key. What the material comes to, as a whole, I do not know. It depends partly, of course, on whether you believe it all. He writes of murders from Kabul to Colombia, but they could be fantasy. Apart from the video we saw – which, on reflection, far from the chaos of that Freeville morning, does little more than make him the first to find Miranda's body – there's no corroboration in Court's videos or photographs that would confirm his guilt. As some of the notes were typed it has not even been possible to establish him, incontrovertibly, as their author. Anyway, Laura is the only person to have read them all. How she could bring herself to read any of it, I will never understand. Reading the passages about his lust for her must have been especially chilling. But then she always was tough.

Laura has refused to watch the tapes she and Court filmed that final night. Brian only just managed to rescue them from an acquisitive Marine sergeant. (I should point out that no-one ever found the knife or the hyena jaw I know I saw.) Laura refuses, in fact, to say anything about those hours. The description of her walk with Court was pieced together from the tapes of that moonlit night and from my admittedly jealous mind.

My friends, what marks does lunacy leave? Something has happened to me, yes. Fear and shock peppered my hair with grey at the temples, but it is away from war that I feel I have truly grown. I know my dreams are quieter and my horizons narrower. Above me is not the boundless sky of Africa, the limitless sensualities and eventualities of war. My possibilities are restricted to the ostensibly banal, the everyday. Though you can be surprised by the conundrums of the humdrum, by how many ways a child of yours can make you smile. There is a haze for me about life that I find impenetrable, but I can face it now without desiring the razor purity of war. I can live without the stimulus of death.

'The more you see, the more you understand.' That really was a network slogan. Some people think by travelling to those places – to the abode of news – by seeing more of the world, more of death, you learn more about life. I am now convinced that's just plain wrong. I saw plenty – more than most people – and, if anything, I understand less.

It is the conflicts in our childhood, the battles in our own backyard that really matter – and that really scare us. Many newsmen flee to the frontiers of existence from those difficulties of everyday, approachable reality. They point that light of investigation, of righteous indignation, so diligently into the darkness, mainly to avoid pointing it into themselves.

War does not teach you bravery, compassion, composure. If you have those things you will soon know. Maybe all you learn is whether you can hold it together under fire, or lose it. That is a test passed or failed. I am not sure how the results are of use where they count – in a relationship, in the classroom, in your bed.

Is it a worthwhile lesson to know, say, that when men are shot they simply fall, that they are not blown backwards like in the movies? Is it useful to know that a bullet flying past your ear does not whistle, but makes a crack like a bullwhip? Does the sight of death, the smell of it, bring wisdom? I don't know. All I know is that the more wars I took part in, the more questions I had. The most common word in war reporting is still 'why?'

Perhaps the lesson is just that – there are no answers. But it is not the style of news reporters to say 'I don't know.' It is doubtful that the global truth-bringers, those civilizing informers of our new digital colonialism, are planning to adopt that line any time soon.

And Miranda Williams? Miranda Williams is dead.

And time passes.

And we all age.

THE END

ACKNOWLEDGEMENTS

I have had help from many quarters in writing this book:

Unfailingly supportive, perceptive and professional, Stephanie Cabot, Simon Taylor and their teams made it happen. Hossein Amini gave early and expert advice.

Much of the book's journalistic detail is drawn from generous friends and colleagues including Paul Woolwich, Edward Behr, Aidan Hartley, Hassan Amini, Sam Gracey, Yasar Durra, Nazih Hijazi and the talented, daring teams at *Channel 4 News* and the BBC series *Correspondent*. Many of them will recognize stories they've told or things we've seen while on the road, up against a deadline, or in the bar.

I have also been guided by the writings of Andrew Boyd, Fergal Keane, Leslie Cockburn, Michael Nicholson and others. Edward Behr's moving and hilarious *Anyone Here Been Raped and Speaks English?* was an inspiration. It is scandalous that it is out of print.

Travels through West Africa by Mary Kingsley was full of rare detail. Gérard Périot's record of his walk across Liberia, *Dans la nuit des grands arbres*, provided me with the description of a traditional burial and a lot of anthropological insight. Kipling's *Jungle Book*, with its archetypal wolf pack, lurks behind this book's journalistic one. Conrad's *Heart of Darkness* and the film it inspired, *Apocalypse Now*, were constant points of reference.

Many trusting people and courageous local journalists in West Africa, the Balkans, the Middle East and elsewhere have been unwitting grist to this mill. I thank them. Especially, I offer belated thanks to Qasim Basma and his family for their unquestioning hospitality in the diamond badlands of Sierra Leone.

My family has encouraged me throughout, especially my mother Kate Lee, despite the book giving her bad dreams. The beautiful Tannaz Fazaipour has been just the right blend of thoughtful reader, patient sub-editor and loving wife.

WHITE MALE HEART
Ruaridh Nicoll

'BRUTAL AND BEAUTIFUL'
Val McDermid, *The Express*

'SPECTACULAR, PAGE TURNING . . . SWEEPING AND ASSURED'
Scotland on Sunday

In the sublime wilderness of the Scottish Highlands, Aaron and Hugh have been friends for as long as they can remember, bound by an affinity for their natural surroundings and a shared alienation from the remote community in which they live.

Then a stranger – a woman escaping a broken love affair – moves to the area, driving an emotional wedge between the two boys. As the strain on their friendship builds, so the violence that is endemic in the land begins to infect them. Turning on their world, Aaron and Hugh vent their frustration, anger and despair in the only way they know . . .

Dark, visceral, beautifully written and with an irresistible, brooding sense of place, *White Male Heart* delves deep into the male psyche and heralds the arrival of an exceptional new literary voice.

'A NOVEL OF STARTLING ORIGINALITY, AN ABSORBING PSYCHOLOGICAL THRILLER AS WELL AS A DEFT, PORTRAYAL OF FRIENDSHIP AND BETRAYAL'
The Times

'EERILY IMPRESSIVE . . . NICOLL PRODUCES PROSE BOTH RHAPSODICALLY BEAUTIFUL AND RED IN TOOTH AND CLAW, MARKING OUT THIS MODERN GOTHIC TALE'
Sunday Times

'WILL LEAVE YOU BREATHLESS. THIS IS A BLEAK NOVEL WHOSE TENSIONS BUILD FLAWLESSLY INTO A SHOCKING DENOUEMENT'
Literary Review

0552 999016

THE TREATMENT
by Mo Hayder

'One of the most frightening books I have ever read'
Guardian

Midsummer, and in an unassuming house on a quiet residential street on the edge of Brockwell Park in south London, a husband and wife are discovered, imprisoned in their own home. Badly dehydrated, they've been bound and beaten, and the husband is close to death. But worse is to come: their young son is missing.

When DI Jack Caffery of the Met's AMIT squad is called in to investigate, the similarities to events in his own past make it impossible for him to view this new crime with the necessary detachment. And as Jack digs deeper, as he attempts to hold his own life together in the face of ever more disturbing revelations about both the past and the present, the real nightmare begins . . .

Horrifying, unforgettable, intense, *The Treatment* is a novel that touches the raw nerve of our darkest imaginings.

'Chilling . . . compellingly drawn . . . Hayder's horrible ability to make you fear for your life is a very modern achievement'
Daily Telegraph

'Hayder's gory insights into the dark side are compelling. the finale is an extreme emotional catharsis, involving both redemption and terrible irony' *Guardian*

'Mercilessly realistic . . . *The Treatment* is exactly what the crime genre needs: a book that treats cruelty with a new moral seriousness' *Metro*

A Bantam Paperback

0 553 81272 6

MYSTIC RIVER
by Dennis Lehane

'Dennis Lehane establishes himself as one of the greats of crime writing with *Mystic River*'
Maxim Jakubowski, *Guardian*

There are threads in our lives. You pull one, and everything else gets affected.

When they were children, Sean Devine, Jimmy Marcus, and Dave Boyle were friends. But then a strange car pulled up their street. One boy got in the car, two did not, and something terrible happened – something that ended their friendship and changed all three boys forever.

Twenty-five years later, Sean Devine is a homicide detective. Jimmy Marcus is an ex-con who owns a corner store. And Dave Boyle is trying to hold his marriage together and keep his demons at bay – demons that urge him to do horrific things.

When Jimmy Marcus' daughter is found murdered, Sean Devine is assigned to the case. His personal life unravelling, he must go back into a world he thought he'd left behind to confront not only the violence of the present but the nightmares of his past. His investigation brings him into conflict with Jimmy Marcus, who finds his old criminal impulses tempt him to solve the crime with brutal justice. And then there is Dave Boyle, who came home the night Jimmy's daughter died covered in someone else's blood . . .

'Enormously impressive: page-turning but thoughtful . . . One of the finest novels I've read in ages'
Peter Guttridge, *Observer*

'A stylish, genuinely gripping whodunit that will keep even the sharpest thriller fan asking questions until the very last page' Andrea Henry, *Mirror*

A Bantam Paperback

0 553 81222 X